Reviewers Love Melissa Brayden

"Melissa Brayden has become one of the most popular novelists of the genre, writing hit after hit of funny, relatable, and very sexy stories for women who love women."—*Afterellen.com*

The Forever Factor

"Melissa Brayden never fails to impress. I read this in one day and had a smile on my face throughout. An easy read filled with the snappy banter and heartfelt longing that Melissa writes so effortlessly."
—*Sapphic Book Review*

The Last Lavender Sister

"It's also a slow burn, with some gorgeous writing. I've had to take some breaks while reading to delight in a turn of phrase here and there, and that's the best feeling."—*Jude in the Stars*

"I have loved many of Melissa Brayden's characters over the years, but I think Aster Lavender may be my favorite of all of them."—*Sapphic Book Review*

"*The Last Lavender Sister* is not only a romance but also a family saga and a journey of transformation for both characters."—LezReview Books

Exclusive

"Melissa Brayden's books have always been a source of comfort, like seeing a friend you've lost touch with but can pick right up where you left off. They have always made my heart happy, and this one does the same."—*Sapphic Book Review*

Marry Me

"A bride-to-be falls for her wedding planner in this smoking hot, emotionally mature romance from Brayden...Brayden is remarkably generous to her characters, allowing them space for self-exploration and growth."—*Publishers Weekly*

"When I open a book by Melissa Brayden, I usually know what to expect. This time, she really surprised me. In a good way."—*Rainbow Literary Society*

To the Moon and Back

"*To the Moon and Back* is all about Brayden's love of theatre, onstage and backstage, and she does a delightful job of sharing that love... Brayden set the scene so well I knew what was coming, not because it's unimaginative but because she made it obvious it was the only way things could go. She leads the reader exactly where she wants to take them, with brilliant writing as usual. Also, not everyone can make office supplies sound sexy."—*Jude in the Stars*

"Melissa Brayden does what she does best, she delivers amazing characters, witty banter, all while being fun and relatable."—*Romantic Reader Blog*

Back to September

"You can't go wrong with a Melissa Brayden romance. Seriously, you can't. Buy all of her books. Brayden sure has a way of creating an emotional type of compatibility between her leads, making you root for them against all odds. Great settings, cute interactions, and realistic dialogue."—*Bookvark*

What a Tangled Web

"[T]he happiest ending to the most amazing trilogy. Melissa Brayden pulled all of the elements together, wrapped them up in a bow, and presented the reader with Happily Ever After to the max!"—*Kitty Kat's Book Review Blog*

Beautiful Dreamer

"I love this book. I want to kiss it on its face…I'm going to stick *Beautiful Dreamer* on my to-reread-when-everything-sucks pile, because it's sure to make me happy again and again."—*Smart Bitches Trashy Books*

"*Beautiful Dreamer* is a sweet and sexy romance, with the bonus of interesting secondary characters and a cute small-town setting." —*Amanda Chapman, Librarian (Davisville Free Library, RI)*

Two to Tangle

"Melissa Brayden does it again with a sweet and sexy romance that leaves you feeling content and full of happiness. As always, the book is full of smiles, fabulous dialogue, and characters you wish were your best friends."—*The Romantic Reader*

"I loved it. I wasn't sure Brayden could beat Joey and Becca and their story, but when I started to see reviews mentioning that this was even better, I had high hopes and Brayden definitely lived up to them." —*LGBTQreader.com*

Entangled

"Ms. Brayden has a definite winner with this first book of the new series, and I can't wait to read the next one. If you love a great enemies-to-lovers, feel-good romance, then this is the book for you."—*Rainbow Reflections*

"*Entangled* is a simmering slow burn romance, but I also fully believe it would be appealing for lovers of women's fiction. The friendships between Joey, Maddie, and Gabriella are well developed and engaging as well as incredibly entertaining...All that topped off with a deeply fulfilling happily ever after that gives all the happy sighs long after you flip the final page."—*Lily Michaels: Sassy Characters, Sizzling Romance, Sweet Endings*

Love Like This

"Brayden upped her game. The characters are remarkably distinct from one another. The secondary characters are rich and wonderfully integrated into the story. The dialogue is crisp and witty."—*Frivolous Reviews*

Sparks Like Ours

"Brayden sets up a flirtatious tit-for-tat that's honest, relatable, and passionate. The women's fears are real, but the loving support from the supporting cast helps them find their way to a happy future. This enjoyable romance is sure to interest readers in the other stories from Seven Shores."—*Publishers Weekly*

Hearts Like Hers

"Once again Melissa Brayden stands at the top. She unequivocally is the queen of romance."—*Front Porch Romance*

Eyes Like Those

"Brayden's story of blossoming love behind the Hollywood scenes provides the right amount of warmth, camaraderie, and drama." —*RT Book Reviews*

Strawberry Summer

"This small-town second-chance romance is full of tenderness and heart. The 10 Best Romance Books of 2017."—*Vulture*

"*Strawberry Summer* is a tribute to first love and soulmates and growing into the person you're meant to be. I feel like I say this each time I read a new Melissa Brayden offering, but I loved this book so much that I cannot wait to see what she delivers next."—*Smart Bitches, Trashy Books*

First Position

"Brayden aptly develops the growing relationship between Ana and Natalie, making the emotional payoff that much sweeter. This ably plotted, moving offering will earn its place deep in readers' hearts." —*Publishers Weekly*

Soho Loft Series

"The trilogy was enjoyable and definitely worth a read if you're looking for solid romance or interconnected stories about a group of friends." —*The Lesbrary*

How Sweet It Is

"'Sweet' is definitely the keyword for this well-written, character-driven lesbian romance novel. It is ultimately a love letter to small town America, and the lesson to remain open to whatever opportunities and happiness comes into your life."—*Bob Lind, Echo Magazine*

Heart Block

"The story is enchanting with conflicts and issues to be overcome that will keep the reader turning the pages. The relationship between Sarah and Emory is achingly beautiful and skillfully portrayed. This second offering by Melissa Brayden is a perfect package of love—and life to be lived to the fullest. So grab a beverage and snuggle up with a comfy throw to read this classic story of overcoming obstacles and finding enduring love."—*Lambda Literary Review*

By the Author

Romances

Waiting in the Wings

Heart Block

How Sweet It Is

First Position

Strawberry Summer

Beautiful Dreamer

Back to September

To the Moon and Back

Marry Me

Exclusive

The Last Lavender Sister

The Forever Factor

Lucky in Lace

Soho Loft Romances:

Kiss the Girl

Just Three Words

Ready or Not

Seven Shores Romances:

Eyes Like Those

Hearts Like Hers

Sparks Like Ours

Love Like This

Tangle Valley Romances:

Entangled

Two to Tangle

What a Tangled Web

Visit us at www.boldstrokesbooks.com

LUCKY IN LACE

by
Melissa Brayden

2023

LUCKY IN LACE

© 2023 By Melissa Brayden. All Rights Reserved.

ISBN 13: 978-1-63679-434-1

This Trade Paperback Original Is Published By
Bold Strokes Books, Inc.
P.O. Box 249
Valley Falls, NY 12185

First Edition: March 2023

Credits

Editor: Ruth Sternglantz
Production Design: Stacia Seaman
Cover Design by Inkspiral Design

Acknowledgments

Redemption is tricky. And forgiveness can be complicated. But I've always been a sucker for the exploration of the things that make us human, relatable, fallible, and real. Most of my books fall into the fun and flirty category, but Peyton Lane's story lies somewhere outside of that. It didn't matter. It was an arc that I felt compelled to write along with her unique set of circumstances. She isn't a typical romance novel character. She has baggage, a past, and a lot to overcome. I think we can all relate to grappling with the results of a mistake and working to come out of the darkness of its shadow. Even when we're the ones punishing ourselves most. In the end, it's my hope that this story resonates with you in some small way as you move through Peyton and Juliette's romance.

I want to thank Sandy Lowe for the kernel of an idea that blossomed into more. Inspiration sparks from a variety of places, even your senior editor!

Much gratitude to my own editor, Ruth Sternglantz, who helped these characters grow into all they became. Thank you to the production team at Bold Strokes Books (Cindy, Stacia, Toni, as well as Inkspiral Design) who brought this book to life.

It takes a village, and I have a great one that includes the meticulous proofreaders who devote their skills to catching the things I did not. You're invaluable.

When Radclyffe is your publisher, you know you're in good hands, and as always, I'm humbled and happy to learn from the best.

Hugs and relief that I have wonderful friends to pick me up when I'm down and to share a laugh with along the way. Writing community, you're amazing, generous, and entertaining in the best sense. To my people, I love you. There are now too many of you to list! What a fabulous problem! I'm blessed.

To Alan, my children, my family, my dogs, my potted plants, and favorite TV show characters—you make my life worth living.

Lastly, thank you, fantastic readers, for continuing to pick up my books and share a little bit of your day with me. You have no idea how much I value our connection. I'd hug each of you if I could.

For anyone in need of a second chance

Prologue

Three years ago

Free air felt different than prison air. Lighter with all sorts of competing aromas. Tree bark, car exhaust, baked goods, rain. They mingled together in an overpowering jumble. Not unwelcome, just all consuming. There also seemed to be lots more of it, air, hovering in the wide expanse of freedom. Peyton Lane couldn't imagine ever taking free air for granted again. She'd been released from prison exactly eight days prior, and in that time, only the air had been hospitable.

She'd put in applications at twelve different businesses, only to have four of them inform her it was against their policy to hire her after they perused her application. The other eight had yet to call. That was an ominous sign. She'd need money soon and had to make something happen for herself. A nonprofit program for recent parolees set her up with a studio apartment located above a pretty hopping burger joint, which left her place smelling like freshly cooked burgers she couldn't afford. Didn't mean she didn't long for one, imagining the melted cheese curling to the edge of the burger in a torturous daydream. Even her clothes carried the smoky smell of the grill, which likely didn't help her job search. She had four outfits in total, also courtesy of the do-gooder program, and a hundred and ten dollars left to her name. Next month's rent was all on her, and the slightest bit of panic eased in as she walked the sidewalk in front of a strip mall. She often selected those because she could hit half a dozen businesses on foot, increasing her chances of someone taking a chance on her. She'd practiced smiling in the mirror, because there hadn't been much of that where she'd been the last four years. Remembering the basics took a lot more effort than she'd anticipated. The world was so much bigger, so much louder, and full of complications she'd forgotten how to juggle.

Peyton paused her search on the sidewalk, depressed because the cosmetics store two doors down had seemed so promising. The dashed hope hurt more than no hope at all. But she hadn't cried. She'd been numb to true emotion for years, moving through each day like an automaton. The practice had made the time she had to serve easier. The owner had chatted away with Peyton, who still struggled with conversations with strangers after having been absent from the larger world for so long. She'd withdrawn into herself, and now it took work to pull herself back out one piece at a time. Surely, others could immediately tell something was wrong with her, which only made Peyton all the more self-conscious. She used to be good at connecting with other people, and dammit, she would be again. She'd make sure of it. If only someone out there would give her a chance, even a small one.

"I'm so sorry," the woman said after five minutes of what seemed like a great interview. But then she'd scanned the application, understanding registering on her face. "We just don't seem to have what you're looking for right now. But I'll hold on to this." She held up the sheet of paper with Peyton's handwriting all over it. A lie.

After a short pep talk, and a gathering of her socials kills, she'd headed into the juice bar next door. Peppy, bright, and fun. She could imagine enjoying her days in a cheerful place like this one.

She tossed the owner her best smile, hoping to show that she could match the place's vibe. "I'm looking for full-time, but part-time would be fine. Anything, really. I'm happy to pay my dues." A pause. "And I love juice. I learn fast, too."

The woman in the lime-green Juice or Die T-shirt studied her like a bug. "You're eager."

"Yes." A smile that she prayed sold her confidence. "I need a job."

"Bless your heart," the woman said as she scanned the application, sympathy all over her face. That had to be a good sign. "How long have you been out?"

"A little over a week."

She placed the application facedown on the counter. "I wish I could help you, but I just don't have the need for extra help. That's not a line, either. I'd hire you on the spot if I could."

"Oh." Her hopeful heart hit the pavement. "I understand." So close.

"I could use a hand."

Peyton turned to the woman in line behind her who'd been studying the menu but also, perhaps, overheard their conversation. "You would?"

"I'm two doors down at the sassiest little underwear boutique you'll ever walk into."

"Hi, Candy," the juice woman said. "Your usual?"

"Yes, with an extra splash of raspberry because this might just be my lucky day." She smiled at Peyton, and in that very moment hope appeared in the form of a woman in her sixties with big white hair and perfectly applied makeup. "Oh, whatever my new employee is having, too. You just toss that on my bill."

"Oh," Peyton said, unaccustomed to kindness. It fit like a shirt that was too big and made for someone else. She embraced it anyway, grateful. "Thank you." She smiled. A real one this time. She'd already caught a glimpse of the menu and, even though she was desperately thirsty, had decided she couldn't afford the inflated prices.

"What'll it be?" the woman behind the counter asked.

She pointed at the Strawberry Banana Explosion featured on the large photo next to the menu. "I guess I'll take one of those." Her taste buds tingled at the thought of the cool, refreshing drink.

"Good choice," her new employer said. "Cheerful and fruity with a stripy paper straw. If you had ordered one of those veggie blends, I would have tolerated it but been sad. We'll grab those, head back to the store, and I'll get you some paperwork. We can start orientation if you have the time."

"I have the time," Peyton said without a blip of hesitation. With fresh juice in hand, she was whisked down the sidewalk to Cotton Candy, which could best be described as a wonderful site for a sexy sleepover. Lingerie of every size, color, and flavor of spice filled the racks and wall displays. Silky sleep masks, garter belts, thigh-length robes, bra and panty combos, and even a section for boxers. It was the softest, most decadent environment Peyton had experienced in her entire life. The nearly loud, upbeat rock music the woman played only made it feel more fun. If there was an opposite to prison, Cotton Candy would be it. Peyton was in heaven.

"First thing's first, I'm Candy, and there's nothing more important than how a woman's boobs feel." Peyton blinked and ran that sentence back. "It's our job to make sure they're living their best life. You get me?"

For a moment, Peyton couldn't speak. "Yes, I do. Very important." It's not that she disagreed—it was just that in the midst of figuring out her life, her next meal, her moral compass, how her breasts felt hadn't entered the picture. About now, she felt like perhaps that had been a mistake, because this store was wonderful. Peyton felt pampered just standing between its walls. She now *wanted* her breasts to look and feel good, and it had only been three minutes.

From that moment on, a small crack of light crept into Peyton's life.

She reported to work every single day and devoted every ounce of brain power she had to learning the business. She was determined to make Candy proud and never once regret her choice in hiring Peyton. When she wasn't doing that, she worked on redeveloping her interpersonal skills, that lo and behold, still existed somewhere deep down in her. With a little workout here and there, she managed to dazzle the customers almost as much as Candy did. In fact, she found she liked talking to people, watching a face light up when she matched them with their perfect piece of lingerie.

"You're good," Candy told her over dumplings and rice at The Golden Panda, three doors down from the store.

"Well, I learned from the best," Peyton told her with a raised shoulder.

"You're also real bright, Peyton. Have you thought about what you want to do long term? You've been with me nearly two years."

"I guess I hadn't gotten that far. My head's above water for the first time since I can remember. I make my rent easily and have food in my pantry. I'm thrilled with both of those things. I've even made a few friends through the shop and have a little bar I like to go to on weekends." She shrugged. "Life is good and manageable. I'm not sure I need more."

"Well, I think you're capable. I have customers who ask for you by name. I'm proud of you, girl."

"That makes me really happy to hear." Most everything good that had happened to her was thanks to Candy and her friendship and faith in Peyton from day one. But in the midst of it all, there was something that pulled at her, kept her flipping from one side of her pillow to the other each night. She had a family out there that she hadn't seen in years. That hurt a lot. And as the days turned to years, it tugged at her, calling her to do something about it. She missed her brother and his kids, who she'd never even met, more than she could process. But for the first time, she was proud of what was happening in her life. Maybe he would be, too.

Candy set down her fork and sat back. "I wonder about you taking it over."

"Taking what over? Do you have another commitment tomorrow?" Candy was scheduled to open, and Peyton would come in about midmorning, but she could always come in earlier. She liked to grab a beer at the bar down the street from her place, but she never stayed out too late. Not on a work night.

"You're my bright star, Peyton. But it's time for me to move my time to where it's needed most and take care of my mom. I got a call last week. The news isn't good." Her mouth turned down. Saying the words must have hurt because she reached for her napkin as a distraction.

Peyton went still, her heart clenching uncomfortably. "Candy. Shit. I'm so sorry."

"Me, too. But it would break my heart to close down." Peyton hadn't considered that the store could close someday. She'd have to find another job, start from scratch again. "I think you should buy the business."

For a long moment, she simply stared. Her brain stuttered. "I couldn't do that. How could I do that? I'm just me. I don't know anything."

"Are you kidding me?" Candy leaned forward. "You know everything. I've never seen someone so bright and quick to expertise. You know your brands, you know what people like, you have relationships with customers who adore you, and you have the best eye for decorating of anyone who's ever worked for me." She held out a hand. "You're a panty prodigy, and I mean that."

The compliments landed and took root. None of it changed the fact that she didn't have the money. "I appreciate that, and I love my job. The store. You. But I'm not really at a place in my life where I'm financially equipped to—"

"Shut up about money. Now listen to me." Peyton paused because she'd learned that when Candy demanded attention, it was in her best interest to give it. "I've done a little research, and there are special programs for business loans for people with your very particular background."

"Is that code for *criminal*?"

Candy ignored her and plowed forward, handing over a couple of brochures from her bag. "Whatever a loan won't cover, I'll finance for you myself, provided you're interested."

While she felt like a kid invited to the grown-ups' table and wildly intimidated, opportunities like this one were rare. How in the world could she turn Candy down? She ordered herself to nod and figure the rest out later. "Yes. Of course. If you really think I can do this."

"Honey, if this was the Triple Crown, all my money is on you."

Peyton had never worked as hard as she did in that next year of her life. She was hustle personified, perseverance in live form. If there was a YouTube video about running a small business, she'd watched it and taken notes probably three different times. If there was a seminar she could enroll in or speaker she could buy a ticket to see, she most certainly did. Not only that, she used her resources, the program for parolees, the bank's small business arm, and Candy, who was only a phone call away and forty-five miles up the road if she needed guidance with anything related to the business or even how to fix a sink. Peyton didn't remember much about her own mother, but Candy had become a bright spot in her life, and someone she would consider family until the end of time. She'd saved Peyton. Picked her up and put her back together until she was quite nearly a whole person again.

"How were this week's numbers?" Candy asked on one of their weekly calls. Peyton was perched on the side of her white and green couch, balancing a carton of yogurt with fruit on the arm before work.

"Much better now that I scaled back on purchases in advance of inventory dip. I'll see a profitable month and then some. That was good advice."

"The early bird does not always get the worm."

"Lesson learned."

"Now let's get serious. Did you hear anything from your brother after the letter you sent?" Peyton deflated and set the carton on the table. The letter had been Peyton's attempt to reconnect, make amends for the stress she'd put on him. The heartbreak. She'd tried multiple times to set up a visit to get to know her niece and nephew more. Each day that passed felt like she'd missed the chance forever. But Caleb continued to brush her off, polite but elusive, probably because he was leery of her. It was hard to blame him. He'd been burned by the younger version of his kid sister too many times and had no idea how far she'd come. If only he'd give her the chance to show him how much she'd grown up in the three years since she'd been out, how much she'd learned and changed.

"He thanked me for sending it, told me Joshua's T-ball score, and promptly got off the phone like it was burning a hole in his hand."

"Goddammit. He needs to open up his mind and his heart. It's been long enough now. I know panties, and his are in a wad."

"Don't blame him. This one is on me." She exhaled, feeling a little shaky. It happened anytime she had to be vulnerable, and discuss things close to her heart. Way out of her comfort zone ever since she'd hit mute on her feelings. "But a part of me can't let go of the fact that Caleb and his family are all I have left. Well, them and you." A hopeful smile tugged. "The T-ball score was an upgrade, though. He usually holds all personal details back."

"Are you sure he's a good guy?" Candy asked. Peyton could hear the squint in her voice. "Seems against any kind of forgiveness or grace, and sweet baby, that's not how it should go."

"It's going to take time. And phone calls and letters might not be enough."

"You gonna visit?"

Peyton was actually considering much more but hadn't yet gathered the courage to voice it. She hadn't been back to Landonville, Ohio, since she'd been arrested there and sent to Dayton to serve out her sentence. In fact, the concept of returning to the literal scene of the crime sounded downright terrifying. Her stomach churned at the thought. She'd only lived there for a couple of years with Caleb and her grandfather before everything in her life went to hell, with a series of bad decisions. It wasn't the *place* that called her back, though, but her one last connection to her family. Her parents were gone. Her grandfather, who'd stepped in to raise them, had passed while she was away. But Caleb was out there, and he used to be her person, the older brother who always had her back. He'd sing her to sleep at night when she was scared. Make her sack lunch. Step between her and any perceived bully. Caleb kept her safe. And after living in an emotional shutdown, Peyton needed to feel something again. Maybe that meant she needed to go backward before she could go forward. She sucked in much needed air. It was too terrifying to consider. The continued rejection. The reaching out of her hand only to have it slapped away.

But with each day that passed, a part of her opened up to the idea of working on rebuilding that connection she'd lost. In many ways, it felt like rebuilding a bridge back to herself. She'd gotten her life in order. She was self-reliant and a contributing member of her community. She'd been not much more than a kid when she'd gotten in trouble, and Landonville was not exactly a small town. People weren't going to remember her. Except of course for her family, the ones that mattered.

They'd be surprised by the changes in her. She smiled most of the time, found the good in most everything she encountered, even the shitty stuff. She'd lost too much time to take any moment for granted. That wasn't to say she wasn't frightened away easily. When things went wrong, she tended to retreat. Ghosted people she was dating. Shied away from anything that made her feel open or exposed or too touchy-feely. Nope. Not for her. She enjoyed people, relished every conversation she had in the store, but she didn't allow them too close. Candy had been the closest she'd gotten, but it was like that part of her was broken. She kept waiting for the fix. In the recesses of her mind, when the night got exceptionally quiet, she knew what she had to do if she ever wanted to feel whole again.

As she chatted with Candy, Peyton balanced the phone against her ear and watched the sign company replace the neon bulbs from atop a ladder now that the shop was closed for the day. "I have a question for you."

"I aim to have an answer."

"How do you feel about me taking Cotton Candy a couple hours south?"

"Sweetheart, that business is yours, and if home is calling your name, I know for a fact you're ready to make the boobs of those Landonville women say hi to heaven."

Peyton grinned. "I was hoping you'd say that."

It was settled. With the last of the roadblocks out of the way, it was time to take her life back.

CHAPTER ONE

The Bureau of Motor Vehicles was put on the planet to punish the innocent. Juliette Jennings had the unfortunate pleasure of having her wallet stolen and now faced the long line of car driving consequences, one of them being filing for a license replacement. She bit the inside of her lip to keep from shriveling into a ball and dying of dread. Some things she would just have to suffer through. The goal: get in and out with the minimum amount of waiting and small talk with other human beings. Shouldn't be too hard. She'd brought her book, the God-given prop that was most instrumental in warding off verbose strangers. She'd also researched what times of day were the least busy and made sure to arrive at ten a.m. as directed by the great and powerful Google.

This was her first time inside the building in a very, very long time. Why? Because it was Satan's house and everyone knew all evil orbited its concrete foundation. Yet the day was here. Sadly, her online request for a replacement had been denied due to the number of years that had passed since she'd last been in. She'd finally lost the lottery, and here she sat in a plastic chair with a loose screw that sometimes tipped her a little to the right just for fun. Satan's late morning amusement.

To top off Juliette's ten a.m. Thursday sundae of joy, it was raining outside. Before she'd left home that morning, she'd watched the big, thick drops cling precariously to the glass of the picture window overlooking her home's front lawn, neatly trimmed and edged just the day before. She blew out a sad little breath in her plastic chair, lamenting the time away from her stationery store and counting the tens of dollars she was probably missing out on by having it closed midmorning.

That's when the merry band of elderly patrons hit up the town's retail circuit. And what did elderly people love if not stationery. Thereby, the weather felt appropriate as she clutched the requisite paperwork, wrinkling the page and not even caring. Not at all like her. She wondered distantly how long she'd be here and, conversely, how long until she could open The Station, her baby, for business. Unfortunately, she was strictly a one-woman-show. She couldn't afford employees, so when she couldn't make it in, the place was dark and dead in the water. Given her dwindling bank account and the extra-small intake of cash the shop pulled in lately, she needed every moment.

She watched a middle-aged couple stand in victory when their number appeared above the counter in neon green. She nodded her congratulations as they scampered arm in arm to the bored-looking clerk. Juliette had been there twenty-four minutes and used each one to assess her professional trajectory of doom. The way she figured it, she had about nine months left until she'd have to close her business entirely, which crushed her soul and kept her up at night. There apparently wasn't a big demand for personalized greeting cards in Landonville, and she was paying for that wrong turn now. She'd stayed afloat this long thanks to the small sales she made from the commercial odds and ends she'd stocked the shelves with for financial cushion— miniature tic-tac-toe games, vanilla-scented candles, a lollipop tree, and refrigerator magnets with sassy sayings from women with hands on their hips. But she had so much more to offer in terms of her art and passion. Somehow her skills with a pen and a brush hadn't translated into a mortgage payment, a problem she'd have to address sooner rather than later. Watching one's dream circle the drain was a bleak image to face.

Shifting to the left to avoid tilting to the right, Juliette took note of a new arrival to the waiting area, who would be taking the number after hers. A striking blond woman close to her age, who she hadn't seen before. It wasn't unusual. Their town wasn't big, but it wasn't small either. There were still lots of people Juliette didn't know, and this happened to be one of them.

"Hey, there."

Juliette took a moment. "Hi." Oh God. The woman had taken up residence two seats down and was speaking. She also smiled kindly. Her lip gloss shimmered and matched the brightness in her eyes.

"Call me a weirdo, but I welcome the opportunity to take a break from life in a waiting room. The downtime is rare. What about you?"

No, no, no. Juliette gripped the edge of her chair. The woman was still smiling, awaiting an answer, and looking too pretty as she did so. Not only that, but she seemed to think a waiting room was Christmas morning. This was bad. Small talk was too daunting to be allowed. Her critical error had been forgetting to bury her nose in the book she'd packed. She never knew what to say, would wind up feeling awkward and socially exhausted. Plus, once those kinds of conversations started, they were impossible to end. You were both sentenced to polite chitchat about her dog named Cookie Monster or why you didn't enjoy the mall food court on Thursdays. Why not just skip it and skate sublimely through the peace and quiet? Wasn't this outing bad enough on its own?

"It's okay, I guess," she said, adding a tolerant smile. "Something we all go through collectively."

"Collectively. I've always liked that word." The woman, who had big hazel eyes, stared happily at the air as if the word sparkled in front of her and then glided off. "I get excited about simple things like this. And the occasion, of course."

"I can't tell if you're joking." But she was serious. Her face would have betrayed her. It was that expressive. "Really? Excited about the BMV?"

The woman raised her shoulders, resembling a hopeful Disney Princess with a side of street smarts. Her jeans had a perfectly placed rip in the thigh, edgy, and her white T-shirt and army-green jacket made her pretty-girl looks cooler than they would have been on their own. The paired brown heels proved she was a fashion-conscious human. "Anytime my day is a little different than normal, I try to embrace the adventure. Trust me. Life is too short. I realize that puts me in the minority of people here, but that's just what I'm like."

"No crime there," Juliette said, adjusting in her chair. "Pardon the irony, because this feels like prison."

The woman laughed melodically, definitely giving Juliette too much credit on that one. "Gotcha. I see how you swerved that one in. And trust me, prison feels nothing like this."

Now she really was being funny. Still. Juliette had to get out of this without seeming rude. Her neighbor's nice smile, which was definitely contagious, was not even close to worthy of small talk. Not that Juliette was in the market for a smile at the BMV. Blond hair with a part on the side and pulled back into one of those fashionably executed ponytails. Juliette eased a strand of straight, layered brown hair behind her own ear. She probably should do more with it. Meh.

"We'll likely be here at least an hour. Don't you think? I'm Peyton."

"Juliette." She supposed they were doing this now. Officially. "I hope to God not. I was estimating forty minutes tops."

Peyton winced. "I get the feeling you're not thrilled to be here."

"I run a small business, and now I have to open late. It's a whole thing." She wanted to stop studying the woman, but it was hard. She had pretty skin with a noticeable freckle to the side of her right eye that was more attractive than any freckle had a right to be. She also had long swoopy bangs that would blind her if she hadn't swept them to the side. That must be hard to achieve, the perfect bang sweep. Was it effortless for this woman or a painstaking process? Juliette could never. Why was she thinking about this?

She decided not to go on because then she was just furthering the exchange, and aside from her curiosity about the bangs, she needed to politely withdraw. She pulled out her book and flipped open to chapter one. *Oh, look—words. In a row. Intriguing.* She prayed it worked.

"Have you ever worked at a place like this?" Nope. Guess not. "I mean, imagine that in the midst of doing your actual job, you also have to shoulder the knowledge that most of the world hates you. You're part of the BMV myth. The unfortunate legend. That can't be easy." Peyton's hazel eyes went wide. She had definite empathy for these workers and expressed it passionately.

"I guess you're right about that. And no, I've never worked a government job. My skin is probably not thick enough for the abuse." She returned her book to her bag, feeling a bit like Bert from *Sesame Street*, failing to avoid Ernie.

"Do you live near here?"

"Oh." She pointed vaguely to the front window. "About eight, ten minutes away. North."

Peyton's eyes widened and danced. "Me, too. Newly."

Why were they on to new topics now? This didn't bode well for her time in the plastic chair of doom.

A middled-aged man arrived in a less than ironed suit, took a number, and sat on the other side of Juliette. He had a book, too. She liked this well-prepared rumpled person. He glanced across Juliette to her talkative blond neighbor, Peyton. "Couldn't help overhearing. Where are you from?"

Something flickered behind Peyton's eyes that didn't match any of her other friendly facial expressions. She seemed to make a decision and sat forward. "Dayton most recently, but I used to live in Landonville a long time ago. I was looking for a new chapter to my story, so here I am."

"That's fantastic. Welcome back." Unfortunately, he was grinning and nodding. They were a group now.

Peyton pressed on. "I also have a family member who lives here who I haven't seen in a while. I was driving to work one day and decided, yep, time to move. Bonus, this is my chance to start fresh, spend some time reconnecting with him. My brother." Her smile dimmed slightly, and she stared at the hands she'd folded in her lap. "It feels good. I'm a Landonville resident again. Surreal."

Juliette had never heard someone so happy to be in mundane, middle-of-the-road Landonville. She was born and raised here, but not many outsiders flocked. "Wait. So you were just driving and up and decided to move. As in pick up your life. Wow." She couldn't identify with the impulsivity. She wasn't that kind of risk taker on average. The interior of her fridge was color coded for a reason.

"Right? I was ready for something new and fucking challenging. And this little city felt like just the perfect spot. It has a small town feel, but also big city perks." She gestured up the street. "Multiple Target locations to choose from."

"Three, actually," the man said. "We're blessed with chain retail."

Peyton sobered, her tone sentimental. "Well, I have not been disappointed. The sun shines a lot here, in a variety of ways." Juliette couldn't help notice that the second Peyton allowed her sparkle to dim, a heaviness immediately took its place. There had been no in between. Almost as if remembering herself, Peyton blinked right out of it again. "Anyway, things are looking up. I hope."

The man, who was maybe ten years older than them, beamed. He was thin both in body style and hair growth. Oh, but he liked himself some hazel-eyed Peyton. That much was clear. In fact, Juliette was probably getting in the way. Maybe she should excuse herself and let these two socially ambitious people speak unencumbered.

"That's the way you do it," he said. "You follow your gut and look on the bright side."

"I'm working on finding a balance." Peyton shrugged. "I learned early that I lead with my heart. That's always been me."

Juliette didn't. In fact, she overthought every decision down to breakfast. She tried not to imagine what leading with your heart must feel like. Or having the ability to naturally chat up strangers. *But go, you, Miss Dayton, Ohio.*

For the next thirty-seven minutes, she listened to her two seatmates shoot the breeze over the actors they liked, foods they preferred on weekends—except anything raw which was apparently abominable, and how cute toddlers looked in the moments before they cried over something ridiculous. The manner and method in which they flitted from subject to subject amazed her. No one really cared about proper transitions during their highly energized exchange. It was a thing to witness. Was she broken, or were these people just carefree about public interaction?

As for Juliette, she kept her eyes on the number wall as it grudgingly rolled over again. Six away. Five. One person after another scurried in relief to the counter and stated the reason for their presence. Finally, number forty-seven appeared. Hers! And wouldn't you know it, number forty-eight was immediately called, too, which had Peyton on her feet, excitement flaring all over again.

"Come on, Juliette. We're both up. Fucking next-door neighbors. Twins." She even seemed jazzed about the walk to the window. Get this girl a pony and she'd likely vibrate and explode confetti. Except she wouldn't because she also had a cool girl vibe simmering just beneath. She interlaced the word *fuck* with her enthusiastic musings. A puzzling contradiction. Peyton juggled them both impressively. Juliette needed those kinds of layers. Alas.

"Twins. That's us." But nothing could have been farther from the truth. Juliette was serious minded, a good two inches shorter than Peyton with boring dark brown hair a quarter of the way down her back. She had no swoopy bangs or affection for weekday food. But she'd made it to the end of their time together and could now afford

Peyton a great big smile from the safety of her own window. "We made it!"

Exhale.

"Paperwork?" the mildly attentive clerk asked as she chewed what had to be three pieces of peppermint gum as she rubbed her forehead with woe. Juliette handed over her carefully filled out form just as next to her she heard Peyton apologizing for not having what she needed for whatever request had brought her in. Surprisingly, she'd never said.

"I can't believe I missed that. Yeah. Wow. I'm so sorry."

Her clerk, a man with dark framed glasses, didn't seem to mind. "Normally, I'd send you back to fill out the forms first, but you know what?" He glanced behind him. "I'm in a good mood and am gonna let you just do that right here."

"I don't have to get back in line?"

He leaned in, his voice quiet. "Nah. But don't say I didn't ever do anything nice for ya."

"Never." Peyton beamed. "You're my favorite, Lance. Can I steal that pen?"

That never would have happened to Juliette, who would have been ordered back to the dreary plastic chair forest to complete her homework like a dutiful soldier. Ah, well. Good for Peyton. Being nice paid off, and she'd do well to remember that.

After standing for her *No smiling!* photo, Juliette left with a new license and a significant urge to get on with her day.

"Juliette, wait a sec!"

She paused and turned, only to see Peyton jogging after her into the parking lot. "I just wanted to say that it was nice to meet you. That's all." She adjusted the yellow leather tote on her shoulder. "I haven't had a chance to meet many people since I moved here, and you seem, well, great."

How was that possible, Juliette wondered. She felt bad now, because the conversation had mattered to Peyton, while Juliette had made only the smallest of efforts. There was a lesson here, and she planned to learn it. "Oh. Well, it was great meeting you, too. I'm sorry if I seemed mired or distracted. It's my default lately. I could honestly be less rigid."

"Well, I think you're awesome. You can carry that with you. Back to work?"

Juliette hooked a thumb behind her. "Yes. Can't afford to stay closed on a perfectly good day of the week."

"I was thinking of checking out the zoo. Maybe you could steal an extra hour or two?" She passed Juliette a hopeful look. "I realize the chances are slim." Peyton seemed a little lonely.

"Oh. Sounds fun." She didn't want to point out that the zoo was really just about four exhibits of small rodents and some birds. Knowing Peyton, she'd probably think the place was magnificent. "But I really can't."

Peyton's perfect face fell, and as if her feelings compelled her, she stood taller. She had a good three inches on Juliette, but then again she was in heels. Her lip-glossed mouth turned downward. "I get it. It's okay. But have a great one."

She wasn't sure, but the dip between Peyton's brows might have indicated that she'd gotten the larger message. Juliette didn't only have to work. She was rejecting the invitation outright and felt bad about that now. Maybe she should have just swallowed back her disdain for forced social interactions and stuck with her new obligatory friend. They could smile randomly and chat all day in front of the anteater hut.

The man who had sat with them in the holding area appeared. "Hey, Peyton. Just got my renewal. I'm gonna grab an early lunch across the street before I head into the office. Want to come?"

Juliette smothered a smile. When you radiated sunshine and happiness, the world flocked to you.

"You can come, too," he said to Juliette by way of an afterthought.

"Gonna have to pass. Work calls."

"I'll go. Thanks for asking," Peyton said, meeting his gaze. There was a touch of sadness behind her eyes before she brightened again. "Maybe I'll see you around, Juliette."

"For sure." For now, she had a greeting card wall to restock and an illustration for a custom birthday card due in three days. "You guys have fun."

"If they have a decent BLT, I'm all set," Peyton said, pointing at her as she walked away. The sun made her blond hair sway even brighter. *Just look at her.* Juliette shook her head at the unicorn she would likely never see again. Probably for the best. Pretty. Confident. Happy. What a way to be.

She had absolutely zero ability to identify.

CHAPTER TWO

Two months later

The Station was hopping for a Tuesday in August, and Juliette couldn't have been more pumped. In-store traffic meant sales, and the more people who came to the front to check out, the more she could send home with a brochure about her custom-made, personalized greeting cards.

Juliette had six whole people in the store, and two of them looked like they were going to buy something. A third, Mrs. Wunderlich, was here to pick up the customized birthday card she'd purchased for her husband, Pete, the week prior. She'd composed a poem, which Juliette had dutifully copied into the card in script, along with a colorful illustration of the two of them on a park bench. Simple, elegant, and personal. She loved the way it had come out and handed it over in its golden envelope with The Station's choo-choo-train logo. Her heart squeezed with pride and love for the cute couple.

"Oh, this is lovely," Mrs. Wunderlich said. "We're like royalty. A picture of us!"

"Thrilled you like it." She grabbed a couple of brochures and handed them over. "Definitely tell your friends about the personalization option. I can handle all types of font requests, too, and if they don't feel comfortable composing the text themselves, I have tons of ideas." She did, too. She was bursting with cute, quippy, sincere, and heartfelt messages to be paired with the illustrations she'd already compiled in her head. Name the occasion, she had plenty of ideas. She was a greeting card aficionado.

"I will tell everyone I know to scoot here like the wind and hand over their money. You take cash, right?"

"Of course."

Mrs. Wunderlich was a resident of the Morning's Glow Retirement Community, and those folks ran in a posse not to be messed with. If Mrs. Wunderlich was pleased, there would likely be more business.

"Good. We love cash. Not a fan of PayPal. Don't get me started. It's not our pal at all."

"I wouldn't dare." She offered a wink.

"Mainly, though, my thinking is that my gals from hot yoga will eat this up. We have all gotten quite good at both down dog and child's pose in extreme heat. The trick is to pretend you're a polar bear in the Arctic."

"I'm impressed."

"So is Hot Timothy, our instructor. His name has nothing to do with the temperature in the room, if you feel me." Mrs. Wunderlich added a wink of her own. "Don't tell Pete. His jealous rage knows no bounds when it comes to Hot Timothy, who graduates from the university next semester."

"My lips are sealed."

"Men will never understand us. I don't know why they try. You should know. You divorced one."

Juliette laughed, understanding all too well. Her marriage, though pleasant enough, often reminded her of a movie with two people speaking in entirely different languages while trying to build an important rocket ship, or in their case, a life together. Nope. She and Thomas had had very little chance of romantic bliss. They were so much better at being best buddies that met up at The Frog and Dog bar for football and Tuesday night trivia. Bowling on Wednesdays. Who knew?

"We should all just date the girlies like you do, Jules. Though that would mean giving up Hot Timothy, and that's a deal breaker in the making. I could drop Pete, though. Don't tell him."

"Sealed lips, remember?" Juliette placed a finger over them just as a very loud industrial-sounding noise roared to life from somewhere nearby. What the hell?

"Dear God in heaven, I thought the angels were coming for me. My time had arrived!" Mrs. Wunderlich's hands were in the air.

But Juliette barely had time to decipher the nature of the noise because something akin to a jackhammer joined what had to be a drill. The sound levels astounded, and she covered her ears, mystified. The strip mall she rented space from had three businesses in a row, and she'd been told nothing about any scheduled construction. That was a courtesy the landlord had always afforded them.

"You're gonna be just fine. Don't you worry," Juliette shouted, then watched her remaining browsing customers make a straight line to the door as if pursued by angry wasps. This wasn't good. "I'm gonna go see what's going on," she said, gesturing over her shoulder as she headed for the door herself. A mass exodus on her busy Tuesday? Disastrous.

"Be careful!" Mrs. Wunderlich called, following her out. "It sounds like a suburban war zone out there."

"Just a little construction," she called back, but the noise drowned her out, which was frustrating, but not as frustrating as the lost business.

The retail space next to The Station had been conveniently empty since the cake decorator with the poodle paintings moved to Spain to live with Markel, the muscular love of his life. While Juliette missed the three tiny white dogs he brought to work with him each day—Lorna, Luna, and Carl—they were surely sharing a doggy churro and soaking up the sunshine. But it seemed like something new was definitely going on next door, and she was interested in finding out just what. And why all the noise in the middle of prime business hours?

"Excuse me?" she asked the man with the low-hanging tool belt tugging on his faded jeans.

He killed his oversized drill. "Yeah?"

"Is there a new establishment going into this space?"

He looked at her like she'd just requested a piggyback ride when he simply didn't have time. A sigh. A shoulder droop. He pulled a folded sheet of yellow paper from his pocket. "Says here we were contracted by, uh, Candy. Wait. Make that Cotton Candy." He shoved the form back in his pocket, crushing it in the process.

Interesting. A confectioner? That tracked, keeping with the whole dessert theme of the location. Maybe the space came with the right layout. She didn't mind the idea. Maybe this new store would bring in more foot traffic than Cake For Days had. Maybe they'd scoop ice cream or make fresh chocolate in addition to their signature cotton candy. She could imagine the wonderful aromas wafting through the walls already. Perhaps it was an entire candy shop, which would be great for browsers to both stores. Greeting cards and a box of chocolates? A match made in heaven. She was liking this reciprocal relationship idea more and more.

"I'm getting a candy shop next door," she told her best friend Cherry Atwater over drinks, a local porter for her and a white wine for Cherry. Thomas, her ex-husband, had been across the bar when they'd arrived but would likely abandon his football game and join them at some point.

"As in fresh chocolate? You are the lucky person of the day. In every bar, there's always one of those." Her eyes lit up like a five-year-old on water playday. "Think of all the sinful splurging I do when I visit you."

"I was actually waiting for something good like this for The Station. It drastically needs a bump." She shrugged. "I don't know. I felt it in the air. That a change was coming my way. Maybe this new next-door neighbor is it."

Cherry nodded with full-on passion. "If the candy place is anything like the one in Willy Wonka, then I'm visiting daily. I wonder if he'll sing." She grabbed Juliette's wrist. "Did you see a ladder on wheels?"

"Who's singing?" Thomas asked. His dark brows dropped as he attempted to follow the fast-paced conversation. He was generally a pretty serious-minded person, which is why they'd lived in such tepid harmony. Very few waves. "I'm late. Bengals are breaking my heart." He slid the porter that matched Juliette's onto the high top.

Juliette squinted. "Sorry about the Bengals, pal, but I think Cherry's literally assuming the candy man from the Wonka film is going to break into song each time she arrives at the new shop going in next to mine."

Cherry rubbed her hands together. "That would be sexy. I might gain weight, which I'm great with."

"The candy man is not sexy. He's cherublike and jolly." Juliette was laughing, though, because that's who Cherry was, innocent and good. If she could bottle half of Cherry's benevolent approach to life, she'd surely be a happier person with probably lots more friends.

"Don't tell me the candy man doesn't get naked on occasion," Thomas said with a casual shrug and grin. "He probably has a candy partner somewhere. Maybe even a sugar sidepiece."

Cherry leaned in. "This is getting good. They probably pour chocolate on each other."

Thomas nodded, mirroring Cherry's lean. A strand of his dark hair fell onto his forehead. It was longer these days than the neatly trimmed haircuts he always sported when they were married. It looked good on him. "Oh, I know they do. C'mon."

"You're encouraging her." Juliette winced through her laughter. "It's getting disturbing. You cannot sexualize beloved characters from my childhood."

"What do you think the Cat in the Hat does for pleasure?" Cherry asked. "Winnie the Pooh doesn't even wear pants. I could take that places."

"Don't." Juliette held up a finger. "We're wildly off topic and careening into the land of traumatic." But she was enjoying herself, loving these kind of laid-back evenings with these two.

"She's not into sex that much," Thomas said as if it was truly unfortunate news.

"Incorrect. I'm a lesbian, Thomas, we've covered this. I adore you, but an asterisk applies to our marriage. May it rest in peace."

He shrugged. "There is that." Juliette didn't take too many risks in life, but facing the fact that her sexuality and her marriage didn't match was at the top of her big moves list. Everyone had their standout moments, and that one had been hers. All in the past now.

It was Cherry's turn to laugh. "One day Juliette is going to find the woman of her dreams, and I have a feeling they're going to smolder."

It was a nice thought. She smiled wistfully. "Just call me Winnie the Pooh. Who knows?"

Cherry always had her back, and she appreciated the gesture of encouragement. Even if she knew that she would likely never *smolder* with anyone. It wasn't in her nature to get all hot and bothered. She wouldn't mind a companion, though. Hand-holding, kissing on the couch, quiet evenings together. Sex was important, too, but it wasn't a driving force in Juliette's life. It was really nice when it happened, though.

Well, most of the time.

But she wasn't like other people. She didn't obsess about all things carnal. Given, she had a much stronger interest in women than she had in men, and Thomas had been gracious and understanding when she told him they needed to end things, but it wasn't like her world radically came alive when the lights went off even after that shift. She was a calm, rational person, and that was fine. She'd accepted herself for who she was, someone who preferred an even keel.

"Are you in there right now?" Thomas asked around his beer. "You're nodding along to your own thoughts again."

"It's kinda cute if you hadn't ignored about five different questions," Cherry added. "Including your pet panda's favorite restaurant."

"I'll have to score myself one of those," she said, hopping back into the conversation. "Anyway, I'm really excited about the new store going in. I plan to patronize it weekly and get my sugar rush on." She grinned and took a long pull from her beer, hanging on to this good news. Needing it. "Maybe we'll be like, I don't know, partners in industry. Do some cross-promotion."

"I can't believe more people aren't snatching up your awesome greeting cards," Cherry said, her big brown eyes soft and pillowy. When Cherry felt for you, she didn't hold back. "It's criminal because they are the perfect combination of whimsical and creative. Who doesn't prefer something unique and handmade?"

"You'd be surprised." She made a money gesture, rubbing her thumb and fingers together.

"Well, it's worth it. I've always loved your artwork since your doodles in chem class. One of these days, though, they're gonna take off."

The dream. Juliette brought her shoulders to her ears. She vacillated between ambition and resignation when it came to her current situation, and which one she landed on just depended on the day. "It's gonna turn around soon."

Thomas lifted his glass. "To The Station."

"Your baby," Cherry chimed in.

These were her people and she loved them. It was moments like these that she realized her luck. Her wealth lay in her good friends. "You guys are going to make me cry, and I finally figured out how to apply eyeliner properly." They had become the most unexpected little trio, but she loved their tiny group and would do anything for either of them. She and Thomas had history, sure, but they'd found their way after years of trying. Cherry was literally just that, the wonderful cherry on their friendship sundae. Perfection.

They stayed for the bar's weekly Tuesday night trivia, which they took a little more seriously than probably called for. Sadly, their team took their customary second place to the table of retired elderly engineers from Morning's Glow, one of whom happened to be Pete Wunderlich, for whom she'd penned the greeting card that day. She was tempted to throw Hot Timothy in his face for spite, but tempered her hot edge.

"Next time, whippersnappers," Pete shot and guffawed with his cronies.

Thomas glared, dripping with defeat. "I hate that they always beat us. We were this close." The prize was a free round for the team, but that was just bonus. This was about more than a prize.

Cherry shrugged. "What are we gonna do? They've been alive longer. They always best us at the history questions. Makes sense. They lived it. Pop culture is our one angle over them. Our shot."

"Study up, you guys," Thomas said, pointing back and forth between the two of them. "See you next Tuesday."

"Wait. Won't you be at bowling tomorrow?" Juliette asked. They were all part of the same small cosmic league, which was really just a chance to get together on Wednesdays and eat nachos and talk smack about everything that happened on Tuesday to some disco music and flashing lights. Rolling the ball down the lane was just a perk.

"Can't. This is kinda news. Are you ready?" He left a dramatic pause. "I have a date." Juliette had no interest in rekindling her romance with Thomas, because it simply hadn't worked, so why was it a slight punch in the gut that he was going out with someone new? Underneath, she knew. It was because her own dating life was at a standstill. No one special had come along, but then she hadn't done much to help the process. She was the tiniest bit jealous of him and his prospects. She also knew damn well it was unattractive and something to work on within herself.

"Who is it?" Cherry demanded, channeling Juliette's low-key annoyance. She was being stood up, too.

"You don't know her. The receptionist at the car place. I met her when I was having my brakes replaced. She makes the best cappuccinos."

"I know that receptionist," Cherry commented with a narrowing of her gaze. "Big boobs. Are you into big boobs, Thomas?"

"I hadn't noticed." He took a pull of his beer and studied the end of the football game on the bar's screen, but it was a blowout and shouldn't have been at all interesting. A ploy.

"Well, enjoy your boobs," Juliette said, striving for good ex-wife sportsmanship. "We'll call Nathan to fill in at the lanes." Nathan had an obsession with choosing the right bowling ball and often smelled strongly of extra-minty mouthwash. She'd get over it. She'd do it for Thomas.

"I don't know that I'm up for Nathan," Cherry said. "The air-kisses. The ridiculous dance when he picks up the seven pin on spare. We can all pick up the seven, Nathan. Relax."

"We'll get through this together. We always do." They exchanged a fist bump, hip bump, shimmy.

"Better run," Thomas said, tossing a few bills to Felix, who was on the bar that night.

"Bye," Cherry and Juliette said in unison.

"Big boobs, huh?" Juliette asked once they were alone.

"And tight green sweaters. I've seen firsthand." Cherry shook her head. "Men. Can't live with 'em."

"Which is why I don't."

"Respect headed your way. Maybe you've got it figured out, Jules." Cherry kissed her cheek with a smack, and they gathered their bags.

It had been a fantastic night in spite of the gut-wrenching trivia loss, and Juliette planned to go home to her cat, make sure Skittles received her late-night snack on time so she didn't attack all the house plants in anger. Then, she'd gear up for another day. It was her goal to be in bed each night by 11:00 and up at 6:24 after two taps of the snooze button. It was eight steps to the bathroom to brush her teeth, and her day would be off and running! Regimented? Sure, but her order and predictability were what kept her afloat. She dined on structure, and it loved her back like a codependent girlfriend. She knew most everything that would happen tomorrow down to Nathan-the-lane-dancer subbing for Thomas and preferred it that way. Did she secretly long for a little shake-up? No. Not really.

❖

Peyton was efficient at picking up her entire life and moving. That was because during her time in Dayton, she'd never fully accumulated the stuff that most people gathered and clung to, making the transition from her apartment to her new house an easy one.

She wondered about that now. Had she just been too afraid of things not working out that she'd never allowed herself to put down true roots in Dayton? It would make sense. She'd experienced a colossal hit, making it hard to trust that things might actually go well for her, even when they were.

She wanted this time to be different, though. This was Peyton's chance to fully live, taste, breathe, and feel something. Well, hopefully that last part. And as daunting as this whole new venture seemed, she planned to relish the little moments throughout the day. Even the hard ones.

First, there was some reacquainting to do. Landonville was a small- to medium-sized city with the appropriate ratio of quaint to contemporary swirling in a mixture through its streets and culture. She imagined that being back would come with the requisite ghosts lurking behind many a corner, but the center of town had shifted so much that it took her a while to even gather her bearings. Her high school still stood on the outskirts. The park where she first tried a cigarette with her friends had received an entire facelift, leaving it almost unrecognizable. She stood along the fence but opted not to go in. A part of her life that hadn't served her well.

Deep breath. All in the past.

She focused on all her new/old city had to offer. Landonville was populated with lots of cute mom-and-pops for charm, but if you needed a Walmart or a Burger King, they were there, too. Medium was where it was at. The best of both worlds. And this city was honestly the perfect place for Peyton to slow her spirit, quiet her fears, and finally find a way to thrive in all aspects of her life. Well, she would give it a go, anyway. Once she'd settled in, however, she allowed herself to acknowledge that she was afraid, lying awake many nights, shaking beneath her new cotton sheet, a splurge.

The renovations she'd commissioned on Cotton Candy's new storefront were 90 percent complete, which left her under a month to unpack her newly arrived inventory, pull the old inventory out of storage, and decorate like there was a lion chasing her through the woods. She channeled Candy and her positivity every step of the way. Semiweekly phone check-ins helped.

"Sounds to me that the design for the space is pleasing," Candy said. "Just make sure you think through the flow of traffic. How the customer moves through the store and what products they'll encounter along their path. Order is everything."

"Right. I should probably physically walk it myself. I get caught up in viewing angles."

"I got ya, sweetheart. You need your enticers up front, your push-up bras, your matching sets, but the larger selection of those goodies should be at the back to force your customers through the space. They'll buy more that way. Bait and catch."

"Brilliant." She nodded, taking notes in her T-shirt and favorite lime green underwear while standing in her newly unpacked kitchen with the white cabinets. She'd always wanted white cabinets, which had been a reason to snatch up the rental then and there. "I'm also working on a boxer, briefs, and T-shirt section, but of the sexy variety."

"A modern approach to lingerie," Candy said. "I love it."

"I imagine women will still make up the largest portion of my customer count, but everyone could use a little something sexy to wear." She saw no reason to limit herself. Men and nonbinary consumers would have choices as well. She planned to advertise the hell out of the variety. Not only that but Cotton Candy would not be marketing with models and sizes that were unrealistic. Nope. Curvy was where it was at, and all sizes would be celebrated equally.

Two days later, amidst the last big push of renovation at Cotton Candy Part Two, Peyton went to work. She wasn't afraid of putting her head down and accomplishing a lot when under the gun. The new storefront was honestly perfect for a lingerie shop, sunny with big, beautiful picture windows that would showcase the very best pieces from the absolute finest brands she could assemble for her collection. The expensive sign she'd ordered would be going up sometime today, and she was pleased with the company's execution of her brand-new pink and brown logo that incorporated the curves of a woman's breasts into the rounded letters. Saucy and fun. Especially since you didn't exactly notice them until, well, you *did* and then never saw anything else. Peyton liked that part. She'd always been comfortable with her body, but through her work with Candy, she'd more fully embraced the sensual side of herself and liked it. She'd learned what she enjoyed and what she didn't.

For one, she very much enjoyed women and their company in the bedroom. She wasn't one to shy away from the right hookup. She never let herself get serious, but she made sure to make each woman she was with know her worth, and her importance. Life was too short for throwaway moments. She relished each human interaction, physical or otherwise.

"You like the spot you picked out?" Candy asked. "Location is everything."

"I really do. Cute little strip mall with a stationery store next door. Sounds corruptible, right?"

Candy laughed in that melodic, uninhibited way that was pure Candy. Peyton missed her.

Researching the city had informed her that she didn't have a ton of competition aside from the big box stores. That meant she could exhale and focus on spreading her wings, cultivating a quality client list, as well as continue to grow her daily customer base.

She relished the clean slate and had no intention of blowing this opportunity. It was her old home, but new. And this time, anything could happen. A fresh, unmarked upon canvas awaited her. She'd used her first few weeks in town to learn as much as she could about her new surroundings and get her head and house in good order. She loved the little garden cottage she'd found in an adorable neighborhood just two blocks away from the store. She could easily walk to work if she wanted to. Her mornings had been full of gardening, redesigning the flower beds out back, and putting in a few tomato plants, which would not only add a splash of color to her salads, but allow her to watch the little plants climb their way to the sky in victory. It was the little things…

But now, on this particular Monday morning, it was time to get serious. She wanted to open in seven days, and that meant hiring an employee or two with an eye for all things sexy, painting the interior in soft purples and grays, supervising the installation of shelves and drawers for additional bra and panty inventory, and setting up her sales racks. The noise had gotten a little loud, but she could drown it out with some music.

She turned on a little Beyoncé, popped in her AirPods, and went to work. A short time later, she was aware of a presence behind her and straightened from the box of corsets she'd just sliced open, her hair in a ponytail, cheeks probably flushed from exertion. Standing there was a brunette with her hands on the backs of her hips and her mouth in the shape of a perfect circle. There was something about her that woke Peyton the hell up.

"Hi," Peyton said. She eased a strand of hair behind an ear and offered a smile. The loud table saw nearby buzzed for shelf installation and shaping. The measurements sadly had been off the first time. The workmen killed the saw when they saw the conversation. "Thanks, guys," Peyton said. "Sorry. Hi, there we are."

"Hi," the woman said. She looked concerned. "Are you the person in charge?"

"That's me."

"Perfect. Just the person I was looking for."

Huh. There was something familiar about this woman, but Peyton couldn't quite land on what. Dark hair past her shoulders, cropped jeans and red top with the three-quarter sleeves. A simple look, but yeah, it really worked for her. Whoever she was, something had her off her game as she stood there, stock-still, as if taking in surprising information. "Well, welcome to Cotton Candy! The future home, anyway. How can I help you? As you can see, we're not open yet. Little construction. But soon."

"It's just loud. A lot loud, actually."

Peyton glanced behind her. "Sorry about that. The shelves weren't fitting, so they're doing a little reworking. Nothing ever goes according to plan, unfortunately."

"It's just that it's in the middle of the business day and we all share these walls."

Peyton felt her grin dissolve a little. "Just temporary. I promise."

She waited. The woman blinked and seemed to reset. That was good. The silence hovered just shy of weird. "I'm your neighbor." She inclined her head to the wall to their left. "From next door. The Station. We sell cards and gifts."

"Oh! The cute little stationery store? Wow, hi. Nice to meet you." That changed everything. "We're next-door neighbors. Twins." The woman seemed less tense now, but also a little bit confused.

"Well, twins might be a bit too…Anyway, nice to meet you, too. I don't know if you've met Mr. Huberson over there. Your neighbor to the other side. He's also the superintendent of the entire building. He's your guy for anything you need handled or fixed," she said, indicating the right wall. "He keeps to himself. Sometimes grumpy, so watch out."

"The dry cleaner? So he's in charge around here? I feel like that's in the paperwork somewhere."

"Yes, that's him. Dry Style. Which I think is a play on *high style*. Never have confirmed that because—"

"He keeps to himself. Grumpy. You mentioned that."

"Exactly why."

"A quiet little row of businesses." And she'd proven anything but. She'd gotten the message but decided to shrug it off because the complaint was honestly a little silly. It's not like this was her normal, and the woman should probably relax that little divot between her eyebrows.

This whole thing could have gone better. She wished it had.

Still, Peyton couldn't quite place why her new neighbor felt so familiar. Even the rigidity resonated with something tugging at her from the past. She reached to childhood and came up empty. Definitely not prison. The woman was friendly enough. Pretty. Probably in her early to mid thirties with straight brown hair, parted on the side, clear blue eyes, and a really great mouth. Full. Her lips could have been straight out of a painting. Oh yeah. Peyton was a mouth expert and those were kissable. She'd definitely seen these lips before. Sadly, not against hers. She'd had zero sex since the move. Something to remedy soon.

"I'm Juliette Jennings."

"Juliette." It hit. "God, thank you! That's it! You're Juliette from the damn driver's license place." Her hand flew to her forehead as she grinned in victory.

Juliette blinked. Recognition flared. "Oh, okay. It's all making more sense. You're Peyton. Yes. Just out of context. So I just didn't make the—" Then her face fell. "I should have been more friendly that day. I was struggling with missing work and the monotony of the process."

"Totally picked up on that part. The divot right here." She gestured to the space between her own eyes. "I didn't mind. You were fun."

"Embarrassing now."

They smiled at each other. The air was friendlier. Maybe Juliette-the-Uptight was a potential friend after all, despite their differences and tolerance for noise. She'd made acquaintances all over town, doing her best to meet people. Lots of folks already knew her name, but she didn't have a true friend yet. Luckily, she'd met no one who seemed to remember the kid who went upstate a handful of years ago. It gave her the opportunity to start fresh.

"I'm sorry," Juliette said, interrupting her thoughts. She was studying the place with the same puzzled expression from earlier. "Where's the candy going to go? I mean, will there be any? Jelly beans. Chocolate bark?"

Peyton studied her, completely lost. "You're going to have to be more specific."

"Cotton Candy. I just figured…but then when I came in, I see clothes." She eyed a see-through nightie. "Well, almost clothes. That one's see-through. I'm sorry. I'm probably making things up. What kind of store is this?" Her voice went up an octave on that last sentence.

"I sell lingerie for all body types and genders."

"I'm sorry?"

"You know, bras, negligees, panties, sexy boxers, and under-garments. Some on the conservative side. Some more sensual. All quite nice against the skin." She crossed to the counter and located a card with her name and logo. "Here you go. I like to make people feel their best in the underclothes."

"Noble." Juliette studied the card and read aloud. "Peyton Lane. Prepare to feel sexy." Her eyes moved to the logo, which she studied for a moment before straightening extra fast. "Oh! So when you say *candy*, you mean…"

"The good stuff underneath, just waiting to be revealed. I love unwrapping a much anticipated gift, personally."

Juliette swallowed, grappled for words, which was honestly cuter than anything she'd done since coming in. Her cheeks flamed and her blue eyes moved from one area of the room to the another, searching for an anchor or an exit sign. She'd seen the same expression before on the faces of daughters who trailed behind their mothers, dragged into a world of silk, satin, and lace before they were ready to embrace and admit to their own curves. Peyton got the feeling that Juliette wasn't an overly sensual person. A shame. Maybe she could help change her new friend's outlook. Over time, of course.

"So, you sell boobs. Busts. Bras, I mean. Dammit. Can't speak today."

"That's okay. Take your time. Breasts have a way of overtaking one's thoughts, no?"

A narrowed gaze. Four blinks. Juliette was clearly processing it all.

Peyton pressed forward. "I do sell bras. And slips, hip-huggers, thongs, corsets, pajama sets, muscle shirts, tank tops. You name it. If it's soft, silky, well-made lace, or just attractive to the human form, we have it."

Juliette swallowed and tucked a strand of hair behind one ear. Peyton held on to a laugh. "You were expecting an honest-to-goodness candy store, weren't you?"

The movement was understated, but Peyton spotted a nod. "I thought maybe. I like chocolate."

"You are the cutest. Well, now I feel compelled to bring you some."

"You don't have to do that."

"I can't have my new friend disappointed, wishing I was someone else. I promise, by the time I'm finished, you're going to like my shop and its proximity to yours. If not, I'll bring you a whole damn chocolate factory."

"I think that you're just kidding. Hard to tell." Juliette didn't hand out smiles easily, Peyton was finding.

"You never know." She lifted one finger. "Hey, maybe we can exchange brochures. I'd be happy to house your marketing materials at my register if you'll do the same. I do special events in the store, too, and I'd love to get the word out to anyone planning a bachelorette party or who just wants to get together and shop with friends after-hours. I provide the champagne and strawberries. Girl parties are my favorite." She had a thought. "Speaking of which, let's have a glass right now. It's a special occasion, after all. We have to commemorate today."

"Oh. We do?"

Peyton tilted her head. "I see the hesitancy on your face and am guessing it's alcohol related. If you don't drink, I very much respect that."

"No. I do, it's just—"

"The fact that it's a late-morning transgression. Just blame me. Fully. Tell yourself that the lace-peddling woman from next door made you partake during the workweek. You'll feel better about it." She tossed in a smile and hoped for the best. She also hoped she wasn't trying too hard. There was a layer of anxiety humming just below the surface when she interacted with people that never quite went away. Could the neighbor girl notice?

Juliette laughed, but there was a stilted, forced quality hooked to it. "You're kind of a whirlwind. I'm just trying to keep up."

"I've heard that before. I tend to try to fit a lot in, probably related to my own weird history. We could ask a therapist someday." She held up a finger. "Be right back."

She returned with two of the new flutes she'd just purchased for the store and poured them two-thirds to the top with the good stuff. "A toast to new neighbors and maybe even—and don't think me presumptuous—new friends. You never know." She bumped her eyebrows on that last part and watched Juliette purse her lips. The really good ones. She was instantly jealous.

"Cheers," Juliette said conservatively and offered another forced smile. Oh, she was trying but seemed a little bummed that the candy store of her dreams hadn't materialized next door. Now that Peyton thought about it, she might have been, too, if she was in Juliette's shoes.

"I'll have to come by your store, take in all the blank paper."

"Well, I sell more than that."

"Oh, I can imagine, but it's the paper that gets me going." She sighed, thinking of the real-life parallel. There was nothing like a clean slate. "Just think of all those uninked thoughts, simply waiting to burst on to the scene and change the world with their meaning. You might be selling the sheet of paper that will one day change the world with an idea."

Juliette tilted her head and for the first time seemed to enjoy something Peyton had said. Progress. "That's a truly an interesting way to frame it. Important thoughts otherwise unvoiced, just waiting for their blank sheet of paper."

"Life-changing ones. And since you're looking at a walking

billboard for a fresh start"—she made a circular gesture around the perimeter of her own face—"I worship at their altar."

Juliette paused. "Was moving here kind of—"

"Another example? Yes. And I don't plan to blow it." Not a topic she planned to go into with Juliette. She didn't share the details about her past and where she'd been with many people. She couldn't. The shame would overwhelm her. Instead, she made a practice of breezing past it. "What about you? Lived here long?"

"My entire life. I did move across town, though. That was big." The way her blue eyes widened on that last word to really smash it home said a lot. She damn well believed the sentiment. "I have about three courageous decisions on my résumé."

Peyton laughed. How could she not? She was beginning to clock her new neighbor: a ball of adorable encased in Bubble Wrap. Her favorite. She'd always been a sucker for uptight souls. She liked to poke at them, make them drop their sharply tied knots and live a little. But this woman was all of that with an extra dollop of something cute.

"We never ran into each other. I bet we went to rival high schools."

"Burnett," Juliette said.

"Yep. We moved here my sophomore year and I went to Hill." Peyton raised a cheerleader-like fist. "Go, Cubs. I should have gone to more games. I regret that now."

"I was in the band." Juliette raised a proud shoulder. "Clarinet."

Peyton nodded because that tracked. "You are too much, and I mean that as a compliment."

Juliette looked pleased yet confused. "If you say so. Thank you." She sighed. "I have to be honest. I wasn't expecting lingerie. I'm still trying to—"

"Do you wear it?" There she went, poking the Bubble Wrap.

"I'm sorry. What? Are you asking me about my"—she dropped her voice to a near whisper—"underwear?"

"Or panties. Bikinis. Jockeys. I'm not sure what you wear, but I'm gonna guess something." She squinted, knowing how to size up a client from the vibe they sent. "You don't seem like the commando type."

Her eyes went wide. "I'm not. God."

"But more specifically, I'm asking if you like to shop for lingerie." She grinned. "It can be a lot of fun. I promise. Nothing embarrassing about it. I will happily assist."

Juliette swallowed. "I'm sure I have before. I mean, of course. But mainly I'm an online kind of girl." She pantomimed a computer and a mouse. "Just click, click. And it arrives."

"Well, maybe once you get acquainted with the store and what I have to offer, you'll change your mind."

Juliette blushed in response and sipped her champagne. "Yeah. Maybe."

"I didn't mean to make you turn pink. We can talk about something else. In fact, let's!" She threw in what she hoped was a warm smile. "Sometimes I get carried away and leap too soon. Zig when it would be much more polite to zag and not talk about underwear. You can ignore me or tell me to back off." She tossed in a laugh. "But know I'm just a harmless person who gets excited about small stuff. If you knew me better, it would make sense." No reason to drop her entire sordid history in their second conversation. Peyton was still cautious about who she told about her past, especially in this town.

Juliette stood an inch taller as if to prove herself. "No. I'm not uncomfortable at all." It was difficult to believe, but she made a display of how loose her limbs were, which was honestly perfection. Peyton wished for a rewind button for a second viewing.

"I can see that. Good demonstration." A pause. "Well, maybe one day you can come in and let me assist you in a purchase. I give hefty discounts to next-door neighbors. No pressure."

"Yeah. Totally," Juliette said. Wide-eyed nodding commenced. "I better get back to The Station. Midmornings, ya know. Maybe ask the guys to minimize the noise as much as possible."

"Another hour. Tops." She paused. "Does it get really busy at this time?"

"No." She seemed to deflate, which was quite sad to see. "Not really. But I work with the traffic I get. Have a great day. I promise to be nicer than I was at the BMV. And when I stormed in here about the noise. And acted depressed about your store."

"You already are. I'm impressed at the turnaround. Bye, Juliette."

"Bye, um…"

"Peyton."

"I knew that."

She watched Juliette push the glass door open and move through it. She had a way of gliding when she walked that Peyton imagined she wasn't at all aware of. With a sigh, she surveyed the mountain of work that sat there, just waiting for her. The visit had been a nice reprieve and reminded her to get out there and get to know the city again and the people who lived here. Maybe tonight she'd hit up that little bistro and bar down the street from the store. She tapped her lips. She loved the crackle of untapped possibility. Plus, she wouldn't be left alone with her own thoughts. Her own demons and self-recriminations. She longed, more than anything, to feel human again. She grabbed her bag and locked her door, wondering to herself if it was even possible.

Chapter Three

Three days later, Juliette walked the four aisles of her store, straightening her products, adjusting displays, and generally just killing time until some new customer arrived. She slid her hands into her back pockets and whistled. She casually checked the door, just in case. She jumped around the corner of aisle two like a ninja. Still no one. It had been ninety minutes since the woman who bought the puppy stationery had left, and that didn't make for a great Tuesday. Not only that, but she didn't have a single custom card to illustrate. That part of her business was shaping up to be a massive failure. Maybe playing it safe and sticking to magnets would have been the right way to go. Lesson learned.

Huh. Look at that. In her boredom, she'd caught a glimpse of Peyton carrying a huge handful of black and pink hangers into the store as she returned from probably her lunch break. She'd waved through the glass, and Peyton had smiled and laughed, because waving back had been out of the question given her fistfuls. They'd developed a friendly relationship in passing but hadn't had more than a few short, casual conversations. She'd give Peyton one thing—she worked hard. She was already at work inside Cotton Candy before Juliette got in and was there still going hard after.

The sound of the bell above the door rang and then, "I need to talk to you."

She turned. Cherry. How did she sneak up? She must have arrived from the other direction on the sidewalk. Cherry Atwater was the catering manager for the Boulevard Hotel several miles away, so it was rare she popped in midday. Something was up. "Yeah, yeah. You got it, Cher. I'm right here."

Cherry's sculpted brows dipped low. "I don't know how you're going to feel about what I have to say. That's the thing. I just don't know." She touched her forehead and zigged one way across the beige and blue striped carpet and then zagged back the way she came. "But I finally have my nerve up and forced myself into my car, and here I am, so I should just go for it, right?"

"Right." Juliette hadn't seen her friend look this upset since tenth grade when she'd sent Jeremy Stracco a shot of her shoulder with a hint of side boob and felt certain he was sharing it with his friends. He hadn't been, but she'd needed talking off the ledge, all the same. "Of course you should. Come here. Relax." Juliette took her friend's hand and pulled her behind the front desk where she could sit in the comfortable chair she used for illustrating at her drafting table. "I have a feeling that there is nothing going on here that we can't fix together. Super duo, power of two, remember?" A throwback to their childhood days. "Tell me everything."

Cherry exhaled slowly. Her dark eyes carried sincerity and a little bit of fear. "I grew my hair out for Thomas."

Juliette held her pose, one arm on her hip. Her mind rearranged the words, trying to grasp their meaning. "Okay. You mean he asked you to grow your hair? Why would he do that? Do you want me to talk to him?" How weird. What was she missing?

"No. No. I mean, I chose to grow my hair out so Thomas might notice it. *Me*, I mean." She covered her mouth with one hand and waited, as if her words were destined to set the room on fire. When they didn't, she released it. "I have a major thing for Thomas, Jules, and I don't want him to go on the date with the green-sweater-wearing boob tart." Another covering of her mouth.

Holy hell. Was this real? She felt the sweat prickle on her neck already. "First of all, let's slow down. Back up. Take it again. You have a thing for…Thomas. A different Thomas or *my* Thomas? Well, my used-to-be Thomas."

Cherry gulped and nodded. "Same guy. Do you hate me? I would totally understand if you do. I've tried to shove it down and beat it in the face with a rolling pin."

"Violent."

She didn't slow down. "But it just won't go away. So is there hatred and is it aimed at me?" She offered a bring-it-on gesture. "I can take it."

There was so much to keep up with, Juliette's thoughts spun like yarn on a loom. "What? No. I don't hate you. I'm floored because you never once let on." She shook her head, grappling hard. "And I know you, Cherry. Why wouldn't you have said something, hinted, sent a singing telegram? I'm your best friend."

"But you're also his ex, and it got so twisted in my brain like the gnarly nets on a poorly run fishing boat, and I did everything to make it stop, but now there's Boobs in a Sweater lurking around the dating corner, and I feel like I need to say something before my gnarly tangled ship has sailed."

The dust settled, and the room quieted. Juliette understood the goal. "You want my blessing first. That's what this is. Before you do anything about it."

"Declare myself. Yes. But I absolutely won't if it's going to hurt you." Cherry chewed her bottom lip as she awaited whatever words Juliette felt comfortable sharing. "No pressure."

It felt like the opposite was true. Juliette hadn't had time to process this, turn it over in her hands, yet at the same time, she was wildly aware of the fact that she couldn't say no. She had zero claim to Thomas, nor did she want any. And if Cherry was so desperate for him, who was she to get in the way and ruin what could be a beautiful future? But a much larger part of her knew that Thomas was not likely to be interested, and that made her heart heavy for her best friend. Cherry was wonderful, but not the type he went for. There was very little risk of her two best friends falling desperately in love, and if it happened, well, she would support them, cheerlead, be their third wheel with a smile on her face because this was *Cherry*. This girl would walk over hot glass barefoot to find you a glass of water if thirsty. She deserved nothing but the best person, and Thomas happened to be pretty great himself, except for his unfortunate toothpaste in the sink habit. So she would swallow the weird kernel of discomfort that nestled in her chest and press on.

She took both of Cherry's hands in hers and, for a moment, saw that spunky fourth-grader on the playground, a friend to every new kid who entered their homeroom. Her heart swelled. "Of course you have my blessing. I will be forthright and say that I didn't see this coming. But I want you to be the happiest person ever. If Thomas brings you that happiness, I say go get him." Not only was she proud of the speech, but she meant every word.

Cherry's mouth formed an *Oh* as she exhaled the air she'd likely kept hostage. "You have no idea what kind of weight that takes off my shoulders. Now I just have to summon the courage I need to open my mouth and speak my truth." She hurried to reassure. "Not that I'm expecting anything back. I just know that honesty is a box I need to check in order to look at myself in the mirror. I can't be a coward, you know?"

"You could never be that. You're the most amazing person I know."

Cherry's face relaxed into the most wonderful smile. "Thank you for being my friend."

"For life."

Cherry didn't hesitate. She hopped out of the chair and pulled Juliette into the warmest, tightest hug. "You're a class act, Jules. I better get outta here." She turned back when she reached the glass door that led to the sidewalk outside. "By the way, you weren't kidding about that lingerie shop. Sexy stuff going up in the window." A final wave and she was gone, a skip in her step, a hopeful smile dancing on her lips.

Juliette winced. The window displays were going in? She couldn't help but worry how the overt sauciness of Cotton Candy might impact her older, stodgier customer list. Because they made up a huge portion of her income. What if the scantily clad mannequins chased them away? She was already floundering. Deciding to satisfy her curiosity and steal a peek, she strolled the few feet down the sidewalk that separated the two shops' doors and turned just in time to see Peyton in the window hanging a *Grand Opening Soon* sign over a mannequin with large breasts and curvy hips in a purple bra and panty combo. Juliette swallowed, because the mannequin was hot. Next to her hung a bundle of helium-filled pink and white balloons. Wow. Peyton'd done quite a bit of work in three days. The space, which had been a sparse box, was now popping with color and product displays. Peyton waved and pointed at the sign as if to say *Isn't it great?* Juliette nodded back enthusiastically, admitting to herself that the display was eye-catching and lively. Ahem, and pretty damn sexy. She moved on to the window display on the other side of the shop, another faceless mannequin who had been blessed by God. The black teddy hugged her in all the right places, and as a mannequin, she shouldn't have sparked heat in Juliette's midsection. Yet did. That happened. She'd just been slightly turned-on by a plastic person.

"You have to come." Peyton held the door open and popped her head outside.

She blinked, processing the sentence that she had to have heard wrong. "What?" Juliette said the word way too loud due to mannequin lust and the likely double entendre, but when she finally caught Peyton's *actual* meaning, her heart rate slipped back into a normal rhythm. "To the opening. Right. Yes. I'd love to come to the *opening*." Why was her voice still forceful?

"I'm having it catered. Sexy foods only, of course." Juliette didn't ask what constituted a sexy food. "Complimentary wine and champagne and door prizes handed out on the hour."

"Let me guess. Sexy ones?"

Amazement swept Peyton's features. "It's like you can read my mind."

She couldn't. Peyton was a different kind of creature than her normal friends and acquaintances. It was like little rays of energy shot off her, sent to brighten the world and make everyone think about half-naked people. There were worse things. She still found her puzzling and the slightest bit annoying. Maybe because she was so hard to predict. She stole a last glimpse of the black-teddy-wearing woman and decided to hightail it back to the land of stationery and mugs, so her body temperature would regulate.

She held up her hand. "Better head back in. The place looks great."

"So do you, by the way. Truly."

Juliette blinked and stalled out. "Me? I do?"

"Yes. I love those ankle pants on you." Peyton's eyes trailed briefly down her legs.

She followed her gaze to the hem of her gray slim jeans. She'd paired them with a sleeveless white blouse that morning and, on a whim, added a low-heeled brown bootie instead of her comfy white slip-ons and had hoped the combo worked. Until this moment, she'd been unsure. "Oh, thank you."

"I'm serious. You're killing the game today, Juliette."

She planned to learn how to take compliments with ease but hadn't exactly gotten around to it. She also wasn't prepared for the tingling sensation in her chest that washed its way to her extremities in a whoosh. That was a brand-new feeling she didn't mind. "Just work clothes." But now she felt so much better about them. "You always look great, though. You get fashion." Juliette meant it. But it didn't stop there. Peyton just seemed *prettier* each time she saw her, and that wasn't just Juliette's opinion. She'd seen the way people reacted to her at the BMV. They'd stolen second looks. Big hazel eyes, blond hair with several different sun-streaked shades. Peyton didn't carry herself the way pretty women always seemed to, however. She was verbose, sometimes silly, but her look was very industrial chic that added a whole separate vibe. Feminine without aiming for it. Confusing. All of it. She had no category. Today, she wore a navy and white striped shirt and short denim jacket that showed off the inward curve of her waist. Beige Timberlands made her look like she could take on any hard job. Twice her hair had been styled with lazy waves, but today it wasn't. Straight as a board. Peyton exhibited all the signs of a girl who knew how to put herself together and keep doing it. It made sense when you took her chosen field into consideration. She used underclothing to make people look and feel their best. Juliette had a suspicion that she was pretty damn good at it, too, if the work she'd done pulling the store together was any indication. Peyton Lane knew what the hell she was doing.

"Thank you for the compliment," Peyton said. A pause. "How's business?"

"Not great." Juliette's spirit sank as she remembered her reality. "I'm keeping my eyeballs above water with the sale of Slinkys and mugs. But my soul sobs about that when I'm alone. It was never the goal."

Peyton's eyes went wide.

"I'm exaggerating, but yeah, my trinkets keep me afloat. There. I said it."

"Nothing wrong with that. What would you rather be selling?"

She hesitated, but maybe talking business with Peyton wasn't such a bad thing. She was likely someone who would get it. "I was hoping to make a go of it with my personalized greeting cards. Handmade. Hand-drawn. The second big risk on my résumé."

"Are you going to tell me the third?"

"Maybe someday."

Peyton seemed to accept that. "Then tell me about the decision to offer the cards."

"I'm kind of an artist at heart and always had a way with words. People seem to really appreciate my work. When they buy one, that is. But that's the problem—only a handful of people do."

"Okay." Peyton looked thoughtful. "Price point?"

"Fifteen dollars a card."

"Consider dropping to eleven ninety-nine until they catch on."

Juliette didn't love that idea. "But my time is valuable. Plus, the cost of the supplies."

"But price point is everything, and they're not selling, right? So you experiment. Make a big deal about announcing the cheaper models. Go nuts on social media. Make it a must-have splurge."

"Oh. Social media is not really my thing. I'm kind of old-fashioned."

"What? Make it your thing. This is your business, not your hobby."

The logic was there. Gone was the enthusiastic, talkative smiler. Peyton was in businesswoman mode and passing on words Juliette likely needed to hear. It was time to get over herself, get her ass in gear, and make a few changes if she wanted a sliver of a chance to save her store. "You know what? I'm going to. Thank you."

"Anytime." Her hazel eyes sparkled. "Will I see you around?"

Juliette thought on that. "I'm not sure you can avoid it. Unless of course you crawl to your car."

"Challenge accepted." Peyton laughed. "You're a unique person, aren't you."

"I can easily say the same."

"Copping to that." But she said it with a soft smile, sincerity creeping in. "But you're loosening up around me. I can tell."

"Confession. I sometimes need a warming-up period." She smiled. "I promise I'm friendly." It felt good to be honest. She wasn't everyone's insta-friend and probably never would be. Even now, she still wasn't comfortable in Peyton's shop. It didn't help that it now showcased satin push-up bras and lacy thongs, but she kept her eyes on Peyton, and that made it easier.

"That's okay. You take a while to warm up, and for my own

reasons, I sometimes seize the day a little too aggressively. Working on it. Maybe we'll find a happy middle."

"Yeah, maybe so." She glanced behind her, seeking refuge in the introvert-friendly shop of hers. "Bye for now. I have two greeting card orders to get started on."

"Well, you'll have a lot more soon. Just wait until people hear all about it online."

"Right. It's something to shoot for."

Juliette had the distinct feeling that Peyton was watching her walk away, and something odd happened. She didn't mind, which was exhilarating and troubling because she wasn't interested in Peyton like that. Was she? She was the wrong type. Slightly annoying. Way too on the sensual side of things for Juliette's personal speed and comfort level and, dammit, just too pretty. She didn't fit the typical profile. She was probably still reacting to that damn curvaceous mannequin, who she decided to call Jacquelyn. All the same, Juliette touched her arm where goose bumps rippled to the surface. She shrugged off the shiver and decided to focus on her business. Peyton, damn her intelligence, had just given her some great ideas to run with, and she planned to put them into action. Maybe she'd get a little social media work done before trivia that night.

"Juliette!"

"Yep?" she said, turning back.

"Are you married, single, joining a convent? We never covered that part."

"Happily divorced. He's a great guy. Just not for me."

"Ah. I'm thrilled for the happy part. Life's too short."

"Word." She paused. "That was awkward. I don't know why I said that. I have an older brother who used to in high school. He's a surf instructor in Miami, and I apologize."

Peyton tapped her smiling lips. "You have to stop saying things that make me want to bug you more. Counterproductive to your quiet person goals."

"Oh. Okay. Wise advice. I'm going to creep away now."

Once safely on the sidewalk, she let the new autumn chill caress her cheeks, which she knew were inflamed. She'd really have to work on her social interaction around underwear and people she hadn't known for years. And also, why couldn't it have been a damn candy store? A nice piece of chocolate here, a peppermint there. Instead, she got breasts, hips, thighs. Oh my.

❖

The Frog and Dog was, in many ways, a standard restaurant and bar, and in so many other ways, not standard at all. Peyton spent her first half hour surveying the place, which was about half full and populating rather quickly. Apparently, this was the place to be on a Tuesday night in Landonville. There were about eight beers on tap and a variety of cocktails advertised in the small menuette the barkeep had handed Peyton when she arrived. The bar itself was a small horseshoe with pub tables surrounding it on two of the sides for extra seating. The restaurant portion of the establishment took up about half the space and came with a series of booths and more traditional tables. Goddamn country music played over the speakers. But the most interesting detail came in the building's decor. True to its name, the place was splashed with images, homages, and cartoons featuring frogs and dogs. Sometimes on their own. Sometimes together. Sometimes on a log, fishing with a beer.

"You guys have really leaned in to the whole frog and dog theme," she told the bartender. She tipped the neck of her Heineken at the frog wearing glasses and thumbing through a newspaper like he needed a frog job.

"Yeah, that's all Lola's doing." The guy had a long dark beard and lively eyebrows to match. His voice was gravelly, and he spoke at his own damn pace. Somehow, he, too, matched the decor. *Way to go.* "Her family's had this place since God was a baby. She's the current owner and manager. Her dad, Rolando, had a few frog-dog tributes up, but goddamn, she's run with it over the last fifteen years." He didn't seem thrilled about it, which gave him character. Like a disgruntled hound dog. Perfection. Peyton, herself, didn't mind the decor. It was memorable.

"You talking about me?" A woman about forty-five with gorgeous dark hair and sparkling brown eyes turned around from a point-of-sale station, a credit card dangling from her fingertips like she didn't care if she dropped it or not. She had her thick hair pulled into a ponytail way on top of her head that made it fall down like a fountain. Presence for days. Peyton could feel her energy flowing from where she stood, a good ten feet away. Lola had on a floral crop top, a denim skirt, and three-inch heels. And it fucking worked.

"I was admiring your frogs and dogs," Peyton said. "I'm new here. Taking it all in."

Lola lit up, returned the card and bill slip to its owner, and headed over with a swish of her hips and hair. She leaned her chin onto her palm and paused. Oh, she was good at pauses. "Who are you? I love new people."

"Peyton Lane." She shrugged. "My dad went to a Paul McCartney concert when he was a kid, became a huge fan, but felt like *Penny* was too on the nose."

"Savvy man. I like him. Are you here temporarily, and if so, business or pleasure?" Lola kicked a hip against the bar and waited. She was really pretty in a feisty kind of sense. The glimmer in her eye said she was here for the good gossip and was entitled to it. A man across the bar watched her like he wanted to take her home. Peyton understood.

"Moved here two months ago. Getting to know the city again. I lived here for a couple of years, once upon a time, but everything's so different."

"Married?"

"Never."

"Straight?" She squinted like she could just sense. "No, you're not. I can tell."

"Not since I was seventeen, and then I was just fucking confused."

"Cheers to that. I think I like you, Peyton Lane." Her eyes carried a very friendly sparkle and her demeanor went calm. "Right now I'm in love with my Bobby. He completes my heart." She looked skyward. "That could change. I don't presume to know."

Peyton laughed. What a force. "I like you right back, Lola. I own a lingerie shop a few blocks from here. Grand opening is next week."

"Well, well. My kinda friend. A business owner. Leave me your card, and I'll help put the word out. So will Bobby. He knows people and does what I say."

"I won't argue with that or Bobby." Their conversation was interrupted by beard guy, who was now on a microphone. What was happening? Some kind of show?

"Welcome, welcome, trivia fans. It's time to find out who knows their facts, and who just knows how to lose." His low voice enhanced the insult, that one.

The bar erupted in cheers behind her. She turned around to see that the crowd had grown significantly in the past twenty minutes. Apparently, this was a *thing*. "Stick around and play," Lola said above the noise. "Every Tuesday. Drink specials all night. People clamor, and that makes me cash."

"We could use an extra player," an elderly man said, as he ordered a beer next to her. "If you don't mind the fact that we're old. Harmless, though. We all have wives with tempers."

Peyton threw a glance back to the high-top table in the corner and saw what had to be real-life equivalents of Statler and Waldorf from *The Muppet Show* waving back at them. "Those two belong to you?"

"Ah, yep. Hank there and Willis. I'm Pete. We all live at the Morning's Glow retirement village, but my apartment is by far bigger than theirs no matter what they tell ya. My wife, Myra, has it decorated in a real nice blue color that we both find calming. Like a beach, but inside. No sand."

"Probably for the best."

"I suppose. She's not much into trivia, so the boys and I meet up and slaughter the young people on the regular."

"Well, I like the idea of joining a winning team. I'm in."

"Okay, then. This way."

She followed Pete to his table and met the other two. "Fantastic to make your acquaintance," Willis said. He seemed a lot more enthusiastic than Pete. "Rules are no cell phones. No discussing the questions with anyone not registered to the team. Pete writes down our answers because he has the best handwriting. After five questions, we turn in our paper. That's one round. There are seven. If we win, we get free beers and the chance to gloat, which we very much enjoy."

"My kind of incentive." She smiled, amused at how seriously these guys took trivia night. But then again, everyone in the room seemed very focused.

"You just be sure to listen real good and help us, especially with any questions about Harry Styles. We're still not real sure who he is, but he comes up a lot."

"The Lady of Gaga trips us up sometimes, too," Pete added in whisper.

"Gentleman, you just leave the pop culture questions to me. I live on the internet." She smiled, shimmied her shoulders because this was fun, and turned her attention to the announcer. Just as he started to highlight the rules of the game in his grumpy delivery pattern, Peyton spotted a familiar face at a table catty-corner to theirs. She smiled because there was Juliette with an uninteresting white guy to her left and a Black woman with a gorgeous smile to her right, both about her age. She tried to wave, but Juliette was concentrating exceptionally hard, biting her bottom lip with her brow dipped low. She really did take life super seriously, reminding Peyton of her mission to inspire Juliette to have a little fun.

"Answer a question for me. Does Juliette over there have a boyfriend?" she asked her elderly teammates. She'd never really answered the relationship status question when Peyton had asked.

"Shh," Hank said. "You're gonna break my intense concentration. If I stare at Felix real hard while he talks on the mic, I can sometimes predict what he's gonna say next."

"Nope. Juliette has an ex-husband, Thomas," Pete said with a proud grin. "She likes the ladies now, though, so he's out of luck."

"Really? Well, slap my ass," she said mostly to herself and sat back in her chair, amusement and surprise bubbling over. "You don't say." Her gaydar had failed her miserably, but the new knowledge caused something in her to shift. Maybe she hadn't cut Juliette enough slack. Sure, she was uptight and complained a little, but there was something about her that left Peyton unable to look away. Perhaps it was the quiet way her mind always seemed to be working or how she tapped her finger above her lip when something caught her attention. The tapping only drew her gaze to the most perfect mouth she'd ever seen. So did the smile that had to be earned, so you knew it was genuine.

"Are you listening?" Hank asked, his voice dripping with anxiety. "We gotta focus. It's go-time."

Peyton came back into the fold of the game. "I'm with you, Hank. I will not let you down. Do we have a team name?"

"We're the Quizzly Bears," Willis shot, his eyes steely and focused, like a predator about to pounce.

"You know, that makes a lot of sense." Her gaze flicked back to Juliette, who looked every bit as determined as these guys, like she was ready to take a fucker down. The tension in the room was thick. Peyton was lost in character study. This city cared a lot about their Tuesday night trivia, and it showed. Taking it all in, Peyton grinned and sipped her beer, enjoying the fierce energy pinging over questions like *What breakfast cereal did Mikey like?*

Fifteen minutes later, round one was complete.

The Quizzly Bears were announced to be in the lead with five out of five correct, and the place broke into cheers from their table and a few heckles and boos from the others. Peyton high-fived her three teammates and passed a flat-mouthed Juliette a wave.

She'd caught sight of Peyton just a few minutes into the game. Her blue eyes had gone wide at the discovery. She'd pointed Peyton out and whispered something to her friend. It didn't take long for Peyton to ascertain that these were the top two teams in the bar, and the rivalry ran deep. The Know It Ales, as she'd learned Juliette's team to be called, "are hungry for trivia blood," Willis explained. "Those clowns aren't stealing the title from us. No way. That's why we gotta study hard."

"Because they can't. They have jobs," Pete tossed in.

Hank nodded proudly. "They don't have the time on their hands that we do."

"I see." Peyton nodded very seriously. "Though I do have a job, I'm happy to help in any way I can."

"You already have. We didn't know the one about chirping bird characters."

"You mean the maximum number of characters allowed on Twitter? Right. And without an account, why would you?" She knocked him one in the shoulder and watched him blush. She really enjoyed meeting new people out in the world and never took it for granted. "Don't sweat it, Hank. I got you."

"I'm opening a bird account tonight," Pete said. "I'll probably need to tell the Mrs. so I don't get in trouble. Ladies love me on the internet. It's a whole thing." He rolled his eyes as if his internet groupies wouldn't let him rest. These guys were fun.

The four of them went on to take the free round of drinks in a pretty sound victory. She'd stolen glances at Juliette, who'd only seemed to grow more focused as the game marched on. But her focused face was really quite endearing, adorable, and more attractive than Peyton would have guessed a concentrating face to be. As the room began to clear after victory had been snatched, they'd run into each other at the bar, Peyton to claim her free drink, and Juliette to settle her tab.

"Hey," Peyton said enthusiastically. "Your team gave us a run for it."

"I don't understand," Juliette said. The little dip in her brow clung. "How do you know the Quizzlies? You're new here."

Peyton hooked a thumb. "Just met them tonight, actually. They're fun. Kind of grumpy, but that just makes them cute. Kinda like you." Whoops. Had she added that part? She tossed in a smile and watched Juliette swan dive into overthinking mode. It was becoming her favorite Juliette to watch in action. Then again, she hadn't gotten a chance to witness her in, ahem, other realms. The ones that were her favorite. Man, she really needed a good lay.

"Me? What?"

"Nothing," Peyton said demurely and accepted the beer. She took a sip. This had been a really good night, much needed after a week of killer hours that had ravaged her physically and taxed her mentally. Her muscles thanked her for the break, and her extroverted personality stretched happily from all the interaction. She could feel her battery recharging already.

"Peyton, come back in soon. I'll tell you more about frogs and dogs," Lola said with a smile. "Maybe you can meet Bobby if he's not busy at one of his meetings."

Bobby's résumé continued to build toward the intriguing. "You're on. I can take you by Cotton Candy, too. You're gonna love it. VIP tour. When?"

"Done, but Monday's out. I have ballroom dancing, and I'm tearing up the floor like I have ants in my pants. Peyton, I can shake my ass like it's my job. Competition is soon. So, I can't miss."

"Nor should you," Peyton said.

"I'll swing by Wednesday."

"Done. I want to see a few of your moves. We can make room."

Lola's eyes lit up with delight. "You get me. I'm off like a bat in the night. Duty calls." Lola whirled around, her ponytail flying, off to tend to another customer. Peyton imagined that hair on the dance floor, tossed this way and that. Hairography was no joke. She had a new friend in Lola and could already tell their energies matched. She couldn't say the same about her matchup with Juliette, who might hate her a little bit. Still, there was a flicker of energy between them that kept Peyton on the edge of her seat, like watching two pieces of flint rubbing against each other just ready to spark. The question that lingered? What kind of spark. The two of them might end up screaming at each other in the parking lot some afternoon or, given what she'd just learned, making out in the back seat of Juliette's Prius with the windows steamed up. Oh, what a decadent thought. Juliette, who stood next to her signing her credit card slip, was hard to pin down. But the idea of kissing left Peyton hot and bothered. She really needed to get laid, apparently.

She tossed Juliette a look, still processing what she'd learned that night. "So, you date girls, huh?" Peyton raised an eyebrow, examining everything from a full new angle. "You never said."

"I left my marriage to be true to who I am. Risk number three on my résumé. Now you have them all."

"You're a lesbian." Peyton marveled at how she'd missed this. "But I'm really impressed with you for taking the leap. We have that in common, by the way."

"Leaps?"

"Women."

Juliette's hand went still on the bar. She squinted. "Truthfully?"

"Why would I lie about that?"

"Good point. Wow." She was absorbing Peyton's own revelation. "Hey, you didn't say anything either."

"Yeah, but I scream gay. Or fluid. Or at least fancy-free." She'd been told she had an appreciative eye when a beautiful woman walked in a room and wasn't that great at hiding it. She didn't mind broadcasting who she was. It fell squarely in the live-life-to-the-fullest category, which she embraced.

"No." Juliette squinted. "Nothing about you screams gay. You wear heels in the middle of the workday without customers, and not that it disqualifies you, but it's hardly a scream."

"Well, get to know me a little better. I'm just me and happy about it."

"You also didn't mention that you're best friends with half the city already." She said it with a half scoff. "You're a magnet for friends."

"Acquaintances. Is that bad?"

"Not at all. But it's not something I've been able to accomplish, and I've lived here all my life. People don't chat with me at bars or sidle up next to me in waiting rooms."

"I did."

"Yes, but you're the outlier I'm studying in this conversation. You don't count."

"Well, that's not fair. I want to."

Juliette kept going. "Lola barely looks in my direction, and I'm a regular. She's probably said eight words to me this year."

"I'm sure I could set up a friend date for you. Do you dance?"

"Not well. And the Quizzly Bears? You're on their team now. You won trivia tonight, and this was your first time here." Juliette was getting worked up, and Peyton couldn't stop watching. She was truly beautiful when her cheeks flushed pink like that and she ran her fingers through her hair without even realizing it.

"Also organic." She leaned in closer, taking note of her height advantage. "I feel like you're upset about our win."

"Well…yeah," she said, coming up with no other word. Hard blinks followed.

"Juliette, I say this was affection, but you gotta breathe more. Have more fun."

Those blue eyes narrowed and zeroed in on Peyton. Oh, that hadn't gone over well. "There's nothing affectionate about that."

"And now you're scoffing again. Look at that. There's no reason to scoff. Let's be trivia pals."

Juliette glared. "You're infuriating, you know that?" She covered her mouth in regret, and then uncovered it. "In, well…a lot of different ways I can't come up with." Her word selection was failing her—she was that keyed up.

Peyton held up her hands, palms out. "It comes down to this. I like people. They seem to like being spoken to. And I do okay at bar trivia when old guys cover the hard parts. Can we be friends again now, please? I miss you."

Juliette uncrossed the arms that acted like the gates of reason. Finally. "Of course. I'm not even upset."

Peyton grinned. "Really? Why are your eyebrows so straight? Let them bend."

"That's just how they look, okay?" She covered them with her hand. "Are you making fun of my eyebrows now?"

"This has taken a turn." But Peyton was more amused than anything by this shiny-haired, easily affronted individual. And even more so, she was intrigued by how this woman ticked. She was stringent and too serious for her own good, but still impossible to dislike at the same time because she tried so hard. She just couldn't get out of her own way. Sure, part of Peyton's fixation was because Juliette was very pretty in an unassuming sense. Sexy in the way she carried herself, formed her words, calculated her next move. Everything was thought out. The other part was due to how earnest Juliette's feelings were as they emerged from every pore. She meant them. Nothing was fake or put on. That was rare these days. "I think we have to continue this dialogue in the future. Your social norms versus mine. Our own unique study. I'll pour the wine."

Juliette sighed loudly. "Or we could just accept that we're very different people."

"I promise there are reasons for the way I am." She heard the shift in her tone when she'd said it. She felt the heaviness settle on her chest anytime she let herself think about the past, where she'd been, and how she'd struggled.

Juliette must have sensed the change in temperature. Her features relaxed as she held Peyton's gaze. "I believe you." She offered a soft smile. To her credit, she didn't push for details and left things there. Peyton exhaled and regained her trajectory.

"Anyway. I'm gonna get outta here, and get some rest before it's back to the grind tomorrow."

"See you at the shops."

"Yeah, see you."

As she moved through the bar, she felt Juliette's curious gaze on her. Maybe she evoked just as many questions in Juliette as Juliette did in her. She shrugged off the tingle and let the night air envelop her, accepting the day for all the good it came with. Something she'd learned to do once upon a time, treasure the mundane joys and take a silent moment to celebrate them. She held tight to Juliette's straight little eyebrows, and Lola's exuberance for a good frog statue. The Quizzlies had made her laugh that night. Her shop was beginning to look like a real store. Now, if only she could convince her brother that she was a good person with positive intentions. Well, maybe then she could regain that part of herself she'd lost. It was the thing she wanted more than any other.

CHAPTER FOUR

There are people in life who hold on just a little too tight. It was even worse when they weren't people Juliette had picked out for herself. Juliette's stepmother, Dolores Fichter-now-Jennings, had been a little too hands-on ever since she'd married her father seven years ago.

"She's a lot at first, but I need a lot," her father had said to her over coffee on the day he'd announced their engagement. Juliette had nearly spit out her almond latte, because she simply couldn't imagine her quiet father with such an overbearing woman. Yet, seven years later, she seemed to still make him happy.

Early on, the attention Dolores focused on *Juliette* had been jarring and unexpected. Now, she just found it tiring. Dolores was meddlesome, smiling, and vibrating with hair dye and social ambition. She worshipped Dolly Parton and spent hours on her own margarita recipe. Juliette had learned to just smile and hand over whatever information Dolores sought.

"Hi! Make space. I'm here and I mean business," Dolores said, followed by a boisterous laugh that echoed through the entryway of Juliette's small home.

She arrived everywhere with blond hair piled on top of her head, and makeup too thick to get a good sense of what she might look like in the morning. She had do-good energy oozing from every pore, to Juliette's conservative discomfort. She was a hovering hen, intent on mothering Juliette half the time and assuming the role of sister figure the rest.

"Oh, hey, Dolores." She pushed a smile through. "Didn't know you were stopping by today. Let me clear off the table. I have my monthly bills covering the place."

"Neatly sorted," Dolores said, studying her paper columns.

"Just by due date and section of my life."

"Only you, sweetheart. And we're family, so I don't think to announce myself, right? Hope that's okay."

"Of course," she lied, accepting her fate.

The problem was Juliette had a mother. She just didn't live in Ohio and, okay, rarely came to visit and didn't call often. She'd always been a little self-focused. Dolores, however, who assumed 90 percent of the words exchanged in her marriage, was eager to fill her shoes, often to Juliette's chagrin.

They'd been chatting for thirty minutes now, while Juliette's bill-paying day slipped through her fingers.

"I think if the greeting cards you draw aren't taking off, you just move in another direction," Dolores said around a blueberry muffin from where she sat at Juliette's kitchen table. "Increase your stock of those ready-made greeting cards, sweetie. That's where it's all at. I like the ones that come in the plastic." She brought her broad shoulders to her ears. "Makes me feel like it's been wrapped up for me personally. A little present." She laughed deep and jolly. "That's pretty silly of me, but I don't care."

"They are pretty popular," Juliette said politely and poured Dolores another chardonnay to accompany her self-provided muffin. Dolores loved a good white wine, or white wine spritzer, or white wine sangria. Sometimes with ice. And any time of day. She also strangely traveled with baked goods and thrust the always-round Tupperware container into Juliette's hands, usually within seconds of crossing the threshold. Muffins were her specialty. Dolores wasn't the quietest of ladies, but she knew what she liked and had opinions on what you should like, too. Beginning with muffins and chardonnay.

"Your father and I just worry about you, is all." Dolores hauled up the neckline of her turquoise sweater that displayed her ample cleavage. The move didn't alter much. "And though we're here to help if you need us financially, you're a big girl now, too." Juliette stared blandly because she'd been a fully grown person when she'd met Dolores. Big-girl status wasn't new.

"I promise you that I don't want financial help. In fact, I'd hate it. I'm gonna turn things around on my own." She took a half-hearted sip of her own chardonnay but wasn't really feeling it.

"You know what? That new neighbor of yours, the one next to your shop, is looking saucy." Dolores's whole face lit up. "What's it called, Silky Candy?"

"Cotton. Like the theme-park snack."

"I'll say it's a snack. I stopped by and said a quick hello to the woman who owns it."

"Peyton."

"Right, Peyton. Stopped in just before I came by The Station the other day when I brought you those chocolate muffins. By the way, I love my new set of magnets. Très chic." She'd purchased a five-piece set of *The Golden Girls* complete with a magnet cheesecake. "My friend, Rowena, is already jealous. I told her to stop by the store and get her own. Who's stopping her? Unless someone's bought the other one you had. She'd be just devastated."

"Sadly, no." She sat back in her chair, not wanting to point out that Rowena could get the set on Amazon for two dollars cheaper. "So, you know Peyton, too. Seems everyone does. She's making quite the splash."

"She's just delightful." Dolores leaned in for a secret. "She's gonna do a personalized fitting so I can stop arguing with this underwire so often. She really understood my pain. My girls need a break."

"I hear you." She sat back. "Peyton does seem to know her way around an underwear drawer."

Dolores raised a brow. "Why are you so serious over there? You don't like her or something?"

Juliette shrugged. It wasn't so much that. Peyton just had a way of getting under her skin. She'd been circling around why ever since they'd met. She was so damn beautiful. And so damn popular. And so damn friendly. Why were all three allowed? And more than that, for reasons she had yet to diagnose, Peyton brought out Juliette's really intense emotions. Everything she felt in regard to Peyton, whether for the good or bad, came with a towering exclamation point that threatened to topple her. The lack of control was maddening. "I like her, but she drives me a little crazy, too."

An idea seemed to creep up on Dolores. "Oh, look at you, darlin'. This is your girl attraction, isn't it?" She'd officially come out to her parents and Dolores two years ago after her marriage came apart. They'd watched her dating life with interest ever since. Not that she'd given them much fodder. She'd not gone public with any of the dates she'd gone on. All two of them. "You have a crush. I totally get it. I'd crush on that one, too. Great body. Gorgeous hair. You should go for it. She dates women."

"How do you know that?"

"I offered to fix her up with my neighbor's son, Delbert, and she declined due to his Y chromosome. That leaves the door wide-open for you."

Dammit. No. "It's not like that." Well, probably not. She liked to think she held her cards close to her vest, but hearing about Peyton's sexuality two nights ago certainly left Juliette aware and studying the hyperbolic reaction she'd had to the news. As in, she couldn't stop thinking about it. Peyton was like her? Glamorous, vivacious Peyton? Kissing girls and collecting numbers and taking their clothes off? God. *Okay, stop that.* Not that there was any kind of stencil, but they didn't make them like Peyton in Landonville, Ohio. She was a shiny penny who had this effect on Juliette and…just no. She squinted and scoffed, proud of the combo. Surely, convincing. "No. I don't have a crush on the hot lingerie shop owner. I get why you'd think that. I mean, that's the cliché after all." A pause. "But, um, yeah, she does date women. No big deal. Lots of the population does."

"I'm on to you." Dolores's eyes danced like her metal detector had just alerted on a huge score. "Little girl, you just acknowledged she's hot. And she is. She could be one of those runway models." Dolores's face went instantly pouty and dark, an imitation of those angry-looking women walking in fashion week. "Nah, she's too nice. So ask her out. Oh, I can't wait for this."

"Peyton? Not in a million years. Yes, she's very pretty. The whole world knows that. But she's not my type, and she tends to annoy me."

"That's what they do. It's part of it, darlin'."

"It is not. It was never like that with Thomas." She leaned in with a secret of her own. "Do you know she joined the rival trivia team?"

"With Pete and his buds?" Dolores slapped the table loudly.

"Those coots must have been thrilled. They won the good-lookin' girl lottery."

"The worst part? She was really good at the game. See what I mean? It's annoying. That's what it is."

Dolores studied her like a puzzling specimen. "Speaking of panties, yours are in the tightest little wad right now, and I'm not sure whether to hug you or shake you, you hot and bothered little mess."

Juliette's mouth fell open. "What?"

"You wanted to find yourself a girlfriend. Well, this is a really great prospect. What is it they say?" She snapped her fingers and pointed. "Don't sleep on Peyton." Her emerald eyes sparkled with glee as a thought struck. "In fact, sleep *with* her." She laughed good and throaty at her own brilliance, while Juliette gaped.

"C'mon. I will most certainly not sleep with her." She corked the bottle as if to signal that the bar was closed. The conversation had her wildly uncomfortable, which was so stupid. She was an adult, one who was now angry at herself for her inability to roll with these mild punches.

"Sweet girl, you mean well, but you are far too coiled up for your own good. You have to grab life by the neck and run off with it to a foreign country and have a saucy affair full of orgasms you'll never forget."

"Weirdly specific. And highly personal."

"I had a few of those before your dad." Dolores got a faraway look in her eyes. "Scandals galore that I've hidden beneath life's pillow." She tossed in a girl-to-girl wink.

Oh, man. Time to take a U-turn. "I probably shouldn't hear about those."

Dolores deflated. "See what I mean? That was about to be fun. I'm offering you up some decadent gossip that doesn't hurt a soul, and you're running like a scared puppy."

Why did Dolores of all people have to have a point? "I can vaguely agree. But what's wrong with a more guarded approach? It's just who I've always been."

"Other than how boring it is?" She covered Juliette's hand with hers. "Not that *you're* boring. You're not. But the way you carry on, the intense structure, the aversion to any tiny risk or change in routine leaves me all perplexed and worried for you."

She pushed herself away from the table. "Just because I'm not thrilled that the exciting new negligee pusher shows up and scares all my conservative elderly customers away…"

"First of all, has that happened?" Dolores danced her long, fuchsia nails on the table. Waiting.

Juliette paused. "Not yet."

"Second, maybe this is a gift from God on his gilded throne. A hot next-door neighbor who's smart and fun, and to top it all off, a lesbian!"

"Godsent seems a little generous."

Dolores visored her eyes with her hand as if needing a respite. "I'm afraid you're hung up on details and missing the greater message," she explained in a calming tone. "But we're gonna get you there." She stood up. "Time for me to head home and start my chili. Swing by at dinnertime if you want some."

"Thank you. I have a new salad recipe I'm dying to try."

"You're getting wild now," she shouted to the rooftops. "I like it."

Juliette resisted an eye roll, confident in her life choices and that the path she was on was the correct one. "Judge all you want. But no torrid neighbor affairs for me. Just not in my DNA. Thank you."

"Your loss. And hers. I love you and your overly organized face anyway." She gave that face a squeeze. "I'll drop by next week." She wouldn't announce when. She wouldn't call. She *would* bring muffins. Welcome to Dolores. "See you then."

"I look forward to it."

"Liar. Get your sassy autumn on, girl. Bye."

Juliette closed the door and let out a deep breath, relieved to return to her regularly scheduled evening of salad, a little TV watching, and a good book. With every moment that passed, she couldn't help but take note of the fact that Dolores was right. She did everything just the same as the times before. She sliced her vegetables on the same portion of the counter into the same shapes as always. She washed the dishes as she used them and sat in the same spot on the couch to watch one of her three favorite TV shows that she had on a rotation. Bedtime was clockwork. She was a machine. Life hadn't always been like this, but somewhere along the way she'd crept into boring territory. Safe was one thing. Regimented was another. Double sigh and a head flop on the couch.

"I might be a little too predictable," she yelled to Skittles in the next room. Then she decided the problem wasn't exactly on the agenda for the evening, thereby she would handle it later. That felt good. Brilliant planning, if she did say so herself.

CHAPTER FIVE

It was two days before her grand opening, and Peyton deserved a massage, a bottle of whiskey, and a good, slow lay. She'd even take them in that order. She must have been going for some kind of record, because it wasn't like her to go this long without some kind of hookup. But she knew why she hadn't sauntered into a bar and found a willing and beautiful woman to take home for the night until she crawled out of bed before the sun and returned to her life as regularly scheduled. This was supposed to be a new leaf she'd turned over, and it was time to start acting like it. Nameless hookups were the old her.

She wanted to plant true roots this time, grow her business, and establish a life with substance. That meant she had to lean in to the responsible, grounded side of her personality, which *did exist*, and quit seeking out the temporary. But she knew that the concept of an actual date terrified the hell out of her. If only hookups weren't so fucking hot and repercussion free. Didn't matter. If she wanted sex, well, then she should date, put in the time, and swallow the fear of feeling something. She had to go about this legitimately, like regular people.

But it wasn't like Peyton didn't think about sex.

She thought about it too much.

It didn't help that she worked in a shop full of soft garments geared to enhance and celebrate the human form. Talk about self-inflicted daily torture. Breasts, bellies, bared shoulders, and tops of thighs were beginning to haunt her.

She needed to clear her head and get away for an hour. The grocery store sounded like the perfect mind-numbing place to escape. Good clean vegetable fun. She skipped the big box chains and opted for a local store she'd found not far from Cotton Candy called Pop, Shop, and Roll. It had a deli, some artisanal cheeses, and a good selection of wine, all of which would help her limp through this week, sexless and exhausted.

She rounded the aisle to the cold foods section and found that ice cream lived at the end. There was a couple standing just in front of one of the refrigerated displays with the door open. Unfortunately, it was the very freezer containing the Double Chocolate Candy Bar cartons that she desperately needed. Being a patient person, she waited her turn. When they didn't move, she craned her neck to see that they were in a hot and heavy lip-lock that apparently couldn't wait for the freezer door to close. Hot damn. *Look at 'em go. Jesus, find them a room.* What were the odds that she goes grocery shopping to escape her sexy thoughts only to run into a couple halfway to their own sex scene in frozen foods? Was this some sort of sign? These people were either newly together or in the midst of a torrid affair. The guy held a pack of grape Popsicles, which stood out in sharp contrast to the R-rated grope session playing out in front of her. She tilted her head, getting the impression that they were actually attempting to use the door to shield what they were doing from the general public, which was a bold choice given its transparency.

Finally, Peyton stepped forward. There was only so much time one could wait on ice cream. "Do you mind if I…No, you're fine. You can keep doing that with your hands. I can just reach around you and… Perfect. Got it. As you were."

"We're so sorry," the woman said and stepped back, touching her lips like a badge of pride. "Just standing here in the way, carrying on." She was beaming, her gaze still feasting on the guy's mouth, looking for her next meal, perhaps. Peyton recognized her immediately as the friend of Juliette's from The Frog and Dog trivia night. Oh, and hello, her kissing partner was the guy from their team. So they were a thing. A steamy little thing. Noted.

"Our bad," he said and deposited the purple Popsicles in their cart. They'd likely melted them. He had a smear of her pink lipstick across his mouth.

She opted not to mention it and tossed them a smile. "Oh, don't even feel bad about it. Sometimes you just gotta go for it alongside the fish sticks. I say more power." She offered a wink and pressed on, happy for the lovebirds and jealous as hell of the action. They were likely about to close the deal at home. Lucky bastards.

Just as she reached the checkout stand, her watch vibrated, reminding her that it was her brother's birthday. She didn't need reminding. It had been in the back of her mind all day. She'd quietly wondered if she'd be invited to a party. Both Caleb and Linda, her sister-in-law, knew she'd moved back but had dodged every attempt to get together so far. And, unfortunately, no party invite had arrived.

Not really able to convince herself to wait a second longer, she pulled up his contact information and hit the call button from her car in the parking lot. Excitement bubbled. She missed him and couldn't help smiling through the rings to hear his voice. He was her only family, and she needed him more than ever. They'd lost their mother young, before Peyton could remember, and their father held on for as long as he could before a heart attack took him, too. Some people said he was never the same after their mother passed. Died of a literal broken heart. Their grandfather had moved them to Landonville and taken care of them until she, the youngest, reached eighteen. But their grandfather had been older, quieter, and did a lot of learning on the job.

Peyton ran after Caleb like his shadow, emulating most everything he did, including the illegal stuff. In fact, she'd proven herself so good at shoplifting that after he'd gone on the straight and narrow, she'd not only taken the baton, she'd run circles around the small jobs he'd once pulled. Planning went a long way, and she excelled. She drank. She skipped school. She ran with all the wrong people. If there was a way to act out, she seized it. Angry at the world for reasons she couldn't quite name, even to this day, she did whatever she wanted without regard for who she might be hurting. When Caleb had tried to talk her down, show her the path she should be on, she'd laughed. Right up until the day that the cops came banging on their door after a risky job had gone horribly wrong. A day she didn't like to think about now. At that point, she'd been nineteen and he'd been twenty-three.

He'd cut her off. For good reason.

She'd been quickly sorry about the trouble, the run-ins with police for theft and truancy. She'd lost her shot at a scholarship, which she'd desperately needed, when her grades tanked. She'd wound up in court on more occasions than she'd like to remember, and embarrassed her brother too many times for his continued forgiveness.

Landonville had forgotten about her, and so had he. He had a new family now, a wife, two kids. Alyssa and Joshua, who was named after their father.

She still tried. Maybe one day, they'd be close again. In fact, it was her number one wish. If only he could see how hard she'd worked to turn things around. She wanted to show him her shop, the house she'd rented, her garden. Caleb needed to know how differently she saw the world now and her place in it. She was good at her job, trustworthy, and tried to be kind to everyone she encountered. It was the least she could do to put things right with the world.

"Hey." Caleb's voice. He'd popped on to the call right before it would have rolled over to voice mail.

"Happy birthday! How are you?" She slid a strand of hair behind her ear. Nervous. Her grin was huge. She couldn't help it. If the conversation went well, maybe she would suggest a visit soon. She'd love to spend time with the kids. They seemed like a ton of fun from the photos online. She wanted the chance to get to know her only niece and nephew.

"Hey, Peyton. Thanks. We're actually just in the middle of a playdate for the kids, so I can't really talk. Linda's got her hands full. Cool of you to call."

"Oh, okay. No problem. Right! Give them a kiss for me, okay? I just really wanted you to know that I'm thinking about you today. We need to do that dinner soon. I'm serious." She waited. The anticipation crawled across her skin.

"I appreciate that. I'll call you soon."

"Okay. Yes. I look forward to that. Sounds good!"

He clicked off the call first. The car went quiet along with her hope. She lowered the phone to the passenger seat of her Mustang, understanding that he likely wouldn't call, and that was okay. Yet she still smiled widely alone in her car like someone trying way too hard to be liked. A common theme. Her loneliness blossomed, feeling exponential and much too big for the space. Then, the happy little balloon deflated, her whole face drooped, and she drove herself home to unload her groceries. When she was finished, it would be straight back to the store for round three of work that day. During the drive, she turned over her feelings, examining them. She felt embarrassed for intruding now. Foolish. It was nothing new. So why was it nagging her today so much more than usual?"

"Hey, have you had any trouble with the internet?"

Peyton blinked from atop the ladder she'd just climbed, a golden swirly sign for negligees in hand. Juliette stood below, hands on her hips.

"I don't know. I haven't tried. Is this thing straight?" she asked, placing the sign approximately where she thought it should go. She had the negligees sorted by sexiness factor, which she was rather proud of. *Just how close to naked do you want to be?*

Juliette squinted. "It's straight, but off-center. About two inches to your right."

"Here?"

"Um, yeah. Wait. No. Sorry."

Peyton glanced behind her in curiosity and smiled at what she saw. "Are you checking out my ass right now? Because that's what it looks like from here." She arched an eyebrow and waited.

"No, no, no." Juliette's eyes went wide. "That's ridiculous. Why would you say that? I was thinking of something. The internet…issue. And probably other things."

"Like my ass." She climbed down calmly. "It's okay. One of my better features. At least, that's what I've been told." She shrugged. "All right. The internet." She took out her phone and tried a quick search to no avail. When she raised her gaze to inform Juliette, she found her bright red and blinking a lot. *Oh, this was good.* It was about the cutest thing she'd ever seen. Her stomach went super tight and she had an intense need to push Juliette against the wall and see if that mouth tasted as good as it looked. She blamed the R-rated frozen foods section. But she quickly swallowed it, because everything had been sending her to Sex Land lately. Juliette did look really pretty today, though. She had part of her dark hair swept back in a curvy brown clasp. Simple. Chic. The royal-blue shirt with the mock turtleneck and short sleeves matched her eyes almost identically. She wondered absently if they darkened when she was touched a certain way. Did she slam them closed in the throes? She had a feeling Juliette's cheeks flushed hot. Did her center—

"Anything?"

"What?"

"On the phone. Now it's you who's missing in action. I was just wondering if your internet had kicked in. Remember?" She reached into Peyton's space and pointed at the screen. The arm that brushed hers inspired a warm flutter that drifted low.

"Oh." She studied her screen and took a few deep and slow inhales. Steady. "Nope. Would you look at that? Nothing but a *working* page."

Juliette sighed. "Dammit. I'll check with Huberson next door. Thanks."

As Peyton watched Juliette leave, she couldn't help but notice the subtle sashay of her hips. That hourglass figure was killer, and Juliette wasn't the type to sway on purpose, which made it all the more delectable. Peyton secretly imagined grabbing those hips from behind, hauling her in, and hearing her murmur with pleasure. That would certainly be something memorable in a streak of mundane lately. She exhaled slowly. It jarred a memory free. "Oh! I forgot to tell you. I saw your friend getting hot and heavy at the grocery store. Saucy stuff. The frozen peas were scandalized, never to be the same." Surely good gossip was currency in Landonville, just like anywhere else.

"Really?" Juliette paused, a smile tugging the edges of her mouth and questions in her stare. She liked a little town chatter herself, it seemed. She inched back into the store casually. "Which friend?"

"The one sitting with you at trivia night. Very pretty. Her dark hair was in twists. Not today, though. It was different. She looked killer."

"Cherry? Shut up right now. Cherry was making out at the *grocery store*? No." Her eyes went wide. She was reveling in this, mouth in the shape of an *Oh*. Peyton had hit pay dirt, apparently. This would surely score her some friend points.

She picked up energy. "Oh yeah. I couldn't get to my ice cream. It was a whole thing."

Juliette's mind was clearly working overtime. "With who? This is wild. Why hasn't she called me?" She checked her phone.

"The other teammate of yours. The guy." She paused and tilted her head because Juliette now had a strange look on her face. Her eyes no longer danced, and that was a shame. Peyton slowed her speech out of caution. Roadblock. "I figured that would have been a given, but I'm sensing it's not. Are they not a couple?"

"No." She shook her head. "It must be new."

"Oh. That would make sense. New romance is often the sexiest time. I get a lot of business off the honeymoon period." She offered a wink, trying to get them back on track because Juliette looked like Peyton had just swiped her lollipop. She decided then and there that she didn't want to see Juliette look that way ever again. She'd work at it if she had to.

"I just can't believe this." Juliette shook her head, but it wasn't in amazement, it was in sorrow. This wasn't good at all. Peyton had clearly trodden unknowingly onto something and wanted to rewind the entire scene.

"Well, what do I know? Don't take my word for it. Maybe I'm confused about what I saw."

Juliette's shoulders dropped. "Um. No. I think you're probably right." She met Peyton's eyes, relenting. "He's my ex-husband. Thomas." Her voice was quiet now.

"The trivia guy?" What? Why hadn't Pete pointed him out at the bar when he'd talked about her divorce? This was catastrophic. "Fuck. I'm so sorry."

"We don't have to make a big deal."

"The fuck we don't. He's kissing your best friend and you had no idea?"

"I did and I didn't. She told me she had feelings. I just didn't really expect…In reality, I should have…but I didn't *actually*." She couldn't seem to get the words in the order she wanted them, which meant she was in downshift mode. Peyton knew it well. Juliette hooked a thumb behind her. "You know what? I'm gonna go."

Peyton felt horrible. Hated herself for having said anything. She had to fix this in whatever way she could. "Juliette. Please, wait. I feel like this is my fault."

She turned back and shook her head once. "Nope. Not true. This is just a thing I need to deal with, and I will. It's going to be fine."

But it clearly wasn't. At least in the short term. Juliette's voice had that wobbly quality that signaled someone was close to crying, and her eyes looked extra large like they were trying to contain tears before they spilled. And when Peyton saw someone cry from a wounded, sincere place, she often had to join them. It was weird, but Peyton could feel the feelings of others, just not fully her own. Something she was still trying to work through. Yep, here came the empathy tears. Her bottom lip trembled.

Juliette studied her with the smallest of frowns. "What's your lip doing? Are *you* crying? Peyton, are you crying? Why?" Juliette wiped the three tears from her right cheek and came closer. "I don't understand."

Peyton waved her off. "Your ex-husband is kissing your friend and you're sad."

"You're crying for me?" Juliette squeaked, her own tears spilling onto her cheeks.

She swallowed, the lump in her throat painful and insistent. "Empathetic disposition. It's new in the last few years. Gets me every time. You cry. I cry." A shuddering breath. "It's a whole fest when one of my clients cries in a dressing room. I have extra Kleenex for the occasion."

"I know empathy. I've just never seen it on display quite like this."

"I'm sorry." Peyton tried to slow her breath, gather control. "This is your moment. Not mine."

"Well, I don't own sadness." She dabbed her cheek with a tissue from the box Peyton handed her from behind the counter.

"Good point. You're sad about your thing. I'm sad about you. We can all have our own separate sessions."

Juliette seemed struck for a moment. "I don't think I've ever met anyone like you."

"Seemingly confident and fun-loving, but cries at the drop of another person's sentimental hat?"

"Exactly that." Juliette seemed to remember the original reason for her tears. "It's not that I don't love them both. Cherry and Thomas. They're wonderful. It's just…"

"You were his person."

"And hers," Juliette said.

"And now it feels like—"

"They're each other's."

That did it. Juliette promptly burst into a new round of tears. Peyton couldn't take it. Something had to be done. She had lots more work to do and not much time left before her opening, but this called for big action. "We're going out for drinks. I'm declaring it. Close up shop."

Juliette frowned. "I can't. I have twenty-five minutes left before closing."

"You own the place, Juliette. You can do whatever you want. Is there a soul in your store right now?"

"No," Juliette said tearfully. "Because I suck at stationery." More tears from Juliette. And in response, more welling up from Peyton. They were a soggy pair.

"That's it. Lock up. We're getting out of here early." Peyton was a woman on a mission, and Juliette was not in a state to argue with anyone. She nodded dutifully, went next door, closed for the day, and met Peyton on the sidewalk a few minutes later.

"To The Frog and Dog?" Peyton asked.

"No. No. I don't think I can chance running into my..."

"Got it. Anywhere else good around here?"

Juliette seemed to search her brain. "There's a bar near my house. Shindig. I've never gone inside, but it looks nice enough. I mean, the sign is neon."

"Neon? Well, now we have to go."

A small smile. Progress. "You're making fun of me," she said, trailing after Peyton, who led the way to her special-order sky-blue Mustang convertible. "Neon pops at night. It means they made the investment. A business owner who cares. I, for one, can respect that."

"Then you must adore my sign. Lights up bright pink beneath the night sky, beckoning any and all sexy people to seek out lingerie and my services. Plus, if you look hard enough—"

"Boobs," Juliette said. "I've seen them. Over and over again. It's all I can see now."

"See? You do appreciate my sign." She passed Juliette a wink.

"I do covet its electrical features."

"Wow. You really just said that and, I fear, meant it."

"I did." A second small smile. She knew she was being teased and took it well. Peyton gave her credit. Juliette took everything so very seriously that it had to be tiring. It exhausted Peyton just watching her do it. Tonight, she hoped they would relax out of it. It was Peyton's goal to let Juliette drown her sorrows in booze and sympathy and maybe even let off some pent-up steam. She needed it.

"I've seen you drive through the parking lot in this car, but it's really something up close. Very...you." Juliette ran her hand across the baby-blue and white leather of the door.

"Maybe if I get you a drink, you'll tell me in precise detail what makes it me. Who I am to you. Inquiring minds."

"The way I'm feeling, you might get your wish." Ah, Juliette had hit the I-don't-give-two-fucks portion of the day. That could be enlightening. She would stay tuned. Beyond all that, however, she planned to be a friend for Juliette because everyone could use one of those in harder times. Uptight neighbor she sometimes lusted after or not.

Juliette popped on a pair of white-rimmed sunglasses and faced the window, likely lost in dreaded thoughts of the ex-husband and best friend tongue-wrestling in the aisles.

"Are you thinking about things you shouldn't be?" Peyton asked, a few minutes into the ride.

"Probably."

That was all Peyton needed. She tapped the steering wheel and broke into a verse of Kelly Clarkson's "Since U Been Gone." She wasn't a belter but gave the melody her own soft, bluesy spin.

"You can sing, too?"

"I can't."

"I just heard you. Your voice is beautiful."

For some reason, the basic, probably generous comment landed squarely where she needed it and nestled in her chest. Her afternoon hadn't been all that great either. That helped. Juliette joined her, and for the rest of the drive they sang heartbreak tunes, which served to both distract and bond them.

Shindig, as it turned out, lived up to more than just its neon sign. Not that it was even glowing yet. But the night was young. The bar was small inside with lots of browns and grays making up its decor. Framed cartoons lined the walls, and Peyton pieced together that they were drawn in the image of local officials and popular places around town. A nice touch. In the center and taking up most of the room, there was a horseshoe-shaped bar with cocktail glasses of all varieties hanging from a rack above, catching the lights and glimmering in a lovely show.

"Welcome in," the bartender said and literally adjusted an imaginary bow tie. He was the pretty-boy type with perfectly thick brown hair and height for days. Likely a model or actor trying to supplement his income with big tips from customers trying to take him home. "I'm James. I'll be at your beck and call tonight. What'll it be?"

Peyton placed a palm on the bar and met his gaze. "Know this. We're nursing a bad day, James, and taking no prisoners."

He mimicked her palm gesture. "Then you're here just in time."

"I'll have a beer," Juliette said in the demure way that said she wasn't here to bother anybody or speak in general.

Peyton glanced over. "The hell you will. Two manhattans, strong."

Juliette winced. "Hard liquor though? It's a Thursday. Should we think this through?"

"Would you like to make a list while James and I wait?"

"I mean, if he has a pen."

"No pen. I was kidding. It's sad you thought I wasn't." Peyton turned to Juliette and her tightly pursed lips. "I'm gonna need you to trust me on this. Totally my area. And let your lips relax, okay?"

Juliette offered a carry-on gesture and moved her lips around. "I defer to the blond woman," she told James. "I'll drink whatever she drinks."

"You got it," he said with probably too much enthusiasm. He needed more customers to fawn over him. They watched him go to work mixing the rye whiskey, vermouth, and bitters. He poured each into a coupe glass and finished with a booze-marinated cherry on a swizzle stick lying across the top with the beauty of a naked woman on her couch.

"Oh, Jamesy. Those are pretty." Peyton held up one of the dark cocktails. "You killed it."

"What's your name?" he asked with a sizzle behind his eyes. Flirting. She knew it a mile away. He wasn't even close to her type, but that didn't matter for an entertaining back-and-forth.

"I'm Peyton. New in town."

"Well, Peyton-New-In-Town, let me know if you need another round." He headed to the other side of the bar and Juliette gaped.

"Why are your eyes so wide? Did I say something inappropriate? We weren't even close to discussing underwear this time."

"So this just happens to you everywhere you go?"

"What?"

"People are immediately interested in you. They ask questions. Want to talk. You're a walking magnet for attention."

Peyton shrugged. "My theory? I think I give off a nonthreatening vibe. I talk back. I smile. I show interest. I ask questions of them, too. You should try it sometime."

"Let's be honest. It helps that you look like…you. Blond, tall, and fashionably put-together."

"But you're gorgeous." For Peyton, it didn't compute. How could Juliette not know how pretty she was?

"No. Not like that."

"Look at me." Juliette did. It seemed hard for her to hold that eye contact, though. "I'm serious about how beautiful you are. It was one of the first things I noticed about you, and still do. Every day."

"Pshh." She looked away. "You're being nice, which I appreciate. But know it's unnecessary. I'm perfectly content in my skin, but I'm also well aware of—"

"There you go, rattling on again with about eighteen sentences of overthinking. Just be. Listen. Accept."

Juliette exhaled. "That's hard."

"It's worth it." She sipped and savored what turned out to be a delicious manhattan. The alcohol warmed her midsection. "If I didn't think you were incredibly attractive, I would have just stayed quiet on the topic. You're stunning, okay? And people notice that about you. They're just intimidated by that don't-fucking-come-near-me vibe you send out."

"I have one of those? And it curses?"

Peyton winced, feeling a little bad about the injured look on Juliette's face, but she was a straight shooter. "Maybe a little one. Totally reversible."

"Great." Juliette went still, like a person sitting on their hands, bursting to argue. To her credit, she did not. "Guess it's good to know from someone on the outside looking in."

"It's not that big a deal. For bonus points, you have this shiny hair and killer mouth. I'm jealous. My lips could never." She sipped the drink, letting the rye settle and slide down her throat, blazing a warm path. Strong and perfect.

"Well, thank you," Juliette said with a reluctant laugh. "That's something."

"You're welcome. And I have a feeling you'd get even farther than I do if you'd let people in a little easier. Most don't mean any harm. A lesson I learned a few years back. The realization changed my life. I went from a kid with a chip on her shoulder to someone who seeks out the value of each connection." She nudged Juliette's shoulder. "Talk to a stranger sometime."

"I talk to my customers at the store all the time."

"That's not the same. You're in work mode. Try it out in the wild. For no reason. See what happens."

Juliette's eyes went wide and she looked like a baby deer, afraid for its life. "That sounds atrocious. Small talk?"

"I know." Peyton laughed. "It gets easier, if that helps. I enjoy it now."

"I'll take it under advisement." Juliette took a sip of her manhattan, and held it up. "I feel a little fancy. It's boozy. But not awful."

"Doling out the enthusiasm now."

Juliette laughed, and it was nice to see. So much better than the tears. They sat side by side, close. Feeling looser, Peyton took Juliette in and wasn't shy about doing so. Adorable profile. Who knew her nose turned up that little bit? And of course, that generous bottom lip that never disappointed. But Peyton already knew that. It worked in tandem with the thick dark hair. Juliette was the perfect winter. She was lost in thought presently, with a faraway look in her eye. Maybe instead of admiring her externally, Peyton could wake the hell up and remember her goal, to distract Juliette from her thoughts and problems. She was clearly failing exponentially. "Play a game?" She was improvising.

Juliette's eyes went wide. "Here?"

"Right here. Right now." She sent a challenging smile, remembering the version of Juliette from The Frog and Dog. She was a competitive person. "Take another couple sips first."

"You don't have to ask me twice." It seemed to go down easier this time. Juliette was bonding with the drink. She'd gulped rather than sipped, leaving very little in her glass. Juliette smiled with pride. "Ready."

"Well, look at you."

"I know. Look at me."

"Biggest fuckup. Go."

Juliette paused, and the edges of her mouth pulled. She blinked too many times and deflated. "The Station. It's the best store and it's quaint and charming, which should have been a match for a town like this one. I don't know what it is I'm doing wrong, but it's definitely something. A colossal fuckup. So there. Now you know."

Peyton closed her eyes momentarily. Another epic swing and a miss on the cheer-up-your-friend front. She thought for sure Juliette would say something trivial and past tense, like she'd cheated on a test in the sixth grade or something equally as obscure. But there she'd gone again, dredging up debris from Juliette's actual present. No turning back now. She pressed on with regret in the back of her throat. "Does that mean the store is in financial trouble?" she asked delicately.

Juliette took her final generous swallow and nodded. "I have months at most before I have to close the doors and find a new profession. Maybe the BMV is hiring. Guess you and the candy boobs will have a new neighbor. I'll miss Jacquelyn."

"Who?"

"No one."

"Okay, well, don't panic. I'm sure there's lot of things to try before we get to that point. So the custom greeting card thing is a bust, too?" She couldn't actually say so to Juliette, but the concept sounded a little unexciting, especially when there were ready-made cards available a few feet away. What made them different?

"I have a handful of regular customers, and the cards are actually well reviewed, but word of mouth hasn't really caught on. I guess greeting cards aren't great fodder for dinner conversation."

"Have you tried the X-rated variety, though?" She tossed in a laugh and an eyebrow bounce.

"You would say that." Juliette shook her head, but it was clear she found humor in the quip.

"I like to apply the saucy factor whenever possible. Everything is better when it's sexy." Peyton took a sip. Then it hit her. "You know, I was kidding, but it's actually not a bad idea."

Juliette frowned. "I'm not illustrating pornographic greeting cards. Not gonna happen."

"Oh, let's not be hasty, sweet neighbor. Let's examine this." Peyton sat back, held up one finger. "First of all, they don't have to be pornographic."

"Okay." Juliette watched her dubiously.

She was in her groove now, chasing her thoughts where they led her. "But they could be. They could also be just a little suggestive. Or better, the heat level could be up to the client. Totally customizable. You could have a heat specific rating system on your order form." She tapped her chin. "Word of mouth on something saucy and forbidden like *naughty* greeting cards would spread like mono in the eighth grade."

Juliette sat back, took another drink. "This is ridiculous. I can't believe I'm actually entertaining the thought. It's the booze. I'm a booze victim."

"Really? Because I love the idea. You need to go viral, right? Desperate times." She banged the side of her hand on the table like a knife slicing vegetables. "This is the way to get the people's attention."

She could see Juliette trying it on, her wheels turning. "People do love gossip," she said quietly. "They love scandal even more."

"When the sweet little stationery shop owner starts turning out sex cards? Holy hell. Cue the blushing. Cue the behind the scenes chatter." She sat forward again, on a mission. "You have to do it."

Juliette waved a hand in front of her face. "I'm too tipsy right now. I know that because this sounds like a half-decent idea, and that can't be."

Peyton sat taller, in love with the concept. "It can, too. It is." The more she thought on it, the more the plan seemed to gain momentum like a sled downhill on slick snow. "We could do a cross-promotion. I'll send my bachelorette party planners over for a discount. They always want the R-rated content. We'll get this ball rolling."

Juliette took a deep breath. "Not yet. I need to marinate while sober."

"Fine." A pause. "I'm excited now."

"Your face lights up when you are. It glows."

"Really?" That made her sit a little taller. A nice thing to hear about herself. Why was she nervous now? She looked for courage. "My drink is low. Yours is gone. Let's have another on behalf your grocery store ex and the sexy new plan to save The Station." But she had to be careful. She hadn't been drinking much these days because she had the business to get up and running. But it felt so nice to be out with Juliette, who intrigued her more than anyone in recent history. Maybe because she was Peyton's opposite in most every sense of the word. She wanted more and more to know how she ticked. And what she looked like naked. Her mind stuttered. She'd gone there.

"It's the least Thomas can do."

"Agreed."

Peyton sent James a smile, and he promptly abandoned the couple he was serving and dashed over. "Another round?"

She tilted her head, letting her hair drape her shoulder. "I think we gotta. You're too good at mixing drinks."

He puffed up like a proud penguin in the most dapper tuxedo. Peyton felt Juliette watching her, likely gaping at her elbow rubbing.

"That's it," Juliette whispered as he walked away. "I'm taking notes."

"Well, I hope they're naughty ones. I hear they're moneymakers."

"You stop that."

"I will not." She turned and immediately found her face startlingly close to Juliette's, who'd leaned in a moment ago for that whisper. Peyton was in no hurry to adjust their proximity either, not when she was this hypnotized by whatever jolt of electricity flowed without restraint. She met Juliette's eyes and held on. Her hair tickled Peyton's shoulder. She smelled like fresh laundry and cool summer rain. What kind of underwear did she wear beneath those clothes? She had her pegged as a high thigh briefs kind of woman. Were the days of the weeks stitched inside? Why did the concept turn her on to such a startling degree? She shifted in her chair.

The arrival of James, who mixed their drinks in front of them, interrupted her incredibly enjoyable thoughts. But that was all they were. She would never take liberties with Juliette for professional reasons and because she was hopefully a new friend. Not one of her many acquaintances, but an actual *friend*, and she only had a couple of those in her life. But it was more than a little fun to think about over manhattans and conversation.

Juliette studied her. "Your hair is pretty like that. Does it have a natural wave?" That got Peyton's attention. It meant that Juliette was watching her, too.

She touched her hair absently, wishing she'd done something special with it. It hung loose, halfway to her elbow, with the slight wave she'd given it that morning. "Not even close. That's the painstaking work of leave-in conditioner and a styling wand."

"You're good at it. The whole beauty, styling thing. Your nails match your accent colors on your shirt that match the rugs in your car and probably your dog's collar. That's too many balls in the air for me."

"Wow. I don't have a dog."

Juliette waved her off. "You get the picture, though."

Peyton decided to explain, rather than balk at the probably accurate hyperbole. "I think it's just an area that interests me. There was a time when fashion wasn't an option, so now I dive in with an extra dash of motivation." She stared hard at Juliette, questions of her own swirling. The buzz smashed her inhibitions. "So, what's your story, Juliette? A husband you're done with, but not ready to hand over. You date women, but not actively. Risks aren't your thing except the three on your résumé."

"I'll answer in reverse. Risks generally don't pay off in my experience. I think dating is daunting. For more on that one, see my answer to taking risks. And Thomas and I were not meant to be in the romantic sense." She ran a finger absently around the rim of her glass. "It hurts to imagine Cherry in my spot. Part of the duo that used to be mine."

"It's not the same. You know that, right? She's not replacing you. She's creating something new."

"That's a helpful way to frame it." A soft smile. "Thank you. And I love her, but now I'm on the outside." She shook her head and stared up at the glasses hanging above the bar. "I didn't expect to feel this way."

"You seemed shocked to learn about them. Were you?"

"Actually, yes. She asked for permission. I gave it. I just didn't think he'd feel the same."

Peyton rolled her lips in. "Can I offer you some advice?"

"You're doing great so far. Dive in." She was halfway finished with that second drink and it showed.

"Try and concentrate on all that you have ahead of you."

Juliette nodded. "Rather than on the new lovebirds? Maybe I should avoid supermarkets for a while. I hear delivery is nice." She stared glumly at the table.

"I know that sounds hard given today, but it will ease up."

She nodded. "I better prepare for third-wheel status. I don't know how we got here. Life has a way of throwing out twists and turns that feel more like sucker punches."

"I know more about that than I want to."

"It sounds like a story. I'm ready to hear it." She pointed her finger at Peyton the way drunk people do when they emphatically want to communicate something important. "Another round?" Juliette asked with an arch of her eyebrow. Now she was the one leveling a challenge. There was no way in hell Peyton could say no. Juliette had a way of twisting her around her begrudging little finger.

Time to put an end to story hour. She signaled their overly eager bartender. "We should probably get that check." There were parts of her past that were scary, precious, and hard to share. She didn't know what Juliette would think of her if she knew that particular story, where she'd been, what she'd done. The shame overwhelmed.

"Wait. It was just getting good." She rested her head on Peyton's shoulder in a pout.

"Another drink and there's going to be nothing good about the way this night ends."

"I do hate hangovers." Juliette grinned like a kid at Disney and sank into her chair. "But I sure do feel nice right now. Can I just hover in this place forever and ever?" She extended one arm to the side as if basking in the freedom she'd found. "Everything is so happy here. I write sex-related greeting cards and hang out with really pretty people like you."

"You can do that in the real world, too."

"Not like this," Juliette said, shifting closer, brushing her breast absently against Peyton's arm, and shooting her libido through the roof in the process. She understood her meaning. They'd been extra tactile tonight, and it felt good. It also made the room feel exponentially warmer than it probably was.

"I better take you home now," she said reluctantly. She needed to play it safe. "We'll get the car tomorrow."

"That sounds downright perfect," Drunk Juliette said with too much enthusiasm. "Is that Magic Mike guy back with the check yet? I'm ready to get outta here. Take me home, Peyton Lane."

Oh good God. This night was one hell of a slippery slope that Peyton did not trust herself to navigate. She took a swallow of water, hoping it would talk a little sense into her lust-driven brain. She'd do her best to stay strong and get Juliette home safely. She was an adult and quite capable of keeping her damn hands to herself. Capable was one thing. Willing was another.

Stay strong.

CHAPTER SIX

Juliette had needed a night like this one. She'd shockingly watched her troubles melt away with each drop she'd consumed, leaving her lighter, happier, and ready to take on the whole damn world. She also laughed her way from the bar to the Uber and all the way to her home, with Peyton there to enjoy it all with her. She was good people. Juliette'd been wrong to judge her so quickly and so harshly because really she was just so sweet with the prettiest pink lip gloss and gorgeous shiny hair that glowed in the moonlight like a sexy halo. That was a funny phrase. Apparently, inebriated, she found a lot funny.

They pulled up to the stop sign a few houses down from hers. She squinted. "Why in the world is that flower so much taller than all the others. Like, what right does it have to tower?" A burst of laughter. "I had no idea my street was so random when it comes to wildflowers. I wonder if they do battle."

Peyton laughed, too, but maybe not because of flower rivalries.

"I will admit that you're a fun drunk."

"Not a lot of people know that. Do you know why?" She pointed and kept going. "Because I never do the damn thing. Feeling like maybe that's a mistake."

"It's not. I think you're doing great."

"Why aren't you drunk?"

"I'm definitely feeling it." Peyton leaned her head back and grinned lazily as they came to a stop in front of Juliette's two-story duplex she shared with her neighbor Mr. Harrison, who still used an actual clothesline. She'd found it charming until now when it just seemed hysterical.

"What is the deal with clotheslines? I can't even with them."

"You have a vendetta?"

"An acute fascination. The clothes dance around until they're dry. They literally party themselves dry. It's amazing."

Peyton was watching her in what seemed like amazement. "I have no idea what prompted such a statement, but I'm really happy that you made it."

"The world is such an interesting place."

"I will never look at a clothesline the same again. Do you need me to let us in?" she asked, and Juliette realized she was just standing there with the key in her hand, pondering the functionality of laundry.

"Nope. No. This part I got down," Juliette told her, super serious. "This is where I live, so I know the key's job."

Peyton held up her hands. "Got it. Just know I support you."

"You're the best and I mean that. I get why people like you."

In a matter of moments, and after two failed attempts, Juliette let them in. The heat was a welcome blanket from the chill outside. Luckily, her house was clean and put together. She saw it through Peyton's eyes now. Not large. A medium-sized living room, her cute kitchen with glass cabinets that showed off everything inside, which prompted her to organize everything to perfection. Mugs arranged by height. Salt and pepper shakers turned just so. Tea towels hanging from the oven handle, the edges landing perfectly even. It seemed so random now, though. She couldn't remember why those things mattered so much.

"I see a lot of you here." Peyton took a lap around the room, studying the walls, the appliances, the decor.

"This is where I live and prosper."

"Prosper? Oh, you're so gone. Say more stuff."

"I will not." She laughed again. "And I'm actually starting to sober up."

Peyton squinted and rethought. "But maybe prosper is just the kind of thing you say normally. I forgot who I was talking to."

Juliette laughed, enjoying the playful energy. "Welcome to me. Hey, want another drink? I have wine. We can keep this train rolling." It was her way of clinging to the best night she'd had in a really long time. Every time she put up a roadblock, Peyton had taken it down. She found it liberating and downright refreshing to have an excuse to cut loose.

"No, no, no." Peyton placed her palm on the counter and leaned, causing her shirt to ride up the tiniest bit, flashing the smooth skin of her stomach. "We're here to sober up, not fall farther down the booze hole."

Juliette sank into the tall-backed dark purple couch that faced a second identical couch. "Fine. I'm just going to watch the ceiling sway. Kidding. It's only sashaying. Sassy little ceiling."

"That's to be expected. I think I'll get you some water." The shirt went back into place. Criminal. She missed the show.

"Oh! Get some for you, too. My treat."

Peyton easily located the glassware through the transparent cabinetry design and returned with two glasses of water, and in that short amount of time, Juliette found it increasingly difficult to keep her damn eyes open. Why were they broken? She let them close momentarily, and felt Peyton sit next to her on the couch and offer a gentle nudge. "Hey, you. Let's drink this water and then we'll get you to bed." A pause as she searched for the energy to answer, but maybe Peyton thought she was already fast asleep. "You look like an angel right now." Her voice was quiet as if she had been talking to herself.

"We're going to bed?" Juliette asked through hazy eyes. "Ooh-la-la." Had she said that out loud? She wasn't sure she cared. She blinked again to clear her vision and was once again astounded by the luminous hazel eyes looking back at her. Such a unique green and gold combination. She'd never seen anything like them, but they did wondrous things to her body when she allowed it, which was now.

Peyton hesitated. "That sounds nice, but…" Conflict was written all over those perfectly formed features. The words sent a flutter through Juliette's midsection. "Just you."

"Ah."

"I'll order a ride home once you're settled." Juliette didn't need anyone to help her to bed, but somehow she couldn't give voice to the sentiment. "I want you to drink this whole glass, okay?"

Juliette looked up at her with a smile. "You're nice to me. You're always nice to me. Even when I was rude."

Peyton looked off her game. The smile had dimmed. Where was all that bubbly confidence now? "Well, I like you."

"I like you, too," Juliette said softly. "You're so smart. And pretty. I think that a lot."

Peyton found her smile. "Thank you. Now drink."

"Okay." Juliette did as she was asked, well aware that Peyton's gaze had dropped to her neck, which she'd exposed when she leaned her head back. Finally, she handed back the empty glass.

"Wanna show me where your room is?"

"In a minute," Juliette said and sat up. She looked at Peyton, leaned in, and with a hand on the underside of Peyton's jaw pulled her close and kissed her with such intention that she heard Peyton murmur a surprised response. That is, until she started to kiss Juliette back. Holy hell. Without thought, reason, or understanding, Juliette relaxed into it, reveling in the way Peyton's perfect mouth moved over hers. She pressed forward, needing to feel more of Peyton against her body, which craved in a different way than anything she was familiar with. Yes, she'd started this, and she also wasn't sure she wanted to stop. Not when she felt the way she did, not when her body sang, making it clear to her how long it had been dormant. This was a very unexpected runaway train. But the ride was tantalizing and more than a tad addictive. She opened her mouth, and to her delight Peyton's tongue plunged inside, proving her kissing skills rivaled everything else she was good at. Juliette's eyes slammed shut, and her hands had all sorts of ideas about the things they wanted to touch, caress, and work over. They were at Peyton's waist as she leaned over Juliette, taking the advantage, hovering on top, Juliette's mouth pressed beneath hers. The reality of kissing Peyton Lane was startlingly much better than the fantasies she'd only allowed herself to glimpse. Hot, intense, and all consuming. She couldn't stop because nothing in her life had ever felt as physically satisfying, and she had a good memory. She tugged at Peyton's shirt, freeing the hem, addicted to this new project of discovery in her very living room.

That seemed to pull Peyton back to Earth. "Wait. We're a little past sober." She was right. They were drunk. This wasn't real. And there would be repercussions in the morning if they didn't stop now. They were still kissing, but she wanted to take her voice of reason out back and smack it a couple times. "We shouldn't," Peyton said against Juliette's mouth. Her voice was gentle if not a little lower than normal. That's because she was turned on and it was hot as hell. "I know you, and you'll be so mad tomorrow."

"Really? Because it feels a lot like I like you." Juliette was smiling with her eyes still closed. "Come back." She meant Peyton's lips. She felt the profound loss when they were taken from her.

"There is nothing I want more than to honor that request." Instead, she straightened and sat up fully. "But I have to go." She stood and offered Juliette her hand. She took it and stood, albeit a little more wobbly than normal. Peyton glanced down the hall. "Where's your room?"

"Oh, this is getting good. No one's been in there in, God, how long now?"

Peyton paused, closing her eyes as if giving herself an internal pep talk. She finally opened them and regrouped. "Totally PG. I'm putting you in your bed and going home."

"Less fun but okay." Who was this forward, cheeky woman selecting words on her behalf? She wasn't sure, but saying whatever the hell she wanted had to be the most liberating thing since she swam naked in the ocean that one time in college.

Her bed did feel lovely, however. She slipped out of her shoes and fell onto her pillow.

Peyton stood over her, hands on her hips, sleeves pushed up, maybe a little overheated. She looked damn good. She blew a strand of hair off her forehead. The lazy waves of her hair were a little tousled. Juliette tingled with the knowledge that she'd done that.

"We're just gonna leave you like this for now." She nodded a few times, probably telling herself it was the rational decision. Peyton clearly had no intention of undressing Juliette, especially now, after their little interlude on the couch. "Once I'm gone, you might want to get out of those clothes."

"You have the best ideas." But her eyes were closing, and she was on her way to dreamland, ushered there by a full day, sexy thoughts, and multiple manhattans. She needed that recipe. She should make a batch tomorrow. So yummy.

"I'll let myself out. See you tomorrow," she whispered. Juliette only nodded as Peyton placed a soft kiss on her cheek. After the footsteps retreated and she heard the door close, Juliette covered her cheek where she'd been kissed, holding on to that tender gesture for just a moment or two longer before sleep claimed her for the night.

❖

Sitting in the back seat of an Uber and listening to the disgruntled woman behind the wheel complain about local politicians, Peyton struggled to return to herself after what had just transpired at Juliette's place. She blinked, nodding along to the rant about the mayor, while reflecting on a day that had really run away with itself, living just beyond her ability to grasp and take in.

The grocery store, the misstep at her shop, the bar, carefree Juliette whose eyes danced and darkened when turned on. She couldn't believe she knew that now. The culmination of the day, the cherry on top, had been the two of them making out on the couch. The chemical reaction that hit when her lips pressed to Juliette's still had her jolted, hot, and bothered. She was still trying to wrap her mind around the staggering sparks and how they still climbed across her skin uncomfortably, since they'd done nothing to release them. The woman was staring at her expectantly in the rearview.

"I'm sorry, what was that?" Peyton asked.

"The mayor. He doesn't mow his own grass. Pays a bitch-ass company to do that."

In her current state, she had no idea why that was wrong but felt like arguing at this point would be like trying to cut down an oak tree with her hands. "Bitch-ass punk." That should do it. The driver seemed pleased. They were friends now.

She melted back against her seat while the woman rambled about the price of gas station hot dogs, all the mayor's fault apparently. Peyton was back at the bar, laughing with Juliette, studying her very organized kitchen, and exploring Juliette's mouth with her tongue. Then came the unfortunate part. She knew sober Juliette, and that version was going to regret their kiss in the morning. Of that, she was confident. Didn't mean Peyton couldn't enjoy the way her slightly swollen lips still buzzed pleasantly. She'd savor the sensations as long as they held on, and hopefully, she and Juliette would laugh about it all months from now. A story they would tell their friends, about the time they almost hooked up. *Can you even believe that?*

Tonight, she needed a hot bath, some chill music, and maybe some black tea to soothe her back to reality. A vibrator wouldn't hurt, either. She had that new one from her supplier at the store. It would be a nice way to satisfy her firing libido, because quite honestly, she wasn't sure she wanted to go back to real life just yet. Doing so would put an end to this little section that she wasn't quite ready to leave. So, for a little bit longer, she reveled and imagined in detail how things might have played out differently tonight. Where would her hands have gone if she'd let them wander? How long would she have kissed and licked every inch of Juliette's body before finally making her come? What would she sound like when she did? Quiet and breathy? Loud and untethered? Would they have gone again, or just the one time? With a smile tugging her lips, and a fucking sexy movie playing in her mind, Peyton zipped through the streets of town, listening to her bitter driver and enjoying herself very much.

CHAPTER SEVEN

Juliette hated manhattans. They were brewed by Satan in his evil chem lab of doom, and she cursed their very existence. And, yeah, that was a headache, all right. Thick and dull, pulsing from the sides of her temples like Morse code for stupid. Why had she insisted upon that last drink? She wasn't a drinker. She was a hardworking businesswoman with no ability to hold alcohol. Nowhere in her schedule did it say get drunk with your thong worshipping next-door neighbor. Juliette blinked several times and looked around her bedroom, attempting to orient herself. She sat up in bed, waiting for her wits to float down from wherever they'd gone last night. The process was slow. She would need a painkiller and some water, but there was something else hovering slightly out of reach, buzzing around her brain. She blinked down at yesterday's clothes. Lovely. How did she get to bed? It was there, just not quite in focus.

"Oh, fuck, fuck, fuck. No. Fuckity fuckface. God dancing a jig."

The details came roaring back to her, creating a sound too deafening for her ears to bear. "What did you do?" she whispered. She saw Peyton sitting next to her on the couch until she'd reached out with her treacherous hands and pulled her in for that altering kiss. Oh, damn, it had been really good, hadn't it? The memory of Peyton's lips moving against hers settled over Juliette gradually, like slipping into a warm bath, until it was all encompassing. She clenched the sheets in her fists as it all came together. Yes. She'd kissed Peyton Lane. Peyton had kissed her back. They'd made out, and were really, really good at it. That part didn't matter. What else? She stood and walked the length of her small bedroom, fingers shoved through her wild hair. As they'd kissed, hands had been on the move, and she'd felt things. Unencumbered, out-of-control sensations that thankfully she hadn't acted on. Oh, but she'd been willing. Thank God for Peyton's cooler head.

"You're in so much trouble right now," she said angrily to her reflection in the mirror. "This was not okay. Now everything's all screwed up." She'd have to seek Peyton out today, as embarrassing as that would be, and apologize. Let Peyton know that her actions the night before were brought on 100 percent by alcohol and meant absolutely nothing authentic. Her phone buzzed, and she cringed, just sure it was Peyton, who she couldn't bear to think about right now. She was wrong. "Cherry," she murmured, staring down at her phone. "Thank God. Praise young Jesus. I'm not even religious but I'll join one if she can erase all this." She slid on to the call. "Hi."

"Hi back. Do you have time for lunch?"

"Hell, yes," Juliette spat out with maybe more aggression than was warranted.

"Okay, someone's hungry a little early."

She reined it in. They had a lot to catch up on, and there would be time. She'd find air and water and whatever other element would help bring her back to herself, and then she'd deal with all of it. Juliette knew about Cherry and Thomas. But Cherry didn't know that. This was a good opportunity to get it out there, deal with the situation as well as her own…set of circumstances. "Yes. Very. Witches and Brew at noon?"

"Sold. You know how I feel about their tuna on rye with the little eyeballs made of grapes on top of the bread."

"Your lucky day," she replied, pretending to be fully functioning, not at all a flipping-out human being. Clothes. Shower. Food. Deep breath. Things were weird on all sides of her crumbling little life, but she could rise to the occasion and push through to the other side. So she'd made out with Peyton, who probably wore devastatingly sexy lingerie she could never live up to. Just a part of her life now. Her best friend and ex-husband were gonna be all over each other in various public establishments including bowling and trivia nights. When the group outings ended, they were gonna go home together. She'd get used to it.

"It's all good. Everything is fabulous," she said as she banged the steering wheel one word at a time. The old clunker she had in her garage was a hand-me-down from her dad, and the noisy engine and the car's propensity to stutter-start were just the cherry on top of her morning.

When she rolled into work, Peyton was already busy inside Cotton Candy, her sky-blue Mustang in the parking lot. Apparently, she'd already retrieved it. How in the world?

Juliette scurried into The Station not only to hide but to distract herself from her thoughts. She straightened the shelves, replenished the coffee mug section, checked on the small wall hangings that hadn't sold as well as she'd hoped, and got to work at her desk on the one custom greeting card she had on order. A birthday card from a fourth-grade teacher to her coworker. Probably not a coworker she'd ever made out with because she was a responsible human and not a lust driven, manhattan swilling maniac. She illustrated the inside with the duck pond the woman had requested, using various colors of blue and black ink, then decided to take artistic license and add a mamma and some ducklings on their way into the water. Very serene and sweet.

"Not at all porn," she said to the empty shop.

"See, no one said porn. See, you're still hung up on that word."

Juliette tensed. Then went warm. She was about to come face-to-face with the owner of that voice and the lips that she never should have kissed. But could still feel. All over.

She turned around to see Peyton holding the door to the shop open with one hand. "Sorry. I was watching you illustrate that one." Peyton came farther inside. "You get an exceptionally thoughtful look on your face when you draw. It's…nice. Peaceful."

Juliette felt herself relax. Partly because Peyton was. She was also touching on Juliette's most favorite topic in the word. Her artwork. "There's a place I go in my mind where I can see all the colors and pull them together with lines and shapes and feelings. In the end, I have this drawing that materializes. My vision comes to life on the page. I've never fully understood my own practice, but it's the most magical part of my life."

"That's it. You don't have to understand it. You're the magic." There was warmth in Peyton's voice and her stare when she said it. "I didn't see any of your work on display in your home. Unless I missed it."

"No. You wouldn't have. I guess I'm more of a quiet artist. I keep it personal for me and the occasional client I pull in here." She gestured to her desk and its supplies. "This little venture was my first time actually going public with my art." She sighed. "And, well, we see how that went."

Peyton breezed past that last part. "But you have more? Artwork of yours, I mean."

"Under beds. In closets. The garage. Sure."

"I'd like to see it." Peyton's voice was quiet and laced with sincerity, which resonated with Juliette in a manner she desperately needed.

"Okay. I mean, sure. Yeah."

A pause as they stared at each other, feeling things out. "You feeling okay today?" Peyton asked. The question could be in reference to a variety of things from the night before.

This was Juliette's chance to point out the immense amounts of alcohol that had been responsible for her out-of-character behavior. "I've had better mornings. Must have been a wild night last night. I hope I didn't do anything shocking." That's it. Play the demure card.

"Like kiss my face off?" Peyton kicked out a denim-clad hip. The button-down white dress shirt she'd paired with those jeans looked too good.

Juliette's jaw dropped and she stared at her drafting table for an escape. Sadly, no magic door appeared. She faced Peyton. "You can't come out and just say that." What kind of person did? "You're supposed to join me in humiliation and pretend like it didn't happen for the rest of time. The great strip mall secret."

"I don't really work that way." Peyton came all the way over and leaned against the counter close to her desk. The little lines around her eyes pulled, and she offered her smooth smile. Her soft blond waves brushed her upper arm. The buttons on that shirt didn't look hard to pop. *Stop it.* It was like the kissing session had unlocked something within Juliette, and she couldn't see Peyton outside of a very sexy context. How could she figure out how to unknow how they fit together, how Peyton felt up against her? Juliette could also detect the subtle cherry-vanilla scent of her lotion. It was never strong. She'd only ever noticed it when they were in, ahem, close proximity. "I could pretend it didn't happen if you really want me to, but I'm more of an own-everything-you-do kind of person, myself. For the good or bad."

"What's that like?" Juliette asked.

"It has its perks. But it was hard-won."

"So, about that. The, um, thing that happened after—"

"*Kissing.* I think we can say the word. French, even. It was actually really good. But you don't look like you want to hear that."

"No, I do. It's a compliment. Right? Yay, us!" God, she was blushing now, wasn't she? "But maybe it wasn't the right move for you and me. You know? We're so different. And I'm in this weird twilight of my marriage ending, and—"

"Right. How long ago was that?" Peyton tilted her head and waited.

"That it ended? Oh, um, going on two years." She held up a finger. "So maybe not that much of a twilight sitch per se."

"A sitch?"

"Yeah, a sitch."

"You're not talking like you."

"Because I don't feel like me today, but the point is that I'm still trying to find myself and my place, which is entirely this struggle I can't even explain." She held up a reassuring hand. "And certainly nothing personal against you. Because look at you. Totally, um, fuckable. Did I just say that? I'm sorry. And I don't even know why I'm explaining all this and talking so fast."

"It's amusing, at least."

"You're entirely out of my league. That's what I meant to say. I mean, you do lingerie for a living. I'm probably going to adopt an elderly ferret." A ferret? Why had she said that?

Peyton stood. "You don't have to sweat it. It was a moment in time, but it's nice to know I'm fuckable."

"Right. Shouldn't have really said that out loud."

"And yet, you did. Anyway. You want to make sure it doesn't happen again. I can help with that."

"Thank you."

She held up her palm. "I promise never to kiss you again."

Juliette exhaled. "Thank you."

"Unless you want me to."

Silence. Well, what was she supposed to do with that? Certainly not flash to the moment she'd crushed her lips to Peyton's and the whoosh that followed. But that's what she did anyway. "That's so kind of you, but I'm good."

"I know." She knocked one casually on Juliette's arm. "I was being playful. You're safe with me, okay?" She sobered. "You don't have to worry about giving me the wrong impression, either. I'm not the type."

Juliette had to wonder what exactly that last part meant, but she squashed her curiosity. Not her business. Hey, those jeans hugged Peyton's hips perfectly. Dammit. *No.* She was all over the place. An angel and a demon version of herself in one.

"But if you take anything from last night, let it be the saucy greeting card idea."

Juliette hesitated, and Peyton kept moving, on her way out of the shop.

"Oh, and my opening is tomorrow. Giveaways and free food. Who can say no to that? Will you stop by?"

A supportive friend? Hell, yeah. She could be that. "Of course I will," she said with a much needed uptick in energy. Her new role was a comfortable one, and she seized it. "Wouldn't miss it."

"Thank you," Peyton said, tapping the door she held open absently. "This may sound weird, but it means a lot to me that you'll be there. Um, I don't have many friends here. So this is cool."

"What are you talking about? You know everyone."

"Sure, but *friendship* is different. Connection is."

A little part of Juliette loosened. The sincerity on Peyton's face was unmistakable. She valued Juliette and their relationship, and that settled snuggly in Juliette's chest. She went all crinkly and soft at the understanding. "You know what? You're right." A beat. A smile. "We're an unlikely duo, aren't we?"

Peyton hit her with a burst of laughter. "You can say that again."

"Okay, you agreed too fast. Maybe at least think for a moment next time. Just a mild hesitation or glance to the ceiling."

"I'll try." She sent a wink. "And we're starting that saucy business for you. You heard it here," Peyton said, pointing at her as she exited the shop. "And it's gonna turn everything around."

She watched that ridiculously gorgeous friend of hers leave her store and admitted she was hard to argue with. There was something about Peyton Lane that buzzed around her like a bee, confusing her, distracting her, and seeming very dangerous. But interestingly, Juliette happened to like bees and their unexpected complexity. Plus, the honey was extra sweet. Maybe, like the bees, there was more to Peyton than she'd first thought.

❖

"Something's on your mind," Cherry said an hour and half later over her tuna and rye sandwich and purple drink served in a mini cauldron. Witches and Brew took their theme to impressive lengths. The two of them had been coming there since they were kids chaperoned by their parents on the weekends.

"Take your pick. There's a lot there," Juliette said with a sigh and set her napkin down. Here went nothing. Her neck prickled with discomfort, but it was important she was honest with the person she loved like family. "Peyton saw you and Thomas kissing at the Pop, Shop, and Roll."

"Oh, shit."

"Incoming confession. I wish I had heard about this new development from you."

She watched Cherry deflate, which made her feel awful. She wasn't here to steal her friend's joy. Even if that joy made her feel wildly uncomfortable. "And you should have." She set down her cauldron. "When I talked to you about Thomas, you were supportive, but also a little sad. So when things started to pick up between him and me, I panicked like a child. I wasn't sure how you really felt." She held up her fingers like taking an oath. "I promise I was just looking for the right time to tell you. It was supposed to be this lunch." She paused. "Please say something."

"It's okay. I was surprised that I reacted the way I did. I mean, Thomas? Way in the rearview mirror. As in, so far back there. I don't have romantic feelings for him, but at the same time…"

"I just moved in on what used to be your territory. I can imagine. Listen, if you want me to—"

"No! I definitely don't want to whatever you were gonna say. Just give me time to absorb this new dynamic and organize my silverware drawer as a means of therapy, and I'll feel normally about everything again."

Cherry frowned. "Is everything okay? I mean, is something else going on that maybe requires more than knives in a straight little line?"

"Yes. I kissed Peyton Lane from the lingerie shop."

Cherry smiled widely and then it dimmed. "Wait. I can't tell if you're kidding."

"I'm not. I more than kissed her." Juliette stared at the ceiling. "I mauled her on my couch like a hungry tigress."

"Those are not the words I predicted next. A tigress? I'm sorry, what?"

"Too much imagery? I'm so weird with word selection lately. I never know when it's enough."

A small smile appeared on Cherry's lips. "This is the craziest lunch ever, and it's only been five minutes."

"You're kissing my ex. I'm kissing my nemesis. Well, *former* nemesis. Now friend."

Cherry straightened and scooted her chair closer as if cozying up for story hour. "Well, well. There's been a lot of progress since we last talked. I thought she drove you crazy."

"She does. Could that be part of it? The pull?"

"Damn straight it can. It is. She's got you hot and bothered in a fun way. Animalistic from the sound of it. Va-va-voom. I say have fun with that. Take her home and see what kind of lingerie lessons she offers." She fanned herself. "That last sentence got me going."

Juliette's gaze dropped to her plate at the thought of Peyton in lingerie beneath her touch, eyes closed and a strand of blond draped across her forehead. Juliette's everything quivered. "No. I'm not sleeping with her."

"Why not?"

"Because we're so different. She's this effervescent, sex-talking extrovert, and I like calendars with puppies wearing glasses, you know?"

"No one is saying you have to marry her, Jules. She's not taking the glasses off the puppies." She glanced at the table next to them and dropped her tone. "Get yourself a little. That's all we're talking about here."

Oh, and now her face was warm and the edges of the square room a touch fuzzy. Why was the mere prospect of a hookup with Peyton having this monumental effect on her? Other people did this kind of thing all the time. "I don't think I'm built for getting a little."

"Don't underestimate yourself." She took another sip of that witch's brew, which Juliette was convinced was likely grape Kool-Aid and Sprite. Cherry pressed on. "I opened myself up to something outside of my normal comfort zone, and you know what?" She shrugged. "It feels really good." A wince. "I'm not talking it up too much, am I? The Thomas and me thing?"

She waved it off. "I think I need to hear it. If you two are happy, that's the important part." The truth was that Cherry and Thomas were living life, propelling themselves ahead onto a brand-new uncharted course. Yet here she sat, paralyzed and stagnant. Not only that, but everyone in the world had pointed it out to her in the last two weeks, which had to mean she was getting worse. Dolores, Peyton, and now Cherry. They saw her for the boring person she'd apparently turned into. "But I'm gonna say this." Juliette sat back and took a deep breath. "I think you might be right. I need to let go more, experience new things."

"Does that mean va-va-voom Peyton?"

"It absolutely doesn't. I'm not that girl." She held up a finger. "Maybe I should go out more." She looked skyward, imagining it all. "Sip drinks at nightclubs and bop my head until someone comes along and bops back."

Cherry's smile faded. Apparently, that wasn't what she'd had in mind. "Sure. Why not? If that's all you got."

"It's a start." Juliette sat taller, pleased with her new resolution. "There's that club around the corner from The Frog. They have drink specials on Tuesdays and dancing until all hours. I'll give it a try."

Cherry watched her, dubious. "Sounds like you've settled on a direction. Keep me updated on the bopping, okay?" Her voice was tender, and she covered Juliette's hand with hers. Her investment was clear. She loved Juliette but was clearly worried about her. She had to admit, she was a little worried about herself, too. The world felt strange and terrifying lately, almost as if she was standing on the shoreline with a giant wave about to crash down on her back.

She wasn't sure what, but something important was about to give.

CHAPTER EIGHT

After a lot of real hard fucking work, Peyton was ready to do a little happy dance, cut the celebratory ribbon, and bring Cotton Candy 2.0 to the town of Landonville. She'd gotten up early, met the caterers, organized the setup, and put the finishing touches on her displays. Bras of all colors and shapes, slips, corsets, and after-midnight attire were all on sale and ready for her new customers to snatch up at will.

She opened the doors at eleven and was surprised to see a grouping of women on the sidewalk outside, some clutching the opening day coupon she'd distributed around town and blasted on social media.

"Come in. Come in," she said in greeting to her new customers. She had her two new part-time employees there to help with the welcome. Kiva was a brown haired pixie-like college student who loved all things Kardashian and reminded Peyton of that hourly. She was extra exuberant or dramatic, depending upon the moment. Her second new employee, TJ, was tall with jet-black hair and willowy limbs. Honestly, Peyton would have thought she was a model if TJ hadn't informed her otherwise. She crossed the room like it was her own official catwalk. Her voice lacked inflection, which was something they should probably work on for retail, but it amused Peyton so much that she almost wanted to hold back the note. Luckily, the kindness of her word selection overrode the drab delivery style.

"We have mimosas and some of the cutest sandwiches I've ever seen in my life," Peyton told her new guests. "Don't forget to drop your name in the plastic bustier for the free giveaways. I'll be drawing five names before the day's over, and you don't have to be present to win."

"Right up my alley," a middle-aged woman with tons of blush said as she scooted on over to the giveaway table.

Peyton listened as the new customers oohed and aahed over the pink and purple store she'd meticulously designed feature by feature, moving through the displays and speaking animatedly to one another as they sipped bubbly from the flutes TJ handed out.

"You're tall like a goddess," an elderly woman said, accepting her champagne as she stared up at TJ.

"I know," TJ said flatly. "So let me know if you want me to reach something on a high shelf. I got you."

"Now that's what I call good service!"

Peyton grinned, said hello, and enjoyed the high-energy atmosphere. She'd waited for this moment, hardly sleeping the night before. She'd crafted the perfect playlist of kick-ass empowerment tunes and pumped the volume to moderate. The room, just as she had hoped, felt like the best kind of party. This was going well.

A familiar voice grabbed her. "Wow. This place is buzzing. Where did all these people come from?"

Peyton turned to see Juliette standing next to her, nodding in awe. "I did a bunch of social media blasts on some of the big online local groups." She began to tick off points on her fingers. "I contacted some influencers, let the city council know about the opening, and paid for a small insert in the Sunday paper."

"You're officially my hero and a reminder that I should be doing more. You're good at this." She offered Peyton a small punch in the arm. "Pal."

She glanced down at her arm. "Did you just punch me?"

"Too much? I was working on friendly."

Peyton eyed her. "You were working hard."

"Excuse me, Peyton darling, do you have this plunge bra in purple? Preferably with an accent design. The more plunge the better," Mrs. Summerton, the mayor's wife, said with a lean in and a wink. She was a saucy one and unapologetic. Next to her, Juliette gaped. Peyton offered her wrist a squeeze so she'd close her open mouth. It worked.

"You know what? I do have a purple design. And that's a fantastic color for your skin tone. Plus, that plunge also comes with a lift you're gonna sell your soul for. So will your dinner companion." That pulled a laugh from Mrs. Summerton, who already had two slips, a short nightie, and a pair of furry slippers in her Cotton Candy branded black shopping bag. She had a feeling this woman was a tiger in the sack. If this was her purchasing style in view of her political public, she couldn't wait to see her haul when she shopped on her own.

"Next time I'm here, I'm gonna trouble you for the handcuffs with the fur," she said out of the side of her mouth. "Those look like too much fun to live without."

Bingo! She hadn't been wrong. "Perfect. And if you like those, I have other suggestions. I'm your girl," she whispered back. "I hear you don't mow your own grass."

"Who does, dear?" she asked with a grin.

They shared a fist bump. "I like the way you think. You'll find what you're looking for right over here."

Mrs. Summerton gave her arm a squeeze. "Glad you've joined us, Peyton. We needed you."

Peyton was glad, too. Today was a culmination of a lot of things, but it was beginning to feel like she'd found a little groove for herself. Not only that, but no one seemed to remember her from her teen years, allowing this reinvention to go so well.

Across the room, Juliette offered her a smile, sipping her champagne in the corner as Peyton played hostess to the customers, who seemed to keep multiplying. Without even realizing it, she caught herself tossing glances to Juliette, to see if she was still there to witness her big day. It felt like she had a little cheering section all her own. How weird was that? It's not like they'd known each other all that long, but Juliette's presence mattered to her today. For the first time in a very long while, she didn't feel alone.

It made the whole event a little brighter.

A little later, she was sad to turn and see the corner empty. Silly. "Knock that off," she told herself, annoyed that her sensitive side was showing. Better to keep that in check right the hell now. Getting wrapped up in other people was outside of what she was used to, and the concept overwhelmed her. In fact, she wasn't sure she had the skill set to handle the investment. Maybe that part of her was simply broken for good.

In the midst of a short lull in traffic, she checked her merchandise totals and blinked happily at the bottom line. People hadn't just shown up for prizes and free drinks. They'd made purchases, and not just the cheap stuff. The grin felt permanent as she floated through the shop after closing, restocking, straightening, and humming to herself. Her employees had been sent home, and she used the time to simply…bask. Her chest was tight, and her eyes misty.

Today had been the best day. God, she'd needed it, too. "Thank you," she whispered to whatever entity was higher than her. "I'm not going to screw this up. I know I've been given a second chance, and I'm going to work my ass off to make good on it." She sent a smile upward. "I promise."

Her feet still hadn't touched the ground when she ran into Juliette in the parking lot.

"You must be exhausted," she said, leaning against her Prius.

"Let's just say there's a hot bath with my name on it. Hey, thanks for coming today. It felt nice to know I had someone there for me." She bit her bottom lip, feeling the truth of that statement wash over her. Uncharacteristic warm fuzzies and goose bumps hit, which she wasn't sure what to do with. She touched her arm absently. Strange.

"It was really great. The opening." Juliette seemed to be chewing on words, finally selecting some. "I'm even a little jealous. You really know what you're doing."

"Thank you." She had a feeling that was difficult for Juliette to confess. Progress.

"I mean it. I've been slogging in retail, drowning half the time, only to see you come in and make a great big splash. It's mystifying."

"Oh."

"But it means I'm also really proud. Of you."

She brightened. "Oh!" Not a huge grouping of people rushed to be proud of her. There was Candy…and now Juliette. "It was a nice surprise how well the event went. I'm still letting it sink in."

"You should be proud. I have a feeling your store is going to be very successful, Peyton. Prepare yourself. Those women were in heaven. I saw firsthand."

"What about you? See anything on the rack that interested you?"

"You mean the underwear?" Juliette nodded too many times. "So many of those, actually. I was simply overwhelmed. With the underwear. It pulled me in, though. I got pulled in a lot of directions."

Peyton sighed happily. "I love it when you get all flummoxed. Keep doing it."

Juliette nodded glumly. "Not sure I have much choice. I wish I was cool and could roll with the punches like you do. But you know what?" She inflated with confidence. "I'm gonna work on it. You've inspired me."

Peyton leaned in, milking this moment, reveling in their playful vibe. "I didn't quite hear that. Could you say it again?"

Juliette, to her credit, did not flinch and leaned very close to Peyton's ear and in her loudest voice proclaimed, "I said you inspire me!"

Peyton pulled away quickly with a bark of laughter. "Now I've got it, and I'm honored. Want to go for manhattans? I hear you like those."

"Never again in my life on Earth."

"Just checking." She pointed at Juliette. "Oh. I told the mayor's wife about your new secret naughty note venture. She's highly intrigued."

"What?" Juliette squeaked. "You told the *mayor's wife*? You better be joking."

"Press pause on your outrage. I could tell she was the type who would dig it, and she was. She seemed very excited."

"Really?" But Juliette's voice had taken on a new strangled quality. "Because I'm feeling a little outside of my body."

"Do you need some water? I could run back in. I would do that for you in a heartbeat."

"No, no. I think I'm going to live." She swiped a strand of dark hair away from her right eye and made the come-here gesture. "Tell me more. It might help."

"Okay, so after she raised her interested eyebrow, I told her to only speak about it to people who could keep the operation hush-hush. That it was a new venture for only the most discreet. An elite list of clients."

Juliette showcased the hint of a dimple that appeared when she shifted her mouth to the side, one of her thoughtful faces. Sigh. A total gem. "But why would I want a business venture to be kept quiet?"

"Because people will eat it up all the more if it's just out of their reach. Do you know how popular speakeasys are these days? The whole password system, the hidden door. Human beings want to be in on anything elite. A club that's hard to get into. A hot ticket to a show."

"That seems to go against all of your other marketing strategies."

"Look into my eyes." Juliette did and their connection clicked into place. "Do you trust me?"

Juliette sobered, her features relaxed, and she nodded. "I can't believe I'm going to stay this, but I do. You're my friend."

Something blossomed in Peyton's chest that she chose to ignore. Not the right moment. "Good. Then you should get brainstorming and practice those brushstrokes. Or is it pen strokes?"

"Depends on the project."

"Well, you might have some work ahead of you if all goes well. Operation Save The Station commences."

"What have I gotten myself into?" Juliette bit the inside of her lip, and Peyton flashed on what her mouth tasted like. *Down, girl.*

"Could be fun. Imagine all the research."

"I think you just gave me dirty thoughts homework."

"Oh, that makes me so proud of myself." Peyton floated away in the direction of her car. "It was nice rendezvousing with you in the parking lot again. Until next time."

Juliette took a deep breath as if gearing up for her new, daunting venture. "See you tomorrow, Peyton."

She passed Juliette her most winsome smile. "And the next day after that. And the next. You can count on it." The permanence felt good. She was finally somewhere she planned to make a life, and now if felt like it was well underway.

She used the ride home to decompress, reflect, and celebrate quietly. No loud bursts of music, just the quiet of her thoughts, the understanding that she was hopefully going to be okay. But she'd been in this situation before only to see it all slither down the drain when she'd made bad choices. No more. "Holding steady this time," she told the road, the grip on her steering wheel growing tighter. "It's gonna work. I'm going to be happy. I'm going to win my family back. And be just like everyone else." The wobbly smile on her face and hope in her heart said that yes, there was a real chance. "Holding you to it," she said, by way of a glance at herself in her rearview.

❖

Juliette had experienced a heap of interesting customer interactions in the time she'd owned The Station, but today definitely topped the chart. The sun was out. The store was open. And she had a customer she'd never seen before asking for…what, now?

"I'm not sure I understand." She cleared her throat, shifting uncomfortably. "Can you be more specific about what you're looking for?" She had an inkling but wasn't quite ready to go there.

The woman nodded energetically. "I'm looking for a card that says we need to get it on and soon."

"Get it on?"

"Right." The woman plowed forward. "I'm thinking no nudity on the actual illustration, because this is our third date, but if you could draw a pair of pretty great-looking knockers with a generous amount of cleavage, that would be perfection." The woman wearing three necklaces and standing across from Juliette nodded without even a hint of a smile, which likely meant she was serious. Wait. She was?

Juliette gave her head a shake to wake it from the surprise of Tuesday morning. "You want to place an order for a get-it-on card. Gotcha." The only issue was she couldn't decide if this was a real request or a practical joke sent from next door.

"Yes. Do you have room?" She studied the custom brochure and pricing sheet. Juliette's cards weren't cheap. "I'd need it by Friday. I know it's short notice, but I'll pay extra. As the card will state, I need to get it on soon, as in this weekend. Why doesn't Hallmark make these kinds of things? Would be a lot easier."

"Right? I've often wondered the same thing." Juliette played along, keeping it breezy, just another day at the raunchy card office. "No problem. I could get it to the front of the line for a, um, rush fee."

"Done. I'll order sooner next time. I bet you get slammed at Valentine's."

"Totally. It's a popular holiday." Juliette's mind raced. This wasn't a prank. Peyton's little idea had just taken a step forward.

The woman handed over her credit card and perused the aisles of the store while Juliette rang her up, mystified, giddy, and a little nervous about how to go about crafting this card.

"Can I ask where you heard about my…services?"

"Oh," the woman said, returning to the counter with a couple of coffee mugs. "These, too. My aunt told me about you. Cathy Summerton."

The honest-to-goodness mayor's wife. Wow. "Right. She's pretty great. Cathy." Juliette didn't actually know the woman.

"A treasure. But don't worry. I know it's a little hush-hush, so I won't blow you up too much. I did tell my sister, though. I hope that's okay."

"It'll be fine," Juliette said and handed over the credit card slip for signing. "Don't spread this around, but I'm sure I can work her in."

The woman scrunched her shoulders. "I'm excited. See you Friday. Big weekend!" She threw her fist up in victory.

Juliette watched in awe as her first naughty card customer left the store. And that's when it hit her. She was about to spend a portion of her afternoon working on a card that depicted generous boob action. "Not porn, though," she reminded herself with a little skip in her step, but honestly that transaction felt so good, she'd draw whatever the hell was ordered with a grin on her face.

"What are you working on so quietly in here?" Peyton asked, a few hours later.

"You're not going to believe this, but a naughty card."

Peyton tilted her head so she could observe the image Juliette worked on right side up. "Wow. They wanted boobs? Good ones, too. Damn."

"Generous ones. Probably much like the pair she brought into my shop. A referral from, drum roll please"—she extended her hand in a ta-da gesture—"the mayor's wife."

Peyton's mouth fell open. "That little minx. I was right."

"You were. I keep saying that lately. What is that about?"

"Listen, I know my lane. I won't try and give you golfing advice. But sensual marketing is my forte, and I will not steer you wrong." She stared at the drawing. "I have a whole new appreciation for your talent right now. Look at those things." She studied the boobs.

"She's fictional. Well, kind of." She did base the drawing on what she'd seen of the woman in her shop. Size, shape. It was for her partner, after all. She had to use her imagination for the rest, but she was aiming for flattering and sexy. This card had a mission.

"Send her next door. I'll get her set up with lingerie to make her night a memorable one."

Juliette saw a series of sexy images. Peyton wearing the purple bra and panties set she'd seen on Jacquelyn the day of the opening. Dammit. The boob drawing was affecting her. She closed her eyes briefly to steady her lusting ship.

"I will certainly hand over your twenty percent off coupon when she picks up her card."

"We are a great team. Ta-ta."

"Is that a boob reference?"

"Hot damn." Peyton's hazel eyes danced. "Well, it is now."

Juliette was definitely thinking about ta-tas now, too. Namely, Peyton's as they pushed against the blue and white striped shirt she wore, which was way too tight to be helpful to Juliette's cause. She blinked, struggling to pull herself out of it. "Wait. I need to come up with the text. I can't just hand over a boob shot and collect."

Peyton winced and walked back over. "Oh, that's not my area. That's yours. What are you thinking?"

She bit the bullet. She scribbled the phrase *Come and play?* on a sheet of paper and slid it to Peyton.

"Oh, I like it. You're gonna need to change that spelling, though."

Juliette closed her eyes. God, was this happening? "I was afraid you'd say that. Fine. What about with this playful font?" She added a few swirls on the new version: *Cum and play?*

"I had a feeling you were going to be good at this."

"Me? With writing sex cards? That makes one of us."

Peyton headed for the door and took her breasts in that shirt with her. A tragedy. "People who kiss like you do don't disappoint in the sex department. I better get back."

Alone, shocked by that sentence and already turned on, she was at a loss. So she sat there with a rapidly beating heart, loose limbs, and an aching center. This was torture. That meant this was the moment to put her naughty card aside for a little inventory check. There was plenty of time to finish between now and Friday. Spontaneously combusting in her stationery store was probably not the best vibe.

But those R-rated thoughts and the heat they inspired followed her from task to task. The images that flashed in her brain developed into full-on fantasies, the likes of which she was not at all accustomed. Who was she, all of a damn sudden? She was not someone who daydreamed about sex and scenarios and positions, and certainly not the toe-curling variety she'd embarked upon today. One thing was for sure—all of the movies in her mind starred one woman in particular, and she was only a short distance away through the thin wall of the strip mall. Sigh. Why did they have to call it that? All roads led back to sex today.

Later that night, Juliette didn't hesitate to place her beer order at The Frog and Dog when she arrived for trivia. She marched right up to the bar and laid down a hand. "Miller Lite, please."

"You got it, Julia," Lola said, and slid her a bottle.

Lola had called her a variety of names of the years—Jolene, Jennifer, Juniper—but she never corrected her, accepting her faceless status. She felt driven to now. "It's Juliette." She lifted her beer. "Good to see you. Love the new glasses." Old Juliette would have kept the compliment to herself. But she was feeling out of sorts and bold these days and sought out a connection. A tip from Peyton. Why the hell not?

Lola glanced down the bar at the pint glasses with the fresh etching. "Just got these today. You're the first one who's noticed. That beer's on me."

"Really?" She looked down at the bottle.

"Yep. You want a cold glass? I'll get you one." She reached below and pulled up one of the new ones, only frosty and cold.

"Thank you." A grin made its way onto her face. Not bad for going the extra mile.

"Enjoy, and best of luck to your team tonight. I have faith."

"Thanks. We'll need it." She turned back around to face her team, also known as the newly happy couple. This was their first trivia night since the infamous freezer kiss. She hadn't seen Thomas at all, but surely Cherry had filled him in on their conversation. At least he had the decency to look nervous as she approached the table.

She decided to let him off the hook. "So, you two are sucking face, and it's weird, but it's fine."

Thomas sat taller. "Nice opener. Wow. You just grabbed it by the throat."

"I figured we should address the elephant before he ate everything in sight." She gave his arm a slug and met the eyes that used to make her smile on a glum day. He'd been her person, the one who'd sing her to sleep when insomnia hit, make her homemade blueberry pancakes that he could never manage to flip without incident. Now he'd likely do those very things for Cherry while Juliette ate Reese's cups in a stack on her couch and then searched for the napkin she should have brought with her.

Cherry beamed. "Well, I think it's safe to say that we both adore you, and nothing really has to change."

Cherry spoke for both of them now. They were a team. She let it roll off her back with a slight lift of her shoulders, the physical helping the mental follow suit. "Great. Let's just focus on the trivia. Right? That's what we normally do. Let's just be everyday."

"Hell, yeah," Thomas said with a tilt of his beer.

Within minutes, their host Felix, the gruff slow-talking bartender, was on the mic and kicking off the game. Smack in the middle of his spiel about the rules, Peyton strolled across the room and took a seat with the Quizzly Bears. Instead of experiencing the customary flare of her competitive drive, Juliette was flattened with a burst of excitement. Peyton had pulled her hair back into a ponytail and wore a denim jacket with a white scoop-neck tee underneath. She looked like one of those carefree sneakers ads. Her heart thudded in applause. She was suddenly a sneaker fan.

"Look who's here," Cherry said, swiveling back to Juliette with a triumphant smile. Her eyes sparkled.

"Who's here?" Thomas asked.

"He doesn't know," Cherry mouthed and then made a lock and key gesture in front of her lips.

"Thank you," Juliette mouthed back. "She just means Pete. He received one of my greeting cards from his wife."

"Oh," Thomas said, blank faced, not fully understanding.

The next hour consisted of Juliette consuming another half a beer, ignoring the eighteen attempts at subtle touching between Thomas and Cherry, and about thirty-nine glances of her own at the Quizzly Bears' table. Probably just because she wanted to see how the opposition was faring. Except that was a total lie. She was fixated on the way Peyton picked up and held a pencil. Her soft hands with the slightly long fingers curled around the portion close to the point as she wrote out her team's answers with concentration across her features. She occasionally laughed to herself as she penned the group's official response, flashing the men a grin, and after five questions, handing off the paper to Pete, who would deliver the slip to Felix at the front of the room.

"You seem distracted tonight," Thomas said to her between questions. He dropped his tone as Cherry chatted with the table next door. Their eighth-grade science teacher, Mr. Cavasos, was talking smack about the game. "Is it us?" He inclined his head in Cherry's direction. His hair was longer these days than when they'd been married, and it curled onto his forehead.

"Um, no. Yes, but no." She shook her head. He wasn't the enemy, and she had to remember that. "I just feel like I'm on the precipice of a lot of new things lately, and I'm trying to keep up."

"Does that mean you're dating or…?" He studied her, one of the people who knew her best on the planet. Surely, he could sense her lustful preoccupation.

"Dating? Not really." Making out? Sure. Fantasizing gloriously? You bet.

"It can be intimidating. You'll know when you're ready." His gaze lovingly shifted to Cherry, and Juliette blinked. What did that mean? She wasn't afraid. Were these two feeling sorry for her? *Poor little lonely Juliette.* That was outrageous. She was happy. She was exponentially fine. She was lip-locking with a beautiful blonde just days ago in a torrid splash of passion. Speaking of which, she caught Peyton hop up from her stool and head toward the restroom. Without a thought, Juliette followed, tired of holding in her every little worry and feeling like she might just lose it in this bar if she didn't just let it all out. Driven by lust and indignation, she doubled her steps until she caught up.

"Oh," Peyton murmured just as Juliette pressed her up against wall of the dark and empty hallway. She inclined her head and without hesitation pressed her mouth to Peyton's. Their lips fit together perfectly. Hot. Soft. Sexy. After a second or two, she felt Peyton relax against her, their bodies pressing closer, eager for contact. Juliette went onto her toes, evening out their height difference and sinking farther into Peyton's lips and embrace. Better than she'd remembered. She needed more of this in her life. Peyton's hands slid from Juliette's waist down to her ass just as she slid her tongue into Peyton's mouth. A quiet moan greeted her. There was a train roaring in her ears, and her body had to have been throwing off literal sparks because that's how on fire she felt.

Footsteps. Juliette took two steps back, her gaze still locked with Peyton's, who stared right back at her from the other side of the hallway. It was Mr. Cavasos. Damn. Not her adolescence calling in the middle of her sizzle fest.

"Juliette, I meant to tell you…"

She nodded and widened her eyes, signaling interest, when really, she just couldn't locate her vocabulary.

He didn't seem to mind. "One of my students had the same reaction to frog dissection as you did. I told him about the picket sign you made in protest, and I think it was a great lesson about activism over disobedience."

She blinked, trying to center her brain around dead frogs and not the surge of arousal moving through her and downward. "Right." She nodded. "Much more productive. Tell him to fight the good fight. Or for what he believes in. Something close to that, maybe." Was she making sense?

"I certainly will. Nice to see you."

Peyton eyed her once they were alone again. "You picketed frog dissection day?"

She nodded. It was coming back to her now, diluting her lust with reality. Not fair. "I believe the practice results in unnecessary trauma for many students and is disrespectful to the frog. We have technology now. Use a simulation."

"You're too sexy right now." Peyton flew to her side of the hallway and warm lips once again lit Juliette the hell up from her toes to the roots of her hair. Peyton's touch had a way of consuming her in a manner no one else's ever had. It was like she'd been plugged into a wall socket, immediately on and buzzing with desire like a hot-to-trot Christmas tree. There wasn't any warm-up needed. If Peyton wanted to take her in this very hallway, her body would be primed and ready.

"You kissin' the enemy?" an older man's voice asked, their privacy shattered yet again.

This time Peyton took the two steps away, pressing her back to the wall, just like Juliette's. "Willis, you aren't supposed to sneak up on people having a moment." How did she manage that playful voice so quickly? Juliette's was still caught in her throat.

"Well, you're smooching in the middle of the route to the head. What's a fella supposed to do?" He kept walking, though, muttering to himself.

Juliette closed her eyes and felt Peyton join her on her side of the hallway and give her hand a squeeze. "What prompted that kiss?" she whispered quietly.

She kept her eyes closed. "So many things that I don't know where to start."

She opened them and turned to find Peyton watching her from very close proximity. It was actually kind of nice, their quiet interaction in this dimly lit hallway. Maybe the differences they had weren't so extreme after all. In fact, from right here, they felt pretty amazing. Her stomach swirled and her hands itched to touch smooth skin, round breasts, and dip into places she'd only fantasized about. She wanted to do things to Peyton that would make her eyes slam shut and her hands move into her hair. *God.*

"Look at you," Peyton whispered with a sly smile. "You're all wound up tonight, aren't you?"

No point in lying now. Juliette nodded. Her center ached and her legs shook slightly. Kissing had done a number on her after a day of torrid thoughts.

"That greeting card didn't help matters, did it?" Peyton whispered, trailing her fingertip down Juliette's cheek. She seemed in her element. Juliette was not. She shook her head. Just as she tried to explain, one of the servers rushed past with a tray of empty glasses, interrupting them yet again.

"Fuck it. Follow me." Peyton took her hand and tugged Juliette through a door marked *storage*. They were now in a darkened closet lined with shelves. The only illumination came from the faint moonlight that floated in from the small rectangular window at the rear of the space. Peyton backed her against a freestanding cabinet, her body pressed against Juliette's. She wanted to protest. She couldn't. Wouldn't. She swallowed as they stood there unable to see much, breathing in the same air, drunk on arousal. She was very interested in how the next few moments would go.

Panic flared. "The door?" she whispered.

"Is locked," Peyton said back quietly in her ear. "I made sure."

"Oh," was all she could deliver. They were utterly and truly alone, safe from interruption. The air hung thick, and the anticipation danced wonderfully across her skin. She allowed herself to enjoy it, which was everything.

Peyton lifted the hem of Juliette's stretchy black top, the one she'd purposefully worn to try to look a little edgier than she would have in one of her standard brightly colored cap-sleeve T-shirts.

Felix had returned to the mic, calling everyone back for the final round of trivia. Peyton's palms landed on her bare ribcage. People would be missing her. Peyton's lips pressed to Juliette's as her hands slid upward. A round of applause as the round kicked off. Juliette opened her mouth, accepting the kiss that went from exploratory to hungry in 2.4 seconds. A shuddering breath, hers, as Peyton's hands pressed against the fabric of her bra, lifting her breasts and pressing them back against her body, sending shockwaves and tremors. Felix asked the first question. Something about dairy cows. Juliette couldn't tell you her own address much less answer a trivia question.

"What are you doing to me?" she murmured, pulling her mouth away, needing air. "Oh God."

"Hopefully, what we both want."

Juliette nodded. It was. One of Peyton's hands went missing, and she felt the button on her jeans go. Holy hell. This was happening. She sucked in air. Her eyes had adjusted, and she could make out Peyton's perfect eyelashes, her lips, the underside of her jaw, but just barely. Raucous cheers just as Peyton's hand slid into her underwear. Appropriate. She bit her lip so as not to moan at how amazing it felt to be cupped just like that. She pushed against Peyton's hand, rocking, closed her eyes, and dropped her head back. Peyton began to move against her, a circular pattern, and it was the best reward. Nothing had ever felt as satisfying. The pleasure built from somewhere deep and powerful. She savored every second and concurrently longed for more. She inched her legs apart, granting Peyton better access as she rocked with her hand in a hypnotic dance all their own. "How's that?" Peyton said with her mouth very close to Juliette's ear. Her warm breath tickled deliciously.

"Yes. Mm-hmm. More," was all Juliette could supply.

Peyton obliged by sliding her fingers inside to a whimper from Juliette, who was very aware that there was a bar full of people not fifteen feet away. She stifled a whimper and instead focused on breathing her way through it, reveling in the climb, longing to reach the top and release the pressure that built to oppressive levels. She heard the next trivia question. Europe. Country known for chocolate. It was Belgium.

"Belgium," she breathed.

"Smart and sexy," Peyton said, with her fingers inside, pumping. "A nice combo."

Juliette increased her speed, inviting Peyton to join her. She did. They were furious and focused as if hurrying up a long spiral staircase. With how far gone she already was, it wouldn't take much longer. Just two strokes higher. Then one. Peyton pushed hard into her, and she broke hard and intense, clinging to Peyton's shoulders for support, reveling in the wash of pleasure that hit and continued to give. Juliette's lips found Peyton's throat and pressed, marveling in the racing of Peyton's pulse, linking herself to it, to Peyton. This was everything.

"I was right. You are the sexiest woman. Do you know that?" Peyton said quietly. Juliette exhaled a shaky breath, realizing that her pants were down around her hips. Before she could do a thing about it, Peyton was there, dressing her carefully, gently.

"Thank you."

Peyton's response was to kiss her lips slowly as if memorizing the feel of them. "You go first," she whispered. "I'll meet you out there soon."

Juliette nodded, straightening, gathering her wits, and headed for the door. What was proper in such a scenario? She'd never had an encounter like this in her life. Did she say thank you? Bow? Curtsy in exchange for the most powerful orgasm she'd ever experienced? "I had fun," she said and then laughed because it sounded so ridiculous.

She shrugged when Peyton laughed as well. "Five stars. Going on my résumé in that case."

They held eye contact in the low light of the room for a couple of moments longer before Juliette excused herself and returned to her table.

"What happened to you?" Cherry whispered as Thomas penciled in the team's answer to a question she hadn't heard. "There were cow questions and we were dead in the water."

"Sorry. I got distracted."

Thomas turned in their answer sheet and then looked from Cherry to Juliette. "I told Cherry about what we talked about."

Her brain was still lounging in the land of bliss. "And what was that again?"

"That you should get out there more, live life to the fullest."

"I should. You're right. I'll get on that."

"Not that you're boring or anything," Cherry said, rushing in.

"No. You're right." She dabbed her mouth with her napkin, enjoying the feel of her swollen lips and the way they still buzzed pleasantly from Peyton's kiss. "I should take a few more risks. Venture outside my routine."

Thomas placed a hand over hers. "Anything we can do, as your friends, to help, let us know."

She nodded. "Thanks. But I think I got this."

CHAPTER NINE

Later that week, Juliette's very first naughty client surveyed her boobtastic greeting card with a series of nods and smiles. "This is amazing." She held it up. "Look how sexy. A commissioned work of art."

"I'm glad you like it," Juliette said. She'd also worked on two regular greeting cards that week, but she had to admit, this one had been more lucrative and more fun…and that's not even taking into account the series of events it set in motion. Nope. There was nothing boring about this potential new side-hustle of hers.

"I actually brought my cousin in because she'd like to place an order."

The redhead standing next to her brightened and leaned in. "I'm looking for a raunchy limerick and a drawing that will accentuate the great art of lovemaking without being too overt. But on a couch. An orange one with stripes."

"Oh," was all Juliette could say to that one. "Maybe I should take some notes." By the end of it all, they agreed upon a premium price, and she marveled that she was actually selling a few of these things.

"Is it true?" Mrs. Wunderlich asked the next day. "You sell forbidden greeting cards here? You do that?"

Juliette hesitated. She didn't want to bring scandal upon her store in the eyes of one of her best, most supportive customers. "Oh. Where did you hear that?"

"Pete told me. The bra pusher next door told him. He said it's a secret, but you and I are like sour cream and chives in a warm baked potato, so I knew I could ask directly, and you would shoot it to me straight."

"I appreciate that. And I will." She couldn't lie. It just wasn't in her makeup. This was going to be hard. "It's true. I do offer a naughty card service to select clients." She held back the wince while she waited for a response.

"Could I buy some? I'm thinking three that I can pull out whenever I want Pete to feel randy."

Juliette eyed her. Oh, for God's sake. Her, too?

"And my next door neighbor Jean is gonna want to buy one for her sweet boyfriend. He lives on the south hallway, and she can't seem to find any alone time with him. His name is Carl, and he has about three hairs on his head. I hear they're expensive. The cards, not the hair."

"They are," Juliette said, holding her ground on the price structure she'd established. She pulled out her newly designed one-sheet from the drawer behind the counter.

Mrs. Wunderlich scanned the list. "I can handle this. We have a lot of sex at Morning's Glow."

Juliette's brain stuttered. "I'm sorry. You do? That's great. Oh, wow." She gave her head a shake. "I mean it. That's awesome."

"So I can I tell Jean? About the naughty cards. Carl might need the inspiration."

Juliette held out a hand, as if granting access. "Sure. Jean sounds like a good person."

"Who really needs to get a little."

Juliette cleared her throat. "Understood."

"Charge my card for my three, and we can discuss details as they come to me. Do you have naked people refrigerator magnets in some hidden closet?"

"I don't. No."

"Well, let me know if you ever get any, okay?"

"Deal."

"I'm off to Pop, Shop, and Hole. There. I made a dirty joke." She winked.

"You're on fire."

Mrs. Wunderlich threw a small fist skyward. "I can't be stopped today."

With the store empty, Juliette had to take this moment to share what just happened with Peyton. Cotton Candy had two customers in the process of checking out, so she waited patiently, doing a little checking out of her own. She waited each day to see what Peyton was wearing. A little good morning gift to herself. Today, it was slim black pants with black pumps and a purple sweater with puffy shoulders. Correction, she didn't just wear those items, she owned them, slayed in them. She'd never known a woman who could make an outfit sing like Peyton Lane. She was a creature to envy and, Juliette was coming to learn, enjoy.

They'd made out on her couch.

Peyton had taken her in a storage closet.

They'd flirted on and off ever since.

Yet they hadn't done a whole lot of talking about that middle one. But they also hadn't pretended like it hadn't happened. Peyton objectified her in the open with an appraising stare here or there. They casually touched, a lingering hand on a shoulder or small of the back, usually followed by a knowing smile tossed this way or that. It certainly kept Juliette's days interesting. Especially because their connection only seemed to gain sizzle as they went. They were still entirely different people with one very potent thing in common: chemistry.

Yet they hadn't acted on it again.

When the women left, Juliette kicked a hip against the counter, taking their spot across from Peyton.

Peyton took her finger and moved it up and down in reference. "Red is a great color on you. Especially that deep shade. Really pops with the dark of your hair."

The long-sleeved red top with a smart collar was a new purchase. Just that week, in fact. Juliette sent her a smile, and not the polite variety she so often doled out. This was her ultracourageous, possibly-maybe-sexy smile. "Thank you for noticing. I came here to tell you that I've sold more naughty cards and have the feeling this might be a new trend."

Peyton's mouth fell open. "I knew this town was bursting with unrealized sexual energy. You're doing God's work, Jules."

Peyton had called her that once before. Jules. She'd never been a Jules to anyone but Cherry. In fact, she'd never been a huge big fan of nicknames in general, but this felt different. She tried it on and liked it. "You're good at that."

"Tapping into underrealized sexual energy? You noticed, did you?" She tossed in a wink and pulled out a stack of tissue paper for packaging purchases.

"I might have. How are things?"

"A little boring but better now."

"You say that to everyone."

"Yes, but I mean it when I say it to you." Peyton's smile dimmed. "In case you haven't noticed, I like you." She studied Juliette, sincerity gracing her features. She was trying to say something here.

"I like you, too."

"I'm bad at big feelings but I can do *like*."

Juliette exhaled because Peyton didn't exactly fit her checklist of qualities she needed in a partner, but she was most certainly on Juliette's radar in a big way. This was a relief. "I think we're in agreement there. We like each other."

"We like doing things to each other."

Her face heated. "We do. Right. So…what is it we're saying?" She wiggled her shoulders to keep them loose, a reminder to herself of how low-stakes this was. No big deal.

Peyton shrugged, nonchalant and together as always. "Let's enjoy ourselves. Keep it light. More fun that way." The way she said it made the idea sound like a wonderful one. She had a way of packaging things. "I mean, why get hung up on the conventions that bind most of the world? There doesn't have to be love in order to have a good time."

"There can be respect."

"Exactly." Peyton grinned.

"Okay, yes. I was hoping you'd say that, actually." Juliette whooshed a strand of hair behind her ear. "Friends, who, you know, see where the wind takes them." A nice way of saying *with benefits*.

Peyton lit up. "I like the project."

That night, Juliette ladled herself a bowl of her famous homemade chicken noodle soup and tore a big piece of fresh bread from the baguette she'd picked up from the Pop, Shop, and Roll. It was the third Thursday of the month, which was bill-paying night, so she settled in at her dining room table and got to work. Just before eight, her phone rattled from its spot on the table. A text.

Nice night. Want to grab some frozen yogurt and sit outside?

Peyton. How incredibly random. She studied the message for

a moment, before snatching up her phone and replying. *But it's bill paying night.*

All the more reason to put toppings on frozen yogurt. Get out here. Now.

"Out here?" She swiveled, and sure enough, idling in her driveway was a sky-blue Mustang. She touched her hair automatically and wondered about its state. That was new. Even when she'd been married to Thomas, she hadn't been a girl who fussed with her hair or clothes. Speaking of, she still had on her work outfit, which Peyton had already seen her in. This was silly. They were friends. They'd just established this. She stood, stared at her tabletop full of paperwork. Could she actually do this? Walk away from a very important task for frivolity?

Another text. *I'm waiting, Jules.* Okay, that one inspired those tricky little butterflies to appear. She hurried into her closet, threw on a pair of jeans and one of her new sweaters since it would be chilly. She didn't hurry down her walk, but it felt a little like she floated, asked out by her fling on a weeknight, and she was *going.*

"Hey, beautiful, feel like dessert?"

"Take me there," Juliette said, embracing the slight chill in the air. She hadn't even brought a jacket. Who the hell was she? She wasn't sure, but she kind of liked her.

❖

They weren't even to the yogurt place, and Peyton was already relaxed and enjoying herself. She'd convinced Juliette to buck her routine and had kidnapped her for selfish reasons. She was feeling lonely lately, and Juliette Jennings was her new favorite way to spend time. For a lot of reasons.

"Did you watch *Sesame Street* as a kid?" Peyton asked as they drove.

"Didn't everyone?"

She looked over at Juliette. "Good. Then you'll get this reference. I was thinking about it on the drive over. You're the Bert and I'm the Ernie."

Juliette laughed. "You can say that again. Nothing has ever drawn an arrow sign over my Bert-like tendencies as much as spending time with you has."

"But it feels like you might be channeling a little more of your inner Ernie these days."

"Well, someone is a bad influence." She held up a finger. "Or maybe I should say a good influence. Because…it's been nice. Letting go more. I don't know. Trying things I wouldn't otherwise indulge."

Peyton laughed quietly. "Frozen yogurt on a weeknight. Wild and crazy stuff." She tossed in a wink, and when she turned back to the road, she could feel Juliette watching her as she drove. She liked that a lot. Not only did it give her a prickle up her spine, but it felt like the most natural thing in the world. How could both exist? Somehow they did.

"Have you seen my latest business venture? I think wild can certainly be attached to my name these days."

"You do get points."

They arrived at the Yogurt is Life, which certainly seemed like a lofty name for a business, and strolled inside, musing about the foot traffic to their shops.

"My craziest time is always lunchtime," Peyton explained. "Women are dashing in on their hour off to grab something for date night."

"We're so different. Mornings are it for me and my older patrons," Juliette explained.

"Well, maybe that's a good thing for borrowing each other's…" But her voice trailed off. She stared straight ahead, her eyes locked on the recognizable family at the counter. Her brother, wearing a green ball cap and cargo shorts, must have sensed the attention. He flicked his gaze in their direction and held. Caleb. Right there in front of her. She'd seen pictures online and marveled at how the boy had become a man in the years they'd been apart. His face was fuller now. His jaw more square. He looked like a dad in the most wonderful way. A little bit like theirs.

"Hey," Peyton said, trying her best to stay cool and casual, but her heart hammered and adrenaline rushed. Juliette stared over at her in curiosity.

"Hey, Peyton," Caleb said. "Good to see you. Joshua, you remember your Aunt Peyton, right?" Her brother didn't make a move toward her. There would be no hug. That was okay. She understood his anger and would work whatever little shred of courtesy he'd extend her.

"Are you the one that sent the fire truck with the siren and blue stripe?" the little boy asked with wide eyes. He had turned five just a few months back. Her niece stood next to him, shyly clutching the fabric of his shorts for protection. Her blond hair was in pigtails and her big eyes peered up at Peyton. Alyssa was almost three.

"That's right," Peyton said, a smile blossoming. "You remember that."

"It's super cool."

"Hi, Peyton," her sister-in-law said. Linda had been Caleb's high school girlfriend and responsible for making sure he made something of his life before it was too late. Peyton was grateful to her for that. She was a good person. "I was wondering when we'd get to see you. You look wonderful." She seemed warm and honestly quite happy to see Peyton, which could not be said for the man she was with.

"Linda. Look at you. It's been so long." The two moved to each other and embraced while her brother watched, adjusting his jaw.

"Hey, big brother." Peyton turned to him. Juliette's gaze shot to her fully on that one. She'd have explaining to do later. "Wow. I can't believe I'm actually in the same room with you." It was fantastic. She tried not to let his obvious discomfort take away from that.

"Just grabbing some dessert since everybody ate a good dinner." He ruffled his son's brown hair, attempting to busy himself with the kids. That was okay. Peyton looked to Juliette at her side, silently taking in the action with a polite smile.

"Us, too. My friend, Juliette. She owns the shop next to mine."

Linda lit up. "And how's business? I need to stop by. I've heard great things."

"I've been open for a couple of weeks now, and sales have been great."

"By the dry cleaner's, right? I've taken my nicer work clothes to them before. The woman, Heather, always takes care of me. She even gave me her personal number in case I had any questions, which reminds me that I need to swing by and drop off my blazer. Hey, maybe I can see your shop." Caleb glanced in their direction, the lines of his forehead on display.

Peyton didn't sweat it. She was thrilled. She'd been waiting for this opportunity. "Anytime. I'll give you the grand tour. I'd love it."

Juliette jumped in. "You'd be amazed at what this one has

accomplished. I can't believe how popular Cotton Candy already is. Not only that, but the message the store sends out is so refreshing. All sizes represented and on display. Gender-fluid marketing, too. A lingerie shop for literally everyone."

"I'm already impressed," Linda said. She'd always been a kind, gentle soul.

Juliette wasn't done, clearly on a mission. "I've been next door for three years and am still working on pulling in that kind of foot traffic. Wow."

Peyton smiled and her cheeks warmed. "Thank you. I guess I filled a hole in town."

Her brother was busy paying for their yogurt and didn't seem to be taking much in. Linda, however, nodded along enthusiastically, her dark ponytail bobbing and her lips pulled wide in a sincere smile.

"We better run. School night," Caleb said. His mouth was tight and he nodded at Juliette as he passed, barely tossing Peyton a glance. His family followed him out the door. A squeeze to Peyton's arm from Linda and curious stares from the children.

"Bye," Joshua called over his shoulder.

Peyton held up a hand. "Bye, kiddo."

Once they were alone, the only two people in the shop, Juliette turned to Peyton. "Everything okay?"

She exhaled. "It will be. One day."

"Okay." A pause. Juliette's voice was soft. "Is there a story there?"

She nodded, her ability to smile missing entirely. "Let's get settled first, okay?" She'd hoped to hold out on pulling Juliette into the true reality of her life and her past, but after the supportive move she'd just pulled in there? Maybe she was someone Peyton could truly trust.

Juliette nodded. Certainly she'd felt the all-encompassing chill pass through the room. This was sensitive territory. Peyton hadn't been this shaken in a long time, and it had all gone down in front of someone she'd come to care about. Embarrassing, yes. But also maybe helpful, to have someone there to turn to. There was no time like the very obvious present.

As they sat in front of the shop, Juliette with strawberry yogurt with almonds and Peyton with lemon-coconut to keep her happy, Juliette gestured with her spoon in a circle. "Correct me if I'm wrong, but that was your brother we ran into?"

"Yeah. My older brother. Caleb Lane."

"I vaguely remember you mentioning family when we first met, but nothing since. I guess I forgot. I'm sorry about that."

She shrugged. "Don't be. Caleb. His family. They're the main reason I moved here. He's not thrilled about it, though, and has been avoiding me actively. You probably picked up on that."

"Yeah," Juliette said. "His wasn't the warmest reception. Why is that?" She winced and set down her dish. "I'm being nosy. You can ignore me."

"No. No. It's okay." Peyton sighed. "I don't tell a lot of people this. It never goes well." Peyton's gaze moved from Juliette's to the pebbles that made up the flooring of the outdoor patio. She hated this part. Revealing who she'd been, what her past consisted of. She knew the importance of owning her mistakes, but the idea that it could all change Juliette's mind about her was a crushing prospect. All the same, she refused to hide forever.

Juliette touched her hand and that pulled her back. "Try me."

"I was in jail for a while."

"A while?" Her brows dipped. A totally appropriate reaction, but it still caused her heart to sink.

"Four years. A long time."

Juliette looked like she hadn't seen that one coming but steadied her reaction. "Oh." A pause. "Was it a mix-up or did you—"

"Oh, I *did*. Totally guilty. My brother and I were left on our own more than we should have been growing up. Our grandfather kept us fed and clothed." She stared at her hands, not enjoying the topic. "Caleb was older and drove around a lot with these guys that always had some sort of scheme to make money, and mostly wasn't the kind of stuff that one would call...noble."

"They were breaking the law."

"More than just one, and I wanted to be just as cool. Impress my brother in front of his friends. It worked. Turns out, I was really good at shoplifting anything they needed."

Juliette nodded. "And you got caught."

"Not for a long time." Peyton chewed the inside of her cheek. "Caleb got smart and broke away, spending lots of time with Linda instead. He tried to get through to me."

"I take it he wasn't successful."

Peyton shook her head. "I was addicted to the thrill, which seems so awful now. But it's true. There was this heady power in doing whatever I wanted, *taking* whatever I wanted. For the first time, I felt in charge of some aspect of what happened to me."

To her credit, Juliette hadn't left the table yet. But she did observe Peyton with a indescribable look on her face. Part surprise. Part confusion. But there was a sliver of sympathy there, which was kind of her. Peyton wasn't sure she deserved it.

"I wish I could explain it better, but it still bewilders me to this day." She dug her thumbnail into her palm, hating the conversation.

"But shoplifting. Four years seems like a lot."

"So, here's the thing. If someone gets hurt in the course of committing the crime, you invite a whole host of other charges."

"And that happened."

She nodded. This was the most regrettable part. "It was an audio-visual store, the one that used to be over on Henderson. I don't know what we were thinking, but I was way overconfident."

"High-end stuff?"

"Big time. The surveillance was top of the line, it tipped off the owner who ran over from two blocks away, and we were caught. Mr. Capito. He was having dinner with his family. He had a second-grader at the time."

"I'm not sure I like where this is going."

"Me neither. One of my friends, a guy I didn't know as well as I should have, panicked and pushed a shelf full of speakers onto the guy so we could get away."

"Oh no."

"Yeah. It was pretty awful. He was injured badly, but it could have been so much worse. We were all so lucky. He did recover without any lasting physical damage but spent a couple nights in the hospital. I know he's still suffers from the emotional effects, though. That's hard."

"What happened to you and your friends?"

"Short story was that we were apprehended within twenty-four hours, and because someone was hurt, I went away for a decent-sized sentence. Upstate."

"That happened here? On Henderson?" Peyton nodded. "I don't think I heard about it."

"There was a lot of talk in the community. But the story was a blip on the news. They knew who did it, and we pleaded out. No real mystery to delve into." Before Juliette said more, Peyton needed to make one thing clear. "I want you to know that I take full responsibility for my actions, and going to jail was the best possible thing that could have happened to me or I might not be sitting here right now."

"That bad, huh?"

"I was out of control and on a teenage power trip. It was honestly awful looking back. I cringe with shame. But I own what I did, and how I was. It's part of me, unfortunately."

Juliette took a moment, lost in her dish. The seconds ticked by like years. Peyton couldn't imagine what she might be thinking, but she prepared herself, because everyone reacted differently when they heard her story. That was their right. But it was possible Peyton just lost a friend. Or the respect of one. It wouldn't be the first time or likely the last. She bit her cheek hard and waited. It really never got easier, this part.

Juliette finally raised her gaze, her eyes solemn and serious. "Thank you for trusting me with all that. You didn't have to tell me."

"I did." She raised one shoulder. "If you're going to know me, you need to know everything. It's not all pretty. In fact, a lot is downright awful."

"You were young. I'm sure that was part of it."

"Of course. But I don't write myself a pass because of it."

Juliette was studying her, probably trying to figure out who the hell she was. "I'm glad you found your way out of that form of...I don't know, darkness."

"That's a good word for it."

"It couldn't have been easy."

"My take? I had to fall to my lowest. That was the only way I was going to understand what my life had the potential to be. After a few months of solid depression, I started reading a lot that first year. It was almost like a tour of what the world could be. Those stories opened me up to the possibility of more for myself." She touched the table forcefully with her forefinger. "I could write *my own story* when I got out. Start fresh. And I did."

"I'll say." Juliette shook her head, bewildered. "I did not see this coming. If you had asked me, I would have put you in a sorority five years ago."

"Well, I guess I was, in a way." She barked a laugh. "Not one I'd recommend rushing."

"So I take it that Caleb…" Juliette paused. "That's his name?" Peyton nodded. "Is not ready to forgive you."

"I'm sure he's wary as hell. He tried really hard with me for a long time. Eventually, he had to let go of the rope and let me drown before I took him with me."

"Got it."

"I imagine he's not thrilled to have a reminder of his past so close to his new, happy life." She shook her head, a dark cloud hovering. "It's not like I have any intention of upsetting what he has going. I just miss…having family. Someone in my corner."

She watched the sky that just twenty minutes ago carried a sliver of light. Stars twinkled back at her now, and the recriminations swirled. The experience tonight had been a stark reminder that she still had a long way to go. Good week or not, her life was her life, and her mistakes would continue to follow her. She could be patient. She would continue to be honest. But maybe it was time she put a lid on the hope she'd allowed to simmer, and accept that she was on her own in many ways and always would be.

Juliette was stunned. In fact, she couldn't remember a time when someone surprised her as much. Peyton was smart, put together, and wonderful with people. Juliette never would have suspected she had such a heavy past. That bias was on her, though. People weren't the clichés that were so often assumed of them.

"My advice? Don't give up on him. Your brother."

"That's my plan." A pause. She looked sad, and that wasn't an emotion that Juliette readily associated with Peyton, but she wasn't sure she'd ever forget the haunted expression on her face in this moment.

Peyton opened her mouth to speak, paused, and then tried again. "I hope you don't think of me differently now. It's okay if you do, but I promise, I'm not that same person." Peyton had always struck Juliette as someone with thick armor, but maybe that had been out of necessity. There was clearly a lot more to Peyton than she'd realized, but it didn't deter her. It tugged at something very human inside Juliette and made her long to know more. In fact, she wanted every detail that made Peyton who she was.

Juliette slid her half-eaten cup across the table. "I just see my friend, okay?"

Peyton blinked. Stared at the night sky. And came back to settle her gaze on Juliette's. A smile blossomed and it was like the sun coming up on a gloomy day. "I wish everyone was as forgiving."

"He'll come around, Peyton."

Her eyes shone with tears. "That's why I'm here."

"Have others made it hard for you? Since you got out."

"There's always going to be a faction that put you in a category when they hear you were locked up once upon a time. I've gotten the disapproving stares when I check the felon box, been refused employment, and even had someone I cared about just stop taking my calls."

Sobering. Juliette's heart ached as she imagined what it must be like to try hard and have doors closed in your face. People who became your friends suddenly ghosting you when they learned a detail they didn't like. "I can't even imagine." Juliette touched the top of Peyton's hand, and she turned it over, accepting Juliette's palm against hers. The feel of their skin pressed together brought a sense of calm over the moment like a much needed security blanket. How unique and indescribable. Juliette had still not figured out their connection, but there it was again, showing itself with a new and surprising manner.

But it was only a moment before Peyton pulled her hand back again. That was typical Peyton, she was learning. She offered glimpses of intimacy, but sooner rather than later the window would slam shut, and the fun and games would resume. She preferred levity, positivity, fun—and maybe that came from self-preservation. It made a lot more sense to Juliette now.

Peyton pushed her half-empty bowl of lemon-coconut yogurt until it came to rest next to Juliette's dish. She crossed her arms in front of her. The move seemed part defense, part protection from the gust of autumn wind that hit and swirled. The night had already been a jumble. Whimsical at first, but they'd certainly taken a right turn into heavier territory, leaving Peyton's features troubled and pensive. Juliette watched the ends of her blond hair lift and settle in a haphazard and perfect conglomeration which felt like a fitting metaphor for Peyton herself.

"But the adversity I met out there in the world was what first gave me the drive to take over the original version of Cotton Candy from my mentor. If I was in charge, it gave me full control over my own destiny. If I failed, that was on me."

"But you're not failing, Peyton. You're not only doing well, you're killing it. Thriving."

"Yeah, well, you have the prettiest eyelashes."

That shut Juliette up. Peyton seemed to catch herself. "I'm sorry. You were saying something really nice, but I'm captivated every time you blink and had to get that out so we could move on."

If only Juliette was good at picking out words when caught off guard. The way Peyton disarmed her was unique and a new experience for Juliette. Thomas, when they were together, had been full of compliments, but they never stole Juliette's entire vocabulary selection the way Peyton so easily managed. "I put on a little mascara," she answered, realizing she could have done so much better with a response. This entire conversation had her off center. Peyton's brother was awful to her. She'd been to jail for stealing. For dishonesty. For causing an injury to someone else. Yet she liked Juliette's lashes.

"Mascara or not, they're beautiful. You were saying?"

"I don't know anymore." Her brain went into project mode, scurrying to right itself and participate appropriately. Juliette gestured as if to erase a whiteboard and start over. She made a cutting gesture with her hand. "Here's the boiled-down version."

"I'm listening."

"I believe in redemption. I don't think one's past has to define their future."

Peyton's gaze held tight to the surface of the white plastic table. A closer look told Juliette that her bottom lip trembled, probably against her will, and her eyes had pooled with fresh emotion. She was wordless. A new development. After a long silence that Juliette allowed to fill the whole space, Peyton wiped her left cheek and met Juliette's gaze for a strong beat. "I appreciate that. I hope every day of my life that it's true."

She laced their fingers. "You don't have to be afraid with me, okay? I'm not going to judge you, or make any kind of assumption."

Peyton nodded. "I may get annoyed with you and the way you charm the pants off everyone you meet."

That pulled a grin. "I only charmed *your* pants off, to be clear."

Juliette sputtered over the sentence she'd yet to utter, changing gears. "I guess I earned that."

"Oh, I think we both enjoyed the reward."

A soft smile. "I can't argue." The night went still as they lingered on the memory of Peyton and her exceptional skills in a darkened storage room.

"Would you do anything differently?" Peyton asked. "Knowing what you do now. About me."

She couldn't admit it out loud, but the version of her from just a couple of months ago might have. That would take examining. But not the person she'd shifted into in the last few weeks. She answered with that version of herself in mind. "I would not have."

"You're either a good friend or an wonderful liar. Either way, I believe you." The moon was only a few days away from full. "And you were adventurous enough to accompany me tonight, even if the mood was torpedoed."

Juliette stood. "I, for one, am glad it was. I think I needed to hear your story."

Peyton nodded. "I'll call Caleb in a couple of days. See if I can chip away at his anger. He really doesn't want me here. I don't think I was aware of how strongly he felt until seeing his face." They strolled to the car at a slow pace, and Juliette let Peyton talk it out. "The anger. The way his face went to stone. It was…eye opening."

"Fuck him." The words even surprised Juliette. She didn't swear a lot, and she certainly didn't come at perfect strangers so aggressively. Peyton raised an eyebrow, but the side of her mouth also pulled, which was a relief. "I just mean, he dabbled in the very same things that got you in trouble at one point."

Peyton scratched her shoulder and leaned against the car. "True."

"So where's his compassion now? Maybe I'm out of my lane because I'm all fired up on sugar."

"Maybe." Peyton seemed bolstered. "I've thought the same, but it helps to hear it from an outsider's perspective." She shrugged. "In spite of it all, I just want my brother back. I want to hit reset. More than anything. And now I'm feeling a little wobbly about it all." She took a deep breath and flipped all the way around, buying a moment of privacy.

Before she did, Juliette caught a glimpse of her face, streaked with hurt, and it prompted her to do something. She wasn't at all sure what. Out of desperation, her arms went around Peyton, and she held on. It was all she had to offer. Her own problems seemed small by comparison, and it just illustrated how you can't possibly know what another person might be going through, because honestly, Peyton seemed happier than anyone she knew. Yet she wasn't. At all. "I hope you get that chance."

"Me, too."

Before she let go, she was treated to Peyton's cherry-vanilla scent and soft skin, a reminder of the pull she felt whenever she was in Peyton's orbit these days. It wasn't that kind of night, though, not that kind of tension. They were quieter, reflective, and had gotten to know each other in a whole new way.

As they drove home, she watched Peyton behind the wheel, nodding subtly to the music, probably without knowing she was doing so. She was in her own head, lost in what was probably a circus of overlapping thoughts. How interesting that they'd only known each other a short time, but Juliette struggled to remember life without Peyton in it. When she did, everything came up as colorless. Boring. She was glad Peyton Lane and all her complexities had moved back to Landonville. She'd affected Juliette and her small corner of the world in more ways than she probably even realized. Also…she had a feeling there just might be more to come.

Chapter Ten

The red leaves were Peyton's favorite, followed by the oranges, then yellows. The rainbow that was the season's changing colors was almost too beautiful to look at. Yet she did, leisurely, every morning on the way to work, craning her head, peering through the windshield, rolling down the windows for a quick hit of chilled air that gave her a quick upshot in energy.

Peyton refused to take autumn for granted. Not after all those years missing out on the season entirely—the decor, the excitement, the changing landscape, the emerging of jackets. Cliché or not, she coveted everything cinnamon and pumpkin spice to a fault. After the first major cold front of the year in Landonville, scarves were everywhere, and folks seemed to smile all the more at the people they passed on the winding sidewalks. Who knew where they were headed? But collective energy had Peyton motivated.

She woke every morning ready to take on the day and work on herself. This season more than any other brought it out in her. She had goals that she categorized on lists, hopes and dreams that kept her awake on her pillow, and long-term plans that weren't going to happen on their own. In order for any of those plans to come to fruition, she needed to be the best version of herself. Thereby, she worked in a reflective meditation early each morning, then took extra-hot coffee on her back patio where she could check in on her small herb garden before hopping in the Mustang and opening shop, new fall colors on display in many of her products. If she was lucky, she'd catch sight of Juliette and wave through the window, setting her day off on the right foot. It really worked, too. Mornings without a Juliette sighting left her unsettled and adrift. She looked forward to them.

The recent weeks only validated Peyton's early business success. It hadn't just been a busy opening. Cotton Candy was definitely on the map now. The shop was populated every hour it was open with customers of all kinds. Afternoons were busiest, and the demand for attention had prompted her to rely more on Kiva and TJ, who reported for work after lunch, or in the morning should Peyton need the time off. She did what she could to assist her customers in fittings and matching up their styles to her merchandise. She'd been asked out twice, too. Interestingly, by two different women, which meant she was putting out the correct vibes.

"Did you say yes?" Lola asked, as Peyton sat along the bar at The Frog and Dog one evening after watching Lola get her waltz and tango on in dance class. Intense stuff, and Lola was better than good. Peyton had newfound respect, watching her spin and march and rise and fall in perfect time to the music.

"I didn't, but one of them seemed super great."

Lola squinted. "Those words don't go together. They fight like bickering teenagers. Explain yourself or I'm cutting you off." She gestured to Peyton's longneck.

"I've had half a beer."

Lola shrugged. "It's all the power I have."

"All right. Hold on." Peyton looked around to be sure there was enough distance between them and the other patrons for privacy. "Here's the thing. I kind of have a situation I don't want to disrupt."

Of course she was referencing Juliette, but at the same time, the sexy side of her relationship with Juliette had been placed on pause, given how busy they'd both been. That only seemed to stoke her fire higher. The idea of touching Juliette again, or having Juliette touch her, had her constantly on her toes and lost in fantasyland. They flirted, they insinuated, they touched, and they smoldered. All unspoken promises of things ahead. The possibilities tapped Peyton on the shoulder daily. But since that momentous encounter at trivia night, they'd fallen into the PG-13 category. The more time went by, the more Peyton craved a revisit. Parameters had been put in place, so all systems were go. Why hadn't she made it happen? She more than wanted it. Needed it, even.

Beneath it all, Peyton suspected what might be holding her up. And it wasn't necessarily her crowded calendar. Underneath the conservative excuse, she was unnerved by the capacity Juliette had to make her feel something after years of going through her days numb and all the better for it. That was a difficult hurdle to clear.

Lola placed both hands flat on the bar. "Is it with that girl Heather from the dry cleaners? Don't get mixed up over there. I speak from experience."

"Hold on." This was good. "Aren't you straight?"

Lola shrugged and grabbed a rag to wipe down the bar. "Is anyone fully straight? Heather, man. She does a number." She crossed herself and blew a kiss to God.

"Maybe I should write that down." She gave her head a shake to clear it. "I was actually talking about Juliette."

Lola paused her cleanup and squinted. "Give me more. Juliette. Drawing a blank."

"Really? How do you not know Juliette? She's in here for trivia night every Tuesday." She pointed at Juliette's team's customary table. "With her ex-husband and best friend?"

"Oh, right. The brunette. A little uptight. She has opinions."

Peyton smiled at the description. Lola wasn't wrong. But what used to make Peyton roll her eyes was now incredibly endearing. And also kinda hot. Maybe because it was so much fun to loosen her screws and watch them fall away one by one. She fanned herself because someone had jacked the temperature up. "No crime in being uptight."

"Oh, you like a good librarian, too, don't you?" Lola bounced her eyebrows. "I see you."

"Not everyone is what they seem once you get them alone, Lola."

Lola placed a hand on her hip. "Ain't that the truth. Stumpy Greathouse was the love of my life. Sexiest man I'd ever seen with the wavy blond hair and the chiseled brow. A total disaster when we got naked." She nodded sagely. "And I never would have guessed."

Peyton frowned. "I might have. His name was Stumpy."

Lola waved her off. "Juliette Whatshername is pretty, though. I can certainly agree to that part. Subtle makeup. Pouty, full mouth. Probably fantastic for kissing. Goes for simplicity with her hair. If you can just get her to loosen her feisty little fucking grip on everything, you might just have a keeper."

"I don't know that I'm capable of permanent with Juliette. She's different."

"In a good way?"

"In a terrifying way." She didn't share with Lola that she'd been moving through life like an automaton, and Juliette and all that came with her would overwhelm everything. She wasn't capable of handling that kind of emotion. She didn't have that capacity.

Instead, she kept it simple. "She makes me feel more than I'm used to, and it's not what I'm interested in." She exhaled slowly. "I think it's better that I keep a certain amount of distance between libido and heart. You know the kind of arrangement, right? No complications. Nothing messy."

"Those are my favorite. They go home. Thank God! And I can stretch out on the couch and eat grapes naked while I watch my shows."

"Why do I feel like I'm doing life wrong when I talk to you?"

Lola just winked and offered a little cha-cha in place, probably in celebration of who she was, which was awesome in every way. Lola didn't give a fuck, and that sounded pretty awesome to Peyton.

"Juliette Jennings is hard to look away from, but I have to be careful."

"Can you do that?"

"I want to try. We vibe. We support each other. And I'm wildly attracted to her." She took a final pull from her beer and slid the bottle. "I just need to make sure it doesn't go too far."

Lola whirled around and pointed a delicate finger at Peyton. "That's because you're a runner when shit gets real. I'm right about that, aren't I? I love you already, but even I can see that much."

She sighed, recognizing Lola's intuition and copping to her conclusion. "I think I'm just trying to focus on one set of goals at a time." Annoyance flared, at herself and at Lola for figuring her out so damn quickly. "And yes. Fine. I'll say it. I get uncomfortable when there are too many emotions flying. I'm not good at them. Not a newsflash. I'm trying to change, but it's so much easier to just fucking not go there. Juliette's the only potential threat in that department." She was saying too much. Even she knew that.

Lola squinted. "You related to Caleb Lane?"

Where had that come from? "You know a lot. My brother."

"I keep meaning to ask. There's a resemblance. In here." She gestured to her eyes. "Used to come in here a lot before the kids. Still once in a while."

"He's not my biggest fan, but I'm working on that. We used to be close. We're not now."

"I see the love in your eyes, though." Lola placed a hand on top of Peyton's head. "Don't you worry. It's all gonna work out. I can tell." She leveled a hard stare that meant business. "But don't you run. Hear me? You come find me, and we'll dance it out. I'll twirl you like a top."

"You have yourself a deal."

"Can I come by for that amazing bra you mentioned? With the super lift."

"I already set it aside for you. You will die and never return."

"My kinda boobage." Lola blew her a kiss, and Peyton was reminded that there were good people everywhere. You just had to find them and lean on them when there were question marks. It was starting to feel like she had more than one of those in town, a foundation she could build upon. She happily stored away some of Lola's helpful but stern words and would try to be less shy about her emotions and maybe, once in a while, lean into them. Let them occur. Terrifying. Exhilarating.

Juliette, however, was an untied pair of shoelaces in Peyton's life, and it was time she stopped ignoring them before she fell flat on her face.

The next day, she waited until the customer Juliette was ringing up had fully left The Station before leaping in. "This is going to sound like a line, but it's not. I swear."

Juliette raised an eyebrow and waited.

"I never told you this, but you were the winner of one of my free giveaways the day of my opening."

"And you've held my prize hostage?"

Peyton hooked a thumb. "Tied up in the back. Claim whenever you want." The funny part was that Juliette had been one of the names selected and Peyton had neglected to inform her, thinking she'd laugh it off. It felt like an opening of sorts, so she went for it.

"I'm claiming it right now. What do I win?"

"Twenty-five-dollar gift certificate."

"Do you have dollar undies?" She stood with a flash of joy.

"Sadly, no."

"Then I'm taking a new bra. Mine hurt."

Peyton squinted and led the way back to Cotton Candy, waiting for Juliette to flip the *back in five minutes* sign she'd invested in. "Bras shouldn't hurt."

"Mine have my whole life. We're at war pretty much daily until I can toss it when I get home."

"This is the most upsetting news of the week."

"Only the week?"

"It's been a busy news cycle." She cocked her head. "I can help if you want." They arrived in the bra section and she lifted a white satin hanger with a pretty blue bra that might be Juliette's style. Not too revealing, but not at all boring. The detail on the cups had been stitched with gold thread and the color contrast was beautiful. "I do fittings. I don't know how you feel about that, though."

Juliette didn't hesitate. "Yes."

"Yes?" She checked in because there was an element of intimacy in a fitting, and she didn't want to cross any lines that would make Juliette uncomfortable. "I can be completely professional."

"I know you can." She nodded once. "I want an official fitting."

Juliette's eyes glimmered with confidence. This was Peyton's chance to showcase what she could do. "Follow me to the fitting rooms, ma'am. I'm about to change your life."

Peyton told her the fitting would take under five minutes and that she could leave her bra on the entire time. Juliette shrugged off the ripple of extra energy. She'd be partially clothed in what easily equated to a bathing suit top she'd waltz down the beach wearing. Plus, Peyton was already, ahem, familiar with her breasts. At least by touch. She swallowed back an acute memory that scratched for attention she simply couldn't give it in this moment. Not when she was about to have Peyton's hands so close, her eyes free to roam, and Juliette's libido in hyperdrive lately.

They were alone in the store and stowed away in one of the two small dressing rooms with the amazingly soft white carpet.

Peyton waited patiently as Juliette unbuttoned her dress shirt. She'd been going for sharp business owner that day and had selected her royal-blue number and paired it with black heels. Two inches. Nothing crazy. Peyton's gaze remained on the cloth tape measure in her hands. Respectful. It amused Juliette for some reason, given their history.

"Tape measure first, just around your bra line," Peyton said, stepping forward when she was ready. There was a mirror in the dressing room, and Juliette took in the scene. She stood facing the mirror in her black dress pants and raspberry lace bra. It had been so pretty on the website when she'd ordered it, but just like all the others, it tortured her as the hours ticked by. Peyton encircled the top portion of her ribcage with the measuring tape and took note. Juliette reminded herself to breathe. What sounded like a practical task, maybe even a little bit flirty, now felt incredibly...erotic. Almost like she was living one of the fantasies she'd imagined in her mind for so many weeks now. Isn't this how they started? A seemingly innocent encounter like a bra fitting that turned intoxicatingly sexy once they got down to it until fingertips were brushing skin and slipping beneath fabric they were never supposed to slip beneath. God.

"Are you okay?" Peyton murmured, meeting her gaze in the mirror. She'd been doing another measurement. Juliette's mouth had gone dry, and surely that would give her away. She nodded instead. Peyton sent her a soft smile, which likely meant she knew Juliette was feeling more than just the soft gust of air from the heater above them.

"Me? I'm so great." She choked on those words because they were too enthusiastic. "I mean, just fine," she amended in a quieter tone. "I'm good."

Peyton smiled. "Excellent. I'm just going to grab a quick measurement across the deepest portion of the bra cups, and we'll get you sized."

"Perfect," Juliette said, taking in the cherry-vanilla scent that she was now obsessed with. Whether she was aware of it or not, Peyton's hair tickled her bare shoulder as she reached around Juliette.

"What are you smiling at?" Peyton asked quietly. Her voice had taken on this half whisper quality that Juliette liked very much.

"I'm just impressed at your very professional demeanor. Just look at your strict concentration."

Peyton exhaled slowly. "Well, I can't alienate my potential new client."

"What if she didn't mind?" For some reason, this whole exchange made Juliette feel very powerful.

"That might be different." Peyton raised an eyebrow. A question. The air in the room had gone thick, and Juliette felt the weight of it on her skin.

"Why don't you show me why my bra doesn't fit. A demonstration. Harmless, wouldn't you say?"

A slow grin emerged. Peyton nodded. "You want me to show you? And you're giving me permission?"

"So much permission."

Peyton took a step into Juliette's space, sending a small shiver. Juliette held her ground. "Here." Peyton traced a circular pattern on top of the fabric covering Juliette's right breast. "Your cup size is too small. You're not giving your breasts the space they need." She pulled the cup back slightly, revealing more of both of Juliette's breasts. "Less spillage that way. See?"

"I do."

Peyton moved around behind her. "And the band? It's too big and not offering the support you need in this middle section. So we need to be tighter around here." She trailed a finger across Juliette's back. "Looser here," she said, running her fingers over the front of the bra's cups, grazing her nipples. Juliette's eyes fluttered. The action sent a white hot bolt between her legs that caused her lips to part in surprise. But she shouldn't have been. She was in another enclosed space, half dressed, with Peyton Lane. This was becoming their thing.

"You're a little too good at your job, you know that?" Juliette said, turning, meeting Peyton's gaze. There was little to no chance she could disguise what those slight touches had unleashed in her. Nor was she sure she wanted to.

Without a word, Peyton moved a strand of hair off Juliette's shoulder, leaned in, and placed an open-mouthed kiss on Juliette's neck. Good God. Her knees almost gave out as her arms went to Peyton's head, cradling it, pulling Peyton closer, gripping her hair as her tongue did wondrous things along the column of her neck. Bam. Her back met the wall. Just as Peyton's lips were pulled away so they could meet Juliette's, the bell above the door rang, signaling the arrival of a customer.

"Fuck," Peyton said, dropping her forehead onto Juliette's bare shoulder. Her breathing was ragged, and Juliette could feel the rapid beat of her heart. "This was too good. Of course someone walks in."

"Go. It's okay." It wasn't. She was on fire and ready to do something about it. She wanted to touch Peyton this time, explore every inch of her until she broke and cried out.

"I'll tell them to leave. Kick them out forcibly."

"Peyton, it's Cathy Summerton. Are you here?"

Peyton's eyes went wide, and Juliette knew hers mirrored them. "The mayor's wife. You can't."

"Then stay half naked in my dressing room forever. In the back, Cathy. I'll be right out."

Juliette laughed. "Just until I can put my shirt on and get back to my store, which is also unattended."

"We're bad business owners."

"The worst. We're gonna get fired."

"Good. More time for this," Peyton said and nipped at her shoulder as she left the dressing room, the slightest graze of her teeth sexier than she would have ever guessed. She had a feeling her afternoon was about to feel long and lacking in the lust department. When she quietly moved through the store, she passed Mrs. Summerton and Peyton speaking animatedly about the many uses of a good corset. Who knew? The knowledge she coveted, however, was the secret moment she'd just stolen with Peyton alone in that dressing room, a little secret all their own. In many ways, it made the exchange feel all the more charged and clandestine. She spent the afternoon drawing a woman from behind holding a robe open, flashing whoever was about to come through the door, and she felt a kinship to that woman, wearing it like a exciting little Girl Scout badge. Fooling around in public? Check. Acting all-around saucy? Double check.

She knew they'd fall back into their friend mode once regularly scheduled life took over. But there'd likely be another time, and she, for one, hoped that when it did happen, they'd have space and time to entertain the desires they'd only just touched on.

"No interruptions," she told her nearly completed naughty card. "None."

When she checked her email shortly after, she had another eight card orders from a variety of different cities. Apparently, her website had gained some traction. It turned out that she might not have such a boring afternoon, after all. With visions of dollar signs, and lacy bras, and bouncing breasts dancing in her brain, Juliette hummed a sexy little tune to herself and got to work on some naughty little presketches. How was this her life?

CHAPTER ELEVEN

Juliette relished the quiet afternoons spent drawing. She even stayed late to finish up a project, finding new ways to bring out color and texture. She had a feeling she would never stop growing as an artist.

With The Station currently empty, she'd lost herself in the three greeting cards with looming deadlines and the illustrations awaiting her attention. She'd been working uninterrupted for about forty-five minutes when the small bell above the door sang out. She lifted her gaze and found Peyton starring back at her.

"I'm on break. Ignore me." She took a seat at the checkout counter and swiveled in the tall chair so she could watch Juliette at her drafting table a few feet away.

"You have curls today. I like them."

"No." She held up a finger. Her nails were a soft mauve. "You're supposed to ignore me."

"Can't. You're not invisible, you know. Did you think you were invisible?"

"This is a letdown." She stared curiously at the hand she placed in front of her puzzled face and shrugged.

"What is it that you are doing on your break exactly other than your invisibility act?"

"I thought it might be fun to come over here and watch you work." She made a sweeping gesture as if to say *continue*. Juliette did. But it wasn't like she couldn't feel herself being watched. Or, rather, enjoyed. Her skin prickled, and she tucked a strand of hair behind her ear, trying to imagine herself from Peyton's perspective.

"Can I ask what you're working on, Ms. Jennings? Your viewing public demands details."

Juliette raised her head and turned to her right, meeting Peyton's wide, interested eyes. She sucked on the straw from her large gas station cup as she waited for Juliette's answer. The straw was the perfect arrow sign to her always interesting lips. She pursed with the best of them.

"Well, public of *one*..."

"I'm special."

"I won't disagree." She gestured to her drafting table and the supplies laid out like soldiers. She tried to keep a neat workstation. "I have seven more naughty cards due this week, and while there's a lull at the shop, I thought I'd take advantage of the time."

Peyton used her cup and straw to point. "You have seven this week. The numbers are increasing."

"No. I have seven left to complete."

"Wow. There were more?"

"Quite a few more." Juliette folded her arms, a smug smile tugging. "It's possible I put them for sale online and had my stepmother's brother, a web designer, work in some keywords for search engines. The orders are coming in from all over, and they seem to have no problem with the shipping costs." She threw a hand toward her laptop off to the side. "I also have a list of inquiring potentials to get back to. Plus, at the local level, everyone who comes in to pick up their card peruses the shop and picks up a few ready-made cards or some other item."

"Maybe you need sexy stationery."

"I hadn't even thought of that. Is this my brand now?" Her mouth fell open and she pondered the possibilities. "Maybe I do. Am I about to be that sexy little stationery shop?"

"God, I hope so." Peyton beamed. "You took the idea and ran with it. This is amazing. With more potential everyplace you look. Who needs a regular stationery shop when you can shop at a risqué one? I know which I'm choosing."

"Being next to a lingerie shop certainly doesn't hurt, Jacquelyn turning up the heat as always."

"Look at us. A team already. Also, who is Jacquelyn? You keep mentioning her."

"Never you mind." Juliette smiled and relaxed. "I do think we now have a through-line to the two businesses, and I never would have imagined it. When your sign went up, I had no idea how it would change, well, my trajectory."

"Say trajectory again."

"Trajectory." She damn well overpronounced the word on purpose. "Happy?"

Peyton scrunched her shoulders. "Your mouth never disappoints."

"You wouldn't exactly know the full extent of that yet, would you?"

Peyton dropped her head back, her hair falling down her back in sexy waves. The fun beach kind. "Now you're teasing me."

"Am I?"

She went back to illustrating the pair of luscious lips her client had requested, even matching the lipstick shade and hair color to the photo the woman had uploaded. Apparently her girlfriend would be receiving a really nice birthday gift from those lips after dinner, and her card would be making that clear. But all Juliette could think about was doing the very same for Peyton, whose gaze left her hyperaware of her own skin.

Finally, "Yeah, you're going to have to go." Juliette turned back around. She was also overly warm now, and her shirt collar felt oppressive.

Peyton sat tall. "No can do. I have ten minutes left on my break, and Kiva will think I don't trust her with the shop because she loves dramatic declarations. Plus, I'm having a fabulous time. Do you have bouncers around here?" She made a show of trying to locate one. "If not, I'm pretty sure I can take you. First of all, height advantage. Second, you're scrappy, but I do push-ups."

Because her mind was already in a million different dirty directions, Juliette's only response was to raise an interested eyebrow, communicating all the ways they could put that to work.

Peyton's eyes darkened. She got the message, all right. She folded her arms and kicked out a sexy hip. "Now I'm definitely not leaving. Want some of my drink? It's a coconut slush from the gas station on the corner. I'll let you suck on the straw."

Juliette focused on the raspberry lip liner she was giving her subject. "Stop it. You're bad."

"Well, that wouldn't be any fun." Peyton lifted a shoulder. "This bra is tight. I might need a fitting. Or I could just take it off."

Juliette closed her eyes. Heat rushed to her face and she set down her pen. It was the middle of the workday, and with no actual outlet for the very powerful desires that swirled and beckoned, she had to mind over matter the situation. Or else be forced into another uncomfortable afternoon full of lustful thoughts and distracting fantasies all starring her sexy, blond neighbor. Juliette needed a cure. She thought about Dolores talking her ear off, her father ignoring her, Thomas signing divorce papers at her request, coffee that had been oversweetened, Peyton standing topless in front of a mirror, searching for a better fitting bra. Dammit. The record scratched. She'd done something wrong. "You cause trouble."

"So? I love trouble." They couldn't go on like this. Juliette was at her limit. Something had to give. "Okay, I better get back to the store. Think about me while you draw. A lot. In a variety of positions." She followed that up with a sassy smile.

Juliette swore under her breath and watched her delectable next-door neighbor sway her hips in a pair of perfect faded jeans all the way out the damn door to stand in the midst of lingerie for the rest of the day. Juliette had gone without full-blown sex for way too long, and now these damn cards! Even if they did save the shop, they were not helping her plight as a woman on this planet.

Again, she slogged through the damn afternoon hours, drawing, and assisting Mort Martinez with his selection of the perfect birthday gift for his wife, a fan of anything with rabbits. Luckily, she had two high-end Hummels that included rabbits and a few bunny-adjacent mugs and magnets.

By the time she'd made it home for the day, she wanted anything but time alone. What she wanted was Peyton. Undressed. Beneath her fingertips. She was a little annoyed about it, too, stalking through her kitchen like an indignant teenager, blaming the universe for this new distraction one minute, and thanking it profusely the next. The truth was that as tortured as Juliette was, she felt alive, hungry, and full of new energy. She didn't want it to end.

"Should I go for it?" she asked the worked-up woman in the mirror looking back at her. The left side of her mouth hinted at a grin. "You only live once, right?" An attempt to bolster herself. It just might have worked. She raised her shoulders to her ears and harnessed the kernel of courage it took to make the drive to Peyton's house, which she'd only experienced from photos, and that one time she'd passed the neighborhood on her way to her favorite coffeehouse. She could have announced herself but didn't. It was a seven-minute drive and a twelve-second trip from her car up the sidewalk to the door. She rang the bell without allowing herself to think, propelled by lust and the fear of missing out on what could be a new awakening or valuable life experience. She heard Dolores, of all people, telling her to get her sassy autumn on, and dammit, she might just try.

Peyton swung open the door, wearing pink track shorts with a white stripe on the side, a long-sleeved white T-shirt, and her volumes of blond hair piled on top of her head with a large brown clip. She'd never looked better. Fuckable. Juliette opened her mouth but didn't get the chance to speak.

"Yes. Get in here. Now," Peyton said, reaching out, grabbing a fistful of Juliette's shirt, and pulling her in. How were they always on the same damn page when they employed wildly different approaches to life? Maddening. Gratifying. Hot.

Music was playing loudly as Juliette walked into the square living room with tons of funky personality. The color scheme involved lots of warm hues. Oranges, yellows, off-reds. The song, which came with a male singer wailing the lyrics with a strong drum beat below, pulsed beneath her feet. She'd never heard it before, but damn if it didn't feel wildly appropriate. She turned around, and Peyton nodded. She knew exactly why Juliette was there, and with three steps invaded her space. Their height difference had never been more evident than when they stood this close. Peyton's lips hovered over hers, leaving enough time to protest or step away. Juliette had no intention of doing either because for the first time in weeks she felt like she was exactly where she was supposed to be, as if their connection was ordained by an unseen force. How? The feeling of completeness enveloped her, and she hoped to live in this perfect moment for as long as possible. The sound of the drums joined with the beating of her heart. Peyton inclined her head, moving closer but oh, so slowly. Too slow. When Juliette couldn't stand it another second, she went up on her toes and covered the distance in a whoosh. Her lips met Peyton's, moving over them with selfish intention. She was taking what she wanted, which felt so foreign, yet so damn good. "I'm afraid I'm using you right now," she murmured. "And I like it."

"And I'm afraid I'm totally okay with that. Wear me out. I'm here for it. God, you taste good."

More kissing. Goose bumps covered Juliette's arms as they stood in the living room, pressed up against each other, trying to get closer, savoring the contact. Juliette's hands itched to explore more of Peyton's skin, her curves. She slid them into Peyton's hair, which made it tumble from its clip in the most wonderful way. She wanted to scream to the masses that she was making out with the hot new woman in town, and look at her goddamn hair, but she was too busy enjoying it.

"What the hell took you so long?" Peyton asked as she went to work on the buttons of Juliette's navy dress shirt.

"You knew I was coming?"

"Hoping."

"You didn't leave me a lot of options today." More kissing.

"Good. I was doing something right. We're getting naked, aren't we?"

"Please."

Peyton's tongue slipped into her mouth, and she murmured her appreciation. Peyton had astounding skills. It was as if they couldn't stay apart for too long after finally coming together. Her shirt was only half unbuttoned when Peyton walked them—kissing and bumping into furniture, walls, and who knows what else—on the way to what had to be her bedroom. Their pace was fast but thorough. Each kiss was finished, each touch fully executed, and damn it all, it hadn't even happened yet, and this was already the most heated exchange of Juliette's life. She was on fire, her center aching. She tried to figure out where she went from here, because it didn't seem like there was room for any more sensations in her body. Yet her nerve endings screamed for more. "Oh God," she heard herself say.

Peyton moaned and pressed her lips to Juliette's neck. The feel of her breath against Juliette's skin quite honestly made her breasts throb. That was new, too.

"I love the way you smell," Peyton said, nuzzling Juliette's neck. Her hands were under her shirt at her hips, not high enough. As if reading her thoughts, Peyton finished the work she'd done on Juliette's shirt and expertly dropped it to the floor. "Lie down." Her eyes were dark as she traced the underside of Juliette's bra, waiting.

Oh, damn. Juliette sat obediently on the bed, held eye contact, and lowered herself onto her back. She was trembling and wondered if Peyton noticed.

"Best visual ever," Peyton said, bracing herself above Juliette on her forearms. "You. In my bed. Just waiting there to be touched."

Juliette grabbed Peyton by her white shirt and pulled her down, refusing to wait another second longer for Peyton's body to be pressed, with its full weight, to hers.

"I like a woman who knows what she wants," Peyton said with a laugh, just as Juliette caught those cheeky lips in a searching kiss.

"She wants you to shut up already," Juliette said around this kiss, feeling a little cheeky herself. That ended the second Peyton rolled to the side and brought Juliette with her so they lay facing each other. With one hand, she worked the clasp of Juliette's bra and slid it down her arm. Peyton didn't say anything, but her gaze flicked to Juliette's breasts, then her nipples. Yes, that was appreciation. Her fingertips danced softly across the tops of Juliette's curves, savoring. This slowed everything down.

She could hear the sounds of their breathing, altered and short, and the music left playing in the distance. A forefinger circled her nipple as she watched. Another tremble. A bolt of heat moved through her. She felt the urgency between her legs and did her best to remain steady, present. She didn't want to miss a moment. The air was immediately thicker, like a storm was about to roll in, deep and low. Juliette felt Peyton all over, which was a sensation she couldn't quite process.

This wasn't them in the storage room on the fly, or trying on a bra in a small, semipublic place. There was no clock. This was all them without restraint. They were purposeful, driven, and unhurried. Time and privacy secured.

"You're so fucking sexy," Peyton said, her gaze holding and fogging Juliette's thoughts. The words and their meaning finally bubbled to the surface. No one had ever said anything like that to her before. But in that moment, Juliette felt like she *was* sexy, and it was the most empowering moment she could recall. She crushed her mouth to Peyton's as her bra was tossed into the wild and, for the first time, her typical restraint with it.

With her tongue in Peyton's mouth and her breasts now free, she lowered herself until Peyton's back hit the bed. Juliette hovered on top, watching eagerly as Peyton removed her own shirt. She loved watching her undress. A hot-pink bra with lace appliqué greeted her. Fancy. It looked expensive. The curves beneath left Juliette's mouth dry. She wanted to lick, suck, and explore. Anticipation was a marvelous and powerful drug.

"This, too," Juliette said, gesturing with her chin to the bra. It was beautiful but in the way.

"What? You don't want to admire my lingerie?"

"Next time." She didn't recognize her own voice that had taken on a husky, commanding quality.

"Promises, promises," Peyton said in the same moment she unclasped her bra and slid it down her arms. Unable to wait, Juliette leaned down. Her tongue swirled a nipple, and they were underway again. Desperate. The heat flushed down her midsection to her limbs, and she relished it, fueled. Her hips pushed against Peyton. On a mission now, Juliette systematically undressed her until she lay naked with hooded eyes and swollen lips, waiting. Skin, curves, and beauty all for her. Their eyes met, and Peyton gave a nod, a clear indication of her desire. Unspoken permission. "Touch me," she said, patient as Juliette's gaze swept over every inch of her first. A marvel. She didn't seem real. Half of Juliette wanted to devour Peyton's body, to learn every inch of her, and how to bring it to life. Another wanted to seal away this moment. She didn't want to ever forget all the acute sensations overcoming her senses to the point that she couldn't articulate all she felt.

Instead, she focused on the task at hand. She'd take pleasure in each second they had together. She eased Peyton's legs apart and lay alongside her as she slipped her hand between the heat of Peyton's thighs. Juliette's eyes slammed shut because Peyton was more than ready. The knowledge that she'd taken Peyton there, inspired her state, left her heady, turned-on, and feeling like the air had gone thin. As her hand pushed, explored, played, teased, Peyton began to roll her hips, slowly at first. An intimate dance. She also made the most intoxicating, needful noises when Juliette moved closer to where Peyton wanted her most. Not just yet. Reverent power flowed freely, leaving Juliette drunk on it. Peyton trusted her. She allowed herself to be vulnerable. Juliette wanted, needed, craved more than she ever had before. Her limbs trembled and tingled. It didn't detour her. She crushed her mouth to Peyton's breast and sucked, pulling a moan. Yes. Peyton slid her hand into Juliette's hair and gripped extra tight. *Fuck.* Peyton had sensitive breasts. She added that to the list of all things Peyton.

Juliette was half on top as her hand continued to caress Peyton intimately. She kissed her neck, inhaling the scent of raspberries mixed with fresh soap. "I want you to come," Juliette whispered, shocking herself. She'd never said anything as provocative in her life. It felt good.

Peyton nodded, words seeming to fail. She swallowed as her hips pushed against Juliette's hand, begging. "Inside," she said, finally. "Please."

Juliette did as she was told, sliding two fingers inside tentatively, thumb stroking circles around Peyton's most sensitive spot. Another kiss. Deep and long with Juliette's tongue in Peyton's mouth. Peyton began to move with the desperation of a wild animal, going up on her knees. Juliette followed, gripping her around the waist as Peyton clung to her shoulders. Peyton took the lead, moving up and down, setting a steady rhythm. Her head was tossed back and the ends of her hair tickled Juliette's shoulder. That little detail alone snagged her focus and made her wet all over again. She caught an earlobe and sucked. "Do you like that?" Juliette whispered, pumping harder.

"Mm-hmm," Peyton said. She picked up her pace, lost in the climb. Juliette found the moment overwhelming, the beauty, the abandon on Peyton's face. Her body slightly glistened, perfectly created. She was art if Juliette had ever known it. The onslaught of sensations, both physical and emotional, crashed upon her in the exact moment Peyton cried out and squeezed Juliette's shoulders tight, her nails digging in without care. The bursts of pain they caused turned to pleasure. Juliette shook and damn near came right alongside Peyton.

"Dear fucking God," Peyton said, crashing back to the bed and taking Juliette with her. "You just took me on the ride of my life, literally. Come here." Her voice was breathy and she seemed on a high. That loose, carefree quality told Juliette how comfortable she was, how at home with sex.

Juliette joined her on the pillow, still in a daze. Peyton's gaze dipped immediately to her breasts. She slid onto her side, palming them both, pushing them up and releasing slowly. Juliette forgot to exhale. "You have perfect breasts," she said. "I could tell that much in the store, but touching them does things to me. I came so hard just now. You're going to make me do it again just looking at you." She gave each nipple a pinch, and sharp little sensations danced across Juliette's skin. She heard the change in her own breathing pattern. She was wet and aching.

"Can I touch you now?"

Juliette nodded. Peyton slid her hand between Juliette's legs and palmed her. Her hips pressed back instantly. Her eyes slammed shut. Good God. She saw light and felt the pressure begin to build as Peyton began to stroke her, softly at first and then with authority.

"Grab the headboard," Peyton said in her ear.

She blinked, processing the words, and did as she was told. She turned around and went up on her knees, holding the top of the white wooden headboard. Peyton entered her from behind, and she heard her own voice whimper.

"Don't let go," Peyton said softly, as she began to move. The position allowed Juliette to control the rhythm, and she started her climb quickly as a result. "Is this good?" Peyton asked, slowing down, purposefully withholding.

"More."

"What do you want?" Peyton asked. "Tell me."

"I want you to fuck me," Juliette said, gripping the headboard harder when Peyton began to do just that. With each forceful thrust she was catapulted to a new height. Peyton's arm went around her waist, which offered her the leverage she needed to take Juliette higher and higher until she shattered so aggressively she lost sound, her voice strangled as the orgasm tore through her. Holy hell. What was happening? She rode out each shockwave from powerful to small, absorbing every ounce of pleasure available to her until she finally let go, sliding back down onto the bed.

Peyton was immediately behind her, encircling Juliette with her arms. She kissed the underside of her jaw as she recovered. "You are the sexiest thing I've ever seen."

Juliette closed her eyes and smiled. "That was one for the record books. Wow."

"We're good together. I knew we would be."

Juliette exhaled slowly. She could think clearly again. That helped. "I think we needed this."

"There was no other choice. Just walking into a room that you're in has me feeling it all over." She covered her eyes with her hand. "And you talking to me like that?"

"Talking to you?"

"During."

"Oh." Juliette's cheeks went hot as she remembered her words, but she said nothing. Mild embarrassment descended when she remembered how carried away she'd gotten. It wasn't her typical behavior, yet somehow…she'd been compelled.

Peyton shook her head as if reliving it. "I did not expect it but found it so very sexy. Turn around so I can see you?" Juliette did and Peyton looked down at her body, taking her time, tracing each curve with her fingertip.

Juliette, who would have classified herself as shy when it came to her body, basked in the objectification, learning yet another thing she liked. She'd never felt more desirable in her life, and that made her want to live in that space a while longer, luxuriate in the excitement, the safety they'd created here. "I'm in new territory."

"Tell me more about that." Peyton ran a finger down the line between her breasts, which sent a shot of something potent between Juliette's legs. She wanted to be taken again, but there was also something about the withholding that got her going even more.

"Well, I'm generally someone who stays on the straight and narrow."

Peyton let the sheet that partially covered her drop, revealing a good portion of her body. "The way you're looking at me right now, you aren't feeling so straight to me."

She laughed. That helped ease some of the stirrings she struggled to fight off. "Definitely not straight. But I've never been one to make a big splash."

"Small splashes then for Juliette."

"Except when I'm with you. I walk out onto ledges. I play with matches." She glanced up. "I hold on to headboards."

"Uh-oh. What are we going to do about that?" A sexy grin. Juliette couldn't get enough. Good Lord.

"There's a little bit of uh-oh. Sure. But it's also exhilarating, like there's more air in the room and I get to feast on it all day and night."

"Do you know what I think?" Peyton asked, crawling closer to Juliette like the slinkiest of cats. She bent down and pulled Juliette's nipple into her mouth. Such a boob woman. "I think that when you and I get together, we bring balance to the universe. I offer you the courage and the push to take those extra chances. And you quiet the vibrations I can't quite get settled."

Juliette looked up at Peyton who was sitting on her knees, cupping the underside of Juliette's breast. "And then, we just…"

"Ignite," Peyton said, straddling Juliette's lap.

She sat up fully and swept a strand of hair from Peyton's forehead. The word seemed to reverberate as their lips found each other in a clash. This was going to be a long and memorable night.

❖

Juliette slept like an angel. Peyton had decided as much in the hour that they'd fallen asleep together, naked, tangled in the sheets of Peyton's bed. Her face was entirely relaxed, every last trace of worry or anxiety washed away. Peaceful. It was entrancing.

Peyton'd woken first and sat up against her cushioned headboard just watching Juliette breathe and slumber, her dark hair fanned out behind her on the pillow as she slept on her stomach, her bare shoulders with the tiniest dusting of freckles on display. She felt the urge to run her hands through it softly, stroke the back of Juliette's head, soothe her, take care of her. The wash of emotion about knocked her over. She opened her mouth and closed it again, unsure what to do or say. She was shaking, shocked at everything that came over her in a jumble. Uncomfortable and grappling, she tried very hard to shut it off. She had to do something to exit this moment and fast. Peyton shifted her weight on the bed purposefully, and Juliette's eyes fluttered open. She looked around, orienting herself.

"We fell asleep," she said, looking up at Peyton. "How'd that happen?"

Peyton shrugged, pulling her shirt on over her head, her back to Juliette. "We expended quite a bit of energy." That's right. Keep it light. All about the sex. No peaceful angels here.

"True." Juliette hesitated. She clearly wasn't sure what to do now. Following Peyton's lead, she began to gather her clothes and dress herself. "Just give me a minute and I will be out of here."

"You don't have to rush." On one hand, she wanted Juliette out the door as soon as possible. On the other, she wanted her to stay forever. How did normal people live in this kind of war zone?

"Work tomorrow. You probably have things to do. So do I."

"Right. I'll just give you space."

She stepped out of the bedroom and placed both hands on her head. What the hell was happening? Hookups in Peyton's experience were usually seamless, easy. Why did the aftermath of this one feel... like everything she ever wanted but couldn't handle. She bucked up, rolled her shoulders, and took a lap around the room to recapture her casual air. She knew how to play this—she just had to do it. "Can I grab you a bottle of water for the road," she called into the bedroom.

"Nah. I'm just a few minutes from here," Juliette said, emerging while dancing into a shoe. Peyton's instinct was to leap to her assistance, help steady her. She should have. But it was like she had no social skills all of a sudden, stripped of all behavioral tools. One thing Peyton was sure of, however, was how sexy Juliette looked after. Her hair was a little wild. Her lips were swollen. And she had the cutest shade of pink dusting her cheeks. She looked like someone who'd been good and fucked, and Peyton bathed in the knowledge that she'd been the one to do it.

Juliette shrugged from about ten feet away. "Thanks for letting me crash your evening." She made a *yikes* face. "And for the rest. Not really sure what to say."

"How about *See you tomorrow?*"

"See you tomorrow, Peyton." As she passed, she touched Peyton's stomach and let her fingertips trail. That's all it took. All the rules, the casual etiquette that she strictly followed when it came to no-strings encounters came crashing down when she grabbed that hand and hauled Juliette in close. She needed just a few more seconds. "Just because," she murmured and captured Juliette's mouth for a kiss she hoped Juliette would remember between now and the next day. She wanted to be remembered, but even more, she selfishly wanted to experience a few more moments of this woman.

And within that touch, everything changed. The awkward film that covered everything around them evaporated, and Juliette's beautiful eyes blinking up at her were all that was left. "Hi," Peyton whispered. They were everything. This was.

Juliette broke into a smile, her arms at Peyton's waist. "Hi."

"I really enjoyed tonight." Why was she talking in that sweet, soft voice? It was definitely hurting her cause.

"I don't even think I have to say it back. You likely already know, which might be a little embarrassing. I could maybe learn to play it cooler. Quieter."

Peyton laughed and looked skyward. "I can admit to maybe having been tipped off by a signal or two. But never change a thing." Holding Juliette close like this while they talked was a first. She was surprisingly more at home in this moment than when Juliette was dancing into her shoe moments earlier. She longed to stay right where she was, indulge her every last whim, which was exactly why she stepped away and sent Juliette a smile from the new distance between them.

"All right. Well, take care of yourself." The look on Juliette's face said she felt every inch of their divide.

"You, too." It was all she had in her to give. The rest she tucked away. Safe. As she watched her walk to the car, Peyton placed a hand over the heart that seemed to know way more than it ever let on. For the first time, she yearned. She reached out. She *wanted*.

Once Juliette was gone, Peyton sat on the couch, pulled her knees up to her chest, and stared at the TV she'd flicked on and not watched. There was something notable swirling in her chest, tapping her on the shoulder, and demanding attention.

No.

She thought about her time in jail, and how she'd struggled to feel much of anything but hurt. She'd expected the rest of her life to be similar. She'd had small victories and joys. She still treasured a well-made cup of coffee or a dish of ice cream. But she'd not experienced this, whatever it was. Alarmed on one hand, and relieved on the other. She *was* capable of feeling. But now that it was here, she wasn't sure she wanted to. How long would it last? Did she have any control over when it would rear its powerful head? Regardless, it was here and real, and for the first time in years, Peyton felt like a human being. Not incarcerated. Not a number.

She placed her hand over her heart and held on, set off-kilter by this foreign sense of incompletion. The need to do something, but not sure what. She stayed that way for the rest of the night. No good. When thoughts of her evening with Juliette barraged her brain, she flipped over in bed, hoping the physical action would shut her brain the hell off. Simple was so much better, and it would be up to her to make sure things stayed that way. Juliette clearly had the ability to make Peyton explode with uncharted emotion. Who knew? She'd even gotten her to break her own rules, which meant she had to either be more vigilant, or end that side of their relationship.

Totally a no-brainer.

She wasn't letting go of Juliette.

But she had to be more careful. She had to manage their connection and hold on to her sense of control. Somehow.

CHAPTER TWELVE

Tuesday nights looked a whole lot different now. Hell, they were thrown on their heads. Juliette's team of three was now a duo... plus her. She used to have Peyton to focus on during trivia night, someone to whisk her away to storage rooms. But Peyton had missed the last two Tuesdays when her shop had been privately booked for the new happy hour shopping promotions Peyton offered. That left Juliette to deal with the happy couple alone, and she did mean happy. They'd started to meld into one of those couple creatures with inside jokes and private looks.

"Jules, you would have loved this little coffee stand right outside of town," Cherry said between rounds. Her eyes laughed. Actually laughed. Her happiness was nice to see. "Nothing frilly. Just a good strong cup. They even have these little..." Cherry snapped her fingers, looking for the word.

Thomas was right there. "Cup stoppers in the shape of race cars." He beamed.

"But they're highly effective. No spills."

"At all." Thomas enthused, "Coffee was out of this world. You'd have died."

"You would have."

Juliette nodded, her attention bouncing between the joint story-tellers. "I'll have to try it out. Take someone with me."

"As in?" Cherry raised her eyebrows, clearly referencing Peyton.

"Yeah, probably," Juliette said, remaining purposefully vague. Her own little sex life had taken a momentous turn lately. Not that she and Cherry had had much opportunity to discuss it. She'd been turned down for girls' night twice because of Cherry's evening plans with Thomas. And they'd been out trying new coffee spots in whatever free daytime availability Cherry had. These were definitely unprecedented times. She and Cherry had always seen every new rom-com in the theater together, but the previous Friday, Cherry had shot her down for the dinnertime showing.

"I'm so sorry. I told Tom that we would try out that new Indian place on Second Ave. Can we catch up next week?"

"Totally. You guys enjoy."

Wednesday bowling had also taken a hit to the point that Juliette dreaded going. Instead of feeling at home, ensconced in her element, surrounded by her friends like she had in the past, she spent the majority of the time watching Thomas and Cherry kiss, cuddle, and make puppy dog eyes at each other to the point that Juliette thought they might spontaneously morph. That Wednesday, Cherry nailed her sixth frame, bringing home the strike. Juliette leaped into the air and held out her hand for the bestie high-five dance, only to watch Cherry fling her arms around Thomas's neck for a celebratory kiss. Juliette smiled and stretched her neck, making a show of how unaffected she was, when the truth was she missed her friends. Her bowling dance. Her normal.

"Come over," Peyton said, when Juliette sent her a Mayday text message that read, *Bowling was trash.*

"It's my fault," Juliette said, arriving on Peyton's doorstep. "My friends are happy and in love, and I'm complaining. Who does that? I'm a monster. Tell the townspeople to gather a mob."

Peyton took her hand and led her inside to the kitchen. "I don't think we need a mob. Let's table that option."

Juliette held up a finger. "Temporarily."

"Deal. First of all, you're in a unique situation. Anyone would need time to adjust to their ex-husband and best friend getting it on. Secondly, you like things to be just so, and right now, Thomas and Cherry are outside of their rightful boxes. Your brain is all scrambled up."

Juliette shook her head. "You're the only person who gets me and doesn't beat me up for it."

Peyton's blond hair was down and wavy as it highlighted her shoulders. The forest-green cotton tank top did her that favor, and she owed it one. This was better than any of her three favorite TV shows.

"I think it makes you Juliette." She dipped her head and met Juliette's gaze. "I know I sometimes try to pull you out of your cycles, but I would hate it if you abandoned who you were to please other people. You like your salt and pepper shakers facing the right and your cooking utensils arranged in height order inside the drawer. That's not a crime. I don't have any other friends like that, so I'm keeping you."

"You caught my drawer structuring?"

"I took a photo."

"I'm hopeless."

"You're adorable. And sexy. And I have brownies in the oven for you."

Juliette paused. "No." Surely, she'd not just walked in on brownie making in progress, because the comfort a warm brownie would bring her in this dim moment couldn't be measured.

"Yes," Peyton said, pulling the box from the top of the trash. "Me and Duncan Hines have formed a tight kitchen-wide partnership. You said you had a rough night at the lanes, so I called 'em over. I'm also going to rub your feet."

Juliette couldn't move. The words were too amazing, and she didn't want to scare them away. She'd expected a hookup. That was the God's honest truth, and she desperately wanted one. She was arriving on her fling's doorstep after ten p.m. on a Wednesday, so she wasn't at all prepared for brownies and a supportive massage. She tried to play it cool, but the combination sounded so wonderful, she quite nearly wept.

"Are you crying?"

Snap. She was! Misting, at least. A failed plan. "Unintentional moisture in my eyes. Allergies. You probably have a cedar tree or something."

"I don't. Come here," Peyton said, pulling her in. She smelled amazing, so it wasn't like Juliette could say no. Once she was there, she wanted to stay in the crook of Peyton's neck with Peyton's arms tightly comforting her for the rest of time. A self-indulgence she admitted only to herself, and only for these vulnerable few moments. But it existed all the same.

"I wasn't expecting brownies." Her voice sounded meek. "You didn't have to make them for me, the wonderful brownies."

Peyton gave her a squeeze. "I wanted to, okay? There was a time when a warm brownie would have made a huge difference in my day.

We sometimes take those little things for granted, but I don't anymore. I never will."

She was referencing prison. The thought of a younger version of Peyton sitting alone and wishing for something as simple as a warm brownie made her heart hurt. Her problems were so trivial in comparison, and the reframing placed it all in a helpful perspective. "When you put it that way, I can't wait for a brownie, and I'm so grateful to you for making them."

"Then we're both excited."

Ten minutes later, Juliette began her love affair with Duncan Hines. Meanwhile, Peyton made good on her promise of a blissful foot massage that sent her to the land of serenity. Her body felt bendable and happy. She regarded Peyton. "You can't pamper people like this. They won't leave your place."

Peyton laughed. "I'm sure we could work something out. I have space."

They were hovering somewhere between friendship and romance, vacillating from moment to moment. This was a gray area that in the temporary felt comfortable although confusing. She tried to remind herself not to analyze everything and take each moment for what it was, staying present and responsive. "You hinted earlier about your time…" She hesitated to say the word.

"In the big house. It's okay. You can say it."

"Right. Okay. Please don't take this the wrong way—"

"Uh-oh." Peyton switched to Juliette's other foot. Soft touches at first. She slipped farther into heaven.

"You just seem like the life of the party type. Not someone recovering from an experience that had to have been traumatic on some level."

Peyton nodded, weighing her answer, her signature smile benched for the time being. "It's hard to feel like a person there. There's a loss of humanity, which is inherently intended, I'm sure."

Juliette closed her eyes. The sentence stuck with her.

"Lots of time alone, thinking, worrying, making plans that may or may never manifest. You pile up a mountain of regret and sit with it. Sort through it with new eyes. I've never experienced that caliber of loneliness or hated myself so much." She shrugged. "When I got out, I was starved for human connection."

"How could you not be?"

"But here's where it got tricky."

Juliette reached down and covered Peyton's wrist. "Tell me."

"It had been nearly four years. I didn't quite remember how to be around other people. It was overload and my skills were…lacking."

"Can't blame you for that."

She rolled her lips in, contemplating. "But it wasn't all that I wanted. It was easier to sit alone in my studio apartment. It was what I was used to. But I wanted out, and I forced myself into the world, making it my life's mission to find a way to connect again."

"You missed people as much as warm brownies." Juliette said it with sorrow in her heart.

"More." She dropped her head back and studied the ceiling, almost as if sucked back in time. "I practiced. Picked out potential jobs for myself that would make me interact with other people. Those were hard to get, by the way. Jobs in general."

"Because of where you were coming from."

"Yeah. Not a lot of business owners are interested in felons."

"Yet you opened your own business. That must have taken such courage."

Peyton exhaled. "Just a ton of homework and someone who believed in me. That last part goes a long way. I can't express to you enough."

"But Candy believed in you for a reason. She saw what you could be. What you now are."

"I was lucky to find her."

Juliette couldn't leave it there. Peyton was selling herself short. "No. You're really impressing me right now. A phoenix from the ashes. Keep going. I want to hear more."

"Are you sure? We don't have to talk about any of this." Peyton glanced at the threads of the couch and back up. This was hard for her, and she seemed worried about what Juliette might think, which made her human, relatable, and someone she wanted to be there for. Root for.

"I very much want to hear."

"It's a little embarrassing." She covered her face, the touch of makeup from her workday now faded. She was gorgeous. "But in addition to taking notes each night on everything Candy explained to me each day, I watched YouTube videos." She paused and cringed. "Total truth. Anything I could find on small business ownership, financing, pitfalls, salesmanship, from basic all the way to niche-specific."

"You taught yourself online."

"No other choice. I couldn't take Candy home each night and pepper her with questions for hours. I was all I had. How did you learn to run your shop?"

"Business degree from Ohio State."

"See?" Peyton beamed. "You're the real deal, Juliette. A smart college girl. I wish I'd gone. I have a lot of regret about that. I liked school. I mean, when I attended."

Juliette sat up and leaned against the couch sideways, putting her in Peyton's space quite purposefully. "You know what I think? I think you're exactly where you're supposed to be."

"In my living room with you eating late-night brownies?"

"Actually, yes. Your journey sounds like it wasn't the easiest, but you shine all the brighter for it. People can change, and you have. Everyone who meets you is impressed."

Peyton didn't say anything. She nodded wordlessly, her eyes pooling with tears. "I don't hear those kinds of things too often from people who know the truth about me, so thank you. I'm not perfect. I never will be. But you still said those words."

Juliette leaned across the small space between them and wrapped her arms around Peyton, and held her, trying as hard as she could to send everything she felt in this moment her way. Pride hung at the top of the list. She was proud of her friend. Moved, even.

"I'm supposed to be making *you* feel better," Peyton said with a raspier voice than Juliette was accustomed to. The emotion had strangled it away.

"I think it can go both ways."

"I'm finding it can." Their faces were close. This wasn't a sexually charged moment, but it was tender. The energy between them flowed generously, and Juliette understood in that carved-out moment on a Wednesday, her connection to Peyton had grown into something unique, something quite meaningful. She'd never anticipated that happening. Especially not when they first met. Her chest clenched in recognition of this person she cared about opening up and sharing a part of herself she kept guarded. Peyton had trusted Juliette enough to confide in her, and that resonated like the warmth of a weighted blanket. Safe and tight. Peyton's gaze held hers. Juliette didn't look away, captivated by the invisible tether that linked them. Her midsection rippled and a wash of goose bumps crept over her skin. What was happening? Whatever it was, she memorized the moment passing between them, cherished it. Peyton blinked and inhaled. She pulled her gaze away and looked around the room, disconnecting purposefully. "We need more brownies."

"Do we?" Juliette asked, her voice weak. But Peyton was up and away, moving through the kitchen, followed by the sound of plates touching. She was running from this, from them. "Oh. Okay. More brownies it is."

They didn't have sex that night. They didn't even kiss. The newly established reverence felt palpable. The unspoken appreciation for what they'd found in each other covered everything like a layer of soft rose petals. Pure. Sweet. Important.

Instead, they turned on Peyton's mellow coffee shop Pandora station and let the world fall off them as they ate brownies and swapped stories about work, friends, and their childhood missteps.

Juliette laughed, having the best time, and held up a finger. "It certainly couldn't top the time I ran around my neighborhood topless as an unwitting eleven-year-old, unaware of my journey through puberty, and had the older boys nickname me Pancake Princess."

"No." Peyton's hazel eyes went wide. "That's harsh."

"I thought so. Luckily, it took me a year or two to get it."

Their laughter faded and they stared at each other. "I liked tonight," Peyton said softly. "Let's do more of this."

"Are you asking to spend more time with me, Ms. Lane?"

"Yeah. I am."

Juliette felt her cheeks heat, and she covered one with her hand to hide the effect that Peyton's simple words had on her. "You know what? I'd like that a lot, too."

❖

Dolores and her muffins were emerging from her minivan when Juliette arrived home from work. Spotting Juliette pulling in, Dolores waved excitedly like there were throngs of people nearby and Juliette might not be able to spot her. She waved back and smiled. Normally, she would have deflated at Dolores's semiregular unannounced visits, but today she was actually a little happy to see her.

"There you are, sweet chicken. I say that because I made chicken salad this morning and brought you some in a little dish with crackers. You can do with 'em what you want." She held up a small Tupperware container next to her larger ones. "We've got raspberry-orange muffins today. You know I like a good muffin with my chats."

"I remember."

Dolores followed her inside wearing floral workout leggings, even though she didn't work out, and a white shirt with a smiling geranium on it, a purple visor which she removed as they neared the door, and lavender tennis shoes to match. It was everything Dolores in one outfit. She beelined for the kitchen table, having no problem spreading out and making herself comfortable. In many ways, it was nice and took some of the hostess duties off Juliette's shoulders.

"I'm here on a mission," Dolores said. "I can be a friend to listen or a shoulder to boo-hoo on, a sounding board to bitch to, and if you want to punch on my arm a little bit, we can discuss it. That's what Dolores is for."

Juliette raised an eyebrow. "What are you referencing?" But she had a feeling she knew.

"Your Thomas and Cherry are an item, I hear. Did you know as much?" She paused and winced.

"I did."

She placed a hand over her heart and fell back in her chair dramatically. "Thank preschool Jesus. How you doing with all that?" Dolores asked.

"It was hard at first." She snagged a muffin, buying into the visit fully. "But I'm working on getting used to the new normal. You know, kissing whenever possible, touching. Goo-goo eyes."

"Goddamn. I'd hate that. My ex-husband carrying on with my best friend? Hell no."

Juliette shrugged. Ever since last Wednesday night at Peyton's house, she'd seen things in a different light, a properly proportioned one. "I miss them as individuals. And I'm the third wheel now. But at the same time, there's a part of me that knows they're both really happy, and that's a good thing."

Dolores paused midmuffin. "That's a very mature approach."

Juliette tapped her fingers on the table and took it one step farther, needing to share with someone the recent developments in her life, her outlook, her bedroom. "But it has elbowed me into something that, I don't know, feels even more important."

"That sounds interesting. I'm all buttered. Tell me more."

Wait. Pause. Should she be saying these words out loud to Dolores, for heaven's sake? The woman who almost literally kicked in her door on the daily to poke her nose in and stay awhile. She was loud, overbearing, and didn't take cues. Juliette flipped that sentiment over. Because that was her old definition of her stepmother, and lately she'd been seeing quite a few things differently. Dolores now felt like one of them. Underneath the hot-pink bravado, she meant well and would give Juliette the loud print shirt off her back if she needed it. And these days, that kind of care and kindness felt more important than harshly drawn social boundaries of Juliette's overly meticulous making.

"Okay. Here goes." The grin on Dolores's face grew to half-moon status. "Remember Peyton from the lingerie shop?"

"Hot Peyton? Of course I remember. She set me up with bras from boob heaven. She's a wizard of lingerie, and my life is peaches and cream now."

All right, Dolores could be funny, and it was nice to allow herself to admit that. "That's a good word for her."

"Hot or wizard?"

Juliette flashed on the way Peyton had played her body like a violin, and her face went warm. "Both." She pushed onward. "We've been seeing each other casually. In the sexual realm. Of bedroom-type things."

"You're hooking up with Hot Peyton?" Dolores's happy eyes went to saucer size and the sound of her voice echoed in the kitchen. "We gotta call your dad."

Juliette reached to cover Dolores's hand but slapped the muffin out of it instead because she was overzealous. "No! Please don't tell my dad who I take my clothes off with. We won't recover. He still says things like *lady parts* because he's afraid of the actual terms."

Dolores went still. Retrieved her muffin and nodded. "That's fair."

"Sorry about the muffin."

"Me, too. But this is good stuff. Color me impressed. I have more muffins." She reached for one.

"Yeah, I was ridiculously surprised, too. But ever since we've been spending time together, I feel…different. Lighter but heavier."

Dolores chewed thoughtfully. "And does she also seem to feel… lighter but heavier?"

Juliette exhaled because it was a question she asked herself. "We don't talk a lot about our feelings, because that's not what this is. It's an arrangement, and it works. I don't want to make her uncomfortable."

"Well, maybe that's what this *was*, but things change all the time. We don't always see the sexy bus coming when it slams right into us. But you have a sexy bus look about you, and maybe next up is a smash with the love bus."

"So many bus analogies happening that I don't know where to go with this. But no bus has hit me—I'm just enjoying a new development. Hooking up might be underrated."

"It's not. Everyone knows it's great. You're the only one who wasn't aware of its ability to give and give and give until you've had three orgasms and an entire bottle of hundred-dollar champagne consumed in hollowed-out coconuts."

Juliette squinted. "That's specific."

Dolores fanned herself. "For another day. My point is this: Welcome to the party, where a little fun goes a long way. That is, until you fall in love and move to the suburbs of Ohio with a man who says *lady parts* but is your best damn friend and the kindest soul alive." She took another big bite of the muffin. "Life is full of surprises, so don't go thinking that you know the ending to every story ever written." She gestured with the remaining half a muffin. "Especially your own."

"That's fair." She didn't like to acknowledge the question mark in her head. The one that wondered if the feelings she kept on low for Peyton were actually a whole lot more. Because if they were, what then? Peyton's history was dark and she had baggage, some of which Juliette couldn't even begin to understand. Hell, Juliette wasn't even sure she had all the information. At the very least, Peyton seemed unavailable, whether by choice or necessity. That much was clear when she fled from the couch the other night.

And wasn't Juliette unavailable, too? Except the reasons she'd so staunchly gathered now seemed to elude her. Eclipsed by the connection she'd found. It was true that she and Peyton were wildly different, but was that such an awful thing after all? She'd discovered a few perks to their dynamic that were hard to ignore. "I'm just really feeling good about things lately, and it's a new feeling. I wanted to share."

"You don't know how badly I've looked forward to this day." Dolores grinned, and the joy that stretched across her features was pure. "I know I joined your life already in progress, and you don't think of me as a mother figure. That's fine with me. You've got a mom. But I'm tickled you let me in on this development." If Juliette wasn't mistaken, Dolores was tearing up. "Ignore me. I'm an old sap."

"I'm glad we're talking, too," Juliette said and offered a smile she meant.

"Well." Dolores took a big gulp of air, an emotional release. "I better get home to your father. He's probably on hour three of his crossword and muttering *damn it all* under his breath in frustration. I'll say one thing for the man—he doesn't give up." Juliette followed Dolores to the door, embracing the blossoming affinity for the woman that she'd never allowed in before. Maybe Dolores wasn't so bad.

"I'll keep you posted."

"I can't even wait." Dolores pulled Juliette in for a tight hug that nearly smothered her. She had more than ample breasts and the hugging skills of a linebacker. Somehow, Juliette found it rather comforting and let herself sink into the embrace, even returning it meaningfully.

"Thanks, Dolores. Say hi to my muttering dad for me."

Dolores's eyes went wide. "Wait. I forgot the important part." Juliette frowned in curiosity. "In all the Hot-Boob-Woman chatter, I forgot to ask if you're selling sex cards out of the shop in secret." A pause, as Juliette pondered the right words. Dolores pressed on. "I couldn't imagine it was true, but I've heard from three people now."

"I do sell sex cards. Time for another muffin?"

Dolores dropped her large yellow purse with a thud. "You saucy panther. Not like we have a choice now."

Chapter Thirteen

It was one of those nights when Peyton had a hard time shutting off her overactive brain. Voices, memories, and ghosts from the past faded in and out in rotation as she watched the tree branches sway in the bright patches of moonlight. Her hands were shaky, and anxiety moved through her blood like a bullet train that wouldn't slow down. She'd made a cup of warm cider and sat on her porch waiting for Juliette.

She knew that once they were together, her soul would settle, and she'd be able to hold life in her hands once again. Somehow, Juliette made the hardest things seem manageable. Maybe she was the Peyton whisperer. Merely her presence calmed Peyton. She clung to the anticipation like a lifeline, squeezing her mug and biting the inside of her cheek. Nights like this one were hard. *Hang on.*

It was Wednesday, and they'd started spending the late evenings together after Juliette finished with her bowling league. She'd made cookies this time. Chocolate chip and pecan. Baked goods were now a part of the Wednesday tradition, and she enjoyed the quiet preparation.

She shoved aside the loneliness that enveloped her and, instead, leaned in to her thoughts. She let her mind wander and stretch out, landing where it might like a spinning roulette wheel. Tonight it drifted to memories of the old house with the white picket fence that hadn't seen paint in years. The driveway that had two sizable potholes, but the coziest bed she could remember sleeping in. Her grandmother's old quilt received the credit. She wondered what had happened to it.

Her brother had honed his skills as a mechanic in that very driveway, which had clearly led him to a successful career. He'd been a prodigy when it came to cars. That's what everyone used to say. Peyton would sit in the round patch of grass, which had likely been a patch of weeds, and watch him tinker away on his friends' cars, fixing them for much cheaper than the auto shop would have charged and learning everything as he went. She'd been maybe twelve, observing in awe as he used his hands to transform a piece of machinery from a broken, inactive piece of metal to a drivable automobile that whirred to life when he stepped back. He'd often give her the honor of turning the key in the ignition until the engine hummed. They'd look at each other and smile, exchange a high five that generally left her hand stinging. She didn't care. He made sure she felt like part of his team, even though she didn't actually contribute much.

"I miss you," she said quietly into the night. She kept her eyes closed. It helped her reach back into the past with staggering authenticity. She was practically there all over again, the summer sun warming her face.

She could still see Caleb grin at her when they'd head inside together, triumphant, and with a few more bucks in his torn pocket. "See? That's why you don't ever give up," he'd said after a particularly tricky job. "You hear me? Because eventually that thing is gonna roar to life again. You just gotta keep searching for the problem and take your time fixing it."

"Yeah. I hear you. Can we get frozen lemonade later?" It was July and the heat never quit.

"Do I look made of money?" he asked her playfully, giving away the fact that he was about to say yes.

"You just fixed a car." She bounced her eyebrows, key to any effective persuasion. "And you just told me to never give up. So... frozen lemonade?"

"Damn, you're good." He slung an arm around her shoulders and gave his light brown curls a shake. "Fine. Let me grab a shower."

"Thank God."

"Evidence of hard work right there."

"I'll give you that," she said, easing off.

"Give me twenty and we'll go."

The frozen lemonade had never tasted sweeter. Days like those had been some of the happiest of her life. She'd felt loved and looked out for. It had been Caleb and Peyton against the world. Her brother had been her steadying force. He kept her safe, gave her a shoulder to cry on when she had a particularly hard day at school, and made sure the rest of the world treated her right. Until she'd gone and blown it.

She heard his voice now. "Even if it's hard. You just gotta be patient and find another way." She nodded. The memory was the affirmation she needed to not give up hope that one day they'd be them again. The breeze sent a chill through her as a pair of headlights arrived at the base of her driveway. She stood, and a relieved smile emerged that she didn't even have to summon. Such a new feeling.

"I made you cookies," she announced as Juliette approached. She wore a hunter-green jacket and had her hair pulled back in a clip as the wind tousled it around her shoulders. Gorgeous. She wanted to eat her up.

"Okay, but I need your lips on mine first," Juliette said, arriving at the top of her steps and moving immediately into Peyton's space. "They've been on my mind."

A tremor of happiness hit, and she leaned in. "Your wish…" As their lips pressed, Peyton released a good portion of her trauma, even if only for a little while. It would be back, but Juliette was the best kind of temporary salve. "How was bowling?" she asked around the kiss. She looked so cute in her blue and yellow color-blocked bowling shirt.

"Boring compared to this. I don't think my pulse raced once."

"You know what would be even more exciting?" They kissed another few seconds, like starving people. The give-and-take was not only perfectly choreographed but just what she needed to feel in sync with someone. Juliette was the perfect yin to her yang on that front.

"What could possibly be?" Juliette asked, her gaze never leaving Peyton's bottom lip.

"Finishing this inside." She gave Juliette's hand, cold from the early winter weather, a tug. "I saw you drawing through the window of your shop earlier and have been counting the minutes."

"Oh yeah?" Her blue eyes darkened. "Us first. Cookies for dessert."

"The reward to our reward." Peyton was already unbuttoning her shirt as she walked backward into the house, enjoying the grin of anticipation it pulled from Juliette. "Coming?"

"Yes, and soon you will be."

Peyton's mouth fell open. "Take me now. Those cards are really rubbing off on you."

"Is that a good thing?"

"Let me show you how good." She crooked her finger. "Get in here."

❖

Juliette blinked and looked around. She'd been sleeping hard, the really good kind of slumber where her limbs felt heavy and one with the mattress beneath. She wasn't sure she wanted to move, but there was something tugging at the edges of her consciousness.

She knew.

She sat up immediately and took in her surroundings. Peyton's house. The first signs of daylight floated in through the large window across from the bed. Peyton's bed. Which she technically wasn't supposed to have stayed in. They'd never done overnight before, an unspoken rule.

She glanced at the space next to her. No Peyton. What was happening? Embarrassed and guilt-ridden she stood, looking around for her clothes, which if memory served were dropped onto the floor one by one as they made their way to bed. The empty plate of cookies sat off to the side on the nightstand, a reminder of the decadent things they'd done with each other before the warm chocolaty indulgence. Had she spent a more perfect night with anyone before?

And now she'd overstayed and likely made it weird. She grabbed her blue bra, the first discarded item she came to.

"You're up."

She straightened. Naked. Bra in hand. Caught.

"I fell asleep. I'm sorry I'm still here."

Peyton frowned. She wore a cream-colored terry cloth robe that looked too good on her. Her blond waves were in a pile on top of her head, which left her neck visible, beckoning like a Siren. Juliette shoved the detail to the side.

"I'm just gonna grab my clothes, and—"

"I made breakfast. Nothing too impressive. A bagel bar. Top your own kind of thing. You up for it? There's also fresh coffee."

"A bagel bar?" That's when the aroma of the brewing coffee wafted her way. Warm bread and coffee. Her knees nearly gave out.

She glanced behind Peyton at the bedroom door that would lead to the kitchen, warring with temptation and trepidation. They were out of bounds, but it felt kind of nice. "Are you sure?"

Peyton squeezed her hand. "We have to eat. Let's do it together." She glanced down at Juliette, who now remembered she was naked. "Clothing optional." A wink. "You can probably guess my vote." She left the room, heading for the kitchen. "Looking good, Jules."

"I'm gonna go with clothing," she called back.

"A shame. But if you want to wear something of mine, help yourself. Closet is just through the bathroom."

It wasn't like she'd say no to a fresh pair of clothes over her bowling shirt. Especially Peyton's. After a quick shower, she selected a pair of jeans, which she had to cuff once due to Peyton's longer legs, and a white blouse with a subtle gray circular pattern. Good enough for the workday, and it would save her a trip home.

When she emerged fresh and ready, she had instant regrets because with Peyton standing there in that robe that had already partially fallen open, all she wanted to do was take her right back to bed and stay there. This little Peyton addiction was taking root fast. She sobered because there were moments like that one when she forgot this wasn't necessarily all real.

"What's wrong?" Peyton asked, adjusting the robe so that it more fully covered her right breast. Juliette felt the loss.

"Um, just warring with sweet or savory on what looks to be an amazing bagel. You continue to pamper me."

"I think we could all use a little of that. Besides, I enjoy it. Come on. Let's have breakfast."

She nodded and allowed herself to be led into the kitchen by the most beautiful and, she was learning, the most thoughtful woman on the planet. It was getting harder and harder to hold back the word *want* because she very much did.

She *wanted* more. From Peyton. From herself. From the two of them together. More breakfasts, more late-night make-out sessions on the porch before they lost themselves in a lust filled journey to the bedroom.

There. She'd admitted it. The mere act lifted the brick of dishonesty from her chest.

Juliette exhaled slowly and slid a knifeful of cream cheese onto her everything bagel, feeling more at peace with the war raging in her brain. "Where do you see yourself in five years?" she asked out of necessity. It was like now that she cracked open the gate, she couldn't hold the floodwaters back.

Peyton popped a finger full of strawberry jam into her mouth and leaned back on the marble countertop. "Maybe buying an island and stocking it with as many margarita machines as I can afford. Of course, I'll need a Cotton Candy location but with a tropical vibe. Maybe even open air. Ooh-la-la." She returned to the jam cream cheese swirl on her bagel. "You?"

She pondered the question for about two seconds before taking the grand leap. "I think I want this."

"You going to open a bagel bar and put me to shame?" Peyton laughed, but Juliette held her ground.

"Us. I want us like this."

The room was silent for a moment, and it was clear from the series of expressions that crossed Peyton's face that it took her a few seconds to understand Juliette's meeting. "Oh."

"That's not the most promising of responses." But Juliette had known. Peyton made it clear from the beginning what she was and was not interested in. "It's really okay. I shouldn't have gone there. Moment of weakness."

"Wait." Peyton pinched the bridge of her nose. "You didn't say anything wrong. I just know that I'm probably not the best person for this kind of, at least not yet, for something as big as—"

"Please stop talking because I don't think I can stand another moment of the humiliation I already feel." She made a point to smile, to hopefully alleviate some of the awkward. "You're great. And this is, too. That's all. Let's just forget what I said and be normal."

"But should we? It seems important."

"Yes, we should." She touched her forehead. "God. Enjoy your breakfast. I should actually take mine to go if I'm being practical. Busy day and I'm already late. Again, thank you, thank you, thank you for letting me crash."

"I didn't mind," Peyton said. Her face was riddled with sympathy, which felt the absolute worst. Anything but that. It was pity's next-door neighbor. "Juliette. Can you slow down?" But she was busy moving about the room, gathering whatever she found that was hers and stuffing it into the tote she'd brought with her. "I don't want you to go."

"I'll see you in just a little while. Neighbors, remember?" That seemed to cheer Peyton up, but there was an ocean between them now, and Juliette hated that she'd been the one to put it there.

"Right. I guess I'll see you in a bit."

There was no formal good-bye outside of that. No lingering kiss. A wave because Peyton looked shell-shocked, and Juliette was running for cover. Why hadn't she just left late last night? Everything would be just as it should be.

As she drove to The Station, the regret over speaking her mind faded to the background as the sting of rejection sprang to the front of the line. Peyton didn't want a relationship with her. She'd said so from the beginning, and nothing that had happened between them since had changed her mind. Her heart broke that morning, and the tears fell to the sounds of Landonville's zany morning radio show. She slammed the thing off just in time for her car to vibrate, and a noticeable flapping sound took over.

Dammit. Really? To top off her doozy of a morning, she had a flat. She steered her car onto the shoulder and swore loudly. It wasn't even nine a.m. and the powers that be were not on her side.

"Yep. It's flat."

She blinked up at Darrell with the shock of red hair and the nose piercing. He'd sat next to her in high school economics and insisted that Eminem would be president within eight years. He'd run for senior class president himself, and handed out, wouldn't you know it, M&M's.

"Right. That part I'm aware. I just need you to tow the car, so I can get the tire patched and open my shop."

"I'll take care of you, Juliette. Since you let me cheat off your test that one time."

"I never did that."

"Damn. Shouldn't have said anything then. Maybe we could grab some toast and eggs after?"

"Work, remember?"

"I hear you're taking a walk on the wild side with those taboo cards. I'm all for it."

She studied him. "Word gets around. But yeah, it's a new thing I'm trying." What was also new? She didn't feel ashamed, embarrassed, or like she needed to soften up what she sold. It felt pretty good.

"I need bachelor party invitations. PG-13. Or R if you're willing. Just don't tell my sister. Can you hook me up?"

She grinned. "I'm your girl. Come by The Station."

"Score."

The short drive to the full service auto care shop Darrell recommended was filled with rap music played at way too high a volume. She was pretty sure she knew the artist. Some things never changed.

"These guys will take great care of you," Darrell said as she headed inside. "Best shop in town, and service comes with free ice cream if you want it. I'll let Caleb know we're friends."

She paused, glass door half open. "Caleb Lane?"

"That's him. Fair guy. You've met?"

"Briefly." Darrell tended to her car, and Juliette presented herself at the counter, just in time for a very smiley girl in a tight sweater and cleavage to arrive. Juliette flashed to the trivia night when Thomas had announced his date. The receptionist. The car place.

"You're the sweater girl," she blurted, because apparently her brain was not working. These had to be the boobs Cherry was referencing. How could they not be? She stared hard at them.

The woman must have noticed and dropped her gaze to the boobs in question and grinned. Luckily, she hadn't been offended. "I might be. I like sweaters."

"Well, you look great in them," Juliette said, vamping now. She offered the A-OK sign like a loser wanting to crawl under the table.

"What can we do for you today?"

"You have a nail," a male voice said. She turned. Caleb Lane arrived behind the counter with a pretty smile. He didn't seem to remember her, but she was out of context. Same hazel eyes as Peyton. His hair was slightly darker, but they also shared those subtle waves. He adjusted the cap that said *Lane Auto Services* in red block letters. "We can patch it if you can wait. Suzanne makes great cappuccinos."

"Um, yes, to all of it."

"Great. I'll get my guy started." He headed back through the door behind the counter, and Juliette did something unexpected, fueled by adrenaline and a nothing-to-lose outlook. She'd had a morning from hell. So why not? She walked behind the counter and followed Caleb to the back to Suzanne's raised eyebrow.

"No cappuccino?"

Juliette stuck her head through the door sweetly. "I'd love one, actually. Be right back."

"Oh," Caleb said, turning around to find her in his garage. "Did you have a question?"

"I recognize you from Yogurt is Life. I was there with Peyton."

"Oh, right." He said it with a smile and nodded along. "You do look familiar. Good seeing you again." But something behind his eyes shifted, and he stole another glance at her. "Everything good?"

"She's doing such an amazing job with her shop. I think she'd love it if you stopped by someday."

"I plan to. Life just gets crazy. If you'll excuse me."

"She's not who she used to be," Juliette called after him, knowing she was crossing all sorts of lines she had no permission to cross. "She's learned a lot. She cares about being a good person and making you proud."

"That's great."

She couldn't get a read on him. He hadn't fully looked at her since she'd mentioned Peyton, but he also hadn't thrown her out. Her heart thudded. "But she's sad. She gets quiet when she thinks no one notices, and it's hard to pull her back in. She feels like she ruined her life, and she carries so much regret that sometimes I see it taking over her whole body."

He paused and turned, hands on his hips. "I'm glad she has a good friend. I appreciate you being around. I want to be. Not quite sure how." Right then she saw it. He cared a lot. It wasn't anger that came over him, it was a soft sincerity of emotion. This was her opening, and whether it was hers to take or not, something ushered her along. Compelled her.

"All she wants is a chance to know her brother again. I think she'd give anything."

He swallowed, taking in the sentence. "There's a lot of history to sort through, and um"—he placed his palm over his mouth—"I might need time to get myself there."

"I get that. Just don't forget about her, okay? As far as family goes, she's on her own. She tries to put up a brave front, but I think she could really use a familiar face."

His gaze fell to the ground and back to Juliette. "And she seems like she's doing well for herself?"

"Better than that. When I heard about her past, I couldn't quite believe it. She's wildly different now. Responsible, thoughtful, funny. And pretty much all-around wonderful."

He studied her. Nodded. "I better get your car going."

She'd taken enough of Caleb's time, and even though she had more to say about Peyton, she respected his cues. "Thank you. I appreciate it."

She didn't know if she'd left an impression on Peyton's brother, but she made the decision not to mention the conversation to Peyton. If nothing came of it, she'd hate to be the source of another disappointment. She sent a request to the heavens that day that Caleb found a way to forgive Peyton. Something told her that he needed Peyton every bit as much as Peyton needed him.

As for her, well, she'd be okay. Her heart hung heavy after the telling kitchen encounter that morning, and that meant she needed to get her emotions under control and tucked the hell away before the damage went any farther.

After all, life on her own hadn't been so bad. All she had to do was stop wishing for more...

CHAPTER FOURTEEN

The entire day sucked. The week did. Peyton dropped an armful of hangers into the box on the floor with too much force on purpose. Felt good. She also typed too aggressively on the keyboard when she reconciled her register for the day. At lunch, she blasted music in her car and gave the door a hearty slam on the way back in. She was frustrated and out of sorts.

Everything changed the moment Juliette confessed that she wanted more. Peyton's response, while honest, had clearly resonated with Juliette, and she'd been distant and quiet ever since. She missed their afternoon chats, the little ways they'd find to flirt with each other. She missed their alone time at her place or Juliette's even more.

It had been over a week now, and the tension between them left her frustrated and not at all herself. She wasn't sure what to do about any of it.

"How's your day?" Juliette asked, strolling over just after lunch that Thursday. They'd skipped bowling night. Juliette had said she needed to catch up on sleep. It had made for a dull week without any kind of spark. No baked goods, no sex. She thought of Juliette more than ever in her absence. But a relationship? Absolutely terrifying. She wished she knew why. Perhaps feeling something so overwhelming after years of living in a numb little existence fried the whole system.

"It's been slow, actually. I think as the weather inches colder and winter descends, I have to market twice as hard. People aren't thinking about barely there clothing items when the winter wind whips."

"Lacy long johns then?"

"I'd rather die than put my name on that recommendation."

"Wait. They exist?"

"Let's hope not."

"Poor lumberjacks."

Silence hit and swirled uncomfortably. This wasn't the companionable silence that they used to have, but the kind that drew an arrow sign over the gap between them. Peyton couldn't stand it anymore, and the main reason was because resisting a deeper relationship with Juliette was plain stupid, because never had she wanted anyone more. She opened her mouth to try to fix it, but the words died in her throat, which was stricken with equal parts fear and panic.

"Are you okay?" Juliette asked, touching her hand lightly. That was their first physical contact since the morning it all changed. Like water to the thirsty.

She smiled. "Yeah. Figuring some things out, but I think I'm going to be."

Juliette hooked a thumb. "Better get back to my side of the building."

"Sure you have to go?" she asked. The nonchalance was pretense. The softness in her voice was real. She didn't want Juliette to go. Ever. That had to mean something, right? Why couldn't she hurdle the mental roadblocks and allow herself to experience what they were creating together full-on? Jack the volume all the way up and feel.

"Yeah. It's busier than ever these days. I might actually make it out of the giant hole I was in." She lifted an arm. "Thanks to you."

"Juliette."

"Gonna go."

"Wait."

And before she could say another word, Juliette was in her arms. She wrapped her up instinctually, breathed her in, collapsed into the moment, because it felt like coming in from the cold.

They held eye contact before Juliette finally broke it, taking a piece of herself back as she left the shop. Peyton stood still, allowing the regret to rain down on her like the pelting rain.

As she finished the day with a private girls' group party, she felt Juliette all over. While assisting her customers with colors, sizes, and words of encouragement, all while keeping their champagne flutes full, she wondered what Juliette was doing back at home, wishing she was there with her, snuggled under a blanket, maybe watching a movie until they abandoned it to make out like sixteen-year-olds.

She needed Juliette.

She longed for her.

And she wasn't about to miss out on something amazing only because her own emotions weren't on her side. Everyone deserved a shot at happiness. Didn't she? Maybe it was time to let herself off the hook, stop punishing herself for things that she couldn't go back and change, and deal with the risk in front of her that just might pan out.

She needed time, though, to harness her courage. When her private party took their leave, she allowed herself four swallows from the open bottle before she slid to the floor of the mostly dark shop moving through the stages of her life, the people who'd touched her, the recriminations she carried, but most importantly, she thought about the very real question Juliette had posed to her in her kitchen. Where did she see herself?

"With you," she whispered to the empty room. "Only with you."

❖

Peyton was shocked when she arrived home that night. There, waiting for her on the steps of her front porch, haloed by the golden light overhead, was her brother. She took a moment to orient herself to the very surreal moment.

He raised a hand and stood as she approached. "Hi." The hand went right back in his pocket. "Fair warning. I've had two beers. Not drunk, but definitely not entirely sober."

"That's okay. It's good to see you." She was smiling but nervous, now super aware of her hands and not sure what to do with them. She blinked a few times to clear her quickly moving thoughts. What if he was here to tell her that her presence in town was unwanted? What if he hated her? She wasn't sure how to withstand either of those things, not when her heart hoped and reached and wanted nothing more than a second chance. To a certain degree, it felt like everything in her life hinged on her making amends with her brother and finding peace. If she couldn't do that, then what?

"Do you have time to talk?" He still wore his Lane Auto Care shirt, and though they were hard to make out fully, his eyes looked red. "I don't mean to barge in unannounced. But it was a whim."

"Come in. I can make us some coffee."

He quietly followed her into her home as she saw the place through new eyes. She wished quietly that she'd folded the white blanket on the back of the couch more neatly, and that there wasn't a bowl in the sink. The curtains weren't her favorite. None of these details mattered, but they felt like everything when she'd dreamed of this moment for so long.

"Nice place."

She turned around, finding her smile. "I'm working a little each day to bring it to life, make it feel like mine."

"You seem to have a knack for it." Both his hands were in his pockets this time. She remembered when he'd used them to pull her in for a quick squeeze whenever he got home, followed by an intentional mess-up of her hair, which she would pretend to be annoyed about.

"Thanks. Regular or decaf?"

"Better make it decaf. I gotta be at the garage by seven."

She went to work making the coffee, attempting to keep her hands from shaking. She filled the time by rambling about the traffic in town and how much she needed to get back to Tuesday night trivia. When she turned to deliver Caleb's coffee, there were tears streaming down his cheeks.

She paused, attempting to process what she was seeing and how to handle it. Her brother didn't cry. He comforted others. She'd never seen him shed a tear, now that she thought about it. Needless to say, her hand found momentum and she placed the mugs on the counter for safety.

"I'm sorry," he said quietly. His voice wasn't his.

"It's okay. Here." She slid him a box of tissues from down the counter.

He raised his gaze. "No. I'm sorry I wasn't there. I'm sorry I let my own feelings of failure come before my job as your brother."

That pulled her up short. She tried the last sentence on again, still mystified. "You didn't fail, Cay. I did."

"I pushed you away because your story was a constant reminder of all the ways I came up short. You were trying to be like me."

"Maybe at first. But you tried a million different ways to get through to me. No one could have. I had to learn those lessons on my own. In a room with four cinder block walls and a door without a knob."

He shook his head, his gaze pulled to the ceiling as if he couldn't face her. Her head was spinning as she tried to keep up at the same time as she tried to be present for Caleb. All these years, she had convinced herself that he was angry at her, when in reality, it was himself he couldn't face? That was a mindfuck.

"Without me in your life, none of it would have ever happened."

"Maybe something worse would have. It's very possible. Who knows where I'd be?" She shrugged, realizing that her cheeks were wet, too. "You tried, Caleb, and I'll always be grateful to you for that."

"Yeah, well, a big part of me has spent all this time hating myself, and until you got here, I don't think I fully looked it in the eye." He pushed back from the counter and circled the living room, as if the movement would help steady his ship. "Ah, God."

She took it all in, absorbing and sorting the new information into stacks to manage. This all meant she'd unleashed a lot of Caleb's personal emotion when she'd arrived. No wonder he ran every time she tried to reach out.

"I think about Mom and Dad. What they would think of me."

"Of you? They'd be proud of you. I am. You have a beautiful family, Caleb. A great career." She held out a hand. "And I don't want to mess any of that up for you. I refuse to do that."

"You've been very respectful. You shouldn't have had to be." He touched his chest with his palm. "That's on me."

She nodded a few times only to sort out her own thoughts. Her voice was a shred of a whisper when she attempted to use it again. *Steady. Go slow.* "But if you'd maybe give me the smallest opportunity to be a part of it, too, I'd really, really like that."

"That's why I'm here. I want to fix things. To be here for you. But I don't know how to make up for the time lost."

She came around the counter. "I don't think we have to. It sounds like we both went through a lot."

"I'm an asshole."

"And I'm a reformed felon." She shrugged. "Let's try to move past it. When's Joshua's next soccer game, and can I come?"

A hint of a smile hit. "Last one of the season is on Saturday morning. The kid loves an audience. He'd be excited if you did."

"Done. I'll schedule one of my part-timers, and I'll be there. Step one. Now sit in this chair and let's drink this coffee. I think we could both use the comfort."

"You got it."

They settled in to tentative conversation that slowly eased into the comfortable back-and-forth of two people who loved each other catching up. Weird? Yes. But also not at all. They were the same people. The conversation made that more than evident.

"But you hate peanut butter." She inclined her head. "Why is Linda packing you PB and J?"

"That's my point. I can't tell her that *now*. She's been making me those sandwiches every day for work since we got married."

Peyton laughed out loud. "Do you understand how wild that sounds?"

"I didn't until I just said it all out loud." They were both laughing now. "But it's my life now. Till death do us part."

"Which could happen when Linda learns the truth and kills you."

"Our little secret." He placed his palm on the table. "Speaking of Linda, she probably thinks I'm still at the bar. Better go."

"Cool." She walked him to the door. "I'll see you Saturday then." She placed her hand on the top of her head and marveled. "I'm glad you came by. Still can't believe you did."

"Well, your friend got in my head. Couldn't get her words to leave me alone."

Hold all her calls. What? "That's weird. What friend would that be?"

"The one with the flat tire. She came by the garage." He snapped his fingers. "I forget her name. The brunette."

Peyton squinted, trying to decode his words. She didn't know anyone with a flat tire. "Lola from The Frog and Dog?"

"No, younger. Pretty. But insistent as hell."

Light bulb. "You talked to Juliette?"

"Yes, that was the name on the paperwork. More like she talked to me. Sang your praises like a forceful little canary on a mission."

"A determined canary. It tracks." Peyton sat with the new information, wondering why Juliette had yet to mention any of it. But then again, they weren't exactly chatty that week. While she didn't need anyone to go to bat for her, Caleb was here because Juliette had. It felt nice, someone in her corner. That hadn't really happened since Candy.

"You got a good friend in that one. My advice? Keep her. I like the way she looks out for you."

She exhaled. "We're kind of seeing each other."

His eyes widened a hint. "Oh. Congratulations."

"It's pretty unofficial."

"Didn't sound like it to me. You should have seen her face, too."

She smiled to herself. "I can imagine it."

And as she reached for that piece of the emotional puzzle, her brother's arms went around her for the first time in close to six years. Her eyes slammed shut, and she absorbed the barrage of love, relief, and elation that came over her. Juliette was no longer the only person capable of making her feel. Somehow, she was coming back to life, a full person, and everything good and hopeful in this world came rushing back to her, too. It was all happening for her at last. She couldn't run. She didn't want to.

She was renewed.

She was eager.

She was ready to finally live life.

CHAPTER FIFTEEN

Juliette hadn't looked forward to an event like this one in quite a while. The Landonville Small Business Association held a vendor fair every year at the town's convention center. Because the fair fell so close to the holidays, they seized upon the opportunity to theme the hell out of the thing, decorating the place with nutcracker soldiers, giant candy canes, and humongous snowflakes dangling from the ceiling.

While it was always a fun event, she arrived on the scene to set up her booth with a newfound confidence. Her business was on the rebound, and she'd never experienced this new level of ambition. She also loved getting to know the other business owners and relished the opportunity to introduce The Station to a whole new audience. This year, she'd added a stack of naughty brochures to the corner of her table because, after all, they were keeping the lights on. Secondarily, she was embracing this new side of herself and enjoying the ride.

The fair would end that night with a dinner and a holiday dance, which—cliché as it had the potential to be—was handled really nicely by the association. Weeks before, she'd made sure Peyton had snatched up a booth across from hers, which meant she could spend the day staring at her. Now she wasn't sure if it was a gift or a punishment. She looked too damn good in her tall brown boots and bright red sweater to usher in the season.

They weren't going to be the couple she dared hope they'd be, but her feelings for Peyton were as real as the wind in the trees. Invisible. Beautiful. The distance between them the last week drew a blinking arrow sign. There was a gaping hole where Peyton had been. The reality was that she yearned for Peyton on her couch telling her stories from the lingerie world. Relaxing after a long day and letting the stress fall off them. Shooting the breeze between customers. Making out in small spaces and ravishing each other in bed. Peyton's smile brightened her day. Her soft scent swept Juliette away. Her confidence and vivaciousness challenged Juliette to step outside of herself. No human had ever challenged her as much as Peyton. Or had such a staggering effect. And wasn't part of Peyton better than no Peyton at all?

God, yes. She knew that now.

She would happily take what she could get at this point. Their arrangement would be enough. She would make peace with it, embrace all the good that came with it, and there was a lot.

She just had to find a way to convince Peyton that she didn't have to be afraid of Juliette demanding more. She'd gone and punched a hole in their universe that now she had to carefully patch. She was falling slowly in love with Peyton, but she'd hold that part in. Her own little secret.

"What do you think?" Peyton asked, appearing at Juliette's side. "My first time decorating a booth, but I'm kinda digging it."

Juliette abandoned her own setup and walked the twenty feet to Cotton Candy's corner booth with Peyton on her heels. She smothered a smile at the purple lights that highlighted the short little nighties and bra and panty sets she'd placed on display. She'd selected a fuller-figured mannequin to feature in the booth's most prominent spot. The decor was sexy yet accessible to everyone. Juliette liked that so much about Cotton Candy and Peyton's approach to store culture. No size received more attention than any other.

"I think it makes me want to make my day a little sexier."

Peyton smiled but didn't leap at the opportunity to flirt with Juliette like she used to. Telling. Depressing. "Well, that's the goal." She touched her chest. "I'm nervous. Is it normal to be nervous? This is my first one of these things, and I want the town to like me."

"Everyone likes you. Move your brochures down the table a bit and make two stacks, one at either end, so people don't have to reach."

"You're brilliant." She executed the suggestion and turned to Juliette. "Will you be sticking around for the after-party?"

"There's fruitcake and I'm the only one who eats it. My duty in life is to attend and make sure it's not left out."

Peyton laughed and her eyes sparkled. Something was different about her. She seemed...lighter somehow, as if a burden had been lifted. That hit hard, because it was starting to seem like maybe she'd been that burden. "Great. Maybe we can talk over...fruitcake. That has to be the most tragic sentence ever."

Juliette scoffed. "Or the coolest."

"Only you, Jules."

The day went by in a flurry of customer conversations, stolen bites of baked goods, hot chocolate delivery from the Chocolate Monster Chocolatier, and of course, stolen glances at Peyton, who seemed to be charming the pants off Landonville. As the afternoon hours ticked by, it was almost like she couldn't take it anymore. She had to speak with Peyton and put things right. Nothing would feel okay until they were them again. She was living in a pressure cooker about to blow, the unsettled energy manifesting in overly friendly small talk with customers. She was compensating. It all felt weird. By the end of the fair, she was exhausted from talking, an emotionally depleted shell.

As the vendor booths broke down, the catering company hired for the event swept in to transform the room into a holiday wonderland with ten-top tables, gorgeous holiday centerpieces, and fancy lighting. Giant projections of snowflakes and candy canes danced along the wall and the scent of cinnamon wafted through the air from the cider table.

"You had quite the little crowd around your booth," Peyton said as they returned to the venue after striking their displays.

Juliette covered her face. "It's the saucy cards. People either want one or they want to know all about them for juicy fodder." She shrugged. "I figure either is good for business. I sold all the pre-made ones I brought with me. A win. You?"

"Booked a couple of parties and gave out a ton of coupons. We'll see. Oh, and I saved you a seat," Peyton said, indicating a chair at her table.

"Oh."

Peyton glanced behind her and back in question. "Unless you didn't want me to." The smile dimmed. "I should have asked."

Juliette could have smiled and had a polite dinner, but the words coming from her lips had a mind of their own. A speeding train en route to a station. "I need to talk to you."

Peyton's eyes widened. "Okay. What's going on?"

"Can we go outside?" It was a ridiculous suggestion. The weather in Ohio was the coldest they'd seen all season. Yet she needed to be alone with Peyton, and this bustling holiday snow globe of a room wasn't delivering privacy.

"Of course. I'll follow you." She didn't question the mission for a second. Juliette needed her, and she made herself available instantly.

"Thank you," Juliette said, grateful. As they walked to the side door, she attempted to untwist the words that had bounced through her head all day and put them in order. Snatches of *I just want to undo the past week.* And *Can we just go back to being the us I love and miss.* Scratch that. No love. Nothing that screamed commitment. That's not what they were going to be.

Was it raining? She glanced up at the dark sky as lines of precipitation flew past the streetlamp overhead. No, that was unfortunately sleet, also known as rain that hurt, but as they stood on the sidewalk, she didn't shy away.

"I pulled you out here because I miss you." She touched her chest, her words coming faster than she wanted them to, her pulse quickening with each second. Adrenaline. "I want you to know that I'm happy with what we have."

"You said that. But ever since that morning, we've been—"

"Weird. Distant. Awkward. Awful."

"Those things. Maybe I have a solution." She slid her hands in the back pockets of her jeans, probably because they were freezing and neither of them was wearing a coat.

"I do, too. We stop being weird, distant, and awkward and just be happy and fun again. I'd love to scrap the rest and get back to the fun."

"The fun is not enough," Peyton said with way too much confidence. Juliette's heart sank, and she felt herself downshift. Sounded like Peyton was done with this little experiment, which was sad because they worked really well together. At least, she thought so. Apparently alone.

"Gotcha. That's unfortunate. But I hear you." She was searching for other words, better ones, and failing miserably.

"I haven't met anyone like you before," Peyton said, tilting her head as she took Juliette in, little pearls of sleet clinging to her hair.

She was the perfect ad for winter. "And I've been so off base about us. I know why now."

Juliette frowned, not sure she wanted to know, but going for it. "Why?"

"Because until you came along, everything was bland enough to keep me moving forward. I didn't have to wrestle with feelings, because mine had been paused years ago." She extended her hand and Juliette, took it, allowing herself to be pulled closer. All the while she raced to understand.

"I make you feel?"

"So much. When nothing else could," Peyton said, touching her forehead to Juliette's. She wasn't sure what was happening, but she liked it very much. "It wasn't comfortable at first. Then it was downright terrifying. Now it's everything I want in life."

"Me?"

Peyton nodded. "You." A soft kiss as the sleet became snow, gracefully layering itself over every inch of them as the distant sound of holiday carols floated from inside. Juliette's body went slack, her bones liquid, her blood warm. She was holding Peyton's face in her hands, cradling it through their kiss like the most precious of gifts. The moment felt like someone had turned the volume of her life to full blast after years of searching for rhythm.

"Are we dating?" she asked around the kiss.

"I hope so. If there was a school dance, I would ask you to it."

Juliette looked over Peyton's shoulder to the building behind her. "There kind of is."

Peyton's eyes sparkled and she laughed. She stole another lingering kiss that certainly warmed Juliette up from the cold. Their lips clung as if designed for such perfection. They fit so well. Peyton pulled away but kept her eyes closed for an extra beat. "Be my date. Be my girlfriend." She smiled and squeezed Juliette's hand. "Be mine."

"Okay," Juliette said simply, unfamiliar with the new levels of excitement and trepidation that battled it out. "To all three." She wanted to be worthy of this special moment, to be everything Peyton deserved in a girlfriend. This was finally a real chance for them, and she planned to give it everything she had. How unexpected this all was. How wonderful. Every part of her sang. She gave Peyton's hand a small tug, asking for another kiss. Peyton grinned and obliged, prompting Juliette to go up on her tiptoes and angle her mouth for better access. "The woman from the BMV is kissing me in the snow."

"Not a sentence one hears everyday. But I like it. Maybe you can make us a sexy BMV card."

"I'll make you anything you want."

She tossed her head back, still holding tight to Juliette. "Oh, the possibilities. The night is young, you know."

"How about we start with that dance?"

"Fa-la-la-la," Peyton said in the sexiest voice ever. It made Juliette want to skip the whole thing and take her right home. There was time for that later.

To say that the rest of the night was fantastic would be an understatement. They missed most of dinner because they were too busy staring at each other, trading smiles and smolders, touching each other subtly under the tablecloth. A brush across a thigh. The squeezing of a hand. They tossed back too much champagne because this was, after all, something to celebrate. On the dance floor, the alcohol permitted Juliette to cut loose. She danced with an abandon she was unaccustomed to, thrusting her arms in the air and moving her hips to the beat of the bass. Peyton was right there with her, showing off impressive moves until the two of them nearly shut the place down. At midnight, the last song was announced, and they found each other on the still fairly full dance floor and stole what they'd been longing for for hours, a kiss under the multicolored lights that pulled applause from the slightly drunk people dancing around them.

"You better take me home now," Juliette whispered in Peyton's ear. "Because I'm not sure I can wait much longer for you."

"Check, please?" Peyton called to the air around them.

❖

Peyton Lane woke up with a grin on her face. It took her a few moments to remember why. Her body still hummed pleasantly. Her clothes were…somewhere. The bed was warm and Juliette was awake and staring up at the ceiling. Peyton turned to face her, sliding her cheek onto the arm she fashioned as a curled-up pillow.

"You're here. I had a dream that we'd kissed in the snow and made love in the early morning hours."

"That actually happened," Juliette said, and stretched like a cat. Adorable. She turned on her side until she was facing Peyton. "And it was amazing. How are you feeling about it all?"

"Is that what you were doing just now? Lying awake and coming up with all the ways the morning could take it all away?"

"It's like you've met me before or something."

"You've got to quiet that brain of yours." But her own heart was pounding, too. They were in new territory, and Peyton didn't have a map. Yet in the midst of her disorientation, she also knew that this was where she was supposed to be. Juliette calmed her seas and made her smile. "But I do understand that it's crucial for you to think your way through any situation."

"I don't have any doubts," she said, stroking Peyton's hair, studying her features. "I'm happy. I just want to make sure you are."

That did it. Peyton melted. How could Juliette not know? *Because you haven't fully told her.* She sat up, taking the sheet pressed to her breasts with her. "When I wake up in the morning, I think of you first. I wonder how long I'll have to wait to see your face. I look forward to talking with you, teasing you mercilessly, and simply being in the same room, because that's when I'm myself. That's when I'm my most happy. You bring light into my dark room."

Juliette didn't say anything. "I don't know what I thought you were going to say, but it wasn't that." A smile spread across her face and she held out a hand. "Come here."

"Happily." Peyton slid beneath Juliette's portion of the sheet and positioned herself on top. The feel of their skin pressed together sent a stirring to her midsection. She checked the clock. There was time. She raised an eyebrow, looking down at Juliette.

"Oh, I know that face. I know exactly what it wants." Juliette nodded permission, and Peyton slid her hips between Juliette's thighs and closed her eyes at the onslaught of sensation. It was something she never got used to, the way her body reacted to Juliette's.

"We have to be quick," Peyton managed, slipping her hand between them. Juliette tossed her head to the side, her eyes closed.

"Not really going to be a problem."

Peyton chuckled and went to work. Her world had righted itself the minute she confessed her feelings to Juliette the night before. She could live with the intimidation, the fear that she wasn't equipped for the staggering connection to another human. What she couldn't live without was Juliette, and she wouldn't have to. Thank God.

They drove to work together that morning. A first. They arrived before either shop opened and shared a lingering good-bye kiss just inside Cotton Candy.

"Before you go, I want to say thank you."

"For what?" Juliette took a step back, her eyes curious.

"The things you said to Caleb. He came by. I don't think things are magically perfect, but it was a nice step in a positive direction."

Juliette's eyes went wide. "That's fantastic news." She rolled her lips in, thoughtful. "I'm sorry if I overstepped. Sometimes the words, they just fly out."

"It sounds like they were good, well-intended words."

"I swear. It's everything I feel about you."

Peyton shrugged. "I like who I am in your eyes." And that was it. In that moment, she understood that it wasn't just about how amazing she thought Juliette was, it was also how much she liked herself when they were together. Juliette made her feel like she could do anything, and maybe she damn well could.

"Good. Because I happen to think you're kinda great."

"You didn't always."

"Nope. I wanted to murder you a few times. Eight at least." She grinned. "Now I'm glad I didn't. Go, me." A pause. She sobered. "I'm really happy about Caleb. Do you feel like you might want to tell me more about that later? We could have dinner. I'll buy."

"I can't say no to free food. And escaping homicide eight times?"

"Impressive, Peyton. I feel like it's something to celebrate. What are you going to wear?"

Peyton grinned. She loved getting to experience this side of Juliette. She was happy and flirty and wonderful. They'd removed the barriers, the question marks, and took away the prickly tension, leaving only the sexual variety, which was quite honestly her favorite tension of all. "I'm not telling you. That ruins the whole date. It's like you haven't been on one."

Juliette folded her arms, leaning back against the door, which pushed open slightly against her weight. "Well, I haven't been on many. You forgot who you're talking to. Hi. I'm new here."

Peyton tapped her own lips, thinking of the future rolled out in front of them. All they had to do was snatch it. She was ahead of herself, obviously, but she couldn't help but dream the big dream. Forever felt possible. "When I'm done with you, you're going to be a pro, and if I'm lucky, you'll retire." She almost couldn't believe the words coming out of her own mouth. A month ago, she couldn't have said them. Thought them, sure. But not said them. But the Juliette effect was staggering. It had changed so much. And after Caleb's appearance on her porch, she really did think herself capable of making a true success of herself. Personally. Professionally. She wanted it all.

Juliette seemed as moved by her words as Peyton was. "Wow. Okay." She nodded a few times. "This feels like a really good morning now." She rushed the four steps between them. "One more to last me through the morning." They kissed as the sun layered in through the window as it made its rise higher in the sky. Juliette's arms wrapped around her neck, and their bodies pressed together. The best. Peyton felt the loss the very moment that Juliette released her. She missed the warmth, the curves against hers, the flutter of exchanged energy.

There was always later, she reminded herself.

Hundreds of tomorrows just waiting for them to scribble in the details. She lit up from the inside out at the concept. There was so much more to come. Vacations. Holidays. Milestones.

"Bye, Jacquelyn," Juliette said on her way out the door.

"Wait. Hold on. For the last time, who is…" The words died on her lips when she followed Juliette's appreciative stare. "Oh my God. You've gotta be kidding me. Really? That's my competition?"

Juliette blew a kiss through the display window, and Peyton laughed, dropping her shoulders in mock defeat. Finally, and because she couldn't not, she blew one right back.

Chapter Sixteen

The Upper Crust was a fancy restaurant on the north side of town and very much worth the longer drive through the city. Juliette had been lucky to snag a canceled reservation the day of. The intimate restaurant was known for its dim lighting, fresh baked bread, and opulent menu selections made with generous butter and everything decadent. Juliette wanted nothing more than to spoil Peyton as much as possible. She wondered if the need would eventually subside as she grew accustomed to having a girlfriend. Honestly, she didn't think so.

Because they'd each needed to change, they'd agreed that Peyton would drive. Juliette emerged from her house at the sight of the blue Mustang pulling into the driveway. As she turned from locking her door, her breath caught because Peyton leaned up against the car in a maroon dress that could only be described as soft, elegant, and beautiful. The sleeves were three-quarter and the black pumps added another three inches. Her curls had been tamed and pulled into a knot at her neck that seemed both simple and complex in its construction. Juliette briefly imagined that hair tumbling to bare shoulders and swallowed back a rush of want. *For later.*

"Good evening, Juliette. I'm very much looking forward to dinner." The soft smile that played on Peyton's heart-shaped lips devastated Juliette's chaste resolve. Another swallow. This was going to be harder than she thought.

"You look so beautiful," she said, covering her mouth.

Peyton beamed. "Thank you. But it's you I can't stop looking at. I love you in this dress."

She paused in front of Peyton in her own black cocktail dress. She'd opted for sleeveless, but brought a soft peacoat to keep her warm. The necklace was new, and Peyton's eyes dipped to it before sliding lower. All part of the plan. Those naughty greeting cards had certainly sharpened her skills when it came to flirting and foreplay. She damn well couldn't get enough. How had she lived without it for so long?

Peyton walked around the car and opened the door for Juliette, kissing her softly before she slid into her seat. Their hands, fingers intertwined, rested in Juliette's lap as they drove through the darkened streets of Landonville to the restaurant. The quiet of the car complemented the reverence of the night. This felt special. As it should be.

The host seated them at a prime table along the window, which allowed them to take in the twinkling lights of the garden just outside. Once they were settled with an open bottle of Bordeaux and a basket of the most amazing warm bread anyone had ever tasted, Peyton told her the story of Caleb's visit.

"The soccer game is huge. That's a legitimate invitation."

Peyton nodded along, buttering a small piece of bread for herself on her miniature plate. "I'm going to play it low-key. Go in without any true expectations. Rome wasn't built in a day, and my brother and I still have our issues to wade through. But I can't articulate to you the weight that was scooped right off my chest the moment he hugged me on his way out. I mean, good and hugged me. He meant it, Jules. It was everything."

Juliette took a moment to simply absorb the glow that surrounded Peyton. She'd waited a long time for what was left of her family to give her a chance, and now she had one. "I feel like we all have our own unique baggage," Juliette explained, hoping she wasn't drawing any comparisons between what Peyton was dealing with and the average person. "Some of us more than others. He seems like a good guy just trying to deal with his own stuff."

"The guilt was a shock."

"We internalize more than we should. Overthink to the point of self-harm. I'm guilty of that as well. Better lately, though." She sent a soft smile of gratitude to Peyton. "You get me out of my head."

"I think we do a lot of things for each other."

"We do. And speaking of family, my dad's sixty-fifth birthday is coming up. Dolores is throwing him a big party. I was hoping you would come. You know, officially."

"You want to parade me around as the girlfriend?"

"Hell yes. And I'd love for my friends to get to know you better, too."

"I mean, I beat you guys at trivia nights most weeks, but it would be nice to get know them under different circumstances. I suppose a double date would be weird."

"Are you kidding? I'd be thrilled for one. So much better than the third-wheel status I've been living." With Peyton next to her, the concept seemed inconsequential. In fact, she rooted for Thomas and Cherry. When you're in love, it's as if you want everyone else to be, too.

Oh. Was she in love?

"I'm working so hard at listening to you, but you look really beautiful right now and it's hard not to say so. The light from the candle is doing wonderful things for your eyes."

Juliette could really get used to this. "I just got lost there for a moment myself." She wasn't quite prepared to say why. One step at a time. Slow and steady was best. They needed time together.

"I have an idea." Peyton opened the menu. "Maybe we should focus on what we're going to order. I think it's going to be the cordon bleu for me." She studied the menu. "Not sure I've ever had Parisian ham."

"I hope I'm not intruding, but are you Peyton Lane?"

They turned and saw a nicely dressed woman standing at their table. Her date or husband stayed a few feet back.

Peyton brightened, always friendly. "Yes, I am."

"It's nice to meet you. I was actually planning to call you tomorrow, but here you are. I'm Annie Dokes from *Landonville Sentinel*." Juliette knew her name from the paper and watched the exchange in curiosity. Why would a reporter be interested in Peyton? "I'm working on a story about your release and return to our town and would love your cooperation on it." A pause. Peyton had gone very still. Juliette closed her menu. This wasn't good at all. "Can we set up a time to talk? I'd be happy to come to your store."

Peyton turned to the woman. She did a fantastic job maintaining her composure, but Juliette saw the shift most notably behind her eyes. "You know, I'm not sure I would be interested in something like that."

"It's a great story," Annie said, her voice sympathetic. "Your journey is a compelling one that I think a lot of people would be interested in." She had really dark lipstick, which felt appropriately sinister for the encounter. Juliette's head began to ache, which happened anytime something unexpectedly awful occurred. Peyton was upset, and that made Juliette want to put a stop to all of it.

"I just want to live my life. I don't want that kind of attention." She heard the slight tremor in Peyton's voice. Not like her. She hated this.

"I will be moving forward with the piece with or without a quote from you. But this would be your chance to insert your voice."

"If you don't mind, I think she's already provided you with an answer to your request. Maybe we could just all enjoy our evenings now?" Juliette asked in her most polite voice. But it wasn't the one she wanted to use.

The woman nodded to Juliette and then turned back to Peyton. "I certainly didn't mean to disturb you. I'll just leave my card." She placed the forest-green business card on the table next to Peyton and rejoined her companion for their exit.

For a weighted moment, they were silent while they watched her leave. Then Peyton raised her gaze to Juliette. She was pale and took a brief sip of water, which showed off the slight tremor of her hand. She seemed changed by the whole conversation. Haunted and attempting to recover in a room full of people. "Thank you," she said quietly. She shook her head and dropped her gaze to her menu, though she was clearly not interested in it.

"Of course." Juliette reached across the table, took her hand, and offered a squeeze. "We can go."

Peyton's eyes shifted quickly to hers. "No. We are absolutely not letting something like this ruin our night. I can't change who I am, and I won't hide from who I was. But there's only so much I can do about it. And all I want now is to enjoy a meal with you in a dress like that. We're going to eat, and flirt, and you know what?"

"What?"

"We're even going to order dessert. Dammit." Her eyes flared with fire again, and Juliette smiled. Peyton was a fighter. It took a lot to knock her out, and it was clear that she wasn't going to let this article be the thing that did it.

"I second that motion." She lifted her glass of wine, and Peyton followed her lead. "To us and damn dessert."

They touched glasses, and Peyton exhaled slowly, coming back to herself more and more by the moment. Juliette couldn't imagine life in Peyton's shoes with a past forever marring your present and future. A story in the paper was like drawing an arrow sign over the mistakes of someone who was doing everything in their power to live a positive existence. What good would come of that? She had questions about Peyton's life and what it had all been like. Maybe one day she would ask.

Though their dinner was noticeably quieter than before the interruption, they managed to salvage the evening, losing themselves in great food and the most amazing mocha pot de crème to cap it off. They spent the night at Juliette's and made love before falling asleep all tangled up in each other. Peyton was restless, however, tossing and turning until at one point, Juliette woke to find her sitting on the edge of the bed and staring up at the moon.

"Hey. You okay?" she asked, touching Peyton's back softly.

Peyton nodded and turned to her with an apologetic smile. "I didn't mean to wake you. Just having trouble sleeping."

"Come here," Juliette said, extending her arm. Peyton came back to bed, and Juliette played with her hair until she heard the long, soft breaths that signaled sleep. It was Juliette's turn to lie awake, as if it was her job to sit watch and keep Peyton safe. She would.

In fact, she'd do just about anything.

❖

For five-year-old soccer players, they really did try hard. Peyton stood off to the side in her jacket and sunglasses, screaming her heart out for her nephew, Joshua, who did everything in his power to get just one foot into the blender of children to touch the ball and move it in the direction of the goal. He smiled each time he managed it.

"He has so much heart," Peyton said, relishing every moment of the game.

Linda laughed and nudged her elbow. "That's one way to put it."

"Dribble, Josh. Don't just kick it." Her brother took the game a lot more seriously than either her or Linda, but he seemed just as happy to watch his son. "There you go. Nice one!"

Peyton couldn't have put her feelings into words that Saturday morning, but the closest comparison she had was the click of a seat belt. That's what it felt like being back in the fold again, with the people she loved and missed.

"I don't know if Caleb mentioned it, but a reporter has called the garage several times."

Fucking wonderful. "Let me guess. Annie Dokes?"

Linda turned to her fully, her brown eyes full of sympathy. "Bingo. You've heard from her, too?"

"I have. She wants to chat." Peyton pulled her hands from her jacket pockets. "The only thing I want to make sure she knows is how sorry I am. That should be included in the article. The headline, even."

"Yeah, but do you want any of this brought up again so publicly?"

Peyton exhaled slowly. "It's my worst nightmare come true. It keeps me awake at all hours." Peyton shook her head, still not quite believing this was happening at all. "But apparently, the story is running soon whether she gets anything from me or not. I don't know if she's talked to Mr. Capito." The victim of their robbery gone wrong had turned into a source of healing for Peyton. She was lucky in that sense. She didn't deserve his forgiveness but had it.

"Have you?" Linda asked.

Peyton nodded. "I sent a letter to him via his son as soon as I was released. He called me. We've talked a couple of times, and I'm forever grateful for his grace. He's a really nice person."

"What's going to make you feel better?" Caleb asked, joining them. He'd apparently kept an ear on the conversation. "Getting your words out there or letting this thing carry itself?"

"I want the world to know that I would do it all differently. That I have oceans of regret."

Cheers erupted as Joshua's team neared the goal. They paused their conversation to shout their faces off, moving to the very edge of the sideline, only to have one of the kids pick up the ball. "It was exciting for a few seconds," Peyton exclaimed. Distractions like this one were so exactly what she needed. The here and now mattered every bit as much as her history. Her relationship with Juliette was another soft place for her to fall and forget about her stresses. The best decision she ever made was opening herself up to the well of emotion Juliette inspired.

"Whatever you decide," Caleb told her, "we will support you. But she's not getting a damn word from me."

Linda smiled and leaned in. "I think Caleb is in protective big brother mode."

Peyton blinked because that's exactly how he was behaving, and it reminded her so much of their old dynamic that her chest ached. She reminded herself of how desperately she'd wished for a day like today just two weeks ago. She had a girlfriend she was crazy about, a business that was off to a great start, and her brother was willing to give her a second chance. She had to stay positive and focus on the blessings right in front of her. The rest was out of her control.

When she arrived at Cotton Candy midday, she found Kiva and TJ, who'd worked the morning shift together, standing on the curb in their coats.

"Everything okay?" she asked as she approached. The store behind them was not only empty, it was dark. Not good for a Saturday when she did a good chunk of business.

"Power's out," TJ said. "We had four customers in the store when it hit. We lost the point of sale station and the whole back half of the shop was too dark for shopping and they left."

"Now we're shivering and alone on the sidewalk." Kiva looked around like a stranded puppy. "I sent you a text."

"Missed it—I was driving. Dammit. This is the third time. I'll get the key to the closet with the breaker box from Mr. Huberson next door. The landlord leaves it with him."

TJ raised a finger and in her standard nonchalant delivery said, "We did manage a cash exchange with a woman hell-bent on a yellow corset for a date tonight. She said she's his little daffodil, and I wasn't about to touch that one. Handed me a hundred dollar bill and said to keep the change."

"Generous little daffodil," Peyton said, accepting the cash.

Kiva shivered. "Do you want us to stick around?"

"No, Kiva. You should seek shelter and an electric blanket before hypothermia strikes. Thank you for sticking it out."

"Bless you, Peyton Lane," she called from midsprint to her car. Peyton grinned after her.

"True or false. You're seeing the hot, uptight stationery lady."

"What?" Peyton whirled around with a laugh at TJ's out of nowhere question. "First of all, it's totally true. Second, I didn't know those were her descriptors. I concur on both."

"Right? The uptight thing really works for her. Congrats on your new sexy romance." TJ shrugged and offered a fist bump. "I can hang out if you want to get on that breaker box issue. Hold the place down."

"Perfect. I'll be right back." She pointed at TJ. "Stay away from The Station in the meantime."

TJ passed her an aloof grin. "I can't promise anything, boss woman."

Peyton shook her head at the joke and headed down the sidewalk. She'd gotten to know her employees in the months since they'd opened, and they'd developed a helpful give-and-take. Kiva was needy, passionate, and dramatic, and TJ was a rock who showed little to no emotion almost to the point of being scary. She could, however, be depended upon in any situation. A big bonus, however, was that women seemed to love to be told how amazing they looked in the merchandise when it came from sexy-as-fuck TJ. Hell, she would, too. Peyton had learned to pull from their strengths.

"We meet again," Mr. Huberson said, watching Peyton as she approached the counter at Dry Style.

"Power's out again."

"So?"

She balked. "You're the super, and I have a business to run. We have to do something about this."

"I'll have Heather call the landlord later."

"Is she your bulldog?" She shot a glance to Heather down the counter, who was listening to every word.

"Don't you worry your pretty head," he told her.

She sighed. "The power? I need it on. Now."

Huberson shrugged. Her problem was clearly not on his radar. "We're busy. I'll get to it in a few minutes."

"I have a better idea. Can I get the key so I can walk the fifteen feet to the closet and flip the breaker myself?"

"Heather, find my building key!" he yelled.

The woman, who she'd heard about from Lola, pushed up from a leaning position and stalked down the hall with a noticeable swish of her hips. She shot Peyton what could only be described as a half flirtatious, half superior glance over her shoulder, as if to say, don't you wish you could get with this? Peyton simply smiled in response. Because Lola had, and she was right. Heather was a number. All curves. Overly made-up. And wearing way-too-high stilettos with her painted-on jeans. Disdain for everything and sexy charisma dripped from every pore. Not at all Peyton's cup of tea.

"What do you need?" Mr. Huberson barked at the customer who'd been standing across from Heather. "Come down here and talk to me now! She's busy."

Damn that man. Damn this place. Peyton found herself stressed just hanging out in here for a couple of minutes. The whoosh sound of the machine in the back coupled with the hostility up front made it feel like jail for clothes. They must do one hell of good job cleaning them for people to put up with being ordered around, abused, and objectified.

"Here you go, darlin'," Heather said, approaching. She flashed what felt like a fake smile. Peyton got the feeling that Heather wasn't a fan of hers, but instead wanted to be admired. Maybe even envied.

"Yep. Thanks."

Mr. Huberson intercepted the key before Heather could hand it over and passed it off to Peyton himself. What a little control freak. "You never bring your clothes in here for dry cleaning. Heather's great with the unmentionables you're so fond of. Treats them with care."

"No. You're right. I don't bring my things in," she said simply. "Have a nice day." She wiggled her fingers at him and Heather, whose brows drew in as her lips formed a petulant pout. She was literally a poodle in human form. Peyton shrugged off the weird vibes and headed for the small room between Dry Style and Cotton Candy marked by a nondescript door. She located the breaker box and got to work resetting the switches that fed her shop. She knew she had to wait five minutes to let them rest first, which seemed ridiculous, given the amount in rent she paid. That's when she heard the door open behind her and turned to see Juliette's face quickly lit by sunlight before going dim again when the door clicked behind her, leaving them in semidarkness.

"Perfect timing. I have five minutes to kill, and you're here." She pulled Juliette in and kissed her, smiling against her mouth when two arms went eagerly around her neck. Always in sync.

"Are tiny rooms our thing?" Juliette asked, coming up for air from the really satisfying kiss.

Peyton was always startled by how good they kissed together. She craved it constantly. "I don't know, but I'm beginning to look forward to each new one I walk into."

Juliette looked skyward. "That's why I'm here. Best we not let a single one go to waste, even though I have a client on her way to pick up a card depicting a man dancing in a towel."

"Let me guess. She yanks it off when you open the card."

"You are the most astute woman I've run into in a small space all day. But I drew the moon side, not the twig and berries. I have limits." She grimaced.

"Well, I like pushing them," Peyton said, kissing the underside of her jaw. "I haven't told you this, but I have an X-rated drawer in the back of the store for interested clients."

Juliette's mouth fell open. "You peddle sex toys, and you're just now telling me."

"Nothing too outrageous, unfortunately."

"Handcuffs?"

"Yes. A few different vibrators."

Juliette gasped and slipped a hand between Peyton's thighs, which nearly made her do the same. "Ma'am. You're getting handsy."

"You're the one who brought up sex toys. I'm just going about my day in this tiny closet. Why are we here, by the way? I follow you without question." She glanced around. Clearly, *her* power had not gone out.

"I'm sorry. I can't think with your hand on my inner thigh when I so want it—"

"Here?" Juliette asked, adjusting her caress so that the seam of Peyton's jeans worked with her in tandem. "Is this better?" She stroked Peyton softly. "Is this where you want it?"

Peyton sucked in air.

She was instantly on her way. How did Juliette take her there so quickly and without any warm-up? Peyton closed her eyes and sank into the touch that she now desperately needed. With her free hand,

Juliette lifted her shirt and found her right breast, which she palmed eagerly, matching the rhythm she began to establish below. Peyton was lost but also impressed because she'd never achieved orgasm with her pants completely buttoned and in place. Wonder of wonders. What was happening? Yet the onslaught of yearning, aching, and constantly rising pressure told her that one was on the way. Her face went hot, and her thighs shook slightly. Her lower abdomen went tight, and that was a clear sign. She placed her palms on the wall behind her and let Juliette take her to heights she hadn't planned on for their afternoon. "What are you doing to me?" Peyton asked, desperate, ready, and amazed.

"Wait and see. It's a surprise." Juliette placed an open-mouthed kiss on her neck. "You moving next door has certainly given my workday a boost. I get so many much needed breaks."

"I can safely say"—she bit her bottom lip just as pleasure tore through her, a shooting star. She rode it out, whimpering quietly, grasping at the wall. Her knees were not working properly, but her body sang. When reality drifted back to her, she took a deep, steadying breath and nodded—"the same."

That pulled a laugh. Juliette, with a hand behind Peyton's head, pulled her in for a slow kiss. "That's a great way to spend a break. Can you come over tonight?"

"Yes, yes, yes."

"Skittles will be pleased."

"I haven't seen that cat in weeks."

"He observes from afar." Another quick kiss. "I gotta go. My *Back in Five Minutes* sign just ran out."

"I love that sign." Peyton took a moment to knock her sense back into place, checked the breaker, and headed back to work.

"Having fun?" TJ asked from the entryway to Cotton Candy.

"I don't know what you mean," Peyton said, just as Juliette dashed past her and inside The Station. A total lost cause. She knew her face was flushed and she probably was grinning like a cartoon character in love. Or, rather, lust.

"Well, thanks for the watts. I'm going to spruce up the pajama section while you, uh, get yourself together." She offered a wink and went back inside. Peyton had a feeling TJ might be someone's perfect wingman. "Hey, how was Heather?"

Peyton eyed her. "She was a little intense."

TJ shook her head. "Fucking Heather for you. She'll do a number. Stay clear, boss. Trust me."

"Not a problem," she said, marveling because TJ, too?

For now, she had a Saturday afternoon ahead of her, and there were sales to make, women to pamper, and lingerie to worship. She just needed to remember how to do all of those things in a post-sex haze. She laughed to herself. This was what real happiness felt like. It had been such a good day. She wouldn't take a single moment for granted.

"I have constructed a battlefield of thongs," TJ called out. "Pastels on one side. Jewel tones on the other. They battle at dawn."

"See? I can't be mad at that," she told whoever was in charge of the Universe.

CHAPTER SEVENTEEN

The holidays arrived in a wonderful flurry. Juliette had never had so much traffic in her shop as she did the two weeks before Christmas. The people of Landonville definitely knew she was here now and showed it with their credit cards. For the first Christmas in years, she felt like she could relax and enjoy the season. She'd be able to pay her bills and even stash a little away. What a foreign feeling!

On Christmas Eve, she and Peyton spent the morning and brunch with Cherry and Thomas, who they'd found were perfect board game opponents. It had become the foursome's favorite activity. Cherry would cook up a pot of something scrumptious, and Peyton and Juliette would brings drinks and dessert. Thomas was always on cleanup duty.

"And that's three out of four!" Juliette proclaimed, leaping to her feet and high-fiving Peyton, her fellow Codenames champion. "I think we are the victors."

"It was a good fight," Peyton said, reaching across the table and shaking Thomas's hand. "I'd like to thank Yoda and Merlot for this victory." She raised her glass in ode.

"I think you guys telepath the answers to each other. I'm suspicious of how fast you got that last one," Cherry said, arms crossed.

"Don't be sad, Cher. You won Trivial Pursuit."

"That's right, and took down a Quizzly Bear."

"Yes, but I'm without my sloth of Bears."

"Still counting it," Thomas said. "Oh, and Cherry has a thing to throw at you both. Cherry, ask 'em."

Cherry turned, all smiles, hands linked like she was about to sing a solo in a very proper choir. "We want to go on a tropical vacation.

Somewhere gorgeous and with a beach, and we want you both to come." She scrunched her shoulders and waited.

"You want to take your ex-wife on your sexy beach vacation?" Juliette asked, directing her question to Thomas but including Cherry. She was feeling the wine, and the comedy of the whole concept couldn't be ignored.

He shrugged. "I don't see why not. You go most everywhere else with us."

"That's valid." She turned to Peyton, who appeared pretty thrilled at the idea. "Survey says?"

"A winner," Peyton declared, palms out. "I'm a sucker for sunsets and margaritas."

Cherry pointed at her. "A girl who knows the important things in life."

Christmas came and they surrounded themselves with all the right people, but they did it together. Christmas Eve brunch with Cherry's family. The evening was spent opening gifts with her father and Dolores, who couldn't stop hugging Peyton every time she walked by.

"I'm just so happy you're here with us. Did you get yourself a muffin? They're orange-cranberry. My favorite."

"Best I've ever had," Peyton said, grabbing another.

"I love this woman." Dolores smiled gleefully, already wearing her new furry socks that came in the gift bag from Peyton. She'd left the lingerie for later. Peyton certainly knew how to play to her audience. "Let's pour more wine!"

The next day, they woke up and had their own perfect Christmas morning. After snuggling in bed until the sun made its first appearance over the treetops, Peyton made them both hot chocolate and baked the croissants she'd prepared the day before.

"Let's sit in front of the tree," Juliette said, cradling her cup and sipping from the chocolaty warmth, heavy on marshmallows. Just the way she liked it. Peyton joined her there in her adorable green form-fitting pajamas with candy canes all over them. Juliette wore a similar blue pair with snowflakes and chose to top it off with a Santa hat.

"We're using that soon," Peyton said, giving the furry ball a flick.

"You can't make Santa hats sexy."

"Um...I didn't. You did," Peyton said in a sweet voice, nuzzling Juliette before kissing her softly. "Merry Christmas, baby." The nickname had made an appearance recently and stuck. Juliette liked it very much.

"Merry Christmas." The words *I love you* were on the tip of her tongue, but she swallowed them. She hadn't said them yet. Neither had Peyton. But this was *love*. She knew it with every fiber of her being. The more time they spent together, the closer they became. Still entirely different people who just happened to really click. They looked out for each other, brought each other surprise coffees, meals, and gifts to brighten the other's day. They cared about the same things and had grown inseparable. Juliette had never been so fulfilled.

She gave Peyton a nudge. "Open your gift." She'd been waiting for this moment, and her stomach pulled tight, nerves working in overdrive.

"Okay, I'm excited," Peyton said, accepting the gold box with the silver bow. "What did you get me?" In actuality, she'd gotten Peyton several things. A cozy sweater she'd seen her admire in a boutique once. A trio of fancy boozes. A small wheelbarrow for her garden. But this was the gift that Juliette had put the most effort into.

"Well, of course I can't tell you. That's part of this process."

Peyton dived into the unwrapping with a huge grin on her face, all patience out the window. When she revealed the painting that Juliette had done of the exterior of Cotton Candy, her lips parted, and her eyes scanned the detail.

"This is stunning." She looked at Juliette. "Did you paint this?"

"I did. What do you think?" She swallowed back a bit of insecurity. "Inks and oils are more my comfort zone, but something told me that this one needed to be watercolor." In the end, she was proud of the job she'd done.

Peyton stared at the framed canvas in awe. "I don't have words." Her eyes pooled. She brushed her fingertips reverently over the glass. "You captured everything. Even Jacquelyn." They laughed. "I love everything about it."

"It's a gorgeous store, and I wanted you to have something that captured its essence. Its personality. I don't know if I did that, but I certainly tried."

"Juliette Claire Jennings."

"My middle name? This is getting intense."

"It's the best gift I've ever received." She grinned through her happy tears. It almost seemed like she couldn't stop looking at the canvas, which was the best reaction Juliette could have hoped for. "I mean it from the bottom of my heart when I say thank you. Come here." She kissed Juliette, and their perfect Christmas morning became the perfect Christmas afternoon. They spent much of it at Caleb's house, eating until they couldn't fathom consuming another morsel, showering the kids with gifts they'd picked meticulously with Linda's guidance. The best part about the whole day? The happiness that poured off Peyton in waves. Juliette didn't think she'd ever seen her glow quite as bright, and it transferred to everything around her. She couldn't look away.

And when the day came to an end, even though they were beyond exhausted, they made love slowly in front of the fire with Christmas carols playing softly beneath. "Merry Christmas," Peyton said and kissed Juliette's temple before drifting off to sleep right there on the soft navy rug in the living room. Juliette made sure her bare shoulders were warm, adjusting the blanket so that they were covered.

"Merry Christmas," she whispered back. She watched the fire dance for another few minutes, giving thanks for the day and the woman in her arms. Finally, she snuggled in behind Peyton and found her way to rest.

❖

Cotton Candy looked like Cupid had shown up overnight and thrown a rager. Pink and red everything had entered the chat, and Peyton could not have been more thrilled about it. Not only did Valentine's Day mean high traffic with all the potential gift purchases and red hot dates to dress for, but this was the first Valentine's in which Peyton had someone she was beyond excited to celebrate with. Love was in the air every which way she turned, except for the saucier section, which downright dripped with lust. She'd worked late into the night with TJ and Kiva on the Valentine transformation, and she was thrilled with the results. So would the original Candy, who loved a good oversplurge of anything celebratory. She'd have to send her photos later.

"What's a good card caption for *I want to fuck your brains out?*"

Peyton turned at the sound of Juliette's arrival in the store and placed a hand over her heart. "Aww. I'm really flattered. You're already planning my Valentine's Day card."

"While the sentiment is obviously true, this one is spoken for by Sheila from Dorchester."

"Sheila's ready to get her some."

"They all are. You should see my Valentine orders. So how do I say it more poetically?"

"If you're asking me, you don't. I would love a card that just got right to the point."

"So noted. This might be a good time to tell you that topless Tuesdays might be a good promotional move. But only for special clients."

"Let me guess. Just one of those?"

"You're so astute. So just leave the caption as is?"

"God, yes."

For the first time, Juliette looked around. "Whoa. Did all the other colors go on strike?"

"It's Valentine's season, baby, and that means we go red and pink for the next two weeks."

"There are more hearts in here than products for sale." Juliette scanned the room in wonder, attempting to count and giving up.

"I don't mess around with eros, and TJ is a beast when you give her a ladder."

"I don't doubt it." Juliette leaned against the counter. "You didn't hear this, but Mr. Huberson placed a sexy card order."

"He did not. You stop it now." Peyton sank behind the register as if hiding from the awful truth of it. "I can't imagine him having sexy feelings. He's angry at the world. I bet that's how he makes love, with stormy little clouds over his head. Who's it for?"

"He opted not to leave a name, but what if it's for Heather?"

Peyton fell all the way onto the floor. Thank God they were between customers. "I can't. I'm dead. You killed me with this." The idea of Heather and Huberson getting it on while the clothes circled on those automatic racks was nausea inducing. She popped back up. "Do you know, I've had three more power outages since the New Year? He doesn't seem to care enough to look into the problem. I'm gonna write to the guy who owns the place. I'm tired of Huberson Hell." The bell dinged, and two women entered the store. Peyton recognized one of them as a regular. Joanne, if her memory served. Fan of matching pj's sets.

"I think that's a great idea," Juliette said, dropping her volume now that they weren't alone.

"Afternoon, Peyton," Joanne said as she strolled past. "I had no idea you'd been through so much, girl. We've got your back. Screw the rest of them and their talk."

Peyton and Juliette exchanged a look. She turned around and followed Joanne as she walked farther into the store. She could feel Juliette following a little ways behind. "I appreciate that. Can I ask what prompted the show of support?"

"The article. In the paper this morning. You haven't seen it? It goes into your whole journey."

Peyton did her best to play it off, even though an intense tingle of dread moved down her spine. "I didn't realize it had been published. But I knew it was on the way." She nodded a few times, ignoring the fact that her hands felt numb. That was weird.

"Well, in my opinion, we all do shitty things and try to learn from them." Joanne studied a push-up bra and searched for the size.

"Yeah," she said, trying to brighten and failing. "I think so, too." Joanne and her friend continued to browse, and Peyton placed her hand on the nearby circular display to ground herself. She tried to swallow, but her mouth was dry.

"Why don't you sit down?" Juliette asked her in her ear. "Come on. You look pale, and I don't like it."

Peyton nodded and allowed herself to be led to the front of the store, but as soon as they arrived at the counter, she seized her phone and found the Annie Dokes article. There it was in bold letters: *Landonville Woman Strives for Redemption.*

The headline alone seized Peyton by the throat. This stranger, this reporter, was talking about *her*, telling her story for her to her friends and neighbors. Surreal. Awful.

She read quickly, sometimes skimming to understand the main idea of each paragraph. Her heart sank when she hit the section that described the injuries Mr. Capito sustained during the robbery to his store, and the PTSD he still dealt with to this day. She felt sick. The room swam. Seeing the words in print really drove it all home.

Annie Dokes then went on to explain what Peyton was like as a teenager. To illustrate her point, she used a quote from a teacher Peyton barely knew. "Peyton was bright. So much potential. It was a shame she didn't run with it. I think she could have done anything she set her mind to."

"This, right here, doesn't matter," Juliette said, pointing to the phone. "That article does not define you."

"Have you read it? It's not wrong." The problem was that the new leaf she'd been carefully cultivating just received a bucket full of cold water right to the face. Everyone was going to know what she'd done. Where she'd been. Who she'd hurt. "People are going to have opinions," she said to herself just as much as Juliette. "I guess I need to be ready for that."

"Just remember which ones matter, okay? The people who know you love and support you. That's not going to change."

Peyton nodded, fighting the painful lump in her throat. She had to find a way to get it together. She had a business to run.

"We'll take these," Joanne said, placing three bras on the counter.

"Wonderful choices," Peyton said, playing her part. "We just got these in, and I'm in love with them. Would you like to keep the satin hangers?"

The world marched on, and Peyton did her best to march with it. Her world had been rattled, but maybe the damage would be manageable. She just had to hold her head up and keep walking.

CHAPTER EIGHTEEN

Once the article dropped, Peyton wasn't herself, and Juliette's heart ached for her. As the days passed, she was quieter, withdrawn, and the smiles that once seemed to radiate off her effortlessly were rare sights. It made sense. The reaction to the piece had been mixed. Some people were shocked to put two and two together, remembering the crime and just now connecting it with the town's new business owner. Others were supportive and friendly, like Lola, congratulating Peyton on how far she'd come and all that she'd accomplished.

"This is my take. You stole some things when you were a teenager," Lola said. "Not a good move. But you've paid your penance, and you're putting good things into the world to make up for it." She placed a beer in front of Peyton. "On me. Because I adore you and still want to take you to my dance class and make you twirl."

Peyton smiled. "Thank you, Lola. Your words mean more to me than I can express." Juliette smiled from the stool next to Peyton's. It was short-lived. Because, unfortunately, there was another faction that cut their eyes when Peyton walked through a restaurant, or even worse, had no problem telling her just what they thought of her. One such person had apparently been taking in their conversation from a few seats down the bar. The older woman with a surly expression on her face sauntered over like she owned the world.

"I came into your store once, but I won't be doing that again," the woman said and looked directly at Peyton. Juliette now recognized her as that opinionated woman from the school board. Wasn't she the president? "I think it's awful what you and your friends did to that man, and I know tons of people who feel the same."

"I do, too. If it helps," Peyton said, sincerely.

"I hope that's true. You have a lot to make up for. Good luck to you and your business now." She signed her credit card slip and was on her way, taking a piece of Peyton's self worth with her. Juliette felt helpless in moments like those. This wasn't the first time Peyton had been approached in this manner, and it wouldn't be the last.

Later that night, Peyton turned to Juliette in bed. "What's up?" Juliette asked, tickling Peyton's stomach. The room was dark and she could only barely make out her features.

"I feel in some ways that I've been living a lie, telling myself that I was this new version of me. I'll never be able to fully move on from what happened. The things I did."

"Of course you will. You just gotta ride out this little section of time. We don't live in a small town, but sometimes it feels like it. Soon, everyone will be talking about something else."

But when the bright colors of spring began to pop, the news wasn't great. Cotton Candy's second quarter hadn't proven as lucrative as the first. Not even close.

Juliette sipped her wine from on top of the kitchen counter as Peyton stared glumly at her open laptop. "I think the dip can easily be attributed to the excitement wearing off. People flock to new places, and then the newness recedes. You'll pull 'em back in."

"That's not what this is. This is a response, tangible proof of what the community thinks of me."

"You think it was the article."

Peyton shrugged, dejected. "I think it's the most likely scenario. The timing lines up perfectly. My sales receipts took a thirty percent dip the very week following the story going to print. I'm just following the breadcrumbs." She sighed. "I hate them, but they're all I have to go on."

Juliette wanted to argue, but she tended to agree with the theory. "Give it time, okay?"

"I don't have any choice." She nodded a few times at the screen. Juliette wondered if she was giving herself a pep talk. "It's okay. Nobody said any of this was going to be easy, right?"

"Right. And remember that so much of this is about other people and their perceptions. Not you. Not the real you."

"I will remember that." Silence hit and they went back to their own thoughts. Peyton clicked away on the keyboard while Juliette surfed her phone. "Hey." Juliette looked up to find Peyton staring at her. "I love you."

She blinked, replaying the moment because she needed to verify it was real. "You do?" Her heart tentatively squeezed. She'd hoped for the words, and now they were here.

"In the midst of all this, nothing compares to how happy I am that I have you. It's this giant arrow sign to all that's good and true in this world. I love everything about you. You make every day better." She laughed. "And maybe I should have waited for a more romantic moment to tell you, over a candlelight dinner, or standing on a covered bridge. Isn't what they do in the movies?" She laughed nervously. Juliette adored cute Peyton and wanted to gather her up and kiss her face all over.

Juliette grinned. She couldn't hold it back. "I like this better. It's us. Living our life in my kitchen. What you just said was simple in the absolute best sense. Wonderful and heartfelt. I love you, too. Head over heels, hearts in place of my eyes."

"You strike better visuals than me." Peyton stood and closed the distance between them, arriving at Juliette's knees and leaning in, her lips hovering just shy of Juliette's. She gave her goose bumps to this day anytime she came near. No one had ever had the ability before. "You're the most beautiful counter sitter I've ever seen."

"Do you see many?"

"I only have eyes for one. Wouldn't know."

"Smooth."

Peyton ran her thumb gently along Juliette's bottom lip. "Did I mention I was in love with you? I am."

"Like I could forget. I refuse to. It's impossible in the scheme of physics."

She lifted her shoulders in enjoyment. "Now that I've said it, I don't want to stop. Do you realize that every time I take a step forward with you it's the best decision I've made up until that point?"

"I didn't, but hearing that makes my night. Now what?"

Peyton exhaled. She couldn't stop smiling. "I don't know about you, but I'm in this thing." She laughed to herself and looked to the side. "And I never would have imagined I'd be here, so gaga for someone, not afraid of being in an actual relationship, and craving more. Life has a way of surprising me."

She gave Peyton's chin a gentle shake. "I wouldn't have imagined I'd be in my kitchen kissing the annoying underwear saleswoman, but here we are. She's a truly amazing kisser, by the way."

"Keep going," Peyton said, eyes dancing.

"I love the way your hair tickles my bare shoulders."

"That's a good one." Peyton placed her palms on Juliette's thighs. "I love the way you make the best little burst of a noise right before you get ready to—"

"Take a bite of a peanut butter and jelly sandwich. I know. I just celebrate."

Peyton pulled her face back and laughed. The sound was music to Juliette's ears. "Is that a euphemism? We don't even have kids yet, and you're disguising our sex life with food metaphors?"

"Yet?" Everything in Juliette went warm and liquid as she thought about that kind of life with Peyton. Soccer games. Family dinners. It all sounded so wonderful that it almost hurt.

Peyton nodded. "Yet," she said quietly.

Well, that did it. Juliette sobered and cradled Peyton's cheek. "I crave more, too. Lots of life to live, and hopefully, a little family of our own."

"Together." Peyton smiled and nuzzled her nose to Juliette's. "Just a few things to do first. We haven't even made out to eighties music yet."

"Or eaten the brownie batter from the bowl."

Peyton looked around. "The night is young. Two birds?"

Juliette grinned, encircled Peyton's neck with her arms, and kissed the woman she loved reverently. Passionately. Deeply.

In the midst of what had been a difficult month, they'd carved out their own personal refuge in each other's arms, away from the stressors.

Through it all, Juliette's business continued to pick up steam, leaving her breathing a little easier about her future. Peyton's, on the other hand, hobbled along. It wasn't clear whether her customers would be back after the long shadow of the news story faded. Regardless, Juliette noticed Peyton pulling back on the promotional work she was so good at, the same marketing pushes that had rocketed Cotton Candy onto the map in the first place. She'd lost her drive and with it her unique sparkle. It was almost like she was ashamed to put herself out there in the same way, as if she didn't deserve the success, which was disheartening. She had as much right to do business in Landonville as anyone, and Juliette, for one, longed to see her seize her ambition and prove the naysayers wrong.

So far, it wasn't happening.

"I think you should do one of your Instagram promos for the after-hours parties. You haven't booked one of those in a while and maybe it's because people forget you offer them. Throw in some queer hashtags. The community already loves your shop. I say lean in to that side of your client demo more."

"I'd love to. And I will. But I'm not feeling more parties right now." Peyton halfheartedly shrugged from her spot behind The Station's counter as she watched Juliette paint the final touches on a custom card during her break one afternoon. "I just want to come to work and do my job the best way I know how. If business picks up, great. I'm not going to beg people to come to the store. Even the mayor's wife ghosted me."

"She's all about appearances. But you know what? She'll be back. She can't resist a sexy nightie or the woman who's an expert at matching her customers to what will make them feel great."

"You might be right about that." She sent Juliette a much needed grin. "I'm sorry I'm such a downer lately. It will pass. Everything's temporary, right?" Peyton held out her hand, and Juliette took it, standing and moving into the warmth of her arms. There was no better place on Earth, she realized, as she allowed herself to sink into the embrace.

Over the next few weeks, Juliette noticed Peyton's spiral slowly continue until it began to touch her personal life as well. She tried her best to persuade Peyton to go places, see people, do all the fun things they'd grown to enjoy together, but more often than not, Peyton declined. She was depressed, and Juliette felt helpless.

"You are awesome for asking me, but I think I'm just in the mood to read a book at home. Is that okay?"

"Of course it is. I'll just miss you."

"Call me when you're home. I'll come over."

At least they still had their nights where they let their limbs intertwine and their souls relax. They'd been staying at Juliette's nearly all the time, but Peyton stole away back to her house whenever a dip in her spirits took hold. She seemed to need the alone time to pull herself out of it. Most of the time it worked.

But Juliette was growing increasingly concerned. Something was going to give, collapse down on them, if Peyton didn't change course soon. She had taken too much on herself emotionally, beating herself up for things she could no longer take back or control. And because Juliette wasn't able to take any of it away, she was feeling frustrated, sad, wanting Peyton to realize once again how amazing she was. Did she understand that her sparkle radiated to every person she encountered? Juliette just had to figure out a way to get it back for her. And soon…

❖

Juliette arrived at work that warm Friday morning with hope in her heart. The sun was out, and they had concert tickets for the weekend to see a local cover band everyone was so in love with. Maybe she and Peyton would get their chance to make out to eighties music after all.

With her warm chai latte in hand, Juliette headed into work, realizing that she'd beaten Peyton, who'd run by her house for a quick wardrobe swap out. The shop felt strange when she let herself in, and she soon zeroed in on the reason. The overhead lights were on. It was unusual for her to forget to flip them off. With a chill moving through her, she put away her chai and her bag and looked around. Nothing looked overly out of place. When she came around the counter, however, she instantly knew. Not only was her point of sale screen missing, but a glance below revealed that her lockbox was, too. She blinked, understanding that someone had been in her shop. They'd stolen from her. The feeling of violation escalated until her blood coursed hot and fast through her veins, and panic rose in her throat, the acid burning her on the way up.

"Call the police," she said out loud to ground herself in what needed to be done next. While she waited on the line for the dispatcher to gather her information, she walked the few aisles of the store to see if anything else had been taken. She made one more unfortunate discovery. The only high-dollar items sold at The Station were a selection of collector's Hummels that had become increasingly hard to find. Juliette always had a soft spot for the figurines and was sad to see them missing from the small case. It wasn't the monetary loss that burned. The six missing Hummels maybe added up to a couple of thousand dollars at most, but the hit hurt her heart. The money could be replaced but the collector's items couldn't so easily.

"Ms. Jennings, we have an officer en route to your store," the dispatcher told her. "Try not to touch anything further."

"Yes, sir. I'll be outside." It honestly felt like the safest place. Juliette didn't want to be in the store by herself right now. When she hit the sidewalk, she placed a call to Peyton to let her know what had happened, only to get her voice mail. Where in the world was she? Cotton Candy was set to open in fifteen minutes. Peyton never ran this late.

"We were hit!"

Juliette whirled around to find Mr. Huberson stalking down the sidewalk toward her. "My cash register was cleaned out, and the sound system was ripped out of the wall. Cameras are also gone," he bellowed. "One was smashed on the floor."

"My store, too," Juliette said in a much calmer voice. Her heart was still beating a mile a minute. But if Dry Style was also robbed, that meant Cotton Candy might have suffered the same fate. She tried the door. Locked, of course. But her shop had been locked, too. She peered through the glass but couldn't see much with the lights off.

The police were on the scene within ten minutes and began taking their statements. Peyton arrived in the midst and hurried their way when she saw the commotion. "What's going on?" she asked, removing her sunglasses and setting her bag on the ground. She was instantly at Juliette's side, studying her, almost as if checking to make sure she looked unharmed.

"My store was burglarized," Juliette explained. "So was Huberson's. You need to go check inside."

The officer was quick to intervene. "Ma'am, if you'd unlock the door for me, I can make sure to clear the place first."

"Of course." Peyton nodded and did what he told her. "But you're okay?" she asked Juliette, squeezing her hand.

She squeezed back, already feeling calmer now that she had Peyton's hand in hers. "I am. I just feel sick about this. Someone was in my space, going through my things, taking what they wanted. I knew we should have gotten cameras."

"Huberson has cameras. I've seen them."

"System was smashed. Cameras are gone. They knew what they were doing." He stared at Peyton. "Doors were locked. You have an explanation for that?"

Peyton frowned. "No. Why would I have an explanation?"

"Because you're the only one besides me who has a master key." She balked. "I don't have a key."

"I lent it to you last week for one of those power failures, which now that I think hard, maybe you made those up."

"She didn't," Juliette said, placing a calming hand on Peyton's arm. "I've seen her store go dark."

"Either way, she didn't return it. There are two keys. I have one, and so does the felon, here."

"Stop that," Juliette said.

"No, let him go." Peyton folded her arms. "I didn't break in to your store. Or yours," Peyton said to Juliette, her eyes earnest. She searched Juliette's, probably looking for sign of whether she believed her, which of course, she did.

"All clear. You want to take a look around and see if anything's missing or disturbed? I'll come with you."

Peyton nodded and went into her store while Juliette waited, nervous and out of sorts. She bounced her knees a few times to try to lose the extra energy. When Peyton and the officer returned, she offered a conservative smile. "Everything looks good. I can't find anything missing."

"That's great news," Juliette said.

Huberson laughed. "Of course nothing's missing! Why would you steal from yourself?" He turned to the officers. "Don't you find it curious that the businesses on either side of this woman were hit but not hers? I can do that math. She has a key and a criminal record. Please investigate her."

The officer held up his hand. "Sir, I'm going to ask you to stand over there."

"She didn't do this," Juliette said.

"Then you're as foolish as she is dishonest," Huberson bellowed, pointing at Juliette. "I'm calling a lawyer."

"For what?" Peyton asked. "Let these guys do their job, and I'm certain you'll see you're wrong." She turned to the officer. "Please investigate and rule me out as a suspect." He studied her silently for several long moments. That unnerved Juliette. Surely, nothing would come of these ludicrous allegations shouted by an irate man on his worst morning, but what if this brought up even more trouble for Peyton? What then? It felt like storm clouds were gathering overhead, thunder clapping in the distance. The morning had gone from bad to awful. As they stood there, Mr. Huberson continued to shout his opinions about how and why Peyton had stolen from him, while the officers did their best to quell his outbursts. They certainly weren't helping matters.

The scene in front of the strip mall was tense at best, laced with chaos and heightened emotion. It was easy to point fingers. She had to remind herself of that. They all just needed to calm down. No one was hurt, and honestly this could have been so much worse.

"I'm glad they skipped you," she told Peyton once they were alone and able to breathe inside Cotton Candy. The detective who'd arrived on the scene spent the morning inside the stores, talking to each of them, and having his officers photograph the scenes. Finally, he'd left his card and said he'd be in touch.

"I guess I just got lucky. I wish I could trade places with you, though." Peyton shook her head, worry creasing her forehead. "I'm sorry about the statues."

Juliette nodded. "That part hurts the most. The detective seemed hopeful they'd find answers. Do they really prioritize these types of crimes, though? I hope so."

"I can tell you from personal experience that they do." She offered a rueful smile. "I feel like this is going to come back on me until they solve it."

"I was afraid of that, too."

"Tell me you believe me?" Peyton asked in a quiet voice.

Juliette didn't hesitate. "Of course I do. I didn't for one second believe that you had anything to do with this. Plus, I'm sure whoever did can be traced back to that missing key. Dry Style has dozens if not hundreds of customers a day. Any one of them could have been staking the place out, and lifted that second master."

"Exactly my thought. This wasn't an on-the-fly job. Someone planned it out."

Peyton was understandably quiet that night, and Juliette gave her a little bit of space as she cooked dinner for them at Peyton's place. They'd made the last-minute decision to indulge in a couple of steaks Peyton had picked up earlier in the week, a comfort meal to soothe their spirits. Juliette looked around and marveled. They'd spent so much time at Juliette's house lately that she'd forgotten how bright and cheerful Peyton's kitchen was. The garden out back really was flourishing, and the natural light was to die for. The only drawback was that she still wore her work clothes, which were honestly not the most comfortable.

"Do you mind if I borrow a pair of joggers and a T-shirt?"

Peyton tossed her a look. "You know I love you in my clothes. You never have to ask."

Juliette placed a kiss on Peyton's cheek and left her to sauté the vegetables. "Perfect. Don't skimp on the butter."

"Are you kidding? We earned a whole stick today."

Comfortable clothes were just what Juliette needed. She easily located a pair of navy joggers and a worn-down-until-it-was-soft gray T-shirt and nearly cried with joy when her bare feet squeezed the plush carpet. As she went to close Peyton's top dresser drawer, she paused. Something shiny caught the light. She reached for the object, not to be nosy, but as a reflex. She gasped when she saw a key dangling from her hand with the word *master* scrawled on the keychain. She remembered the green border around the key from the many times she'd seen Peyton use it.

Only Peyton said she didn't have the key, that she'd returned it. This was bad. Her brain started and stopped, unsure where to take her thoughts. She stared in the direction of the kitchen, stunned, concerned, overwhelmed. Peyton never in a million years would have stolen from Juliette. Was she being naive like Mr. Huberson said? She swallowed, realizing the only thing she could do was to ask.

"Dinner should be ready in six," Peyton said, sliding a mixing bowl into the dishwasher. "Baby, what's wrong?"

"Hmm?"

"You look like someone just ripped up your favorite photograph."

"This is probably nothing, but this was in your top drawer. The one with your pants?" She dangled the key and waited.

Peyton came around the island, eliminating all barriers between them. She touched the key, taking it into her hand. "I had no idea I still had it. I wonder if it was washed with my clothes." She raised her gaze to Juliette's. "In a pocket maybe."

"Yeah. Maybe." It was a plausible explanation. It was. So why were they staring at each other in this uncomfortable silence that seemed to stretch on for years? Why did Juliette feel the need to sit down or place a cold rag on her forehead?

"Look at me," Peyton said.

For just that split second, Juliette didn't. In fact, she turned her face away because she needed air and a clear head.

"Really?"

"I'm just trying to think," Juliette said, closing her eyes. It felt like her ability to process was two steps behind her need to.

"You think I did this," Peyton said, incredulous. Juliette opened her eyes to see Peyton begin to quickly plate the dinner, all care out the window.

"I don't know what I think!" she shouted, surprised by the force behind her own voice. "I'm literally taking information in in real time. All I know is you said you didn't have a key and now I'm holding a key."

"Which I explained."

"It's also a really convenient explanation!" The words, which dripped with suspicion, came from anger and the fact that Peyton was upset and pressing her. Juliette had blurted them to be combative, not to accuse. Yet, indirectly, that's exactly what she'd done. She realized it seconds later. Too late.

Peyton held up her hands, palms out. "Got it. No, you are completely entitled to your opinion. I would never want to deny you that." She dropped a potholder onto the counter.

"No, no, no. Stop. I didn't mean it the way it sounded."

But Peyton was angry, hurt, and on the move. She grabbed her bag and gestured behind her. "Please enjoy dinner. Stay as long as you want. I don't want to rush out on you, but I need air." Moments later, the door clicked closed. While everything in her wanted to chase after Peyton, this wasn't the time. Juliette knew her well enough to know that Peyton needed her space. That's how she operated, and Juliette would respect her enough to provide it. She spent the next hour cleaning up the kitchen, watching the door, and hating the way she'd handled things.

It looked bad. Peyton's business was the only one untouched by the thief, who'd clearly used a key. She'd denied having one, only for one to show up in her possession. She'd also been weirdly absent that morning when the crime had been discovered. In spite of it all, Juliette didn't buy it. The more she thought on it, the more sure she was that Peyton had nothing to do with any of it. Her one recrimination was not getting there sooner. She should have. Her head ached with regret to the point that she finally excused herself home, embarrassed, sad, and longing for the moment to put things right. Her texts went unanswered, which meant Peyton wasn't ready to talk.

"Soon," she told Skittles, who in a rare show of support snuggled against her side on the couch. She gave his head a scratch. "We're gonna be okay."

CHAPTER NINETEEN

Peyton drove around for the next hour and half on a memory lane tour of Landonville, the city that had been so many things to her. She left the radio off and rolled down a window, embracing the silence that covered her journey. She remembered a time not too long ago when she found it difficult to feel much. Today, she longed for that kind of protection from the emotions that took their turn with her.

She passed the Pop, Shop, and Roll where she'd seen Cherry and Thomas embark upon their epic make-out session, the very one that had led her to the night she first kissed Juliette, the taste of manhattans still on their lips.

She circled around Hill High School where, according to the teacher in the newspaper, she'd demonstrated so much potential. She stared, taking in the white stone buildings that looked so different now. What could have been if she'd harnessed that instead? What would her life look like now? Coulda, woulda, shoulda. She shook her head, refusing to fully go there.

She drove by the audio-visual store that was now a bustling flower shop with a lavish purple bouquet in the display window, remembering the exact moment when she'd ruined her life. Memories shuffled by in a single-file line, blending from one to the next, leaving Peyton in a confusing, disorienting haze. She heard kind words in her ear from the people who loved her. She also heard the voices of her dissenters, those who weren't happy about her presence in town. She parked her car and pressed her forehead to the steering wheel, this time flipping on the radio to try to drown them out. Anything. She shook her head at the accusations screamed at her from Mr. Huberson, and a question she'd heard him sneer to the officer. "Why don't you ask the felon where she was last night?" She turned up the volume, attempting to bop her head to the music. Any kind of distraction. She felt like she was suffocating and squeezed her hands as tight as she could. She realized she might be experiencing a panic attack and got out of the car, located the dark sky, and attempted to hold on to it like an anchor. In the midst of all this, she remembered the way her body had clenched, her muscles wilting, when she saw the small group of police officers in front of her store. She was right back there in custody. Her freedom gone. Her humanity stripped to its core. All power surrendered as years of her life faded like a photograph that was never hers. She shuddered and swallowed, struggling for air and calm.

The only thing that could save her in that moment did. The wonderfully potent words from Juliette floated in next, freeing her from the vise of her more difficult memories. "I love you, too. Head over heels, hearts in place of my eyes." She replayed the sentence over and over, letting the warm blanket settle and comfort her. When her heart rate returned to normal, she got back on the road. Yet she was aimless, tearful, and unsure what to do with herself when she pulled into her brother's driveway. Unsurprisingly, she found the garage door open and the light on. Caleb was bent over a car part, a wrench in his hand. As she emerged from her car, he straightened and frowned. "Hey." He walked toward her. "You crying? What's going on?"

Embarrassed, and doing her damnedest to wipe away any stray tears, she shrugged. "I might have been. It's stupid." The story came tumbling out. The robbery, the master key, the way it probably looked, and how she felt about all the doubts cast her way. "But the way Juliette looked at me when she came out of my room with that key is a visual I don't think I'll ever forget."

"I hear you." Her brother nodded, taking it all in. "Before I weigh in, you know I have to ask."

She closed her eyes. "No. I don't. You're my brother, and I'm telling you the truth. Is that not enough?"

"Did you have anything to do with this?"

"I don't understand how that's a real question. That's not something I would ever do again. I live a good life. I try to be kind and care about others. I don't steal." Underneath, she knew that after all she'd put him through years ago, he had the right to ask. It still hurt like hell.

He seemed to be struggling with the fact that she didn't outright say it. "Can you just answer the question for me?" His voice was gentle. The words weren't.

It took the wind out of her that she even had to. "Fine. I didn't rob my girlfriend's store or the asshole neighbor's. Okay?"

He nodded. "Okay. I hear you."

"You're my brother. I guess I was hopeful that you'd believe me, too." It made her wonder what she was doing here. She loved her brother, making this punch to the gut extra brutal.

"I never said I didn't believe you, Peyton. I'm taking it all in."

"Everything okay out here?" Linda asked, poking her head out. She brightened when she saw Peyton, but only for a moment. "I heard voices. Peyton, are you okay? Do you want to come inside? I have wine. We could chill."

She wanted to, but couldn't. She felt alone and sad and didn't want to bring that to her brother's family. She felt like she'd been living in a fictional fairy-tale world where she'd been given a wonderful second chance, only maybe those didn't truly exist. "I appreciate the offer, but I need to get home. Work tomorrow."

"Okay. Come by for dinner this week. I'll send you the menu that consists of a lot of chicken nuggets, and you can pick a day."

Peyton forced a smile that felt like a cardboard replica at best. A nod to the fact that nothing felt real right now. "Sounds good."

Caleb and Linda exchanged a look as Peyton headed to her car, tossing a wave over her shoulder, and attempting to look like a functioning human. Her phone lay on the passenger seat and notified her of several missed calls and a barrage of texts from Juliette. She dashed off a reply so Juliette wouldn't worry.

I need a break. It's nothing personal.

She stared at the screen. She was sad to step away from a woman that had made her feel like the luckiest person alive, but reality had a way of crashing every party she'd ever had. Why would this one be any different? It wasn't Juliette's fault, and she would find a way to make it make sense to her later, when she was capable. This was a sink or swim decision.

She swung by the store. She stopped at her house. And in just under two hours, Peyton was on the road with Landonville in her rearview. Maybe she'd be back. Maybe she wouldn't. The thing she needed most was time to regroup and gather herself.

She knew just the place.

❖

When Juliette didn't get the chance to speak with Peyton the night before, she did her best to remain calm. Peyton was safe and had sent a text to confirm as much. A cloud hung over her as she got ready for work. Her bed was empty when she woke that morning, and she'd run her palm along the spot that was Peyton's, missing their morning chat, the cuddling, the sex when they had time. Today, she was anxious, averse to food, and not herself. She knew exactly why.

She was carrying the guilt from what had transpired between her and Peyton like a backpack of bricks, when all she wanted in the world was to set it right. To make sure that Peyton understood that she had the utmost faith in her character. Luckily, she'd get that chance at work that morning, a perk of being next-door neighbors.

But it wasn't to be.

She stood in front of a darkened Cotton Candy in mystification and shock. She blinked and read the words again. The sign printed in Peyton's curvy handwriting read: *Closed for a much needed break. Stay safe!*

What was going on? Juliette drove straight to Peyton's home. She could open The Station a few minutes late today, or even not at all, but there was no way she was letting another moment go by without making things right between them. This was the woman she loved, dammit. Desperation crept in with each minute of the drive. Upon arriving at Peyton's garden cottage, the news was the same. Her car was gone. The house was dark. Peyton was missing in action. On purpose.

Juliette called Peyton, only to leave an apologetic voice mail full of questions. "I love you. I'm so sorry, and I need to see your face right now. Where are you? Are you sad? Angry? Depleted? I can help. Please call me."

She tried Caleb next. He relayed his conversation with Peyton from the night before, and Juliette's heart sank farther. Peyton had received doubt and mistrust from all sides. No wonder she'd checked out.

"The thing is, I really do think she's telling the truth," Caleb said. "I should have handled it better."

"Of course she is," Juliette said, pinching the bridge of her nose and attempting to comprehend how she'd let it come to this. "I think we all let her down. What do we do?"

"Give her some time."

No. Juliette liked Caleb, but the idea of allowing Peyton to sit there and go on believing that the people who loved her didn't believe in her was out of the question. She had to do something and would. If Peyton wouldn't offer up any information, Juliette would break out her amateur detective skills because they were all she had.

Step one. Scour Peyton's social media for clues. No-go. She'd been inactive and left no breadcrumbs to aid the search. But wait. A quick check of Cotton Candy's Instagram had a video posted just an hour ago. She watched with interest as Peyton's face appeared on the screen.

"Hello, beautiful people. We're taking a break from in-house sales but are happy to fulfill orders online. Look for all your favorites there. Have the best day." Peyton, in customary fashion, blew a sexy kiss to the lens and disappeared. Juliette watched it again for details. Anything that would tell her where Peyton had gone. She was standing outside the Mustang in the video, with a diner in the frame behind her. The name of the place was out of focus. She started the video again, took a screen shot and zoomed in. *Acapulco* was the first word. What was the second? She squinted and tilted her head because that always helped. *Steve's*? Was it Acapulco Steve's? What kind of a diner name was that? She turned to Google, and sure enough, it existed! Three hours north in Dayton, but why would Peyton go back there?

She had an idea and checked the *likes* on the post. A bunch of random names with the exception of one, Candy Love. Peyton's mentor and friend, the woman who started it all. She clicked through to her profile to find it entirely locked down. It did, however, state that she was from Dayton, Ohio. Bingo!

"I'm like Veronica Mars over here," she murmured.

Now that she knew Candy's last name and the city she lived in, she typed both into the search bar on Facebook. That was locked down, too, but she could see Candy's profile photo, which had her standing in front of what looked to be a house she'd just closed on. The number was visible. Juliette wrote it down and threw a victorious fist in the air. She should moonlight, honestly. Not sure if it would work, she threw all the information she had, including the house number, onto Google, and bless the internet fairies, the white pages delivered her a full address.

Her heart thumped as she returned to The Station, wrote out her own *Back in a Few Days* sign, gathered her card orders and art supplies, and headed for home.

"Wait. A road trip? What are you talking about?" Cherry asked from speakerphone. Juliette tossed her royal-blue suitcase into the trunk and gave it a slam.

"Well, it started when The Station was robbed yesterday."

"Jules! You gotta tell me this stuff. Robbed? Are you okay? Is The Station?"

"I'm rattled but okay. Some money was taken. A few Hummels. Nothing I can't recover from." She slid into the driver's seat and put on her shades.

"Listen to me. I know I've been in Thomas la-la land, but I promise to be more present. I want to be a better friend. I will be."

"I know you will. You're Cherry, and you're amazing. And while I can't wait to catch up over about five thousand glasses of wine, I'm on a mission. So for now, can you feed my cat while I track down the woman I love?"

"That might be my favorite sentence ever. Hell, yeah!"

With her GPS pointed to Dayton, Juliette blared rock music as she caught I-75 and headed north. She didn't know what Peyton might say when she found her, but there were words she had to say before she slept again. They were too important, and so was Peyton Lane.

CHAPTER TWENTY

"What can I bring you to soothe that soul of yours?" Candy asked, placing a bowl of warm buttered popcorn on the coffee table between them. "This is what always works for mine, but what about yours?" Peyton had missed this woman and her glamorous hair and designer glasses on top of her head. Being back in her presence helped anchor her thoughts. Ever since she'd arrived at Candy's sprawling one-story near the duck pond, she felt her thoughts slow down.

"I don't need anything except a vacation from life. Just seeing you helps. I was sorry to hear about your mom."

Candy placed a hand over her heart. "Me, too. But she lives with the angels now and is watching over all of us. Yours, too, you know."

"My mom?" It was a nice thought. She'd never invested much in religion or the afterlife, but there was something about the way Candy said it that resonated. Maybe her parents were with her, helping her every step of the way. She felt a little bad about all the missteps they'd surely witnessed if that was the case.

"Your mom. Your daddy, too. I know for a fact they'd be proud of you. I am."

"Can I ask you a question?"

"Always," Candy said, sitting next to her on the couch and taking her hand in a fierce grip. That was pure Candy. She didn't do anything half-assed.

"Do you believe in clean slates? Do you really think they're possible?"

"Look at me, Peyton." She did. The unwavering eye contact, the kindness she saw in Candy's stare, sent a wave of unexpected emotion.

"I one hundred percent do. Do you know what else I know? People aren't perfect, and we can't expect them to be." She shrugged. "I wish they said all the right things. I wish they were less opinionated. Hell, I wish the teenager at the cinema would put more butter on my popcorn, but he has flaws he can't help." She held up a hand to signal she was aware of her digression. "Do I think this woman you told me about, who's been blowing up that phone since you've been here, believes the worst? Not a chance. Sounds to me from her apologizing six ways to Sunday that she screwed up and knows it."

Peyton nodded. The tears fell and the lump in her throat swelled to uncomfortable. "I love her so much, Candy, but I don't think I could stand seeing that kind of disappointment in her eyes again. Not aimed at me." She dropped her hand onto her lap.

"But it wasn't aimed at you, really," Candy corrected. "A fictitious version of you. Because *you* didn't do anything wrong."

Peyton shook her head. "No. I didn't."

"Now your brother and Juliette, that's her name, right?" Peyton nodded. "Did you show 'em all the ways that they were wrong? Explain it to them?"

"I probably could have said more, but I was so upset that I…left."

"I see. And you gave 'em time to come around, and they still didn't see things for what they were?"

Peyton sighed. This was confusing. "In retrospect, I could have remained patient and given them a chance to sort through everything." None of this changed the fact that she wasn't sure she had skin thick enough for all that came with loving somebody. She readjusted on the couch, facing Candy fully. "But maybe all this has taught me that I'm not cut out for intense feelings. I don't handle it well when—"

"Now hold the hell on." Candy's voice was no longer gentle. In fact, Peyton would characterize it as downright forceful and loud. "You're telling me that you would just trade away this woman you love because you got your feelings hurt by a moment she's since apologized for?"

"I think they were more than just hurt, they were—"

"Hurt pretty bad. Is that better?"

"Yes."

"Okay then. Are you gonna trade away a once in a lifetime true love because your feelings got hurt *bad*?"

Peyton opened her mouth and closed it, having lost her foothold. It was a once in a lifetime love, and the situation was surely larger than just hurt feelings, but that was Candy's way of boiling it down for her. She paused, not knowing what to say, when two minutes ago she'd been so sure. "Maybe not."

"You're keeping an open mind. I like that." She picked up the dish. "Shovel some hot corn in there and you might feel even better. You can't think without food. A full stomach makes for a sharpened perspective."

Peyton frowned. "Did you make that up?"

"Yes, I did. It's true as your ass is cute. I'm gonna hunt down some champagne. This day calls for my favorite afternoon pairing. We've earned it."

Peyton widened her eyes and took a handful of popcorn, as she organized her thoughts with new, focused perspective. Okay, so, maybe she'd fled a scene when she should have stayed and fought a little harder. Let the dust clear. Retreating when things became difficult was her tendency, and something to learn about herself. They'd have to let the police investigate and find the actual intruder responsible for the thefts, but in this day and age, with cameras on every street corner, it shouldn't be hard. The truth would come out, and men like Huberson could choke on their coffee when they read the headline. As for Juliette, she was a good person who tried her best with the details she had available. She'd been nothing short of wonderful for every moment they'd spent together, save one exception when maybe Peyton could extend a bit of grace.

Just as she reached for a second handful of what had to be heaven-kissed popcorn, someone knocked on the door. Peyton peered over her shoulder and then into the kitchen. Candy had yet to appear and the knocker had turned into a banger, and Peyton decided to get the door herself. She swung the huge thing open only to be shocked at who she saw standing there.

Juliette held up a hand. She looked a little frazzled. Her cheeks were reddish, little wisps of dark hair fell from her ponytail, and her eyes searched Peyton's in panic. "I had to come."

"Hi," Peyton said, looking behind Juliette as if that would offer an explanation. Her car sat in Candy's driveway. "How did you…?"

"I went all Nancy Drew and then packed a bag, got Skittles set up with Cherry, and drove straight here with only a bathroom break. I'm starving, exhausted, and missing you like crazy."

Peyton took a moment to use her Juliette decoder ring, which helped with about half of that. She looked behind her, and opened the door farther. "Why don't you come in. You can meet Candy."

Juliette nodded, slid her hands into her back pockets, and followed Peyton inside.

"You must be Juliette," Candy said, sliding a second large bowl of popcorn onto the coffee table and turning around to retrieve three glasses of bubbly. She handed one to Juliette, and then offered up a warm hug with her other arm. "I'm happy to make your acquaintance."

"Wait a minute. Did you know she was coming?"

"We've not spoken," Juliette said, returning the hug. "I'm so happy to finally meet you. You come with a long list of really positive attributes attached to your name." Peyton had to smother a smile because the sentence was so very Juliette.

"Thank you, sweet girl." She reached for the third glass and handed it to Peyton. "While I didn't know for sure, I had a feeling that the woman you described was not the type to sit and wait."

"No," Juliette said adamantly. "She's not."

"So I expected her sooner rather than later. Cheers to you both. I'm going to leave you time to talk." She took a sip and grinned. "I'll be out by the pool if you need me."

Once they were alone, Peyton wasn't sure what to say, still reeling from Juliette's presence. Amazed, really, that she'd gone to so much trouble to find her and promptly drove all the way here.

"You don't have to say anything," Juliette said quietly, taking her hand. The rush of adrenaline from her trip seemed to have slid off. This was the soft side of Juliette, and it made Peyton soften, too. "I love you more than I've ever loved anything. Anyone." She touched her heart. "And it hurts here when you're hurt or upset. I jumped to a conclusion with my eyes closed. But I want you to know that the second I opened them, I knew without question that you had nothing to do with what happened to the shops." Peyton nodded, needing the words, turning them over in her mind, and holding them close. "At the end of the day, it's you I want to be standing next to, and standing by. You're the other half of me I never knew I was missing, and now, as you can see, I can't go another hour without you." She set her champagne down on the table and took Peyton's hand in both of hers. "Please forgive me. Please come home with me. I want you to be my happily ever after, and I want so badly to be yours."

"I hear you." She rolled her lips in and took a moment. "I need to say this first. I shouldn't have run. I should have stood there with you, looked you in the eyes, and promised you that I had no part in the theft. That's what you do when you're in something together. You work through those bumps in the road with patience and forgiveness. You come back to each other. I'm so glad you came back to me."

"Does that mean what I think it means? Because I can't lose you, Peyton. Ever. It's unthinkable to me." Those beautiful blue eyes searched Peyton's, reaching for their connection that seemed to topple all other things. Standing in Juliette's presence reminded her of just that.

"It means you're my best friend, my uptight next-door neighbor, and most certainly my happily ever after. Always."

They moved to each other tentatively, and then with no hesitation at all. When Peyton kissed Juliette, in that moment, it was as if light had been turned on in her dark room. This was all she'd needed. Right here. Her home. Her heart. She was the luckiest.

When they came up for air, they took several long moments just to drink each other in, the sun coming out after a storm. With her forehead pressed to Juliette's, they shared a smile. No words needed.

"I'm sorry," Juliette whispered.

"Me, too. But do you know what I want more than anything right now?"

"What is that?"

"Popcorn and champagne by the pool with you and that wonderful woman in there."

"You didn't tell me you had a glamorous Dolores of your own."

Peyton laughed. "We should throw a popcorn and muffin party and see if they find each other in the crowd."

Juliette laughed, and the stress seemed to slowly fall off her. "I'm so happy to see your face. I love you."

"I love you, too, Jules."

An hour and a half later while they sipped expensive bubbly and Candy and Juliette swapped Peyton stories, a call came in on Juliette's phone.

She slid on to the call. "Hello." A pause. "Yes, sir. Thank you so much for getting back to me." Another long section of silence that seemed to stretch on forever. Peyton frowned, watching Juliette nod along, her eyes going wide at points. Finally, her gaze flicked to Peyton as she pointed at the phone. This was important. Peyton continued to listen for Juliette's side of the conversation, moving closer. "That's... wow. Quite the turn of events. So what happens next?" She shook her head, processing. "Amazing. Well, I can't thank you enough, Detective Gray. Let me buy you pancakes someday. Mm-hmm. Yes, perfect. You have a good night, too. I'll wait to hear." She lowered the phone, her mouth now agape. She looked from Peyton to Candy. "Well, I can safely report that they arrested Heather Minor, an employee from Dry Style, today along with her boyfriend for the robbery associated with both businesses. They've filed several charges against her."

Candy let out a little scream and tossed a hand in the air. "I knew they'd be brought to justice."

"Heather?" Peyton sat with the information for a moment. A small smile blossomed. She was off the hook officially. "I didn't see this one coming. I gotta tell Lola."

Candy grinned and marveled. "They acted fast."

"Cameras from the law office across the street pick up a section of our parking lot," Juliette explained. "They have footage of Heather arriving in her own car with a tall male just after one a.m. The rest of the parking lot is empty. The video shows her walking in the direction of The Station before she leaves the frame. She arrives back at the car, this time coming from the direction of Dry Style, by one thirty-five. This time her hands were full." Juliette shook her head. "They think she skipped your shop on purpose. She knew your history and who still hadn't returned the other master key."

"She was trying to set you up for the fall," Candy said. "I have a few choice words for that girl. You give me two minutes alone with her and she'll hear 'em."

"That's awful," Peyton said. "What if it had worked?"

"I refuse to even think about that." She sighed at the awful reality. "I should be hearing from the DA at some point soon. I have no words. I'm just glad we have answers."

Peyton was up and moving to Juliette, wrapping her in a celebratory hug. They rocked back and forth for several moments in relief. Peyton had nothing to prove. They'd established that already, but now the people who didn't believe that, could see for themselves. There would be no police showing up, asking questions about that key. She could exhale and work at putting the whole catastrophic occurrence behind her.

Once they were back in Landonville, Peyton made a vow to herself to go slower and to understand that she couldn't control the rest of the world or what they thought, but she could celebrate the gifts she'd been given. Juliette was the most valuable gift of all.

Peyton loved her cottage, but in the following weeks, she transitioned it into a workspace where she could steal away and dream up ideas for Cotton Candy. Her home, however, was with Juliette and that elusive cat of hers. She couldn't imagine spending another night apart.

"I want to marry you soon," she said, as they lay in bed, drifting toward sleep one hot July night. Summer was in full force and everything looked sun-kissed and magnificent. It would be the perfect time for a wedding.

Juliette turned her cheek to the pillow and stroked Peyton's hair. "Sometimes I think you can peek inside my thoughts and lasso the important ones."

Peyton smiled and kissed her softly, pressing their bodies together. "You're on to me."

"Is this a proposal?"

"God, no. What do you take me for? You're too special for a blurted-out proposal. I'm simply telling you what's in my heart, and it's you. It's us. Till death do us part. No question has been posed." A pause. She grinned. "Yet."

Juliette smiled back. "I wasn't going to tell you this, but I've actually imagined our wedding before. It doesn't have to be big, but it should be beautiful, soft. Elegant."

"And it will be. We'll just make Candy and Dolores the co-wedding planners."

Juliette's eyes went wide. "You most certainly will not!"

"As long as you always promise to look outraged at my very serious suggestions." They shared a kiss.

"I'm looking forward to tomorrow," Peyton said.

Juliette raised an eyebrow. "It's just a regular day."

"I know. But you'll be there."

They shared a sweet smile and snuggled together, limbs tangled, hearts full as they fell asleep on what was also seemingly a regular night. But Peyton knew better. What she'd found in Juliette was anything but ordinary, and she'd spend the rest of her life savoring every precious smile, each exchanged glance from across the room, and the quiet dinners where they shared every detail of their time spent apart. Yeah, there was no getting used to this. Their connection amazed her every day. She'd found her perfect place. Her home. At last.

❖

Juliette smothered a smile as she listened to Peyton and her nephew Joshua work on his speech for parent-teacher night at his school. The two had been huddled around their kitchen table for half an hour now and had made some progress. Josh and two other children had been selected to speak about the person they considered their hero. Of course, Joshua had selected his father, which had melted Peyton's heart.

"Why don't we start by making a list of the things you like most about your dad?"

Joshua seemed to like that idea and dictated while Peyton recorded his thoughts. "He can fix anything. He's nice to me. He picks me up after school is his cool sports car." His eyes lit up as a new thought hit. "We play soccer together in the backyard."

Because he was nervous about speaking in front of a group, Peyton had agreed to help him write and practice what he was going to say. While they worked, Juliette made herself small and quiet, supplying lemonade and chocolate chip cookies.

"Thank you, Miss Juliette."

"You're welcome, Joshy-Josh," she said, giving his hair an affectionate ruffle. He and Peyton had grown close over the past few months. She'd taken him shopping, to movies, and had even been showing him how to bowl. He'd even come to watch Juliette's Wednesday night team tear up the competition.

"Hey, did you hear from Cherry?" Peyton asked as Juliette passed through.

Juliette scrunched her shoulders happily. "She's still dealing with a lot of morning sickness but doesn't mind at all. I could hear her glow through the phone. She's literally the most adorable."

"You think she'll still be okay for the Cayman trip?" Peyton asked.

"She's already purchased three maternity swimsuits and a pack of seasickness wristbands. I don't think she's going to miss it."

Peyton beamed. "I look up to her more and more every day."

When parent-teacher night rolled around, Peyton made them arrive early so they could snag good seats. Joshua had reported earlier that afternoon that he was feeling confident and excited. Juliette made sure her phone was charged up so she could snag the recording. Ten minutes before showtime, Caleb, Linda, and Alyssa landed in the seats alongside them. Juliette caught Caleb giving Peyton's hand an affectionate squeeze and she passed him a smile. This was his big night, after all.

When it was Josh's turn to speak, he appeared from offstage in slacks and a dress shirt, looking like a million bucks. He also looked incredibly nervous. It didn't deter him. He approached the podium, stood on the stool behind it, and began to speak.

"When I was asked to select my hero, I knew exactly who I wanted to speak about. You see, I like what my mom likes to call a good comeback story." He looked up for a moment after that. "Aunt Peyton is sitting in the audience right now and doesn't know this speech is about her. Everyone else does." That earned quiet laughter and a sentimental sigh from the crowd. Juliette stole a look at Peyton as she continued to record the moment on her phone. Peyton's lips were parted in surprise, and moments later, she covered her mouth with her right hand. The tears were apparent right away, which made Juliette squeeze her hand and hold on. She'd worn the red blouse that always made her features pop with vibrance, and in this moment she simply radiated. Josh's decision had moved her as much as it had the rest of them when he'd informed them of his master plan. "A long time ago, when she was younger, she made some decisions that didn't go so well. We've all done that. But she was very sorry." Josh shuffled his feet but pressed on. "She had a very hard time. But since then, she's worked a lot to make up for it. She does good things all the time. She runs a successful business not far from my house, and she helps me with my homework when I go to her home. She's the nicest, coolest person I know. I'm very proud of her, and I want to be like her one day. She's my hero."

Right then, Josh looked right at Peyton and smiled with pride and admiration. Juliette had never witnessed anything as special. He excused himself down the stairs and ran straight to Peyton, who caught him in a bear hug and hung on while the rest of them dabbed tears.

"You guys knew about this?" she asked the group, wiping her cheeks.

Juliette nodded. "It was very sweet of Josh."

"And I really did use all the advice you gave me. Just on some different words."

"Well, I may never recover from that," she said, giving him another squeeze, as Caleb and Linda watched their son with huge smiles on their faces.

After the event concluded, Juliette called ahead to make sure everything was in place. They were going to dinner as a group at a rooftop restaurant with a view of the city and a live pianist. What Juliette hadn't told Peyton was that she'd reserved the entire rooftop for just their group, and that she planned to propose.

Peyton's words from months before about Juliette being too special to receive a blurted proposal had resonated with her. The more she turned them over in her mind, the more she realized that it was Peyton who was deserving of a special moment, and she wanted more than anything to give her just that. What she hadn't counted on was how nervous she would be when they arrived at the restaurant. It was go-time. There was no way she could make it all the way through dinner, so she had the proposal planned for drinks and appetizers.

"I wonder why no one else is here," Peyton asked, marveling at the beautiful space. "This view is the most gorgeous ever. You can see all of downtown. Just look." She squeezed Juliette's leg, and that helped center her on her mission. Her nervous energy softened to excitement.

"Oh, you know what? I left my purse in the car."

"I'll run down and get it," Peyton said.

"No, no. We're with your family. I'll go. But can I have the key?"

Peyton grabbed her bag, which if all had gone according to plan, now had a stowaway item inside, thanks to Caleb's quick maneuvering.

"Yep. No problem," she said. "Here you…" A pause. "What is

this?" She pulled out the black velvet box that contained the ring Juliette had meticulously designed with a jeweler, with Peyton's aesthetic in mind. Still not fully getting it, Peyton opened the box. Simultaneously, Juliette had taken one knee next to Peyton's chair and watched as she shifted her gaze from the diamond ring to Juliette, who looked up at her with glistening eyes.

"Is this real?" Peyton asked, but her hands were already shaking. She looked back at her family, who watched happily. Caleb nodded at her. Josh was even standing on his chair for a better view, and Alyssa yelled, "Yay!" from her high chair.

"Peyton Lane, there's no one like you," Juliette said. "I wear lingerie now and love it." Peyton laughed, which helped break down some of the nervous energy that bounced back and forth between them. "Ever since you walked into my life, I've felt myself stretched, challenged, and satisfied. What I've come to understand was that everything that happened between us, the good and the more difficult, was similarly the stretching of our hearts to be big enough for two. They say that love chooses you, and it did. I truly believe that you were chosen for me, and I was chosen for you. We were meant to be. Written in the stars." Peyton looked skyward at the twinkling stars overhead and nodded. "But more than just loving you, which I do immensely, I also need you. You make me a better person. You make me laugh and let go. We embarked upon a friendship first, and that has never left us. We've built upon that foundation and created something that no one can topple. Peyton, you are the love of my life and my favorite person on Earth. Will you do me the honor of becoming my wife?"

Leave it to Peyton to take a dramatic pause that couldn't have been more perfect. "I would love nothing more. Yes."

The family of four joined by the line of servers near the door broke into applause. Flutes of the good stuff were promptly poured for all adults, as Juliette kissed Peyton, her fiancée.

"I can't believe you did this," Peyton said. "But I've never felt more special in my life."

"Yet. That's the operative word. I have a whole lifetime to spoil you now. Get ready."

Peyton's hand was still shaking as she placed it over her heart. "This day has been everything. I don't want it to end."

"That's the best part." Juliette dipped her head. "There is no ending. Just every day together. Each one better than the last."

"After a line like that, you better kiss me."

"Anything," Juliette said and happily wrapped her arms around Peyton's neck for a kiss that would catapult them into forever. She was one very lucky woman.

EPILOGUE

Peyton was dealing with the typical nervous energy that came anytime the spotlight was placed on her shoulders. She adjusted the navy blazer she'd picked out for the event by giving her shoulders a gentle roll. Today, however, she didn't mind the butterflies. The cause was near and dear to her heart, and the afternoon felt very much like a full circle moment in her life.

The Hope and Help meeting happening in the room adjacent had been underway for ten minutes now. Nancy, the director of the organization that helped recently released women get back on their feet, popped her head into the small waiting room and smiled. "All set?"

Peyton nodded. "I'm ready." She clutched the blue folder she'd brought with her to her chest. Inside, she'd organized her speaking notes into bulleted points for easy reminders. But something in her said no. She set the folder down and decided to speak from her heart. "I'll follow you."

Nancy led her into the meeting room next door where she found a group of about fifteen women looking expectantly her way. Some were clearly withdrawn, scared, their eyes moving to Peyton and then quickly away again. Peyton's gaze flicked to an older woman pressing her nails into the palm of her hand. A coping mechanism. She remembered a time when she'd likely done the same. Other women grinned at her as she approached the chair Nancy indicated was hers, welcoming and relaxed. They were likely farther along on their journeys.

The hum of the air-conditioning floated over the room, and the chairs had been arranged in a circle, making the space feel intimate and supportive. She knew these women. She was them.

After a brief introduction that went by in a haze of Peyton's basic past and present status, Nancy signaled that the floor was hers.

"Thank you for allowing me to attend your meeting today. My name is Peyton Lane, and I'm a small business owner here in town. You might have seen my shop not far from here. Cotton Candy, named for the woman who showed me a little bit of kindness when I was first released."

"What did you do?" a woman across the circle asked, loud and bold. Her hair was pulled back in a tight ponytail, and she was thin like Peyton had been when she was saving up enough cash to buy a burger from the eatery below her apartment. She could still smell the wonderful aromas that taunted her.

"I was a thief. Shoplifting until the jobs got bigger and bigger. People got hurt. So I'm a felon now, and always will be. But I'm here because that's not all I am, and that's not all you are either. There is a path forward." She studied the unique faces looking back at her with interest. "I got married last month. To the most wonderful woman, who I am convinced was put on the Earth to be my person." She smiled. "I'm convinced I'm hers, as well. I'm also seeing a lot of success in my career. Cotton Candy has been open in Landonville nearly three years now, and I have a dedicated customer base, a steady income, and I feel like part of this town."

"But I imagine it wasn't easy," Nancy said, leading her to some hard truths.

"It wasn't," she said to Nancy. "It was awful at first. People closed doors in my face. No one wanted to hire me. I had to work three times as hard as the average person to prove myself, and even then, some folks in town didn't want to shop in my store because of what I'd done." She shrugged. "I dealt with so much personal shame that I couldn't blame them. That part took a long time. Learning to love myself. Hell, *like* myself." She smiled. "But I have."

Nancy took it from there. "Peyton reached out to us because she wants to join our mentor program and help you all using the knowledge she's gained from walking in the very same shoes you find yourselves in."

Peyton nodded. "Please come by my store. You don't need money. I'd like to set you up with the underclothes that will make you feel like a million bucks. Just bring in this certificate." She took the stack from Nancy and passed them around the circle for each woman to take one.

She watched as the group members, who likely felt discarded and hopeless, brightened a tad. She knew what it was like when just one person cared enough to offer help. She could do that now, and she vowed to continue. She was in a place to give back and would. "I also brought a check for five thousand dollars from Cotton Candy to the Hope and Help Organization." The group applauded, and Peyton handed the check to Nancy. "I asked that it be used to fund gift cards to budget-friendly restaurants or maybe even a clothing store."

"We can do that," Nancy said. "We're not a large organization and customize the support we offer to each person's individual need."

"But most of all, I want you to know that I see you, and I plan to help in whatever way I can."

The woman who sat next to her, who'd not moved a muscle since Peyton had arrived, reached out and squeezed Peyton's wrist. She didn't speak a word. She didn't even look in Peyton's direction. She didn't have to. The gesture said everything, affirming that Peyton was exactly where she was called to be. She'd made it to the other side and would work like hell to bring others along with her.

She went home that evening aware of how damn lucky she was. What she wanted more than anything was to celebrate the gifts in her life, and that started with Juliette Lane. She opened the door expecting to find Juliette cozy on the couch, watching one of her favorite shows with Skittles the cat at her feet and maybe a glass of red wine on the side table. That would have been absolutely sublime. What she actually came home to was infinitely better, but quite frankly, unexpected.

Peyton blinked, her feet frozen to the floor. "What is happening here?" she asked in a voice that sounded like a first cousin to her own. Juliette stood facing the couch. She wore a matching bombshell bra and panty set in burgundy. The lacy ones that came with stockings and a garter set. Holy hell. She was wearing those, too. Peyton knew this combination. They'd just gotten the sets in at the store, and now her wife was giving new meaning to the word *hot* because Peyton needed a glass of water to the face to quell the heat that hit.

"Oh, you're just in time. I was getting ready to paint." She shrugged. "I'm feeling artistic."

Peyton loved watching Juliette paint, and tonight she was doing so in lingerie, which made her want to weep with gratitude before taking her time bringing pleasure to this incredibly intoxicating woman. This wasn't the first time Juliette had moved through their home wearing some of Peyton's favorite merchandise from the store. The month before, she unloaded the dishwasher in turquoise hip-huggers and a demi-plunge. Peyton's brain had short-circuited, and she still didn't look at their plates the same way.

"What can I say?" Juliette had said at the time. "I started to get a little jealous of all the sexy sets you wear around the house."

"Yeah, but this is so much better," Peyton said, blinking as Juliette put away the glasses on the second shelf of the cabinet. "You are."

"Oh, I don't know about that, but I am enjoying the look on your face. You're really cute right now, baby." Juliette swung her hips as she walked. Her ass had never looked more amazing. "I might let you touch when I'm done, but have a seat at the kitchen table first. I have more work to do." That little surprise had ended in the most memorable of ways. The kitchen had been christened, and Juliette had a newfound interest in lingerie.

Tonight, however, with her paintbrush in hand, Juliette left Peyton in an appreciative daze.

"I'll need you over there when you have a chance to catch your breath." She gestured to the couch.

Peyton nodded, fielding the onslaught of desire as it overcame each of her senses one by one. "You want me to sit and watch you paint?"

"No, silly. You're my subject. How do you feel about nudity? Be honest."

Peyton's mouth went dry, but she played demure. "I feel like everything is negotiable. Tell me. What did you have in mind?"

"I've often thought about sketching you topless." The world slowed down for Peyton. "The idea's actually been playing in the back of my mind since the first night we kissed."

"Why have you never told me about this?" Oh, this was too good. She got a shiver that rippled and tingled.

"You can't know everything. Where's the fun in that?"

"You have a point because this is a nice way to arrive home."

"Over there," Juliette said with a smile and a jut of her chin.

"Yes, ma'am." Peyton shrugged out of her blazer and went to work on the buttons of her dress shirt as Juliette watched wordlessly. She let the shirt fall to the floor and unclasped her bra as she walked.

Juliette handed her a book and placed it in her most faraway hand. "This shoulder down. Book up, rest that wrist on the back of the couch."

"I can do that," Peyton said, realizing that she was speaking in quieter tones, almost as if she didn't want to disrupt her wife's creative process.

"This might be hard," Juliette said, taking her place behind the easel.

"Not for me," Peyton said. "I get to relax and enjoy the best view in life."

"You say that because you haven't seen mine." Juliette exhaled slowly and turned to her oversized pad. For the next hour, she sketched, sometimes quietly, sometimes as she asked Peyton questions about the event.

"I'm so proud of you," she said. "Everyone is. You're the town's big comeback story. The world adores you." She shrugged. "But no one more than me."

"All done?"

"Mm-hmm," Juliette said, moving toward her. "But don't move."

Peyton grinned as she approached and allowed the book to be taken out of her hand. "I was hoping you'd come over here."

"As if there was any chance I couldn't." She slid on top, nestled her hips snugly between Peyton's legs, dipped her mouth, and pulled in a nipple. Peyton, who'd been hoping for this moment for the past hour, closed her eyes, lost her words, and sank into the ocean of wonderful sensations. She wanted to tell Juliette how much she loved her, and how very lucky Peyton felt to share in her life, and how excited she was for their future. Her heart felt ready to burst. Her cup runneth over. But first, they were on their way to a night to remember.

The best news of all was that she had forever to tell Juliette those things, and she planned to. In the morning, she saw the sketch. With Juliette still asleep in their bedroom, she took a moment to study her work. Tears sprang into her eyes when she saw the woman looking earnestly back at her. Was this how Juliette saw her? She covered her mouth at the light in the woman's eyes, the sincerity in her stare, and the beauty she'd never quite assigned to herself. Until now. She wanted very much to be this person, and for the first time, she truly believed that maybe she was. If Juliette loved her in this way, something she never would have expected, then she could certainly love herself. In fact, she would. She did.

In the quiet of the morning, with the sketch that she would treasure forever not far away, she made two cups of her famous coffee with whipped cream and took them back to bed with her. It was only a few moments before Juliette stirred.

"Please tell me that's coffee and whipped cream."

Peyton kissed her cheek. She never got enough of Juliette's sleepy voice. "Yes, but you can sleep a little more if you'd like."

Juliette sat up and reached for her cup. "And miss all this? No way." She cradled Peyton's cheek. "Good morning. What should we do today?"

Peyton didn't hesitate. "Anything and everything we want."

They shared a lingering kiss. The whole day stretched out in front of them. The coffee tasted amazing. The bed was warm, and they were madly in love. "Those are the best words ever. Kiss me again."

About the Author

Melissa Brayden (www.melissabrayden.com) is a multi-award-winning romance author, embracing the full-time writer's life in San Antonio, Texas, and enjoying every minute of it.

Melissa is married and working really hard at remembering to do the dishes. For personal enjoyment, she spends time with her Jack Russell terriers and checks out the NYC theater scene as often as possible. She considers herself a reluctant patron of spin class, but would much rather be sipping merlot and staring off into space. Bring her coffee, wine, or doughnuts and you'll have a friend for life.

Books Available From Bold Strokes Books

Lucky in Lace by Melissa Brayden. Straitlaced stationery store owner Juliette Jennings's predictable life unravels when a sexy lingerie shop and its alluring owner move in next door. (978-1-63679-434-1)

Made for Her by Carsen Taite. Neal Walsh is a newly made member of the Mancuso crime family, but will her undeniable attraction to Anastasia Petrov, the wife of her boss's sworn enemy, be the ultimate test of her loyalty? (978-1-63679-265-1)

Off the Menu by Alaina Erdell. Reality TV sensation Restaurant Redo and its gorgeous host Erin Rasmussen will arrive to film in chef Taylor Mobley's kitchen. As the cameras roll, will they make the jump from enemies to lovers? (978-1-63679-295-8)

Pack of Her Own by Elena Abbott. When things heat up in a small town, steamy secrets are revealed between Alpha werewolf Wren Carne and her human mate, Natalie Donovan. (978-1-63679-370-2)

Return to McCall by Patricia Evans. Lily isn't looking for romance—not until she meets Alex, the gorgeous Cuban dance instructor at La Haven, a newly opened lesbian retreat. (978-1-63679-386-3)

So It Went Like This by C. Spencer. A candid and deeply personal exploration of fate, chosen family, and the vulnerability intrinsic in life's uncertainties. (978-1-63555-971-2)

Stolen Kiss by Spencer Greene. Anna and Louise share a stolen kiss, only to discover that Louise is dating Anna's brother. Surely, one kiss can't change everything...Can it? (978-1-63679-364-1)

The Fall Line by Kelly Wacker. When Jordan Burroughs arrives in the Deep South to paint a local endangered aquatic flower, she doesn't expect to become friends with a mischievous gin-drinking ghost who complicates her budding romance and leads her to an awful discovery and danger. (978-1-63679-205-7)

To Meet Again by Kadyan. When the stark reality of WW II separates cabaret singer Evelyn and Australian doctor Joan in Singapore, they must overcome all odds to find one another again. (978-1-63679-398-6)

Before She Was Mine by Emma L McGeown. When Dani and Lucy are thrust together to sort out their children's playground squabble, sparks fly, leaving both of them willing to risk it all for each other. (978-1-63679-315-3)

Chasing Cypress by Ana Hartnett Reichardt. Maggie Hyde wants to find a partner to settle down with and help her run the family farm, but instead she ends up chasing Cypress. Olivia Cypress. (978-1-63679-323-8)

Dark Truths by Sandra Barret. When Jade's ex-girlfriend and vampire maker barges back into her life, can Jade satisfy her ex's demands, keep Beth safe, and keep everyone's secrets…secret? (978-1-63679-369-6)

Desires Unleashed by Renee Roman. Kell Murphy and Taylor Simpson didn't go looking for love, but as they explore their desires unleashed, their hearts lead them on an unexpected journey. (978-1-63679-327-6)

Here For You by D. Jackson Leigh. A horse trainer must make a difficult business decision that could save her father's ranch from foreclosure but destroy her chance to win the heart of a feisty barrel racer vying for a spot in the National Rodeo Finals. (978-1-63679-299-6)

Maybe, Probably by Amanda Radley. Set against the backdrop of a viral pandemic, Gina and Eleanor are about to discover that loving another person is complicated when you're desperately searching for yourself. (978-1-63679-284-2)

The One by C.A. Popovich. Jody Acosta doesn't know what makes her more furious, that the wealthy Bergeron family refuses to be held accountable for her father's wrongful death, or that she can't ignore her knee-weakening attraction to Nicole Bergeron. (978-1-63679-318-4)

Tides of Love by Kimberly Cooper Griffin. Falling in love is the last thing on either of their minds, but when Mikayla and Gem meet, sparks of possibility begin to shine, revealing a future neither expected. (978-1-63679-319-